EDGE OF THE STORM

DRAGONS OF THE STORM
BOOK TWO

ELLE WOLFSON

SALTY ROGUE PRESS

THE MAGIERA (TWISTED)

List of abilities should not be considered complete.

DANCER

Element: Water
Potential Abilities: Read and manipulate emotions. Agility and Grace. Manipulate water. Sense patterns, up to and including most likely outcomes of events. Change appearance.
Rumored abilities: Manipulate Weather

FERR

Element: Blood
Potential Abilities: Strong sense of smell. Can sense energies around people and objects and track them. Scrub disease from blood. Manipulate blood and heart in their own body and in others.
Rumored abilities: The ability to coerce and control people by creating an affinity in their blood.

MESMER

Element: Air
Potential Abilities: Read and manipulate thoughts. Telepathy. Manipulate air in ways that effect light, the composition of air, wind.
Rumored abilities: Flight

STONE

Element: Earth
Potential Abilities: Super strength. Make skin impermeable. Ability to change mass of their bodies. Manipulate dirt, rock, stone, and plants.
Rumored abilities: The ability to detect lies

WISP

Element: Fire
Potential Abilities: Super speed. Call fire. Lend their raw power to others to increase their ability. Manipulate electricity
Rumored Abilities: Create bombs from stored power.

ZEE

Element: Bone
Potential Abilities: Manipulate bodies of others. Healing and Regeneration. Sense types of power in others. Manipulate bones.
Rumored abilities: Coming back from the dead. Resurrecting others.

VASUM

The vessel
Abilities: Can borrow the power of any other type.

CHAPTER ONE

Vinnie had bought too many cookies. Four plastic boxes filled the shopping bag, forcing her to hold her hand at an awkward angle to get her fingers through the loops. It hadn't been uncomfortable when she'd left the grocery store, but five blocks later her hand was cramping.

Her other hand was straining, too. Three large bottles of soda were heavy and the cap of one bottle had punched a hole in the thin bag. As Vinnie walked, the hole continued to tear, causing the bottles to list to the side, threatening to spill out onto the sidewalk.

Just one block to go. The bag would hold up—it had to. She needed this event to go smoothly.

Vinnie breathed a sigh of relief when she reached the entrance to the alley that would take her to the charity library she ran. The plastic bags bumped awkwardly against her legs as she rounded the corner and jerked to a halt. The library was in the building's basement, its entrance was halfway down the alley. Someone was standing at the bottom of the stairs, in front of the door, graying blond hair glowing dully in the afternoon light.

Please don't be Carla. Please don't be Carla. Vinnie kept her Vasum power open all the time now. With it, she could determine if others had power and borrow it if she wanted. The woman was normal and as Vinnie got closer, the rest of Carla came into view, her customary scowl already in place.

"You're late." Carla's scowl deepened. Several plastic shopping bags rested at her feet and Vinnie could just make out some bright colors.

What was Carla doing here? And with what looked like party supplies. Carla had suggested the fundraiser but hadn't said anything about helping.

"We don't open until one today. There's been a sign on the door for a week." Vinnie stepped back from the top of the steps. The stairs were narrow, and she needed Carla to move so she could unlock the door.

"We agreed I'd come early to help you set everything up," Carla said.

No, Vinnie had not agreed to that. Zandia was going to help Vinnie set things up. Carla had been in the same room.

And she wasn't going to move.

Vinnie transferred both of her bags to one hand and fished in her front pocket for the key as she went down the steps. She wedged herself between Carla and the door and stuck the key in the lock, only bumping into Carla twice before she got the door open.

"The fundraiser starts at one. Getting here early to help set up would be now." As Vinnie stepped through the door, the bag carrying the drinks gave way, spilling the three large bottles on the floor. They tumbled, thankfully they didn't break open as they hit the ground.

"You can't set up for a party in 30 minutes." Carla stepped around the bottles on the floor and plonked the bag she'd been carrying on the counter and started pulling out streamers that looked like they belonged at a children's birthday party.

Vinnie opened her mouth to protest and then shook her head. It didn't matter. She doubted anyone who came to the library would care what the streamers looked like, and Vinnie was grateful for the fundraiser idea. Carla was tired of the same old books and wanted new ones, but Vinnie had a different motive.

She'd used what little money she'd had saved to put a deposit and the first month's rent down for an apartment. Her first paycheck from working at Walt's convenience store wouldn't be until next week, and the rent for the library was due Monday. If she didn't make enough, she'd be calling her landlord and begging for an extension, and he was not known for his generosity.

The bell on the door jingled again. Vinnie snatched the third bottle of soda off the floor and scooted out of the way as Zandia entered.

Zandia was Vinnie's most frequent patron, and she'd been here even more in the last few weeks. She was the closest thing Vinnie currently had to a friend, which wasn't saying much. She didn't know much about Zandia, aside from her love of romance novels, and was trying to keep it that way. She'd moved away from her other friends so no one could use them against her, and making new ones would just repeat the cycle.

Zandia's eyes crinkled in a smile, deepening the lines around her eyes, and she propped open the door.

One of the bottles in Vinnie's arms started to slide and she tightened her arms.

"Where's your table?" Carla's sour voice asked. "Where are you going to put those?"

Vinnie looked at the bag of packaged cookies at her feet. "I'm going to put them on the counter."

"That's too high up. You need food to be at waist level. Tell me you have a table."

"They'll be fine. I don't need a table."

Zandia looked from Carla to Vinnie. "Don't you have a table in the back, Vinnie? I'll help you bring it out."

She had a table in the back, but it was heavy and Zandia was at least seventy, and while this whole thing had been Carla's suggestion, it was still Vinnie's fundraiser. "It would be awkward to move. The counter will be fine. Or we can move the coffee pot."

Against the far wall was a small table with a coffee pot.

"Nonsense. If you're not up to it, Carla can help." Zandia was already around the counter. She paused to look Vinnie up and down, and Vinnie self-consciously tugged the end of her sleeve over her thin wrist. She had lost a lot of weight in the last few weeks, but she could still lift a table.

"I can lift the table," Vinnie said.

Ignoring her, Zandia opened the door to the back room, which had been a large closet before Vinnie opened the library.

It was harder to say no to Zandia since she was kind where Carla was critical, so Vinnie stop trying and followed her to the back room.

Zandia had already picked up the books that were on the sorting table and moved them to the floor. Vinnie helped her move the rest of her supplies to the floor and together they maneuvered the table into the front room. By the time they set it down out front, Vinnie was a little winded, but Zandia just slapped her hands together and moved on to setting up the cookies and drinks.

Fatigue drew Vinnie's shoulders down. Sitting would be nice, but she couldn't let her patrons do everything. Maybe just one cookie to give her energy.

She opened the paper plates and one package of cookies.

One of the giant pink frosted confections went in her mouth where she held it while she arranged the rest on a plate. Once she had them arranged, she allowed herself to bite down on the cookie and chew, almost moaning with relief.

"Really, Vinnie," Carla said. "If I had known you were going to buy that garbage, I would have baked some nice homemade cookies. It's like you're not even trying."

"I love these," Vinnie said. "When I was a kid, my dad would never let me have them. Everything had to be made by hand." Their personal chef made the cookies, but she didn't want to say that. "Even for school bake sales. Most of the other kids brought store cookies, and I was different."

She took another big bite.

Carla pursed her lips. "You're not a child anymore. People blame their parents for every little thing."

Then she turned and pointed at the streamers and the welcome sign she put up, a proud smile on her face.

The streamers looked bright and garish — a perfect complement to Vinnie's store-bought cookies — the elementary school party aura was complete.

"They look good, Carla," Zandia said.

"Very colorful," Vinnie said around another mouthful.

"Are we having a party?" Ed, one of Vinnie's few male regulars, stood in the doorway.

"It's a fundraiser," Carla said. "We haven't had any new books in ages. If you take a cookie, you have to leave a donation in the jar."

Zandia must have seen the horrified look on Vinnie's face because she squeezed her arm. "Why don't you have a seat, Vinnie? You look exhausted."

There was a nice, cozy library chair near the coffee pot. The thought made Vinnie snap her spine straight. She did not want to sit down. Was Zandia manipulating her? She directed her Vasum power at Zandia and dug in to find her spark, that tiny bit of power that everyone had. Stone, Zandia's spark was Stone, so weak it couldn't have even helped her move the table.

She wasn't Ferr. Vinnie knew that, but the memory of Kara putting her hand on her arm and forcing her to be still while she tortured Conor and Cerulean haunted her.

Zandia wasn't trying to manipulate her, she was just concerned.

Carla had dragged Ed off, and Vinnie could hear her extolling the virtues of donating to the library somewhere in the back.

"You know she didn't really suggest this to get more books," Zandia said. "She wants more books, but we know you use some of the donations for a salary, but you don't take nearly enough. You're so pale and tired all the time and she's worried."

"Did she say that?" Vinnie asked. She had a hard time imagining Carla suggested this to take care of her.

"Not in so many words," Zandia said. "You know she's hurting from that little girl dying. She knew her mom. Sit." She pushed Vinnie toward the chair and went to greet a mom with two kids who had wandered in.

Vinnie sat, but she couldn't stay sitting long. She needed to move so she wouldn't have to think about Maddie, the girl who had died. Carla had been the one to tell Vinnie she was missing, and Vinnie had tried to find Maddie and save her, but she'd been too late.

More people trickled in and Zandia and Carla took turns greeting them. Zandia seemed content to hover by the door, greeting people and explaining that they were having a fundraiser. Meanwhile Carla was rattling off made-up stats about the benefits of libraries.

The donation jar was about half full. Maybe there would be enough to pay the rent and get some more books for the patrons. After Vinnie had rested and eaten more cookies, she got up and wandered, surprised at the number of people who had come. She smiled and talked to people, glad it was nothing like the fundraisers she'd had to go to as a teenager.

When she sat back down, a little girl wandered over to her. The girl, who looked like she was around four, put her hand on Vinnie's knee and looked up at her with round eyes. There had never been any kids in the library before. Almost all of her patrons were older, either retired or close to it. She didn't even have any children's books because she'd never thought about it.

"This is like grandma's house," the girl told Vinnie.

"Your grandma likes books?" Vinnie asked.

"No, but being there makes me feel happy, too." She yawned.

"Emma!" A woman had come around the same shelf the girl had appeared from. "I'm so sorry. She thinks everyone in the world is her friend. Come on, Emma, it's time to go."

Emma took her mother's hand, and together, they headed for the door.

Vinnie stood as well. Time to be social again.

"Oh, excuse me," the woman said, stepping back as a man came through the door in front of her.

"Conor." His name was past Vinnie's lips before her brain engaged.

He stood in the doorway, and his eyes met hers.

"It's my fault," he said to the woman as he stepped into the library and out of her way. "I'm sorry for almost running over you."

The woman laughed nervously and dragged her daughter out the door.

Conor was an athlete who played in the Warrior games. Lots of people knew his face. Even if the woman hadn't recognized him, he was gorgeous. Vinnie's eyes raked over him. From this distance, she couldn't see any scars on his face or neck from being burned by Kara. She hadn't seen him since that day. He had wanted nothing to do with her after that, but he also hadn't reported her for being Twisted.

Zandia, who had been standing by the door with her mouth agape, widened her eyes as Conor approached Vinnie. She didn't know Vinnie and Conor had almost dated.

"You look tired," Conor said.

From up close, she could see his face didn't have the same healthy color it used to, and his usually blinding smile was absent. She could say that he looked tired too. Instead, she said, "Thanks."

His lips quirked and a trace of the old warmth returned to his eyes. "Sorry, I guess that was rude."

Her tongue was paralyzed. Conor had been with her a month ago when she'd finally found Kara, the woman who had murdered Maddie. She wanted to ask how he was and what he remembered. Everything she knew came from news sites since he refused to talk to her. The news reported that he'd been dropped off at the hospital by an unknown person with first and second-degree burns over half his body. He had trauma-induced amnesia and didn't know where he'd been and how he'd gotten there. They weren't first and second-degree burns, though. They were partially healed third-degree burns. Would the doctors have known that? And it wasn't trauma-induced amnesia. Kara had erased his memories, but how much had she taken?

"I see you haven't replaced the wallpaper," Conor said.

"I didn't have anyone to help me." The words were out of her mouth and she wished she could call them back. Conor had said he'd help her replace it before everything had happened.

"Right. So…" He looked around at the five or so people in

the library and the few remaining cookies and soda on the table.

"Fundraiser," Vinnie said.

"Ah. I'm sorry to bother you here. I didn't realize it would be busy." He rubbed the faint pink scars on his neck. "Can we talk?"

He meant alone. There was no place in the library where you couldn't hear what someone said in another part.

Zandia, eyes still wide, nodded toward the door.

"We can talk outside." Vinnie led Conor out the door.

When they were outside, Conor glanced around, movements furtive. "Maybe in my car?"

His nervousness was making her uneasy. Something was going on. "Sure."

They had almost made it out of the alley when Conor spoke again. "No, maybe the car is a bad idea. They might have bugged it. Can they hack car computers? Do they still bug people's cars?"

"They probably do." But why did he think someone would bug his car? Will's warning that people would come looking for a dragon trilled in her mind. She'd left and moved out of the only real home she'd had since the government took her mom, so her friends would be safe, but if Conor was worried that someone had bugged his car, then maybe someone was already looking for her. "There are some benches down near the light."

They walked down the street to the corner and settled on the bench. Conor glanced around again. Vinnie resisted the urge to do the same. Instead, she allowed herself to pay attention to the people in the area to see if there was power she could borrow. She was hoping for a Mesmer, so she could hear his thoughts, or a Dancer so she could feel his emotions. She didn't think he would lie to her, but the extra information couldn't hurt. Unfortunately, the only power nearby was Stone.

Conor leaned forward, elbows on knees, and rubbed his hands together in front of him. His right hand also had some light scars, what remained after he got burned and Jory partially healed him. He was wearing long sleeves, so she couldn't see the rest of his arm, but it was probably covered in scars.

Finally, he spoke, "Some people came by to talk to me yesterday about Kara and Maddie."

Kara. And Maddie. At the same time. As far as Vinnie knew, no one had connected the two — Maddie's death and Kara's disappearance. Kara's disappearance had been all over the news — She'd been a trainer for the Warrior games, and that made her somewhat high profile. Maddie's death had barely been a blip to most of the city. People asking about both might mean someone was putting the truth about what happened together. That was a bad sign.

"The police have come to talk to me, too, about Kara's disappearance." Her voice sounded calm.

Someone — they all guessed Will because he'd told her he'd taken steps to make sure she'd be safe — had erased a lot of the connections that would tie Vinnie and Conor together but a dragon had appeared the same day that Conor turned up with partially burn scars. which was also the last time that Kara McKnight had been seen. That was too big of a coincidence to be ignored. Will also couldn't hide that Vinnie had been looking for Maddie. Someone making a connection was probably inevitable.

"Not the police. They were FID agents. Someone," He paused and let out a breath. "Someone told them I had been asking around about Maddie after she disappeared, and then Maddie was dead and Kara disappeared."

"I'm sorry," she said. "I didn't think asking you would put

you in danger." He'd been asking about Maddie because of her. It didn't matter that she'd thought he might be the killer — this was her fault.

"You were trying to do something good," Conor said. "And I didn't get the impression they thought it was me. They asked a lot of questions about you and the two friends who came with you to the game the day of the explosion."

The FID was looking for TK and Hilda. The three of them had all gone to the stadium so that TK could try to match the power signature to the killer, and Kara had used one of the Twisted teams to create an explosion to get to Vinnie. Will had covered up a lot, but they couldn't hide that they'd been there that day.

These last few weeks, she'd wanted to ask him what he'd told anyone about what had happened or how much he even remembered, but she hadn't had the courage to go see him when he didn't want to see her. Lou, one of Conor's team-mates, didn't tell her why he didn't want to see her, but Lou knew that he'd gone to see Vinnie that day. Conor had to have figured out she and her friends were Twisted, and he could have given them up at any time, but he hadn't. She had told herself that had to be enough of an answer, no matter how much it hurt.

"I didn't have to tell them you asked me to ask around," Conor continued. "They knew."

Of course they had. "What else did they know? What —" She couldn't ask, though. She couldn't bring herself to ask what he told them about that day.

"They were very interested in what you and your friends were doing at the stadium the day of the explosion. How well you knew Kara. Why were you interested in finding Maddie? I just wanted to warn you. If you've got any more tricks up your sleeve, like people who can get me to the hospital without anyone seeing them, now would be the time to pull them out."

Vinnie swallowed hard and nodded. Did they have any more tricks up their sleeve? If the Federal Investigations Department was coming after them, did they have any defense? Will still texted her, trying to get her help, but she hadn't responded. In the fight with Kara, Will had taken over her body and tried to kill Kara. He might still help, but she wanted to stay as far away from him as possible.

"Vinnie," Conor said, his voice threaded with pain. "I told them the truth about the day I was burned."

Her head shot up.

"The truth is, I don't remember any of it," he said. "I guess I might have lied a little. I said we'd gotten into a fight that morning after you texted me and I left. The last thing I actually remember is you asking me to help you find your friend. I'm sorry. I never asked if you found him."

Fire flared in Vinnie's chest and she could swear she smelled the wood of the bench burning under her hand. "Yes, we found him."

"Not alive." He waited for her to nod. "I heard about a memorial. A street artist and when I looked him up, the paintings felt familiar."

"That was him," Vinnie confirmed, but she hadn't shown him Cer's painting until after the text he said was his last memory. The other memories must be there somehow. She didn't know how erasing memories worked.

"I'm sorry," he said.

"You still say your sorry too much."

"Maybe I should stop doing things I need to apologize for. It wasn't my fault, was it?" He closed his eyes. "Please tell me it wasn't my fault."

"It was mine," Vinnie said. For thinking she could save people, for not finding a way to help Cerulean before Kara sucked him in and used his pain to convince him to help her. "Or it was Kara's, if you prefer."

"I want to know," he said. "But maybe it's better if I don't. I don't want to lie if they ask me what I know. I want to be able to tell them she was evil. I knew that. I knew that before you told me just now, but I don't know how I know. Was she the dragon? Did she burn me? No, don't answer that. I told the truth. I woke up in the hospital with burns. I don't know how I got burned or how I got there. I don't know anything about a dragon. I don't know where she is. When this all blows over, you can tell me. Until then, I don't know anything."

Her heart hurt. Conor seemed like such a good, genuinely good, person, and had gotten caught up in all of this because of her.

He sat up straight and turned to her. "You will be able to tell me. You have nothing to do with this. Kara became a dragon somehow and burned me. You're not even Twisted."

The last part was a question. He wanted a response to that, wanted her to deny it. She'd lied by omission, knowing he was afraid of Twisted and not telling him she was, that her friends were.

His face fell. She'd taken too long to answer, but she had to tell him the truth. He deserved that much after what had happened to him. He wasn't even able to finish the season with his team because of his injuries.

"I'm sorry," she said.

He huffed a humorless half-laugh. "I shouldn't have shut you out. Lou said… never mind, it doesn't matter. I should have talked to you sooner. You should have told me what you are before all of this. I understand why neither of us did. We barely know each other, and we have enough baggage for an old married couple. But I don't feel like I barely know you. I feel like I could name your favorite vegetable."

"Weirdo, who has a favorite vegetable?" she said. That was what he'd said to her when she'd told him her favorite vegetable was zucchini.

His mouth opened. "Zucchini. Mine's butternut squash. I didn't tell you that, though, did I?"

Vinnie shook her head.

Conor stood. "I wish things had been different, Vinnie. Be careful. If there's any way to protect yourself from this, please do."

He walked away, head down. Vinnie waited until he was in his car before she stood. She needed to warn the others, and she'd have to go to the house to do it because she'd gotten rid of anything with their phone numbers on it to remove the temptation to call. If she hurried, she'd have just enough time to clean up from the fundraiser and go talk to them before she had to get to work.

CHAPTER TWO

There was a porch swing in front of the house that hadn't been there when Vinnie lived here. She'd only been gone a few weeks, but the bright yellow cushions in the white frame felt wrong. They'd moved on without her.

And yet, the old house still felt like home and all she wanted to do was open the door and climb the stairs to her old room, curl up in bed, and have all the people who cared about her nearby.

She shouldn't be here at all. Kara had used Cerulean and TK to get to her, and then Vinnie had transformed into a dragon and flown over the freeway. Will said people would come looking for her and she didn't want anyone else to be in the line of fire.

But if the FID was looking for Hilda and TK, she had to warn them. She'd just warn them and then she could go. Vinnie put her hand on the gate.

Nell was in the kitchen. When Vinnie had stopped blocking part of her power, she'd realized that she could tell her friends apart from all other Twisted and Nell was the only one home. At least she wouldn't have to worry about anyone trying to convince her to come back unless Nell had forgiven her.

Vinnie squared her shoulders, pushed the gate open, and strode up the sidewalk. The porch swing gave a tiny creak as she stepped next to it and eyed the door. She still had the key, but this wasn't her home anymore. Not that anyone but Nell would mind if she just walked in.

Maybe she should come back when Jory was home. Maybe she shouldn't have deleted his number. Maybe this wasn't urgent.

That's what she'd thought about Cer, too. He'd been in pain and she'd thought it could wait, and he'd fallen prey to Kara's manipulations. Kara promised to take away his pain, and Vinnie guessed she had in a way.

Vinnie squeezed her eyes shut and lifted her hand to knock. A shift in the air let her know the door was open before her fist came down.

"What do you want?" Nell said.

Vinnie opened her eyes. Nell's dark hair looked more ragged than she remembered. They used to have the same hairstyle, but they'd both gotten a little wilder. Nell had kept her bangs cut blunt, but Vinnie had just started shoving hers to the side. Nell was shorter than Vinnie, with darker skin and brown eyes to Vinnie's green. Completely different in every way except the hair.

Plus, Nell looked delicate in a way that Vinnie never had, which proved how deceiving an appearance could be.

"How did you know I was here?" Vinnie asked.

Nell pointed above the door. A small camera was aimed down at Vinnie. Things really had changed around here.

"Has something else happened?" Vinnie asked.

"What. Do. You. Want?" Nell repeated.

This was going to be much harder than she'd thought.

Jory had said Nell would forgive her eventually, but that day clearly had not arrived.

"Can we talk?"

Nell stepped out onto the porch, closing the door behind her, and waved at the porch swing.

Ouch. Vinnie sat on the porch swing and Nell leaned against the railing.

"There were federal agents asking the Warrior games teams about Kara and Maddie," Vinnie said.

"Slow. They were at the station two days ago."

Hurt burrowed its way into Vinnie. Her first thought had been to come warn them, but Nell hadn't bothered to tell her she could be at risk. Embarrassment followed close behind the hurt. Nell worked at the police station in the Holt. It should have occurred to Vinnie that she'd have information already. "Conor said they seem to think there's a connection between Maddie and Kara. They might trace it back to us. "

"Conor." Nell's lip curled.

"This is not his fault," Vinnie said.

"No. It's yours." Nell pushed off the railing.

Vinnie hung her head. She couldn't disagree with that.

"Feeling guilty doesn't make it better," Nell said. "You think if you feel bad that absolves you. Newsflash. It doesn't."

Vinnie tried to ignore the hot flash of anger in her stomach. Nell had been through enough, and she didn't want to cause her more pain, but Nell wouldn't give her the same kindness. Maybe it was time to set things straight.

She lifted her head. "I made a mistake. I paid for it, just like you did. I know there are some things that can never be fixed. But you seem to forget—you agreed with me until there were consequences."

Nell's jaw clenched and her eyes were glassy with rage.

Vinnie continued. "You're a coward. I can admit my mistakes, but you are too busy blaming everyone else. I made a mistake trying to do the right thing. Maybe I did take on more than I could handle, but trying to do the right thing is not wrong. I will always try to do the right thing. Even for assholes like you. You didn't even bother to warn me that the Feds might be looking for me."

Nell looked her in the eyes for the first time since Vinnie had arrived. "It was your decision to cut us all off, not mine. We didn't need your warning, which you would have known if you had taken the time to think for two seconds, but you never do, do you? And please send my regards to Will and thank him for taking my house away from me, too. Also, for the record, I wanted to go through legal channels, but you wouldn't let it go. I tried to help you, to protect you, and look at what happened. I haven't done anything wrong or illegal, and neither has anyone in this house. I'm not worried about what any federal investigators might find."

Hadn't done anything wrong? "You working in the police department and being unregistered is illegal. Of course you've done something illegal. Everyone who lives here has. Everyone would go to a detention camp if found out. And you? You broke into your supervisor's office and hacked his computer."

Nell's jaw relaxed. "I have things to do. You know your way out." She turned to leave.

Vinnie stood, not wanting to let it go, but she had nothing left to say. Then she remembered the camera. "Nell? If you're not worried, why is there a camera over the door?"

Nell looked over her shoulder. "There was a dead rat left on the porch last week. Hilda thinks it was just a neighborhood cat but..." Then she shook her head and went inside.

Vinnie turned and nearly jumped out of her skin. She'd been so focused on Nell she hadn't felt Jory coming up to the gate. He had some kind of duffle bag on top of his shoulders and he was wearing athletic clothes and covered in sweat. He burst into a smile as he stepped through the gate and swung the bag down, muscles rippling in his arms and chest.

She started down the steps, and he came up the front sidewalk. Before she could protest, he wrapped her in a strong, sweaty embrace.

"Why are you here?" he said into her hair.

Vinnie stepped back a bit and had a closeup view of the thick scar on his neck that looked almost like twin snakes under his skin.

She pulled back even further. "I came to warn you that Federal agents may have connected Maddie's death and Kara's disappearance, and they were asking about Hilda and TK. I don't know if they'll make the connection to all of you."

He frowned. "Hilda and TK only talked to Kara briefly the night of the explosion. Probably riskier for you since you were seeing Conor, and she was his trainer. Have they come to talk to you?"

"Not yet. Conor said they were really interested in Hilda and TK. I just wanted to make sure you guys were aware." She hadn't even thought about the FID coming to talk to her, but of course they would if they were asking about her friends.

"Thank you. You'd think Nell would have known they were making connections and told us."

Nell hadn't told any of them? Did she really think they were not in danger? It seemed unlike her. "Maybe she thinks it's nothing to worry about."

"Maybe it's not," he said. "Still would be nice to know. If they didn't talk to the local police, that's even more worrisome."

But they had. Vinnie didn't want to say that she knew Nell knew. Didn't want to out her.

"You haven't talked to Will, have you?"

"No, but he might be able to deflect them again, if he hasn't already."

"We can take care of ourselves," Jory said. "You don't need to put yourself in debt to anyone."

Nell came charging out of the house with a small paper sack in hand. Vinnie tensed as Nell shoved the sack at her.

"Here," Nell said.

Bewildered, Vinnie grasped the sack as Nell turned to go. Had she given her the dead rat in a bag?

"You're too skinny," Nell muttered and then charged back toward the house, throwing one last glare over her shoulder.

The bag in Vinnie's hands was warm, and the smell of cinnamon wafted up from it. Unless Nell had decided to spice up the rat and bake it, this was something else. Something that smelled like dessert. Her stomach rumbled, but she wasn't going to tear into it with Jory here. She could be dignified. She could wait until she got home.

"Don't let the smell fool you," Jory said. "It could be poison."

"Poison?"

He laughed at her expression. "Not on purpose. I don't think it's on purpose, anyway. Nell has taken up baking, but she's not good at it. I'm not actually sure how anyone can be so bad at it. The last batch of cookies she made had too much salt and the one before that, she burned. There was a cake that was somehow a brick. She won't throw out her mistakes and the freezer is full."

Another whiff of cinnamon and sugar wafted up to Vinnie's nose, and her stomach growled loudly.

"I told you she'd get over it," Jory said.

Vinnie held up the bag. "You think giving me poisoned dessert is a good sign?"

"Maybe this batch is fine." He smiled in a way that said he didn't believe his own words. "Since you're here, maybe you can do me a favor. I'm worried about Shaw. She's behaving strangely. Barely home, won't talk to us."

"Jory…" Coming to warn them was one thing, but seeking out Shaw would show to anyone watching that they still mattered to her way too much.

"I know —" He held up his hands. "You think associating with us will bring the doom and destruction, but she's muttering about cities being destroyed when no one is looking, and she's found a way to block Hilda from hearing her thoughts. If you could talk to her. You told me when you left you'd be a phone call away and then you refused my calls. You already came to talk to us. Just one more thing?"

Sneaky. She couldn't blame him, though. Jory was a worrier, and he had asked her to keep Shaw and Cer out of this whole thing. Maybe she owed him at least that. But if she went to talk to Shaw, maybe she'd just make things worse. Jory had always had more faith in her influence than she did.

"Let me think about it."

"Thank you." He gave her a side hug. "I need to shower. Come back anytime. This is still your home."

Nell didn't seem to think so, but she *had* given Vinnie poisoned cookies. Vinnie sniffed the bag and her stomach growled again.

She needed to get to work. The decision about whether she should go talk to Shaw could wait.

CHAPTER THREE

Early weekend evenings at Walt's convenience store usually weren't busy. There was a mini rush as soon as she got there, and then it was dead quiet for a few hours.

Vinnie hadn't had a minute to think since she'd arrived, but now the front door chime jangled, signaling the exit of a young mom and her three kids. They were the last of the rush, and she was alone in the store.

Her stomach grumbled, reminding her it had been a few hours since she last ate. Vinnie felt like she ate almost constantly these days, but she couldn't seem to keep the weight on. She reached into her satchel under the counter and pulled out the paper sack of oatmeal cookies Nell had given her. There were scorch marks on the bag where her fingers had rested, as she'd expected.

She wasn't supposed to be able to light things on fire — She was a Vasum, not a Wisp, but the Wisp ability had grown in her over the last few weeks. Vinnie couldn't control it — she'd almost burned down the library and her apartment. At times, it seemed to take every ounce of focus she had to hold the power back — especially any time she thought about Cerulean.

Vinnie didn't think her new ability was a coincidence, as Cer had been a Wisp.

The bell above the door jingled again and a tall blonde woman walked through. Hilda. Vinnie shoved the bag of cookies under the counter, not wanting Hilda to see the burn marks. She'd felt Hilda nearby before, but this was the first time she'd come into Walt's since Vinnie had started working here. Did she know Vinnie worked here, or was it a coincidence that she'd come in today?

Without so much as a glance in Vinnie's direction, Hilda walked toward the back of the store, making a loop around the refrigerated cases until she made it to the snacks where she slowed, examining the food.

Hilda wore soft gray slacks and a shiny blue shirt. Her cheeks looked sharper, and blue eyes colder than Vinnie remembered. Was she here because Vinnie had gone by the house?

Down, puppy.

Hilda's mental voice startled Vinnie. It felt like ages since she'd heard it in her head.

Vinnie forced her body to relax, slumping on the stool behind the counter and propping her chin in her hands. On the other side of the store, Hilda had paused, head tilting to the side.

What are you doing here? Vinnie asked.

Shopping.

The dismissal stung. For a moment, it had been like the comfort of an old friend coming to check on her, but apparently it was coincidence after all. Hilda seemed as cold and unapproachable as she had when they'd first met.

Hilda approached and dropped three twin packs of

cupcakes on the counter. They were the chocolate kind with cream filling and a white swirl on top. Cerulean's favorite.

"You hate cupcakes," Vinnie said.

"Just ring them up, Vinnie." Hilda sounded tired.

"Sorry," Vinnie muttered. She grabbed one package and punched the item number into the cash register, and the times three button and gave Hilda the total.

Hilda paid, shoved her change in her purse and fished around for something else. When she pulled her hand back out, she kept her fist closed over whatever it was.

"You really don't know, do you?" she asked. "I thought that was the real reason you came by the house today."

Vinnie squirmed. Hilda seemed angry, or maybe sad.

Hilda opened one package of cupcakes and put the two cupcakes on the wrapper. She opened her fisted hand, revealing two tiny yellow birthday candles, and put one in each cupcake.

Power flared inside Vinnie, and it was like Cerulean was right there with her. He'd only been dead a few weeks, and she'd already forgotten his birthday. Her eyes stung. She'd been trying so hard not to think about him because when she did, the power flared. She pushed the thought down, hoping Hilda hadn't heard. If she had to explain that, she might burn the store down.

"October 26," she said. "He'd be twenty-one today."

Hilda grabbed a lighter from a display on the counter and lit the candles. "Happy Birthday, Cerulean."

Hilda's nose was pink with unshed tears. Vinnie had never seen Hilda cry. They let the candles burn for a few moments and then Hilda lifted hers and blew out the candle.

"We don't want to set off the fire alarm," she said.

Vinnie blew out her candle, pulled it out, and laid it on the counter before taking a big bite of the cupcake.

Hilda took a bite of hers and winced. "Why this? Why couldn't he like oatmeal cookies or something?"

"Would have been hard to put a candle in an oatmeal cookie," Vinnie said around a mouthful of cake. "But I have some if you want. Nell gave them to me." She could probably slip them out of the bag without Hilda seeing the burn marks.

Hilda made a face and put the rest of her uneaten cupcake on the plastic. "Uh no, no way, no thanks." She shuddered and then flicked the candle on the counter with her finger. "I wish we could kill her again."

"Nell?"

The look Hilda gave her said she was an idiot. She meant Kara. Kara wanted to learn to use Vinnie's power because it was rare. She'd had a pendant that allowed her to do something similar, but she wanted it to be more permanent. She thought she could use the object to take Vinnie's power, too. The problem was, when you removed a Twisted's power, they died. That had been what happened to Cerulean. Kara had ripped his power out of him while Vinnie watched helplessly. And then Vinnie had taken Cer's power from Kara —

Warmth flared in Vinnie's core, and she stopped the thought in its tracks. "I don't understand why she thought she could keep my power when she couldn't keep any others."

"And you can't keep power, either," Hilda said. Were her blue eyes more intent on Vinnie than they had been a moment ago?

"Maybe she thought between the pendant's power and mine, she could figure it out." Vinnie had tried to find more information herself, but there was precious little she could find on Vasum power or objects that had power of their own. Will might know, but so far, she'd managed not to give in and text him back.

"It's too bad we don't still have her pendant," Hilda said.

Hilda didn't know that Jory had gotten the bottom half of the pendant and given it to Vinnie.

"Really?" Hilda asked, startling Vinnie again.

Hilda didn't read all of Vinnie's thoughts, but she said that sometimes they were loud and she couldn't block them out. She pointed at Hilda's half-eaten cupcake. "Are you going to eat that?"

Hilda's eyes slid over Vinnie's upper body and Vinnie resisted the urge to grab her hoodie off the back of the chair and cover how thin she was. She could feel the thought forming that would answer the question in Hilda's eyes and tamped it down, in case that one was loud too. Confronting the guilt she felt over that was too much to face. She snatched up the second cupcake without waiting for an answer and took a bite.

The crystal is completely inert, she thought at Hilda. *As far as I can tell, there's nothing at all special about it. It's aventurine, according to the internet. I can't see any power in it at all.*

Hilda hmphed. *Damn. Can't kill her twice. Can't take her power. Feds digging around. This is a bad day.*

"When are you moving back in?" she said out loud.

The question caught Vinnie by surprise. "I'm not moving back in."

Hilda's eyes raked over her upper body again. "You look like you can't even afford food. And you moved like, what? Five blocks away. It's stupid Vinnie. You should be home."

She already knew what Hilda's opinion about her leaving was, she didn't need to hear it again.

"Is Shaw okay?" she asked instead. "Jory says she's behaving erratically and wants me to talk to her."

Hilda pushed herself up straighter, and looked out at the store like she was poised to leave. "Her best friend died a few weeks ago. Of course she's not okay."

Grief wasn't necessarily the same thing as being in danger, but Cer had been in pain, and that had allowed Kara to get into his head. But if Cer hadn't known Vinnie, he wouldn't have been in danger anyway.

"She's also learned to block me, somewhat," Hilda continued. "You know I try not to intrude."

Vinnie didn't know any such thing. Hilda never seemed to have any qualms about reading people's thoughts when she felt it was necessary. Fortunately for the rest of them, Hilda rarely thought it was necessary. "Yeah, someone not wanting you rummaging through their thoughts is definitely a sign that something is wrong."

Hilda's lips thinned. *Idiot.* "Don't worry about Shaw. I'm sure it's just her new girlfriend. Nothing that you should concern yourself about, or make you feel bad about leaving. I mean, you were just the one closest to her after Cerulean. I'm sure leaving a second big void in her life to be filled with some drug dealer's sister isn't so bad."

Jory hadn't mentioned anything about a girlfriend. That could explain strange behavior.

"I don't feel bad about leaving." Vinnie lied. She felt bad that she couldn't be there, but she didn't feel bad about trying to protect them. "And you were going to do the same thing."

"That girl, Maddie, died and it could have been you. I was confused for a moment, but I never would have left," Hilda bit out. "That is my family. I thought they were yours too, but hey, if you want to hide out here and pretend you're trying to protect us when you're only trying to protect yourself, go right ahead, and if something happens to Shaw don't cry and say you didn't see it coming." She snatched the cakes off the counter and stalked to the door.

If I hadn't come by the house today, would you have even told me something might be wrong? Vinnie asked.

Hilda jerked the door open and was gone without

responding. It hurt, but what did she expect? Vinnie hadn't wanted to leave the place and people that felt like home, but she didn't know what else to do, how else to live, with what had happened.

She buried her face in her hands. What was the bigger risk right now? Shaw was probably fine, but she'd already taken the risk of going by the house, signaling to anyone who might notice that she still cared.

She couldn't go by the house again, but maybe if she just dropped by the diner where Shaw worked tonight, she could see for herself. It was open later than Vinnie's shift and Shaw would be working the weekend because the tips were better. One more check in, just to reassure herself.

CHAPTER FOUR

Eight minutes had passed since the last time Vinnie looked at the clock on the wall. Her shift would be done at midnight. Manny, who owned the place and could take any shift he wanted, preferred the early morning. Twenty-three minutes to go. For most of the night, busyness had kept her mind off the decision she'd made, but the last thirty minutes had been dull. She just wanted her shift over so she could see for herself that Shaw was okay and remove at least one worry from her mind.

She glanced down at her notebook. On the page in front of her was what she knew about Dancer abilities. Shaw's abilities. She'd never heard of Dancers being able to block a Mesmer's ability, but if Vinnie could block out her own then theoretically any of the other six types could block to some extent, right? Hilda could keep Vinnie from taking her power if she noticed, and she was the one who'd told Vinnie she was blocking her own abilities.

Over her notes, Vinnie had drawn a thick, black spiral. She touched a fingertip to it, feeling the dent. The page underneath it about Stone ability would be damaged too, but drawing the spiral had focused her mind for a few minutes.

She just needed to make it through this shift.

Large windows wrapped around Walt's and outside was the inky blackness of the middle of the night. The lights outside the building only turned the night into shadows and vague shapes. They didn't seem to illuminate much. Meanwhile, Vinnie was here in a blaze of light. Anyone out there could see her, but she couldn't see them.

The shape of a person moved against the window, then the doorbell jingled, and a man stepped into the store. He was tall, medium build, and wore a black hoodie and gray sweatpants. The hood was pulled up over his head, casting his face in shadow. He kept his hands in his pockets and his head down, almost seeming to turn deliberately away from the camera that was behind the counter.

A small jolt of warning woke Vinnie's brain up. She checked the man for Twisted power, but he was normal. The Zee, who worked at the nearby grocery store, was at work. She could borrow his power to defend herself if necessary. With Zee power, she could give the guy a muscle cramp.

She imagined him pulling a gun and her giving him a hand cramp. His hand twitched on the gun, pulling the trigger and shooting her. Okay, maybe not a hand cramp.

Manny had made extra sure to point out the button for the police alarm and told her to just give anyone who came in the money from the register. They were rarely violent, he said, and the insurance would cover it. When she'd asked how often the store was robbed, he'd been evasive, which had made her think twice about taking this job, but Manny was willing to pay her in cash.

Maybe he didn't know that she knew the police in the Holt wouldn't do much. They would arrive long after the robbery was over, but they also wouldn't say anything about workers being paid illegally.

And the type of petty criminal who would rob a convenience store didn't scare her that much. It should. A bullet would kill her just as easily as anything else, but the small spike of fearful energy was already fading. She eyed the energy shots by the register. They would keep her awake too long and she needed to get as much sleep as she could. On the bright side, tomorrow was Sunday, so the library opened late, and she could sleep in.

The man had gone straight for the back corner of the store, where one light had gone out and the other flickered like a dying butterfly. He shifted from foot to foot, staring at the refrigerated case. A nervous movement. Maybe she wasn't being paranoid, and he was here to rob the place. If she gave him an arm cramp and shifted to the side, a bullet wouldn't hit her, right? Shift first, then cramp. Nothing suspicious for the camera to see. Nothing that would get her hauled in and tested for being Twisted.

Because maybe she wouldn't pass the test this time. Her own ability, Vasum, didn't show up on the tests meant to identify Twisted, but she wasn't just Vasum anymore, and she didn't know what would happen.

The man grabbed something from the refrigerated case and slunk toward the register. He tossed one of those gross packaged chicken salad sandwiches on the counter and grabbed three energy shots from the rack. They tumbled onto the counter next to the sandwich. All this without ever once looking up. The only thing she could see was his tanned chin, which was long and squared at the bottom with the hint of a thick lower lip.

And he reeked of alcohol, like he'd bathed in it and let it sour on his skin. He'd been drinking for a while. That might explain the hoodie, maybe the light hurt his eyes.

Vinnie hoped he'd walked here and not driven. She rang up his purchase, and he handed her a credit card. She glanced at the name before running it through the card reader. Mark Jones. Fake. Her mind threw the word at her, but there were a lot of people in the world named Jones and Mark. Just because Will used Jones as his fake name didn't mean everyone with that name was fake.

Vinnie handed Mark Jones his card back and scooped his purchases into a plastic bag. "Have a nice day."

He slid his bag of stuff off the counter and headed to the door, almost colliding with a teenaged boy who had just walked in.

She wasn't scared but seeing him leave was still a relief. Her eyes strayed to the clock. Fifteen minutes and her shift would be over.

The kid had gone to the refrigerated case and was now walking toward the counter carrying a case of beer. Vinnie groaned internally. There was no way this kid was old enough to buy beer. He looked like he was thirteen at the most.

Just follow procedure.

"I.D. please," she said.

He fished something out of his pocket and handed her a driver's license, hands shaking. It looked legit. Manny hadn't told her how to handle this. He'd just said to ask for I.D., and when they gave it to her, ring the purchase up. The driver's license had to be fake, though.

The bell over the door rang again. Vinnie frowned at the card in her hand.

The kid cleared his throat. "Hey," he said, bolder than he'd seemed a moment ago. "I don't have all night."

"Sorry to interrupt," said a light and easy voice. It was hoodie guy back again. His head swiveled from the beer to the kid to Vinnie still clutching the I.D. "When's your birthday, kid?"

The kid puffed himself up. "None of your business, weirdo."

It was a hint. "When's your birthday?" Vinnie looked at the date on the card and waited.

The kid deflated. "Screw you." He snatched the card from Vinnie's hand and the hoodie guy snatched it from his. "Hey, that's mine."

"Should we ask the police about it?"

Growling, the kid stalked toward the door, shoving it hard outward. It swung shut, then swung open again, and Manny stepped through. Finally. Eight minutes to go.

Hoodie guy placed the card on the counter. "There's a holo of the state seal on real ones. You can see it if you hold them up to the light. It's there on some fakes too, but much rarer."

"Thank you," Vinnie said, leaning forward to get a look at his face.

He turned his head away and placed something on the counter. "Someone lost their earring. I found it outside."

He passed Manny on the way to the door.

"What was that about?" Manny pointed at Mark Jones's retreating back.

Manny was an older man, bald and wiry but a little soft around the middle. He had a face that made him look angry, and the giant smile he always wore seemed out of place.

"A kid tried to buy beer with a fake ID. I didn't know what to do." She picked up the card and held it up to the light. Just as the guy had said, no holo. She held the card out to Manny.

He took the card and tilted it this way and that. "You sell it to them. He had I.D. You're not a cop. Not your problem.

Don't get yourself hurt over beer." She opened her mouth to protest, but Manny interrupted. "You have to pick your fights."

Hurt? The kid didn't seem like he would have tried to hurt her. "I asked him for his birthday, it was easy enough. Do teenagers rob stores for beer?

"It was easy enough this time," Manny said. "I've never had someone rob me for beer, but a few years ago, a clerk confronted some boys stealing tobacco. They waited for her to get off work and followed her. She ended up in the hospital."

The Wisp fire tried to light in Vinnie. She pushed it down. "I'll just sell it to him next time."

It didn't feel right, but there were worse things than buying beer. Vinnie ground her palms into her eyes. She was so tired.

Manny came around the counter, set a paper sack down and slid out of his jacket, tossing it on some boxes. "You look like you've had a bad night."

"I'm just not used to being up so late every day. I'll get used to it." She lifted Manny's jacket back up to retrieve her hoodie from underneath.

She was halfway to the door when Manny called out. "Hey, is this yours?"

He held out the bag of cookies Nell had given her. Vinnie went back and collected it, shoving it into her bag.

Outside felt like a completely different world than inside of the bright store.

Vinnie stepped off the sidewalk and pulled her hood up over her hair, imagining she could be invisible in the dark. Her mind popped up an image of the guy who'd helped her with the kid. He hadn't sounded or acted drunk. From the amount of stink on him, he should have been slurring and maybe a little clumsy.

She glanced around, half expecting to see him lurking in the dark, but she was alone.

CHAPTER FIVE

Vinnie crossed the street and looked back at Walt's. She'd always loved the way it stood out, the old 1950s winged awnings surrounded by taller brick buildings. This section of the Holt was quiet at this hour, but it would pick up when the bars closed. The nearest bar, The Rope, was a few blocks away, but people would migrate to Walt's for snacks and painkillers before going home.

Until a few years ago, they might have gotten gas too, but when Manny bought the convenience store, he'd had the pumps removed. Or so she was told. Vinnie hadn't lived here then.

A gust of chill wind lifted her hair, making her shiver from surprise but not cold. She was rarely cold anymore. Still, her hands reached to zip her hoodie up out of habit, but the bite in the air would help her stay alert. She pushed the zipper back down, scanned the darkness, and picked up her pace.

In two blocks, she reached the turn that would take her to the diner. There should be enough time to talk to Shaw before the diner got busy again.

A scuff of footprints on the pavement caught her attention, and she glanced back, but no one was there. Vinnie stopped, eyes scanning the darkness, not caring if she looked weird and paranoid. She *was* weird and paranoid. Another gust of wind pushed some dead leaves across the sidewalk, making a scraping sound like the one she'd heard.

That had probably been the source of the sound, but Vinnie took a deep breath and listened to what her Vasum sense was telling her, anyway. Ferr. There was a Ferr lurking in the darkness, but not moving, two buildings down on the other side of the street. Following her? Or maybe it was just the Ferr from the grocery store on his way home.

Vinnie began walking again, trying to act like she didn't know the person was there. What Manny said about angry kids following a clerk played in her mind. Had the kid been Ferr? She never completely shut off her ability, but it was like a song that constantly played in the back of her mind that she barely noticed. She wished she'd paid more attention to the kid, but if he'd been strong, she might have noticed, anyway. Everyone had some power in them. The difference was in how deep she had to look in people to find the spark.

The nearby Ferr was strong. Power screamed so loud she wondered how she'd missed it before. Now it was like a cut you didn't pay attention to until someone pointed it out, and then you couldn't stop noticing.

Vinnie started walking again. As she continued toward the diner, the Ferr moved too. In the few blocks it took to get to the diner, they stayed an even distance behind her. Maybe she wasn't paranoid after all.

She continued past the diner without even glancing at it. Kara had been Ferr. The strongest Vinnie had ever encountered. Was the one following her strong enough to be Kara? Maybe. If they weren't, it was close. It couldn't be Kara because Kara was dead. Kara. Was. Dead.

Vinnie had pushed her through an anomaly and closed it, severing Kara's pendant. Kara had used the pendant to open the anomaly which meant she couldn't have opened another and come back through. Unless there was a similar power in whatever alternate universe Kara had found herself in. No. Kara was dead. She'd gone through the anomaly, and it had closed, and you can't live for more than a few days in a universe that isn't your own.

This was some other Ferr following her. It had to be. Some other very strong Ferr who was definitely following her. Did this new Ferr need to touch her to control her?

This is something that she'd searched on the internet, had been obsessive about. How did she keep someone else from controlling her? And she found mostly stuff that seemed like paranoid superstition, and the opposite, people arguing that Ferr couldn't control people, which she knew was wrong. Even TK, who was a Ferr, had thought that they couldn't control a person.

Some said they had to touch you, some said if you didn't look them in the eye, you'd be fine. Basically, nothing she'd found seemed like a reliable answer. Kara hadn't looked her in the eye when she'd told her not to move, not to help her friends, not to breathe.

She'd told her not to breathe and Vinnie had stopped breathing. Vinnie pulled a deep breath into her lungs, just to reassure herself that she could.

The burning in her veins wouldn't stop, either. Kara had taken control of Cerulean too and used him to lure Vinnie out to the house. Fire roared in Vinnie's veins, and she pushed the thought away, tried to put Cerulean in a compartment in her mind where she couldn't think about him.

The next cross street was coming up. Vinnie made a left,

not paying much attention to where she was going. When she saw the street she'd turned on was darker and more deserted than the one she'd left, her feet slowed. Was it better to find a crowd, so they wouldn't attack or to find a quiet place where she could fight back without fear of being turned in?

Ferr could be subtle. They could attack in ways no one could see. Kara had gotten to TK in a crowded room. There was no guarantee that a crowd would be safer. Darker and more barren it was, then. If she made a right at the next turn, it would take her into an area with a few office buildings. No one would be working at this hour.

If she was fast, she could strip the power from them and use it to make their heart beat faster, and get away while they recover. The Ferr followed her as she turned down another street. She was so focused she almost didn't notice the Mesmer, who blinked into her awareness, loud and bright, and then was gone.

The Mesmer couldn't just disappear, so they were still there too. Damn Mesmers, blocking her ability.

Did that mean they knew what she was, or were they blocking for some other reason? Vinnie pulled the Ferr's power, just a little so they wouldn't notice, then extended it to sense people that her own ability wouldn't pick up. Just the two of them.

Neither of their personal signatures felt familiar to her, but she couldn't remember different ones the way TK could, so she couldn't be sure. Still, two people made things considerably more complicated than one.

She could probably still pull enough of the Ferr's power they wouldn't have enough to use on her and that would at least give her a chance against them. She needed to surprise them. Pull the Ferr power fast, incapacitate the Mesmer, then run like hell.

Vinnie pulled in another deep breath and when the exhale was complete, she pulled hard on the Ferr's power.

A soft sound came from behind her and she turned to see someone collapse on the ground. The Ferr? She hadn't pulled enough power to kill them, had she? No, there was a heartbeat.

A man came charging out from behind another building toward her and she could feel blips of Mesmer power that disappeared as fast as they appeared. Vinnie sent the Ferr power out to him to find his heartbeat.

And nothing. There was no heartbeat.

He stopped on the street, and a gust of wind knocked her flat on her back. As she lay there, the air around her grew thin and she gasped, trying to breathe, barely aware of feet approaching.

How could there be no heartbeat? She was going to die. He was going to suffocate her. He had power if she could get to it, she could take it. Vinnie tried to pull the Mesmer's power, but she had nothing to latch onto — she couldn't feel his power.

He stood over her now, face covered with a black ski mask. She could see nothing about his features in the dark.

He was going to kill her, and there was nothing she could do. She had the Wisp power, but it was a raging inferno compared to the Wisp power she pulled when she borrowed it from someone. If she let the power inside her loose, she might kill herself.

Vinnie cast her own power out, looking for something else she could use — anything that could help her, but there was nothing.

Dead by her own hand or by a stranger's wasn't much of a choice, but it was the only one she had. She thought of Cerulean, and the power roared to life inside her.

She tried to grab it, focus it, but she could barely feel the edges. Fireball, she moved her hands together, hoping the gesture would be enough to focus her mind. Fireball.

A great gout of flame flowed from between her hands, blasting the Mesmer backward.

The air around her thickened, and Vinnie pulled in a gasping breath. She stumbled to her feet.

The Mesmer rolled on the ground. The flames seemed to be out already. She needed to move before he got up. Vinnie took one staggering step back, still gasping, trying to get more air.

She felt it growing thin around her again. She'd used Wisp power to make herself faster before. It still roared through her and Vinnie did all she could to channel it into her muscles as she turned and ran.

The power raged through her body. The world around her was a blur of dark shapes and fuzzy buildings. Vinnie's muscles felt like they were liquifying, but she couldn't hold back, couldn't stop the power.

She was almost to her apartment building, and she tried to contain the power, pull it out of her muscles, but it wouldn't stop. The apartment building went by and Vinnie ran around the block once, twice. Finally, the power inside her faded, and she slowed as she got to the front of the apartment building.

A sudden heaviness settled into her muscles. She'd overshot, and used up too much of the power, but she had just enough juice to sprint up the stairs, slide the key from her pocket and slip it smoothly in the lock, just like she'd practiced many times over the last few weeks. Within two heartbeats, she was inside with her back pressed against the door.

CHAPTER SIX

Vinnie slid down the door. She caught herself before she'd sunk all the way to the floor and pushed herself back up. The Wisp power seemed to have left her body as soon as she'd stepped into her apartment. She couldn't feel it anymore, but she couldn't feel much of anything anymore.

The smell of burned fabric wafted up to her nose, and Vinnie ran a thumb along the edge of her hoodie sleeve. Charred flakes came off under her fingers. Her legs shook. She didn't have much time if she wanted to remain conscious. She pushed herself up and tried not to think about the lack of sensation in her legs.

Her body knew how to walk. She opened her freezer and pulled out a bag of ice. Something warm squeezed through her fingers, and the bag dropped to the floor — the plastic she'd used to pick it up melted to her fingers. Vinnie blinked at it. That was a first.

Cold water, maybe the tap would be cold enough. She went to the tap, turned on the cold water and shoved her hands under the stream. The water hissed and steamed, and Vinnie stood there bowed over the sink for a few moments.

When her hand stopped steaming, she went back to her fridge and pulled out a gallon jug of sweet tea and poured some into a cup that sat on the counter. Some of the liquid sloshed out, but once she got the cup filled, she lifted it and gulped the tea down before pouring another and gulping that down, too. Wisps needed sugar.

"Hummingbird, hummingbird, fly away," she murmured.

Her bag had been slung over her shoulder crossbody style and she'd forgotten about it. It was squished but not burned. Vinnie slid it off and let it fall to the floor.

She picked up the bag of ice and the jug of tea and stumbled to the bathroom, where she dumped the ice in the tub and started the tap before setting down the tea. Vinnie unzipped her hoodie and let it drop to the floor on top of the jug of tea, then looked down at her feet. Her shoes were too far away and her body was too unsteady for her to slip them off with just her feet.

Another burning flare ripped through her chest, like an after echo, and the tremors increased. She needed the ice. With her shoes and clothes still on, Vinnie stepped into the tub and sunk down.

A squealing gasp ripped from her at the shock of the cold against her burning skin, but after a few panting breaths, she found the courage to sink down, letting the icy water come to her chest.

Her breath came out hitching, and her eyes burned. Vinnie ground the palms of her hands into her eyes. No tears would come. She knew that from experience. Her body shook harder, but not from using power that was too big for her. They could have killed her out there and there was nothing she could do about it. Thank goodness she hadn't made it to the diner and talked to Shaw. She'd been right to stay away from her friends. What would have happened if they'd attacked Shaw?

Who were those people? Why had they attacked her? Part of her wanted to believe it was random kids, but her gut told her it was much worse than that. Enemies, potential enemies, too many to count. How had they found her?

All she had were questions.

The water was already warm. It wasn't helping anymore, but at least the tremors had stopped. The fatigue and brain fog were kicking in, and she needed to get the water draining. She'd learned that the hard way after she'd nearly drowned herself. She flipped the switch to open the drain with her foot and tried to convince herself to move.

If she didn't move, get some sugar, this would all be so much worse. Leaning over the edge of the tub, she put her hands on the floor and then drug the rest of her body out. The jug of sweet tea seemed to weigh a ton, but she got it to her lips and took more big gulps.

Then Vinnie pried her shoes off and slopped off her socks. The zipper on her wet jeans resisted, but she got it down before standing and sliding them down her hips. After that was done, she pulled her wet shirt off and wrapped herself in her one towel before picking up her tea and trudging toward the kitchen.

She poured another cup and drank all of it before leaning forward with her head on the counter. She needed more, but just a wanted a moment to rest first.

Was this what Cerulean had gone through every day? The constant fight to hold back this raging inferno? It was his power in her. There was no other explanation she could think of. She'd ripped his power out of Kara and held onto it — used it to help her become a dragon. She'd thought she gave it back to him in the field. She'd thought it was gone, but the day after his funeral, it was there.

A few days after that, she'd almost burned the library down when a book caught on fire in her hands. And the day after that she'd been thinking about him and it flared so bright she almost passed out. Every day was a fight to contain the power. She had to try not to think about Cer or fire or Wisps. She'd gotten better at keeping it down because if she let any out, it all came out.

Vinnie lifted her head and crouched to pick her bag up and set in on the counter. Inside, the bag of cookies had been partially flattened and grease had soaked through the bag onto her notebook. She pulled the cookies out and popped a chunk into her mouth. Hard as a rock, but the flavor was good, so she dumped some of the bits into her cup to soften and headed toward her bedroom.

Her mattress and a box of books were the only thing in the bedroom. The smell of paint lingered from where she'd painted the walls last week. They felt too white, too stark, but it was an improvement over the stains that had been there before.

Vinnie put the tea and cookies on top of the box of books and tried to decide if she had the energy to move the mattress. She should rest, but this might be the only time she could think about Cer without burning the apartment down.

She crouched, legs shaking so much she thought she would topple, and tugged the mattress, scooting it back far enough that she could get what she needed.

In the corner, the baseboards looked like the wood had split about eight inches from the corner seam. You could learn to do all sorts of things on the internet. Vinnie draped herself across the bed and pushed on the molding. There was a soft click, and she pulled out a drawer. This would have worked better with something more ornate to hide the seams, but if the cops searched her apartment, they probably wouldn't think to move the mattress and look for seams in the molding, right? Making it look like the molding had just cracked had been the hardest part.

Inside the drawer were two things. Vinnie pulled out the half of the green crystal and ran one thumb over it. This was evidence. Anyone who had known Kara might recognize it and know Vinnie had something to do with her disappearance. Beneath it was a small black book. While feeling power in others came to her more easily, seeing the power still required effort. Vinnie took a few deep breaths and shifted her vision. The crystal was dead, completely inert.

She put it aside. It wasn't what she wanted to look at. Vinnie ran her hand reverently against the cover of the book, removing the small accumulation of dust. Cerulean's sketch-book. When Shaw had given it to her right after Cer's funeral, she'd said there were a bunch of them, but this was the last one he'd used.

It was possible one of his fans would be motivated enough to take it if they knew it existed. According to the fan website, some objects he'd painted that were moveable had been taken from their locations. Cerulean had been a graffiti artist, and she hadn't even realized how popular his work had been until he was gone. Just one more way she hadn't been paying attention.

But the possibility of a fan stealing it wasn't why she'd tucked it in this hidden drawer.

Vinnie flipped the book open. The first pages were in Cer's normal style — whimsical creatures with various kinds of wings. Her favorite was a cat with angel wings that was repeated on three quarters of the pages. She smiled as she flipped, pausing on one of the cat flying straight up in the air in a superman pose with one paw straight out.

She sniffed and continued, flipping pages until she came to one of a dragon, curled up, sleeping. As she looked at the dragon, the shivering started again. The style was somewhere between Cer's usual style and something more realis-tic. The drawings that started on the next page were the reason she hid the book. Every time she saw them, fear coiled tight inside her.

She steeled herself and turned the page. A realistic drawing of Vinnie's face stared back at her.

Cerulean's talent was not realism, so the resemblance was mostly in surface details — straight dark hair with bangs, triangle chin. Most of the sketch was done in dark pencil, but her eyes were green. And half her face appeared to be melting like she'd been made of wax and left out in the sun for too long. The drawing wouldn't be that disturbing on its own, but what came after made it seem like a message or a premonition.

The page after that was a drawing of some buildings. The only living creature in that one was a tiny bat near the top. Nothing weird about this one.

But then the next one was of a house sitting by itself in a field. The roof of the house had burst open, and above the house was a dragon. The house didn't look like Nell's brother's house, and she didn't know if the dragon looked like her but that's what had happened. She'd burst out of the house with Cerulean and Conor, trying to get them to Jory so he could heal them.

And Cerulean had drawn it before it happened. She'd found nothing in her research about Wisps being able to tell the future, but Cerulean and Shaw had been close and Shaw was a Dancer. Some Dancers had better than average intuitions, but it would've taken more than intuition to draw this before it happened. Maybe it was a coincidence.

The next page was a return to whimsy, but whatever the creature was, it was only half drawn, and that half was smudged as if someone had taken a wet hand and run it over the page, trying to erase it.

And then the next page. Two dragons trying to tear each other apart in the background, and in the foreground a boy laying on his side, head twisted at an odd angle, and blank eyes with rainbows pouring from them.

Then on the next page was an old bomber plane with smoke pouring out of its wing. She'd looked it up, and she thought it was a World War One plane, but she couldn't be sure.

The last one was the worst. It was Vinnie again. This time, she stood in front of a building with flames licking out the windows. A body was falling from the window and there were more littered on the ground.

Vinnie slammed the book shut, shoved it back in the drawer with the crystal on top, and closed it.

The sketchbook didn't show the future. How could it? The dragon bursting from the house was just a coincidence. Another shudder went through Vinnie's body.

And what if it was the future? She was the cause of people dying. She didn't want anyone else to get hurt because of her. Hilda thought she was being silly and unreasonable, maybe she was, but she didn't know if she could live with herself if another of her friends — or anyone else at all — died because of her. What would have happened if Shaw had been with her tonight?

Vinnie curled up in her bed and drug the cover over her body. One good thing about using Wisp power was that it wouldn't matter how active her mind wanted to be. She was too tired to keep her eyes open.

She'd just drifted off when her phone chimed. That would be Will with his daily text. He sent them in the wee morning hours. She usually saw them when she first woke up.

She never responded. It was hard to forgive someone who'd taken over your body and tried to kill someone. She read every text, though, and wrote the information in her notebook. Knowledge was power. Vinnie could read it in the morning.

CHAPTER SEVEN

Vinnie tapped her pen down on the question in her notebook, as if staring at it would provide the answers, or give her an idea of where to look next. Will's text on the night she'd been attacked had been about a man named Elliot Mustaine, who lived in the early 1800s. By that time, most Vasum had been killed, and entire family lines eradicated to make sure no more were born, but this Mustaine wanted to find one.

"What happened to the girl Elliot Mustaine used?" Vinnie underlined Elliot Mustaine.

Will had continued the story last night. Mustaine had wanted a Vasum to use as a spy and after years, he'd finally located one that he referred to in his diaries as 'Mouse.' He'd held her mother prisoner to insure her cooperation.

And knowing Will, that was where the story would end. He never completed anything he started. Maybe he was hoping he would come up with a tidbit or story enticing enough that she would respond and ask him for more information.

Instead, she had a notebook with more questions than

answers. She'd left two blank pages at the front of the note-book for questions. If she found the answer, she wrote what page it was on next to the question.

Elliot Mustaine was squeezed in at the bottom of page two.

She should have left more pages at the front for the questions. It seemed every answer she found, she ended up with more questions.

Why were Vasum like her hunted and exterminated? She could pull power from others but was defenseless otherwise. At least she was until she'd ended up with Cerulean's power, and that was almost worse than having no power at all. She couldn't control it. She kept burning things, and it was eating her up.

How were objects that could rip away a Twisted's power created?

The questions she really wanted answers to were not in the notebook. Who had attacked her and why? Would they go after her friends? Was it random? Was there anything she could do?

Maybe she could start adding questions to the back of the notebook. Vinnie flipped to the back just as the bell on the library door rang. She hastily scribbled her question before lifting her head to greet her patron.

"I thought maybe you'd keep your head down and ignore me," Shaw said.

"Shaw!" Vinnie slid off her chair and stood there, uncertain. Shaw wasn't supposed to be here. It wasn't safe.

Shaw grinned and approached the counter. She put her hands out and Vinnie reached out and squeezed them. Shaw had changed her appearance and it was a little disorienting. Her hair was shorter and bouncier looking. A strong Dancer could change a lot more than their hair. Some, including Shaw, could alter their physical appearance so much they would be unrecognizable to people who knew them well. Shaw had done that a few times, but only for short periods of time. This time she had just made her eyes bigger, lips fuller and a few other changes that took her from her usual sweet looking self to beautiful.

Unease churned in Vinnie's abdomen, and she pushed it away. It was perfectly normal to want to be more attractive. She should be happy that Shaw looked happy and healthy.

"You're burning up," Shaw said. "And pale. Are you sick?"

Was she sick? The constant fight against the Wisp power meant she never felt well, but she wasn't sick. "No, I just don't get out much."

Some of the smile had gone out of Shaw's face and then her Dancer power flared to life in Vinnie's senses. "You're not sick?"

Shame burned through Vinnie. She'd taken Cer's power and hadn't given it back. If Shaw knew how badly Vinnie had failed, would she hate her? If she'd known how to give the power back, maybe she could have saved Cerulean.

"That question makes you sad and...." Shaw bit her bottom lip in thought. "Guilty?"

Vinnie snatched her hands back. She'd been able to hide the truth from Hilda, but Shaw could see right through her.

Shaw's eyes remained on her empty hands when she said, "Hilda's worried about you."

"Is she?" Or was she just trying to get Vinnie to talk to Shaw by sending her here? Hilda didn't know she'd almost succeeded in getting Vinnie to go check on Shaw, because she'd never made it to the diner.

"She said you were hiding things," Shaw said. "Trying to keep her from reading your thoughts. And too skinny."

"Is that why you're here? She asked you to check on me?" She tried to inject a harsh note into her voice that she didn't feel.

Shaw shrugged. "I wanted to see you, too."

"Did you? Everyone else texted or called me after I moved out. Everyone but you and Nell."

Shaw stared at her hands, picking at her nails. "You left me. If you'd wanted me in your life, you wouldn't have left. I can't force you to care."

The nonchalant way Shaw said the words made the blow feel even harder. "You think I don't care? I left because I care. I don't want anyone to get hurt because of me."

Shaw's head bobbed in agreement, but she still wouldn't look at Vinnie. "So you say. Do you really think the threats stop just because you're gone?"

They didn't. Vinnie knew they didn't. Her being gone didn't stop people from putting dead rats on the porch or the threat of being found out to be Twisted and taken away. It didn't stop them from being connected to whatever investigation the FID had launched because Vinnie had been seen at the Warrior Games clubhouse and so had Hilda and TK. And since Vinnie and Hilda had both lived in the same house as the others, that put them at risk, too.

But what was the greater threat? TK had told her to weigh risks and take the less risky path, and this was it, wasn't it? She didn't know how to fix this or keep them safe from everything. She drew danger to them and was useless when it mattered most.

"I can't change what happened in the past that might hurt you in the future," Vinnie said. "But maybe I can prevent new threats by not being there."

"You think we would just ignore threats to you and not try to help? Is that what you would do?"

"It depends on the threat," Vinnie said. If she thought her presence would make things better instead of worse, she would be there. She didn't want to hurt Shaw, but she needed her to understand. "Hilda asked me to check on you too."

The blow landed and Shaw's face twisted in pain. She'd come to check on Vinnie, but Vinnie hadn't done the same.

"Maybe if Hilda was so worried, she should take care of things herself. If you don't care enough to come check on me —" Then her face closed off, and the hurt was erased, leaving behind something cold and distant. She pushed away from the counter. "It doesn't matter. I had another reason for coming here. Can I have the sketchbook I gave you back? I forgot that was the one that Cer and I worked on together, and my girlfriend wants to see it."

Vinnie had been right. Shaw had helped with the drawings. That still didn't make them premonitions. Did Shaw remember what the drawings were?

"Vinnie?" Shaw prompted. She sounded weary.

The sketchbook was the last thing she had of Cerulean, and the drawings felt dangerous. Vinnie wanted to ask what Shaw remembered about them, and she wanted to know if Shaw had premonitions, but the barely contained hurt was still there under the surface of Shaw's words. Vinnie had lost the right to ask anything at all of her.

"Sure," she said.

"Great. I'll text you to let you know what day." Shaw strode toward the door.

Pain tried to crush Vinnie's chest, and she realized she hadn't asked if Shaw was okay.

"Shaw, wait."

Shaw paused but didn't turn around.

"Are you okay?" Vinnie asked. "I do care. I'm sorry."

"Look, don't feel bad about not being at home. Even if you were there, you still wouldn't know what was going on," Shaw said. "I got fired from my job a week after the Affirmation Day parade." Finally, she turned. "I chickened out at the parade. I was a coward and Nieves got away. I had left my home, my family, because I thought I could make the world a better place, but I was just a waitress at a stupid cafe, and the one chance I had, I blew it. I called in sick a few days and they took me off the schedule, said I was unreliable."

A week after the parade. Shaw had been getting dressed in her uniform and going to work as if nothing was wrong, but Vinnie had been distracted by everything that was going on. Would she have seen the signs if she'd been paying attention? Relief mixed with the worry and guilt. Even if Vinnie had made it to the cafe a few nights ago, Shaw wouldn't have been there. Which meant if the people following her had realized where she was going, they wouldn't have found Shaw.

"You never told us," Vinnie said.

"Everyone had more important things to worry about. I'm just one person and I'm supposed to save people, not have people save me. But I can't even save people. I screw everything up. How can I be the person I'm supposed to be if I keep screwing up? I don't even want to fight. I don't want to be in danger, but I have this power and I'm supposed to do something with it."

She'd had no idea Shaw felt that way. Vinnie thought back, trying to remember what Shaw had said when they'd started the Dragons all those weeks ago. It had been Shaw's idea, hadn't it? She had been mugged and they wanted to make the Holt, their home, a safer place. They'd decided they would help people who the police wouldn't. Shaw had seemed eager, and then when they had all decided not to help Will hunt Kara, she and Cerulean had tricked Vinnie to get Will's phone number. Had she just been doing it out of a feeling of obligation the whole time?

Vinnie wasn't sure how to feel about that, her chest felt heavy thinking about the weight Shaw thought she had to carry.

"Just because you were born a certain way doesn't mean you have to fight." The words tumbled out. "You don't have to be anything but yourself. You are kind and generous and loving. You care about people, and you make the world a better place just by being in it. If more people learned to be the best version of themselves, if they helped their neighbors and were compassionate, there would be no need for people to fight so hard to make the world better, it would just *be* better. My life…" Vinnie said. "My life wasn't better because someone went out and stopped some thugs on the street. It was better because someone gave me a home when I needed one. Because people cared."

"What about all the lives you saved by stopping Kara?"

"We saved," Vinnie said.

"Exactly," Shaw said. "She'd still be out there if it weren't for us, fighting."

Was that true? Someone else could have stopped her. "Maybe she wouldn't have been there at all if the world wasn't so hateful."

"That's naïve, Vinnie, even for you. People find a reason. Some people just want to find a reason hurt others."

That wasn't the point. Vinnie almost growled in frustration. "That doesn't mean you have to fight if you don't want to. There's more than one way to make the world better. Leave the fighting to people who want to do it."

"You don't get it," Shaw said. "As scary as it is, I couldn't live with myself if I didn't try."

The memory came unbidden — gravel against her back, struggling for air. Vinnie never wanted Shaw to be in that position. "There are ways to use your abilities to do good in the world without putting yourself in danger."

"Is that what you plan to do? Hide and not take risks anymore?"

"That's exactly what I'm trying to do." She could only

hope the world would let her lay low, and the attack was just a fluke.

Shaw looked at Vinnie as if she didn't recognize her. "You're not going to help Conor? Even though it's your fault he's in this mess?"

Conor was fine. She'd gotten him to Jory after Kara burned him, got him to the hospital. She couldn't help him get back into the games. There was nothing left to help him with and she would have to live with that. "Conor doesn't need my help."

"Right. I guess you don't know anyone who maybe lives in a hotel and can make evidence disappear. And you certainly don't know what really happened to Maddie."

Evidence? Maddie? "Why would evidence need to disappear?"

Shaw's lips parted in surprise. "Do you even watch the news? Or keep your ears open?"

"I..." Vinnie turned to her computer and wiggled the mouse to wake it up.

Before she could type in the password, Shaw said, "You really don't know. Conor was arrested for murder last night."

That wasn't possible. He didn't have anything to do with it. He'd almost died and there would be no evidence. None. He hadn't even seen Maddie since that day—the day she disappeared. Vinnie froze. He'd been one of the last people to see her. There was a picture of him with her. Still, they had to have more than that, didn't they?

Shaw opened the door. "Let us know if you need any help."

The door clicked closed behind Shaw and Vinnie sat back on her stool and stared at the computer screen. Help? What could she possibly do in a criminal investigation?

She needed more information.

News articles weren't hard to find, but for all the volume

of articles about his arrest, there was very little information. He was the last person to see Maddie alive, and they had other evidence connecting him to the crime. That's it. Nothing saying there was any connection to Kara, or the other murders or the dragon.

Will had removed any connections he could to what happened. He'd erased Nell's connection to the house. She wasn't sure what else he had done, but surely he would have erased any connection Conor had to the situation, too? Because Conor and Vinnie had been seen together, and Will wanted to use her for something. He couldn't do that if she was in a dead-end camp.

Vinnie had done it again. She hadn't paid attention to the dangers because she just assumed Conor would be fine because she knew he hadn't done anything, or been involved at all, but she should have seen the risk. After all, she'd suspected him herself. That's why she'd gone looking for him and how they'd met.

She sat back and stared at another article that didn't tell her much and tried to collect her jumbled thoughts. She just had to prove to the FID that he was innocent without getting herself and her friends in trouble.

Her hand reached for her phone, and she opened the last text from Will, fingers hovering over the virtual keyboard. If he could do something, would he? Did she want to ask him? He'd been asking for her help for weeks and she'd ignored him. Vinnie put the phone back down and stared at the computer screen.

She didn't even know what was going on, what evidence they had, but she knew someone who might. Someone who had sent her messages telling her that Conor wanted nothing to do with her. Someone who hated Twisted.

But Lou might know more about what was going on, and that made her the best place to start. Vinnie picked up her phone and scrolled down to the messages Lou had sent, telling her to stay away from Conor. She should have deleted them, but it was lucky she hadn't. Vinnie wasn't sure she could have found Lou's number on her own. She pressed the call button and waited.

CHAPTER EIGHT

The Sixth Street gym on 54th Street was exactly how Vinnie remembered it. Big, smelling of metal and not much else. Weightlifting equipment took up most of the space — cages, benches, weights, but there was a token treadmill and exercise bike in one corner and some heavy bags along the back wall.

One of the treadmills was taken by a blond woman, walking slowly and tapping on her phone. Three men lifted weights, and a woman punched at a heavy bag. The woman at the heavy bag wore ratty sweats, her brown hair in a messy bun on the back of her head. That had to be Lou. The Warrior Games would have a fancy place for the teams to work out, so why had Lou asked Vinnie to meet her here in the Holt?

Vinnie walked across the gym floor carefully, trying not to get in the way of the man walking up and down the aisle carrying some metal contraption with weights on the end.

Lou had shifted to the side and was kicking the bag, her face intent on what she was doing. Vinnie was almost to the back of the gym when Lou noticed her. Her eyes flicked to

Vinnie and away, but she'd recognized her because her face went from serious and intent to intent and angry.

This wouldn't be fun. She'd first met Lou when Conor had asked her to meet him at the Roundhouse — the small building near the stadium where visiting sports teams hung out. Lou had seemed friendly enough until she'd called the Twisted evil and implied they were less than human. Kara had fought with her, and Vinnie had been on Kara's side in the argument.

"I didn't tell them shit about you if that's what you're worried about," Lou said, not pausing her punching. "Didn't even tell them he was meeting you that day he was dumped at the hospital. Still won't be long before they come knocking."

"That's not what I'm worried about." Not primarily. She'd already told the police she had been looking for Maddie and she'd told them the truth, that she'd heard about it from a library patron. There was no evidence connecting her to Maddie other than that, but there shouldn't have been any connecting Conor to the murder, either. "I'm worried about Conor."

Lou stopped and put her hands on the bag to stop it from swinging and gave Vinnie her attention. "They'll put him in some cushy prison. He'll be fine. At least he won't almost die of smoke inhalation."

Another dig at Vinnie. "He didn't kill her."

"Are you sure?"

"Yes."

"They found her sock in his apartment. Her blood was in his car. Phone GPS puts him in the area she was dumped at the time she was dumped."

A sick heat washed through Vinnie. That wasn't possible. He hadn't done it, but if she hadn't heard Kara confess, would she believe he was innocent?

"Ah, there's the doubt," Lou said, misreading Vinnie's expression.

"He didn't kill her," Vinnie said.

Lou nodded, looking thoughtful for a moment. Then she wiped the sweat from her upper lip, stepped back and threw another half-hearted punch at the bag. "They're saying he and Kara killed a bunch of kids all over the country. They say the evidence is compelling. The FID agents seemed pretty convinced he did it. I trusted him. I defended him."

She really thought he did it. "They were Twisted kids, shouldn't bother you."

Lou gave her a sharp glance.

"What bothers me is that people go around defending something with their mouths. Meanwhile, their fists," She hit the bag hard. "Are the ones pulverizing it in the background. Kara and all her self-righteous bullshit, 'Twisted are people too.' Give me a little honesty any day of the week. Shouldn't be a surprise that people who support evil have no qualms about being evil themselves, should it? Tell me, Vinnie, why do you know they were Twisted children? I haven't heard that said anywhere else. So a little honesty, hm?"

She wasn't wrong about Kara's hypocrisy, but calling all Twisted evil made Vinnie want to punch something too, but fighting with Lou, verbally or otherwise, wouldn't get her any answers.

"I worked for a man who was looking for Kara." That was true enough. Will had asked her to help him find the killer.

"And this man wants to save Conor?"

"I'm not working for him anymore. I don't want Conor to go to jail for something he didn't do."

Lou considered her for a moment, then she stepped away from the heavy bag and nodded for Vinnie to follow her. They walked to a back corner of the gym into a hall filled with lockers. She punched in a code on one of them, opened it, and pulled out a towel and some shampoo.

"Why are you here instead of the private gym for athletes?" Vinnie asked her.

"That place is a madhouse. Tired of all the fighting." She slammed the locker and walked down the hall.

They turned a corner and Lou led her into a room full of showers.

"Take the stall next to me. Keep your ears open."

Lou took off her shoes and walked into the room. Vinnie eyed the wet floor and decided to leave her shoes on. She followed Lou into the back corner, where Lou stepped into a stall and closed the curtain. The towel slung over the top railing, followed by Lou's pants and shirt and a sports bra.

"Tell me what happened the day he got burned and I'll tell you what I know," Lou said.

Water sputtered to life on the other side.

That didn't sound like a good bargain. What more could Lou possibly know? And the information she was asking for would tell Lou she was Twisted and maybe some of her friends too. But what if she knew something that would help Vinnie prove Conor was innocent?

"A friend of mine had gone missing. Conor said he would help me look. He let me use his phone to call my friend. We went to go pick him up. Kara was there. She'd taken him." And Vinnie had just said the people kidnapped were Twisted, which meant she was telling Lou Cerulean had been Twisted. Careful, careful with the words. "Kara had a pendant that let her use Twisted power. She burned Conor and took his memory and then she got away."

The splashing sounds of the shower stopped as if Lou had gone still on the other side. The moment stretched until finally Lou said, "And the dragon?"

She couldn't tell Lou the truth, but she felt wretched lying after the whole speech about honesty. "It came from an anomaly that was in the house."

"She was after Conor, then."

She hadn't been, but that hadn't been a question, so Vinnie kept her mouth shut.

"She warned him," Lou continued. "She said that if he continued the work of his foundation, that people would come after him. They would shut it down, one way or another."

Vinnie was glad that Lou couldn't see the look on her face. She hadn't considered that it might be something Conor had done to put him in jail. She'd come to Lou tonight thinking this was just a misunderstanding, but if it was a deliberate set-up, then this was much more dangerous than she'd thought. She knew the evidence Lou had mentioned couldn't be real, but earlier Lou seemed to believe he was guilty.

"You think this was a set-up?" she asked.

Splashing started on the other side again, and Vinnie waited. Finally, the water stopped, and the towel disappeared. "Conor's not the killing kids type. You say you don't want him to go down for something he didn't do, but they want him to. There is not a damn thing you can do. Except maybe get yourself taken down with him. My advice? Walk away."

"Who is 'they?'" Vinnie stepped out of the stall and waited for Lou to come out.

"Doesn't matter who they are. Someone with power — political power, or money. They do what they want, and they get away with it. "

But if Vinnie had hard evidence and made it public, they couldn't keep him locked up, right? Or would they just say their evidence was stronger? It was the only plan Vinnie had. He'd run back into the house to face off with Kara. He'd tried to save Vinnie. She couldn't just abandon him without trying.

How did she prove that Kara had killed all those people? The only proof she had was Kara's confession and that wasn't helpful. What else did she have to tie Kara to the murders and absolve Conor?

"Did they ever find out what caused the explosion that day at the games? The one that injured the Sloth team and one of the Twisted crews?"

Lou stepped out with a towel wrapped tight around her. "The ungrateful crews caused that."

"Where was Kara at that time?" Kara had caused the explosion. Maybe if Vinnie understood how she'd done it, it would lead her to something. It was a long shot, but she didn't have any other ideas.

"She would have been in the coach area. We were up next. Did she do that too?"

Kara had said she'd caused the explosion so Vinnie would come to the clubhouse and she could get her away from the others, but that hadn't worked. "Yes. She admitted that to me."

"Was she one of them?"

"She was Ferr. Twisted."

"And you still think there's something you can do?" Lou scoffed. "That many trained Twisted all together means the security for the Warrior Games is extremely tight and the vetting process for anyone working with the games is extensive. If she slipped through, she had powerful friends and backers."

This was the second time Lou had implied that there was something much bigger going on. If Kara had powerful backers, what did that mean? Lou seemed to think that this had something to do with Conor's research foundation. The purpose of the foundation was to find a way to more easily identify Twisted. Who would want to stop that from happening so much that they'd put someone in the Warrior games for years, and have her kill Twisted just to set Conor up? What would be the end game? It would be easier just to kill Conor.

Vinnie asked, "Will Conor's foundation dissolve if he goes to jail?"

"If he doesn't have the money to fund it anymore," Lou said. "Maybe."

Maybe. "Can I talk to the crew who caused the explosion?"

Lou smiled tightly and pushed herself around Vinnie, headed for the locker room. "You just have a death wish, don't you?" She called over her shoulder. "They're in a holding facility waiting for a transfer to a maximum security Twisted prison. There's no way they'd let you in to talk to them."

Vinnie scrambled after her. "Wait, all of them? I thought they only thought the Mesmer was to blame?"

Lou looked at her like she was stupid. "If it's one, it's all of them. But you'd still defend them, wouldn't you?"

Vinnie ignored the jab. "Why would it have to be all of them?"

"They're all linked when they work together, but they still have free will."

Vinnie wasn't sure that was true. She'd seen the Ferr power and knew that Kara could convince a person so thoroughly it was like they couldn't choose. She didn't know how the crews for the games worked together, though. Only how her own friends worked, and what was possible.

"Not necessarily."

Lou rolled her eyes. "You're as bad as they are."

Because defending what Lou considered evil made her evil, too. "Why are you helping me at all?"

"Maybe I just want to see you go down in flames trying to save them?" She made a twirling motion for Vinnie to turn around.

Vinnie did as she was instructed so Lou could get dressed. Lou said she wanted Vinnie to go down in flames, but she'd been trying to warn her away. Was there something else there? Something she was trying to protect? "How's your cousin? They found Maddie's body outside her warehouse."

"They haven't even looked at Alice. Haven't even spoken to her. Do you know why? You can turn around."

Vinnie turned around. Lou had quickly dressed.

"Why?" Vinnie asked.

"Because they aren't looking for the person who did it." Lou made a circle with her thumb and index finger and made a motion like she was about to flick Vinnie on the shoulder, but then she pulled back. "Remember that, and maybe you'll survive."

CHAPTER NINE

Vinnie was paralyzed by the array of children's books in front of her. She hadn't started reading until she was a teenager and though she had some fond memories of books the school librarian or teachers had read to her, this was a used bookstore, so who knew if they had the ones she remembered.

Lou's words from last night played in her mind again, and she pushed them aside. She just wanted to do something normal for a moment and not think about people attacking her or Conor being in jail.

Today was the first time Carla would be at the library since the fund raiser and Vinnie had come to get some books so she wouldn't be disappointed.

"Liar, liar pants-on-fire," she said in a sing-song voice. Then glanced around, hoping no one was around to notice her talking to herself. She didn't care that much about disappointing Carla. Carla would complain no matter what Vinnie did, but reading was comforting, and she'd come to the bookstore to hide from everything that was going on—to escape responsibility just for a moment. Shopping for books never felt like responsibility even if it was for the library.

She wanted a few books for kids in case more came in, but she didn't know what was good. Vinnie slid her phone out of her pocket and ignored the text from Jory prompting her for a response. He'd texted last night asking her if she was staying out of it and she hadn't responded.

Now he was telling her there was nothing she could do about Conor. Vinnie shoved her phone back in her pocket. She should just grab some children's books. It probably didn't matter.

"You don't look happy." A man said from the end of the aisle. He came around the corner, head tilted as if curious. "Birthday present for a kid you don't know well?"

He was medium height, somewhat handsome, though his face seemed a little off kilter somehow — square jaw, lips a little too wide, and the hazel eyes surrounded by thick black lashes were a little too round.

"No, I —" The last time she'd told someone she ran a charity library, he'd found her. Not that she minded that Conor had found her, but she didn't want just anyone to know what she did, just in case. "I'm building a small book collection for a non-profit. They're for disadvantaged children."

"Ah." He walked further into the area. "What ages?"

"All?" Vinnie said, expecting him to give her recommendations.

Instead, he began pulling books off the shelf. "Budget?"

She shifted from foot to foot. She hadn't quite decided how much she was going to spend on kids' books. Since she also needed the money for the library rent and adult books. No one had come to the library with their kids, and most of her patrons were older, retired people.

The man had crouched to get to books on the bottom

shelf. He paused and looked over his shoulder at her because she hadn't answered.

"Uhh, ten books seems like a good start."

He put a couple of books back, glared at one, and then pulled another off the shelf. "Did anyone ever come to claim that earring? It looked expensive."

"What?"

He looked up at her, and recognition clicked. She hadn't gotten a good look at him at Walt's that night, but the shape of his jaw and lower lip were familiar when she ignored the rest of his face. Hoodie guy, code name: Mark Jones. She'd completely forgotten about the earring. "I don't know. I left it by the register. I only work four nights a week so someone could have come in."

His eyes were so intent on her, she felt like he was reading her soul and finding it wanting.

"Okay." He rose from his crouch and held up a book. "This is my niece's current favorite." He put it in her basket. "This author is excellent, and this one, well, you can't go wrong with dragons." He put the rest of the books in the basket. He took the book off the top and frowned at it, then rummaged through the basket for another. When he had the second one out, he held them side by side, frowning, before putting the first one back on the shelf. "That'll give you a good start, then."

Vinnie glared at the books in the basket, irritation bubbling up in her. She didn't know what books she wanted to buy, but she didn't need anyone choosing for her.

"Well…" his voice trailed off. "Take care of yourself."

"You too," she muttered, but he was already gone.

She removed the books from her basket and turned back to the shelves, but a kitten on the cover on the one on top caught her eye and she picked it up, opened and read the first few pages. It was cute. She put it back in the basket. The rest of them looked pretty good, too. Vinnie growled and put them all back in the basket. She'd wanted help, and she'd gotten it, and she really needed to pick out some books for adults and to get to the library. Her volunteer assistant, Meg, had come in this morning to cover but would need to get home and do her schoolwork.

And maybe she'd message Will when she got there. Jory was probably right. There wasn't much she could do on her own. But Will hadn't sent his usual text last night, and it felt deliberate. He had something she wanted now and was waiting, and that pissed her off, too.

Vinnie stopped at the mystery section of the bookstore next. Mystery was Carla's favorite. Then she got some romances for Zandia and started toward the hot new releases at the front of the store. Just as she pulled one off the shelf, the sound of raised voices came from the area near the cash register.

She shuffled sideways until she could peer around the bookshelf. Mark Jones faced off with June, the store clerk.

"I told you," he said. "My wallet was stolen. Why would I have someone else's mail?"

June shook her head. "You're welcome to come back when you get a replacement license. No picture ID, no book. I'm sure you are who you say you are but if I break the rules for you, I have to break them for the next person, too."

Vinnie should go to the back, ignore this. It was none of her business. Her feet carried her forward toward the cash register.

Mark Jones ran his hands all the way from his eyes to the back of his head, a look of panic on his face. "I know I shouldn't have put it off until the last minute, but if I don't get this paper done, I'm going to fail. All the copies at the school bookstore are sold out. Please. I will come back as soon as I have the new license, I swear."

There was only one reason Vinnie knew of that June would require identification. She leaned a little to the side so she could see the book he was trying to buy. *The Destiny Papers* by Cole Hanna lay on the counter. The book was on the restricted list for subversive speech. June would have to keep a list of anyone purchasing restricted material.

It was a stupid law. It wasn't like it was illegal to own or hard to get. Plus, Mark Jones — she couldn't seem to think of him as Mark or Mr. Jones — had helped her out twice already.

"I saw his ID," Vinnie told June. "I can vouch for him."

June narrowed her eyes at her. "Are you lying to me, Vinnie? You don't ask for ID at the library."

"I work at Walt's, now, for extra money."

"Jory doesn't care about the money. Did he kick you out?" June's mouth fell open as if she had surprised herself, and Vinnie felt her cheeks warm. "Never mind, sorry, none of my business. I can't sell this unless I see some ID and write a name in the log." Her eyes cut up to the corner of the room, where there was a camera pointed at the register.

When had that gotten there? Cameras, cameras everywhere.

"Hey," Mark said. "You've seen my ID. You could buy it for the library," He put emphasis on the word library, like he knew she hadn't wanted to tell him the truth about why she was buying children's books. "You can buy it and I'll just borrow it. I'll give you the money to buy it, of course."

That would mean that she had to put her name in the log. Vinnie didn't think that anyone ever came and checked those things, and it was just a paper log. She'd seen them sell restricted books here before, but she didn't want her name in the log, considering everything else that was going on.

"Please," he said. "If I don't get this paper done, I'm going to fail."

He didn't say that she owed him, so point in his favor, but she felt like she did, and it wasn't as if this would cost her anything.

"Sure," she said. Vinnie pulled out her ID.

"That's illegal, Vinnie," June said.

It was illegal to buy restricted books for another person. Another silly law, since it wasn't illegal to resell books you owned. "It's not illegal for me to buy a book for the library and it's not illegal for me to resell books. Plus, I get donations for the library all the time." Sort of.

June shook her head and took the ID, even though she knew Vinnie. She wrote her name in the log, rang up all the books and loaded them into two bags.

"Let me help." Mark Jones tried to pick up one of the bags, but Vinnie grabbed them and left the store.

Outside the store, she put one bag down, fished around in the other and pulled out the book, glancing at the cover. She almost winced. *The Destiny Papers* was a manifesto about how Twisted should rule the world because they had greater abilities than the average person.

"That must be some class you're taking." Vinnie held the book out to him.

"Shouldn't I go to the library to check this book out?" He emphasized the word library again. Mark pulled some cash out of his front pocket and held it out to her.

Was he calling her out on her not quite truth? "They really are for disadvantaged children. The city shut down the local library, saying that anyone could go to the main branch, but it's too far away for a lot of people."

"I didn't doubt you," he said. "But it is technically your book, and I don't know the address to the library. How will I return it to you?"

Maybe he was flirting? He knew where she worked if he wanted to give the book back.

"I don't want that in my library. Good luck with your class!" She picked up her other bag.

"You don't agree with the premise?"

She didn't think anyone had more right to rule than anyone else and she didn't think might made right, but that was none of his business. "I just don't want any trouble."

Vinnie turned and strode off with purpose, hoping he wouldn't say anything else.

"I thought you were a by-the-book girl, Vinnie!" He called after her.

"I sold it to you, I'll write your name in my log. Nice and legal."

Only when she got to the end of the block did she look back. He was gone. Relieved, she turned the corner and headed for the library.

CHAPTER TEN

Vinnie ran the duster along the top of the books, wiggling as she went to get any dust out of page cracks. Not that there was likely to be any dust on them since she'd gone over this same shelf three times already.

She'd spend the morning rearranging a shelf near the center of the library to make room for a children's section, which had taken less than ten minutes. Carla had already come and gone and hadn't complained once, which had to be some sort of miracle. Vinnie had spent the rest of the time staring at her notebook and doing random fruitless searches on the internet.

She'd looked at Maddie's social media and she'd looked for information on Kara and she'd tried to find some angle she could use to get into a prison to talk to Twisted crews, but there was no way that she could find.

Nell might know. Or Will. She had pulled out her phone a dozen times, finger hovering over his last message, but hadn't pressed the button. Maybe she could find some other way, but weeks of trying to learn more about her ability hadn't gotten her that far, so the chances of figuring out how to help Conor on her own seemed pretty slim.

Vinnie ran the duster over the shelf again. Maybe she could try some more research. She could try again to figure out how to get into a restricted holding cell for Twisted and fail at that, or she could fail at trying to figure out how someone might block her Vasum ability. The sky was the limit!

But she didn't have anything better to do. Vinnie was almost to the front counter when Zandia came through the front door.

"I thought I missed you today," Vinnie said. "You usually come in the morning."

"Alloute wasn't feeling well this morning, and I had to take him to the vet. Were you out too?"

"I got some new books."

Zandia grinned and headed off toward the back to look.

Vinnie sat on her stool behind the front desk. She'd just flipped open her notebook again when two men in suits came through the door. The FID had finally arrived to ask her questions.

"Hi," the front one with the receding hairline said. "I'm agent Taylor and this is agent Tucker, with the FID. We're looking for Lavinia Forbes."

Vinnie resisted the urge to slide off the stool and stand. She didn't want to look nervous. "You can call me Vinnie."

"I'm sure you know why we're here, and there's no need to be nervous," Tucker said. "This is just a formality. We have to cross all the i's and dot all the t's."

How to get someone to feel nervous — tell them not to be nervous. Tucker probably knew that and was counting on it.

Tucker pulled a notepad out of his pocket and flipped through it. There was nothing on the pages — Vinnie could see that as he flipped, but he paused on a page, anyway.

"You were supposed to meet Conor Hahn the day he showed up at the hospital, is that correct?"

"Yes," she said.

"And did you?"

"Yes."

"And then what?"

"We hung out for a little while. We argued and he left."

"Did he say where he was going to?" Taylor asked.

"No." Her short answers weren't making them happy. She could tell by the set of Tucker's jaw.

"We are not your enemy, Ms. Forbes," he said. "We're just trying to get information."

"You've already arrested him. Don't you have all the information you need?"

Taylor approached the counter and leaned on it, a little too close to her personal space. "You don't think it was strange a man you were dating ditched you and didn't tell you where he was going?"

"We went out once," she said. "And like I said, we fought. He wasn't in a sharing mood when he left." She wished Conor hadn't told them he'd left. She could have told the agents, truthfully, that they'd driven around talking.

"What did you have a disagreement about?" Tucker asked.

Conor hadn't told her what he'd told them about their imaginary argument. She should have asked him.

Vinnie ground the palms of her hands into her eyes, as if she was exhausted. That was true enough. "I don't remember. It must not have been very important."

"Was it about your friend that you asked Conor to help you look for?" Tucker tapped his finger on his notepad. "What was his name?"

"Cerulean." Her nervousness turned to dread. Did they know Cer was wanted for the murder of his parents? TK had faked a death certificate but they hadn't thought it would need to stand up to intense scrutiny. Cer was dead, they couldn't hurt him anymore.

"That's an unusual name. What was his last name?"

Vinnie grabbed her pen off the counter and held it out to Tucker. "You don't seem to have anything to write this down."

He didn't take the pen.

"You already know his name." She put the pen back on the counter. It was a gamble, but she didn't think they'd be asking about Cer unless they knew something. "He has nothing to do with any of this."

Taylor's brows scrunched together. "And yet, Conor Hahn was burned and reports we've obtained say that this Cerulean had the appearance of a Wisp. Strangely, no one seems to have a picture of him. Do you have a picture of him, Miss Forbes?"

"Are you accusing Cerulean of something?"

Tucker's surprise seemed genuine. He and Taylor shared a glance. "Do you know what Conor Hahn is accused of?"

She did, of course, he was accused of murdering Maddie. "Killing a girl."

"Killing Twisted children and young adults," Taylor said gently. "We don't know they were all Twisted, but there are hints in their lives. Conor Hahn ended up in the hospital with burns on the same day that a young Wisp died."

Oh shit. They thought he killed Cer, too. And the evidence was right there. Conor was burned, Cer was dead, and Kara was missing.

"Wasn't there a dragon that day?" She clamped her mouth shut. Brilliant move on her part, just point them at herself so they could take her in instead. Only, she wouldn't be sent to a normal prison. Who knows what they would do with her if they knew what she was?

Tucker smirked. "I don't think a dragon would hunt down Conor to burn him. Just a coincidence."

"Can I see your phone?" Taylor asked.

"Do you have a warrant?" Why had she said that? She had nothing to hide on her phone. No pictures of Cer, because she'd only just gotten it before he died. Now she sounded suspicious. Vinnie pulled out her phone, unlocked it, opened the photos, and handed it to Agent Taylor.

"Sunsets, random children and pets. Do you have any other friends? Family? I'm sure your dad would love to know where you are."

She snatched her phone back. "I told you I don't have pictures of him, and my location is none of my dad's business. I don't have friends anymore."

"Why is that?" Tucker said. "Did Conor threaten them because they're Twisted? Did they blame you for bringing him into your lives?"

The second question hit close to the truth. Fire roared in Vinnie's stomach. She felt trapped, and she wanted to hit something, or say anything, to make them go away and not look too closely at her friends. To not think Conor did this. She pulled a breath in through her nose, and let it out through her mouth, focusing on the breath.

"You said this was a formality, but I feel like I'm under attack. My friends aren't Twisted. My personal life is none of your business. If you want to talk to me further, I'll need my lawyer present."

She sounded calm, like her dad. Maybe she had one small thing to be thankful for. He'd taught her how to act when threatened, because she'd seen him do it.

Agent Taylor sighed. "Of course. We're not here to out anyone. We're just trying to make the connections, rule certain things out. Just one more question? Why were you looking for Maddie Willis?"

"Because I asked her to." Zandia stood at the front edge of the nearest bookcase, looking more uncertain than Vinnie had ever seen her. When all eyes were on her, she dropped her hands to her sides and squared her shoulders. "You don't know what it's like living in this place. No one cares about kids that go missing in The Holt, but Maddie had skipped school to go to the games and Vinnie is young and smart and I asked her to go out there and talk to them. The police wouldn't do anything."

"I'm sorry that you feel that way," Taylor said. "We're trying to do something, ma'am. Do you have any knowledge of the murders that might be useful to us?"

Zandia shook her head.

Tucker pulled out a card and took the two steps necessary to reach her. "If you think of anything?"

"Of course," Zandia said.

The men nodded at Vinnie and Zandia and left.

"Thank you," Vinnie said when they were gone.

Zandia wrung her hands a few times and then held them down at her sides. "You went looking for Maddie?"

"Someone had to," Vinnie mumbled, and stared at her counter. "Obviously I failed."

"You don't think Conor did it. You were too chummy with him." Zandia sidled up to the counter and put the two books she'd picked out down.

"I know he didn't."

Zandia leaned close and whispered, "Was it that woman who disappeared? Did you get her?"

Vinnie knew she shouldn't be telling her this, but Zandia had been having a hard time lately. Telling her the truth — that Kara couldn't kill anymore — was one small thing she could give her.

"She won't hurt anyone else."

Zandia whooped. "I knew it. You're the White Dragon. I

was thrown when you said you'd been tested, but I know there are ways to beat those tests."

Vinnie's mind reeled, and she wasn't sure what part to react to. She could try to deny that she was Twisted, but she didn't want to lie. And she probably shouldn't ask about how to beat a test for Twisted, since Zandia thought she knew and then she'd have to explain what she was — the existence of Vasum wasn't common knowledge. "The White Dragon?"

Some of the mirth left Zandia's face. "You're not?"

When Vinnie and her friends had decided to fight crime in the neighborhood, they'd called themselves the Dragons, not the White Dragon. Could that be what Zandia meant?

"I don't think so," Vinnie said.

Zandia gave her a quizzical look and dug into her purse. After what seemed an eternity, she pulled her phone out, tapped a few times, and showed the phone to Vinnie. She'd opened an app. At the top was a drawing of a White Dragon. There were two buttons below that. One said 'request help' and the other said 'SOS.'

Vinnie was definitely not the White Dragon. "What's the difference between 'request help' and 'SOS'?"

"SOS is if you need help right away, like an emergency."

"How can they get to someone fast enough if there's an actual emergency?" Ten minutes was a long time if you were in serious trouble.

"There's a legal disclaimer that says the app is for entertainment purposes and should not be used in case of a real emergency. The creators are not liable for any harm if the person didn't call 911."

But Zandia didn't think it was for entertainment, so that still didn't answer Vinnie's question. Were people relying on some app for help?

"That seems like a cruel joke," Vinnie said. "Are people relying on this?"

"I thought you would understand." Zandia seemed hurt.

Vinnie could kick herself for her doubt. Zandia was smart. She wouldn't download an app if she thought it was a hoax or that it wouldn't help.

"I'm sorry," she said. "I do. It's just… if you were in an actual emergency, you wouldn't have time to pull this up and press the button."

"It guides you through setting up a voice activated command. You choose your help word. Mine's Roscoe. So I just activate the voice recognition feature by pressing the side button, or using the activation words and then use my code word. I was worried because it seems so slow, but a friend of a friend said her daughter set it up and used it when she surprised a burglar in her house and the police showed up in less than five minutes."

Vinnie was completely confused now. If this white dragon was supposed to help, why were the police showing up?

Seeing her look, Zandia threw her hands up. "Don't ask me. I don't know how it works. Another guy said he called when he heard a noise outside his house and he saw a woman in black, with dragon wings painted on her back, prowling around his house. She knocked on the door and left. That's why I thought you had something to do with it. You really got that woman?"

Vinnie nodded.

Zandia was somber this time. "You're not going to let him go to jail for killing those young people. You failed Maddie, but you've got to make it right."

"I don't know how." How could she stop something when she couldn't even figure out how to find out what was happening?

"You know there's no shame in asking for help." Zandia pointed at her phone.

The White Dragon. Shaw had stood right where Zandia was standing and told Vinnie she had to use her power for good. Could she have done something like that? She couldn't risk asking the White Dragon for help, but there was someone she could call. It didn't matter what her feelings were about Will. Zandia was right, she had to do something.

CHAPTER ELEVEN

Vinnie had felt him nearby a few minutes before she closed the library, but there was only one way out of the alley. She peered carefully around the corner onto the street. He loitered by a nearby lamp post, eyes glued to his phone. If she moved fast, perhaps she could slip away.

She flipped her hood up and turned right, moving fast down the street. The nearest bus stop was too close — she would still be in his line of vision. As soon as she crossed the street, she felt him shift position behind her, and follow fast. If she ran, he'd know she was trying to get away. Maybe if she took a quick turn, she could duck into a shop, act like she was shopping.

Buying things she couldn't afford. Things he knew she couldn't afford. Plan B, talk fast.

He was almost on her. Vinnie slowed her steps.

"Your apartment's the other direction," Jory said.

"I have some errands to run." She didn't want to tell him she was going to meet Will. He wouldn't approve, and she wasn't in the mood to argue.

"You didn't answer my texts."

"You already knew what I was going to say."

"You're not the boss of me?" he asked. "That's what you were going to say, right?"

Her lips quirked in spite of herself. "Something like that."

"What do we know so far?"

She eyed him sideways. "There's no 'we.'"

"You're not the boss of me."

"That's the second joke in less than two minutes. You're going to ruin your dour reputation."

"Technically, it was the same joke. I don't have a dour reputation."

"Yes sir, preacher man."

He grunted. "I guess the question is, what have *you* learned so far, and where are *you* going while being followed by me?"

"No," she said. "The question is, 'how do I get rid of you?'"

She'd meant it in a joking manner, sort of, but Jory wasn't amused. "You've found something and you're currently about to put yourself in another risky situation. You don't get rid of me."

Walking was just taking her further away from where she wanted to go, and Jory didn't look like he was going to give up. "Lou says it's a setup. Kara threatened Conor that if he continued with his foundation, someone would shut him down one way or another. The FID has hard evidence that Conor killed Maddie, which is impossible. You and I both know that's not true."

"Do we?"

Should she even respond to that? When she had been trying to find out who had Maddie, her friends thought Conor was a part of it, but Jory knew Kara hadn't expected Conor to be with her when she went to get Cer and he knew Kara had erased Conor's memory to hide what she'd done.

Vinnie glared at him.

"Fine," Jory said. "Where are you going now? La Mafia? Gonna poke around Alice's warehouse?"

"I made a deal with Will. I'm going to talk to him."

His jaw clenched. "You can ride the bus out there with me following you or we could take the van."

"I don't need you to come with me."

"You don't need me, but I need to be there. For me." His jaw flexed again and then he ground out. "Please."

She was frozen. Her mind flashed to Cer, to the people who'd attacked her a few days ago, and to Jory asking her to keep Shaw and Cerulean out of her quest to find Maddie. He'd been right, and she should have listened to him.

"I'm not easy to kill, Vinnie." His voice was gruff.

Jory was a Zee. The name of his type was some sick joke about them coming back from the dead like zombies. He'd come close to death once, but he didn't die. She still didn't want him involved but he was here and he wasn't going to give up. In the future, she'd have to be sneakier.

"Let's take the van," she said.

They went back the way they'd come. Once they were in the van and buckled, Vinnie said, "I should have texted you back, told you I was staying out of it."

"I would have known you were lying." Jory pulled into traffic.

"Why were you telling me to stop if you knew I wouldn't listen?" Vinnie asked.

"I had to register my complaint. What did you promise this guy in exchange for his help? What is he helping with?"

"We didn't work out the details. I said I would help him if he helped me and he preferred we talk in person." She didn't mention that he'd stopped his daily information texts as soon as Conor was arrested. That was obviously deliberate, but why? He knew she'd ask? He was making a point that he was now the one with the power because she would need his help?

"He wasn't counting on me." The look on Jory's face was a little scary. She wouldn't want to meet him in a dark alley.

The feeling of leaving home was palpable the second they crossed out of the Holt. Will was staying in a cheap motel, just a minute's drive outside the unofficial border. When she'd asked him where he wanted to meet, he'd given her the address of the same place she'd met him at before, which had surprised Vinnie. She and TK and Hilda had gone looking for him and the hotel had been empty. Somehow, he'd set the clerk's memory to erase when anyone asked about him, and yet, he went back to the same place.

In no time at all, they were pulling into the hotel parking lot.

"I can't believe he's still staying here," Jory muttered as they approached the door to Will's. He'd even gotten the same room.

Vinnie knocked on the door. They waited for what seemed like an eternity for the door to open. When it did, there was Will, looking the same — same rumpled brown hair, same bright green eyes that were so much like her own. He was wearing faded designer jeans and a t-shirt.

Will raised an eyebrow at Jory. "Glad you both could make it."

Vinnie had thought he would protest Jory being there, but he didn't even seem surprised. "Why do you insist on staying here when you can obviously afford something better?"

The room looked unused. There were no personal items, nothing in the trash.

"This wasn't cheap," Will said.

"This room is obviously cheap," Jory said. "Even I could afford it."

"Things that seem obvious are not necessarily true," Will said, and started toward the bathroom. "Follow me."

"Into the bathroom?" Vinnie whispered to Jory.

"If he wanted your help for some kind of kink, I'm out," Jory said.

Will peered out through the doorway. "Coming?"

"Let's see what's in the bathroom." Jory followed Will and Vinnie followed Jory.

Inside the bathroom, there was an opening where the toilet should have been. There were rails on the ceiling and floor and a handle attached to a wall piece to slide it to the side. Jory followed Will to the opening. When he got his first glimpse of whatever was on the other side, he whistled softly.

He disappeared through, giving Vinnie space to see what he had seen a moment before.

There was a line of computer banks directly beyond the door. She stepped through into a room that was too large to be a hotel room. Walls had been removed, and thick columns had been placed in what she assumed were places needed to keep the hotel upper floor from collapsing on their heads.

"This is William," Will said, pointing to an old man at one of the computers. "No relation."

"Having the same first name doesn't usually mean people are related," Jory said.

He hadn't gotten the joke. Thank goodness she wasn't the only one who didn't think Will's jokes were funny.

Beyond the computer banks was what looked like a personal gym. In the other direction, the room looked some-what like a lab. There were refrigerator cases, some with test tubes and such, but one held bottles of Dr. Pepper and water. Beyond that, close to the outer wall, was a doorway without a door leading to another room.

"It would have been cheaper to buy a nice house and live there than it was to modify this hotel room," Jory said.

"I'm invisible here," Will said. "People just see me going into a cheap motel. They don't know I have money and being in a motel accounts for the high electric bill."

There would be other problems, like people wanting to check in or noticing there were no other guests the way she and her friends did.

"You think you're Batman or something?" Jory asked.

"Even better." Will put his hands on his hips and puffed out his chest. "I am Poodle Man. Defender of pets and squirrels."

Jory snorted in amusement.

Betrayed. Will still wasn't funny.

"Shall we?" Will led them through the open doorway to a well-furnished room with a kitchen and a dining table that would seat about eight. There was a long sofa pushed up against one side.

"What is all of this?" Jory waved at the equipment in the other room.

Will pulled a Dr. Pepper out of the fridge and held it out. Jory shook his head, but Vinnie took the bottle from his hands and sat at the table. Jory sat with one chair between them as Will took another bottle out and cracked it open.

He leaned back against the countertop. "I'll explain after we have an arrangement."

"Same old jackass, huh?" Jory said. "Humor me."

"I could point out that the two of you are the ones here asking for favors, but I won't. All of this is my current home and the operations of the project I'm working on. I'm not going to explain that to you unless we come to an agreement. The gym isn't part of the project. It's just there to make me feel tough." One side of Will's mouth quirked. "Now, what brings you here?"

The conditions seemed fair enough, and Vinnie had nothing to hide. "If you'll get Conor out of jail, I'll help you with your project. If you can erase property records, I'm sure you can make evidence disappear too. Especially since it's fake evidence."

"Fake evidence?" Will asked. "Are you sure about that?"

"She's sure," Jory said.

Will pushed away from the counter and sat in a chair at the other end of the table. He slid his bottle back and forth with his hands for a few moments. "I had the house records changed before anyone started looking too deeply. If they already have the evidence, making it disappear is just more suspicious and would bring people looking."

"Then help me prove it was Kara. We can take it to the press. They can't keep him if there's evidence out in the open that proves he's innocent."

"I think you are overestimating the power of public opinion. Whether or not that works depends on who is setting him up, and how convincing the counter evidence is. That could end up being even more dangerous, for him, for you."

She could see his point, but that didn't mean she liked it. If someone was after Conor specifically, then getting him released just meant they'd try something else. "I don't care about the danger to me. What would you suggest?"

"Find out who set him up and take them out," Jory said. "He has a foundation that's working to identify Twisted. There are a lot of people who would like to stop that."

Vinnie doubted she could take anyone out, but finding out who had set Conor up sounded like a good first step.

"Lou said Kara threatened him over the foundation," Vinnie told Will.

Will said, "I can get him out of jail, but other than that..."

"And help me find out who put him there," Vinnie said. She was leaving out vital information, but she didn't want Jory to know she'd been attacked. That would only make him more determined to help. Besides, that might be unrelated to Conor's arrest.

"That's a big ask," Will said.

Jory pointed at the other room. "I have the feeling you've got a pretty big one, too."

Will stood, taking his drink with him. "Let's take a look."

They followed him back into the other room, where he paused in the lab. "We know Kara had objects of power of unknown origin, which she somehow used to open anomalies. I don't think any of those objects were made in this world, but even I can't break the private security of the agencies that would know that."

As far as Vinnie knew, she only had a crystal, but her office had been broken into after her disappearance. That had been in the news. "Kara's office was broken into. That was you."

"I was hoping she kept records, where she got the objects, how they were used or at least a clue to where she came from so I'd know where to start."

Jory looked at Vinnie, but neither of them said anything about the piece of the crystal Vinnie had.

"It was never about saving people for you, was it? It was about power."

"The disappointment. The condescension," Will said. "It was about saving people, but no, not the Magiera she was taking. It was about saving the entire world."

Jory scoffed as Will led them to the rows of computers. On the wall of monitors in front of William were maps. "I have retroactive maps of known anomalies. Their locations and natures when I can find that, which is rare. I've built records that go all the way back to the beginning, and it's important."

"There seems to be a line of increasing intensity that goes from here." He pointed at their city on the map. "To here." He pointed to Europe. "It goes both ways around the globe, but it's stronger across the shorter distance, and that tracks with the original pattern of deaths in 1918, which started in France. The scientists know that. What they don't seem to care about is the type. There are at least three types of anomalies, the eaters that suck everything in, ones that are deliberately opened and ones that open spontaneously but are benign. Many eaters fall along this line."

He showed them another map, this one covered in dots of various sizes. It looked like a scatter graph — dots all over the globe with a slight concentration along the line he had pointed out. The line that stretched from their city to France where the deaths had started. What did it mean that it started here?

"Interesting," Jory said. "But Vinnie isn't a scientist or a computer whiz, and you still haven't told us what you want."

"Why would I need a computer whiz when I already have one?" He clicked another button, and most of the dots on the map disappeared. "50 years ago, number of anomalies in one year." He clicked again. "Twenty-five years ago." The number of dots increased. "Last year." Double the number of the dots appeared on the screen. "And then the Holt last year." Click. "And after Kara arrived." The number of dots went from five to fifteen.

"Kara was opening anomalies. That's not a surprise. What does this have to do with me?"

"Isn't it obvious?" Will waved at the screen.

Jory folded his arms, biceps bulging against his hands. "Maybe you should explain it to us anyway, genius."

"The anomalies Kara was opening wouldn't have been recorded. It's not like she opened them where anyone would notice. No, this is the number of eaters."

She'd forgotten the increase in anomalies was one of the ways he'd told her he was tracking Kara.

"When she opened them, she increased the instability of time and space?" Vinnie asked.

"Yes," Will said. "But look, this is the last few weeks." He clicked the button. There had been no anomalies in the Holt.

Was he implying that Vinnie closing Kara's anomaly had made the others stop? "That's not so strange. There were only five the year before. Not that likely there would be one in a few weeks."

"The other places Kara opened anomalies in the last few years continued to see an increase in instability even after she was gone," Will said. "Even barring that, the anomalies are increasing, and if the anomalies keep increasing, more people are going to die. Kara's objects allowed her to hold power and open a portal... like a Vasum. You absorbed the power of her anomaly. It's related somehow. If I can find out how, maybe we can stop them for good."

Jory sputtered. "What makes you think you can do something scientists have been trying to figure out for decades?"

He looked at Vinnie. "I have knowledge they don't."

"You know, if you'd told her this weeks ago, she probably would have helped you sooner. Vinnie's a bit of a crusader."

Vinnie opened her mouth to protest and then snapped it shut. Would she have helped if he'd told her this was what he was doing? That he had used her still made her feel a little ill being around him. But she wanted the knowledge, too. It might have been enough to tip the scales. He didn't need to know that. That would take away whatever leverage she had to get him to help with Conor.

"Lavinia is more afraid of being controlled than she wants to help," Will said. "I broke her trust."

"There is no proof I have anything to do with this reduction in anomalies, and working with someone who'll use people to get what he wants without telling them anything is not high on my list of good times. I'm here because you agreed to help me."

"William will find what he can," Will said.

"I want to talk to the Twisted crews involved in the explosion three weeks ago."

"I can do that," Will said. "And you'll be here daily to learn to manipulate the anomalies, starting tomorrow. It would be best if you weren't distracted." He looked pointedly at Jory.

Jory looked at Vinnie. "You'll keep me in the loop?"

There was a pain in his eyes, something buried deep inside. If she opened the door to Jory, would the rest of her friends come through? Vinnie didn't know how to say no when he was looking at her like that. Could she find time between her job and the library to be here every day? She'd have to figure it out.

"Fine," she said to both of them.

CHAPTER TWELVE

Vinnie tapped her finger on the sketchbook and glanced at the clock. Today was her first day of training with Will and it should have been easy to fit in. It was Halloween, so she was closing the library early, but last night Shaw had texted that she would come by before lunch today to get the sketchbook. It was now 1:15 PM. She'd closed the library at noon today and was supposed to meet Will fifteen minutes ago.

Shaw hadn't shown up and wasn't responding to text messages. Vinnie told Shaw yesterday that this was the only time she had. She had to meet Will and then she had work.

The clock ticked over another minute. Shaw wasn't coming. Vinnie snatched up the sketchbook, grabbed her small bag and headed out, wishing she'd brought a bag big enough to hold the sketchbook. She hadn't wanted to carry a bunch of stuff to training but since she was already late, she would just drop the sketchbook back at her house and would still have time to catch the next bus.

Vinnie locked the library door behind her and ascended the steps. Will's SUV sat at the end of the alleyway. Or maybe the SUV belonged to Greg because she'd never seen Will driving. She was only mildly surprised to see the vehicle, even though she hadn't agreed to be driven. Will liked to assume.

Vinnie knocked on the passenger window and Greg, Will's henchman, looked up from the book he was reading. Greg read books? That should have improved her opinion of him, but somehow it didn't. The door unlocked, and she pulled it open.

"Have you just been sitting here?"

He waved his book. "I have a book."

"Why didn't you come inside and get me? And why didn't someone tell me you would be here?" She climbed in. "I wouldn't have kept you waiting if I'd known."

"It's fine. I make my own choices."

Just as scintillating a conversationalist as she remembered. "Can you swing by my apartment so I can drop something off?"

"We're already late." Greg pulled out, and not toward her apartment.

Vinnie clamped her lips together and kept them that way for the entire ride. Easier not to get frustrated if you didn't even try to reason with someone.

Greg pulled the car up to the same hotel room Will had always met her in.

"Is there no way in from the other side?"

"We keep up appearances, just in case."

She guessed that made sense. When they'd come looking for Will they hadn't looked at the bathroom and hadn't noticed it was anything other than a normal hotel room. If they went in the other side, it opened directly into the secret lair.

After their meeting yesterday, Jory had given her his usual lecture. Will was dangerous. People who weren't dangerous didn't need the elaborate ruse of a hotel to keep people off their trail, etcetera. She could have pointed out that Jory was dangerous, but that didn't make him a bad person. Instead, she'd said that maybe she needed someone dangerous on her side.

Greg didn't follow her when she got out and the SUV pulled away as she got to the door. She knocked, and a lock clicked, but the door didn't open. Will's disembodied voice told her to come in. She didn't see a speaker, which meant either it was hidden or this was another creepy Mesmer trick. Vinnie suspected the latter.

Vinnie stepped through the door, locked it behind her, and went through the bathroom to the secret lair. William wasn't there, but the computers churred along, doing whatever they were doing.

Will sat in the middle of the gym in a meditative pose. He knew she was here, but was ignoring her. Vinnie lay the sketchbook on the computer desk and stepped around the computers into the gym area.

When she reached the mat where Will was, she dropped her bag by the side, slid off her shoes and stepped onto the mat, where she curled her legs under her to sit diagonal to Will. She closed her eyes and pulled in a deep breath through her nose and let it out through her mouth. After four breaths, she let her breathing fall into a normal rhythm and began counting breaths. Her mind was active today, and she didn't even make it to three before it was trying to convince her to ask Will what he was doing and why he was making her wait. She wasn't a child who couldn't wait a few minutes for someone to acknowledge her.

Will let out a breath that sounded like a balloon deflating, then said, "Glad you could make it."

She opened her eyes. "Shaw was supposed to meet me to pick up a sketchbook, and she didn't show up."

His lips pursed. "Did your irresponsibility rub off on her, or was it the other way around?"

Did she want to know why he thought she was irresponsible? Not really. "I think she rubbed off on me, since I think I'm soaking up your assholery, too. I'm just a sponge. Did that come about naturally, or have you had to work at it?"

He opened his eyes. "If impatience at other people's lack of respect for my time is assholery, I guess I came by it over time. I used to let people walk all over me."

Her chest felt hot. She wanted to snap at him, but he had a point, and she hadn't been happy about Shaw not showing up, and she'd done the same to him. "I'm sorry. I didn't mean to disrespect your time. I was upset about being stood up and I don't actually want to give her the sketchbook back."

"She wants something back that she gave to you, or did she loan it?"

"She gave it to me — said she had plenty more. It's Cerulean's." Why was she telling him this? She didn't know him, and didn't trust him, but she didn't exactly have many people to talk to about her life.

"Don't give it back, then."

He made it sound so simple, but she knew she wouldn't do that. Shaw lost her best friend. "Right. What's the plan for today?"

"What do you remember about the day you fought Kara?"

She'd pushed down all the sick feelings from that day, but at his words they came bubbling up. "I try not to remember anything at all."

"Nothing? I put a map in your head, memories that showed you exactly how to use all the powers together."

He moved so they were facing each other, which was something Vinnie had wanted to avoid. She shifted on the mat. "The memory where the woman put the thoughts in your head, and then you did the same to me."

He looked startled for just a second before his face returned to normal. "What woman?"

"She looked like me, a little." The woman had brown eyes and her hair had been wavy where Vinnie's was stick straight and her chin rounder where Vinnie's was sharp and pointy.

"You saw Evie." He breathed the name as if he was saying, 'you saw heaven.' "She taught me how to use my abilities."

In the vision she'd seen, this Evie had kissed him on the forehead. "Your girlfriend?"

"My wife. I didn't realize she was so tied up in my memories. We can use that."

Wife. He'd also told her that the Mesmer who'd helped him learn to use his abilities was dead. She assumed these were the same person, but she wasn't going to ask him anything that personal.

"When I needed to close the anomaly, I remembered her face, but it was still fresh in my mind. I've tried to bring it back since then and I can't. It doesn't feel like it was ever there. I can't picture her face — just remember that she looked a little like me."

"Maybe because we didn't have direct contact when I gave you the memory it didn't take."

Vinnie stiffened, expecting him to suggest trying again, but his eyes had lost focus and he seemed to be staring at nothing.

"Will?" she said.

He didn't move, didn't even seem to be blinking. This wasn't the first time she'd seen him zone out like that, but that didn't make his blank eyes less creepy. After a few minutes, he still hadn't moved. Vinnie leaned over to grab her bag, and drug it closer so she could pull out her phone to check the time.

Five minutes passed. Should she do something? He'd said he was ill. Was this part of his illness? She wished she'd asked more questions. Two more minutes passed. Vinnie waved her hand in front of his eyes. No reaction. She sent her senses out, being more deliberate so she could tell if anyone was in the building. And there, someone was on the floor above.

"I think you are right," Will said.

Vinnie flinched at the sound of his voice.

He didn't seem to notice as he continued, "It is easy for me to give you the memory, but without connections in your brain, it will not be useful. What we will do is find connections and reinforce patterns, starting with Ferr."

"No!" Vinnie blurted. "I mean, maybe we can start with Stone. Something grounding."

"Ferr is blood, blood is connection. Ferr is the best place to start."

She knew she was going to have to get over her aversion to Ferr power. Now was probably as good a time as any. "Okay. Where did you just go? You zombied out for a good ten minutes."

"I apologize. I have a lot of memories to sift through. I did not realize it would take that long. I should have warned you."

Freaking Mesmers and their creepy Mesmer brains. "Please warn me next time."

He nodded. "You should know that I will not intrude in your head, so you will have to talk me through what you see and feel. Ready?"

"Yes." Vinnie closed her eyes.

"Let's begin."

Ferr energy flared to life in one of the nearby hotel rooms. A pinprick of thought tried to surface in Vinnie's brain — something about the people who had attacked her being able to block.

"I want you to pull the Ferr power and my Mesmer

power," Will said. "We're going to see what your mind remembers."

Vinnie put her thoughts about the attack aside and did as Will asked. Pulling the Ferr power was as difficult as she remembered and she had to use the focusing technique Will had taught her — imagining pulling string through straw. If she pulled too fast, it would snag and slow her down. She had to pull slow and smooth to get the power faster. When she had it, she pulled Mesmer power from Will.

"Good," Will said. "We're going to learn how to use these two abilities together to remember more than you thought was possible."

Vinnie lost track of time as they worked. Will talked her through using Ferr power outside of blood, using it to connect memories by the energetic signature they left in her body rather than observable thoughts.

At least — that's what he tried to teach.

"I don't see it," she said for what felt like the thousandth time.

"You're not trying to see," Will said, sounding like he was speaking through clenched teeth. "I believe we are close to the time you said you needed to stop."

Vinnie dropped the power, and the spike of pain in her head was instantaneous.

"I have caffeine and iron in the kitchen," Will said.

Caffeine for the Mesmer ability depletion and iron for the Ferr. The caffeine wouldn't be enough, though. She was going to need a painkiller.

She opened her eyes and her gaze darted toward the kitchen but snagged on William slumped in the doorway, watching.

He started when he noticed her gaze and sat up straighter.

"William? Did you have something for us?" Will asked.

"I have Miss Forbes's clearances."

Vinnie uncurled. Will was already up. He strode over to where William stood and took a card from him, which he brought back and held out to Vinnie.

The card was heavy, with some kind of metallic chip. Her face stared back at her next to the name Anne White and the USSF logo. United States Security Force, the people they called in for direct threats to the country.

"You really think it's believable that the USSF would investigate this?"

"It's risky, but within reason," Will said. "And we shouldn't have to worry about them asking why different investigators from the same agency are there. I'll pick you up tomorrow morning."

He'd done it. He'd gotten her into a holding facility with Twisted inside. The realization excited and disturbed her. Will Darrow was not someone whose bad side she wanted to be on. Following that thought was the havoc she could create in a facility full of Twisted. She almost shivered.

William shuffled forward a few steps. "Mr. Hahn should also be out on bail today. There were quite a few people amenable to monetary assistance."

Bribes. They'd bribed people to get Conor out. Temporarily. Now she needed to find a way to keep him out.

Vinnie stepped back and eyed the barstool she'd just put under the overhang of her kitchen counter. When Greg had dropped her off in front of her building, her downstairs neighbor was hauling the stool out to the trash and she'd asked if she could have it.

The barstool was perfectly fine. There was no need for it to be thrown out. Vinnie tilted her head to the side. It was uneven because one of the nobby things on the bottom was missing, but she could fix that. She put her hand on the barstool, and it wobbled a little.

She'd never owned furniture before. When she'd lived at Jory's house, the only thing that had been hers was her mattress.

There were no countertops at home that were high enough for this barstool. Vinnie squeezed her eyes shut. She had to stop thinking of Jory's house as home. Furniture wasn't that important to her. She could curl up on the floor, her books could stay neatly in their boxes, but she had to try to make a life.

Without people? Vinnie shook the traitorous thought off.

She pried the plastic lid off the clearance cake she'd gotten on her last grocery trip and pulled her butter knife out of the drawer. Her eyes cut to the fridge where she'd stashed some more substantial food. Probably should eat some of that first. But she had work in an hour and she needed the quick fuel. She'd take a sandwich with her.

Decided, Vinnie took a big slice of her cake and plopped it on a plate. As she grabbed a fork, her dad's face popped into her head. What would he say if he could see her standing in a crappy apartment eating cake?

"At least sit down, Nia, don't eat standing up like a heathen," she said, imitating her dad.

She imagined grinning at him, her teeth stained brown with frosting. "The chair is wobbly, dad."

There was a knock on the door. Shaw. She was not supposed to come to Vinnie's apartment. That wasn't the deal they'd made.

The sketchbook. Vinnie's eyes roved the counter. She would have dropped it with everything else when she came in. Her bag was close to the edge of the counter. Cake next to the sink.

Panic flared up in her. When was the last time she'd seen the sketchbook? At Will's hotel. She'd put it on the counter. Vinnie traced her steps in her mind, trying to remember if she'd had it after that. No, definitely at Will's, which meant it was safe, at least.

Another knock, more insistent this time.

She put her fork down and went to the door. Mentally bracing herself, she turned the lock and pulled the door open. Shaw looked amused, but the girl next to her had a hard stare on her face. The girl had dyed her hair ruby red, which clashed with the smattering of orange freckles across her nose.

Vinnie smiled, thought of frosting in her teeth, and snapped her mouth shut. "Hey, I've been texting you."

Shaw stepped past Vinnie into the apartment. "We have a rule. No cell phones when we're together."

The other girl had followed Shaw inside and was looking around the room with a curl of her upper lip. This must be Shaw's girlfriend. She looked familiar, but Vinnie wasn't sure why.

"I thought you were coming by the library to get the sketchbook." Vinnie could understand not wanting the intrusion of text messages, but they'd had a plan and Shaw hadn't shown up.

Shaw scratched the back of her head and smiled sheepishly. "We got caught up in something else."

At the look on her face, Vinnie decided she didn't want to know what something else was.

"This is Minka," Shaw said, pointing at the other girl.

Minka finally looked at Vinnie and her face shifted from disgust to an amused smirk.

"Hi," Vinnie said and turned back to Shaw. "We had a deal. You broke it. You should have texted me or called."

"It was totally my fault," Minka said. "Hey, mind if I make something to eat? I'm starving." She didn't wait for Vinnie's answer, but headed for the kitchen.

Shaw grinned, "She's not shy."

Vinnie opened her mouth, but she wasn't sure if she wanted to point out to Shaw that she was upset at the lack of communication or tell Minka she did mind if she ate her food.

Minka pulled open her refrigerator door. "Holy shit, that's a lot of sugar. You know those sweetened drinks are the worst thing for your health?"

Shaw turned to Vinnie, a small frown line appearing between her brows. "Why do you have so much sweet tea?"

Vinnie's chest burned, and she felt her whole body flush, the Wisp power rising with her unease. "I don't get much sleep and I don't like coffee."

Minka had pulled out some ham and was rummaging around again. "You only have mustard?"

"I don't like mayo," Vinnie said. She turned to Shaw for help, maybe convince her to stop her girlfriend from being rude, but Shaw's eyes were on the ground, and Vinnie's frustration turned to anger. "I have to leave for work soon. Maybe you can get food somewhere else."

Minka had already found the bread and squirted some mustard on it. She slapped the sandwich together and took a big bite. "We won't be here long. We only came to get the sketchbook."

"You were supposed to come by the library to get it," Vinnie snapped. "I don't have it here."

Shaw lifted her head. "I can go to the library to get it, since you need to go to work. I'll bring the key back to you at work."

"Why don't you just come by the library Sunday afternoon?" Since she was meeting Will tomorrow, that would give her time to retrieve the sketchbook.

"You can trust me, Vinnie," Shaw said in a small voice.

Could she trust Shaw, though? She hadn't come by when she said she would and her girlfriend seemed to be someone who insisted on having everything their own way. None of that mattered, since the book was not at the library. "It's not about trust. The sketchbook isn't at the library."

"You lost it?" Minka said around another mouthful.

Why would she jump to that conclusion? "I didn't lose it. It's in a safe place." Probably. How could she have been so careless? Shaw would be justified in being upset with Vinnie if she knew. Vinnie rubbed her eyes, hoping to dispel some of the fatigue that came from too much power use and not enough sleep.

Minka tilted her head and frowned. "Where?"

None of your business, she wanted to say. Instead, she said, "I left it with Will."

"Oooh. That's the creepy dude who took over your body, right?"

Why did she know that? That was dangerous information, and Shaw could only have known this girl for a few weeks.

"That's the guy," Shaw murmured. "We can get it from Vinnie another day."

Minka slapped the sandwich down. "She's just as selfish as all your other friends. It's all about what's convenient for her."

The pressure that had been building up in Vinnie snapped. "I'm selfish? If you had shown up when you said you would. I would have had it."

"So you say," Minka said. "But maybe if we'd shown up, you would have conveniently forgotten to bring it. Maybe you're just trying to keep it from us the same way you won't tell Shaw how to transform into a dragon, even though you know how much it means to her."

Vinnie's mind roared with confusion for a moment and then cleared. Either Minka was dumb or didn't care about Shaw at all. It was clear Shaw had given her information that put them all at risk. Vinnie wasn't sure which one made her more angry.

"Is that what you think?" Vinnie asked Shaw. "That I'm keeping it from you out of... what... malice? That I'm being mean?"

"I..." Shaw's eyes darted away.

"We don't have to think it," Minka said. "You transformed

into a dragon and haven't told Shaw how you did it. True or False?"

It was true. She hadn't told Shaw how she'd transformed into a dragon, but Shaw had never asked either. Shaw had wanted to transform into a dragon for as long as Vinnie had known her, but Vinnie thought she'd changed her mind. They hadn't talked about what happened that day at all, other than some mutual comforting about Cer's death. The guilt twisted Vinnie's stomach. She should have had this conversation with Shaw and now Shaw had told a stranger secrets she shouldn't know. Vinnie didn't remember how to pull the power of an anomaly, which was how she'd gotten enough power to become a dragon. Even if she did, she didn't think it was something that Shaw was capable of doing.

"It almost killed me," Vinnie said. "And it did kill our friend."

Minka rolled her eyes. "Sure, it almost killed *you*. You're not supposed to be able to transform, but Shaw is a Dancer. She was made for it. You're just trying to hold her back like everyone else in her life."

Vinnie wanted to ask Shaw if that's what she thought again, but her head was down — chin almost on her chest. She probably wouldn't respond again, and Minka would bulldoze the conversation. What she wouldn't give for the ability to talk mind to mind right now.

Instead, she faced Minka. "Her body may have been built to transform, but it wasn't built to hold all the other powers. They would still tear her apart."

Minka's lip curled. "She doesn't have to hold them. She just needs that crystal. You have it, don't you? It's not at Nell's house."

"Minka," Shaw said so softly Vinnie wasn't sure she heard her.

Shaw was obviously upset and Vinnie didn't want to hurt

her, but she'd told Minka things she shouldn't know and had apparently taken her to a house they were trying to distance themselves from, potentially putting them all in danger.

"How does she know the crystal is not at the house?"

"We can trust her," Shaw said. "She's Zee."

Vinnie turned her senses to Minka. She was Zee. She'd been so caught up in her own guilt and frustration, she hadn't even noticed. She had to stop doing that. But right now, she needed to deal with Shaw. Her secret, what she could do, what all of them could do, was now exposed to a girl Shaw barely knew. "Being Twisted doesn't automatically make someone trustworthy. You think it's safe to tell people other people's secrets based on knowing them what? Two weeks?"

Shaw wouldn't look at Vinnie. "Five."

Five. Vinnie reeled. Not only had Shaw been fired without telling them, she'd been seeing Minka while they were in the middle of all that turmoil.

"Were you giving her a play-by-play as it happened? While we were all scrambling to save Maddie?" Vinnie wished she could take the words back as soon as they were out of her mouth.

"No... no... I— "

"Hey!" Minka came around the counter. "You can't push her around anymore. If how long you knew someone determined if you could trust them, then she should have been able to trust you. Instead, as soon as you got a little power, you cut her off. And then the one thing she asks of you — to get the sketchbook she worked on with her *best friend*. You can't even manage that."

Shaw seemed to shrink into herself.

The flames lit up inside Vinnie, and her head roared. Minka skewed the facts to support her argument, but the facts were still correct. She wanted to talk to Shaw, ask her what she really felt, find out why she trusted this angry girl, but that was impossible as long as that angry girl was standing here.

"If Shaw has a problem with me, she is perfectly capable of telling me herself," she said. "Maybe the issue is yours."

Minka laughed derisively. "Oh, sure. Just keep pretending."

A wave of unnatural calm washed over Vinnie, and she recognized Shaw's influence, sending calming waves to get them to stop fighting.

Minka rounded on Shaw.

"I told you not to do that. I'm allowed to be angry. Don't mess with my emotions without permission." She stalked to the door and didn't look back as she jerked it open and left.

Shaw's watery eyes met Vinnie's for a moment before she turned.

"You know I would never keep knowledge from you on purpose," Vinnie said.

She thought Shaw nodded as she followed Minka out the door, but she couldn't be sure. Vinnie wanted to call her back, ask if she was okay, but she only seemed to be able to stand there.

The Wisp power had stopped raging when Shaw had sent her calming waves.

"Fire and Water," she whispered.

What she wouldn't give for a nice long run to soothe her confused brain, but she had to get to work.

CHAPTER FOURTEEN

Vinnie sat on the steps outside her apartment and cinched the laces on her running shoes. She should probably have stayed in bed this morning. After only five hours of sleep, she was exhausted and Will, or maybe Greg, would be by to pick her up in an hour and a half, but she hadn't been able to get the thought of a run out of her head since last night.

Even though she'd eaten a ton of Halloween candy, she didn't have physical energy to burn, but mental energy? With the fight with Shaw still fresh in her mind, she had that in spades. Stretching her legs and lungs sounded like heaven.

Her breath escaped in a big, steaming puff, but she wasn't cold in her shorts and hoodie.

Vinnie stood, flipped her hood up, and pulled it low over her eyes before descending the steps. She started at a slow jog, legs stiff and heavy. After a few minutes, her calves started to burn, but she ignored the sensation and let her mind run along with her feet.

Did the others know Shaw had told Minka all about them? She was supposed to keep Jory in the loop about what was going on, but so far she hadn't told him anything — not even that Will had gotten her in to the holding cells. She could ask him about Shaw if she did.

What she was trying to do — save Conor, keep her friends safe — seemed impossible. Even if she could prove that Kara had killed Maddie and broadcast the information to the world, there was no guarantee the truth would make any difference at all. If someone with more money, clout or resources wanted him to take the fall, he would.

And no matter what she did, her friends were in pain. Why was Shaw with someone who was obviously making her miserable?

A soft shuffle that sounded like jogging feet came from behind her. Someone else running in the Holt was rare. Vinnie looked over her shoulder. A tall man in a gray hoodie ran not far behind her. He had his hood pulled low, and something seemed to be covering the lower half of his face.

Whoever it was was trying to hide his appearance and seemed to be keeping an even distance between them. For a moment, Vinnie felt weary, tired of the threats, but anger replaced it. She really was tired of the threats. It was time to make it stop.

Maybe she was being paranoid, but if she was, he wouldn't follow. She picked up her pace and made a sharp turn down a road that would have less traffic. Before long, she heard the shuffling behind her again. She checked him for power, but he appeared to be normal.

She didn't need to look to know it was him. Fire flared in her abdomen. It was light out. There were people on the street this morning. Would he attack, or was he just trying to scare her?

If she could use the Wisp power for speed, could she use it to hit someone? The impact of something moving fast would be more devastating than something moving slow.

Probably she'd just break her hand since hand bones were more delicate than the bones of a chest or jaw. She didn't want to do this again, didn't want to fight.

But she was tired of being afraid. This jerk wasn't going to get away with trying to scare her. She scanned the area for power. There was a Mesmer in the distance, which would be safer than trying to use the Wisp power.

Time to find out what this guy was made of. He seemed to be normal, but he might be blocking her.

Vinnie picked up her pace again. Her muscles screamed at the sudden movement, but she ignored them. Hoodie man sped up, he was definitely following her. She turned another corner, stopped, and pressed against the side of the building.

The man followed her around the corner, looking straight ahead. His feet faltered to a stop when he saw the street was empty. He turned around and Vinnie launched herself at him, using air power to push him back against the wall and followed with her hands, hoping it seemed like she'd just moved fast enough to overpower him.

"Vinnie," he gasped. A pair of startled blue eyes peered at her from under the hood.

"Conor?" Vinnie stepped back but continued holding him with the power. "What are you doing here? Why are you following me?"

"I was just running in the neighborhood and I saw you. You're a Mesmer?"

Was that fear on his face? Vinnie dropped the power and took another step back. She'd let emotion get the better of her. What if it had been someone who intended her harm that just figured out she was using Mesmer power? She'd been tested for being Twisted several times as a child and Vasum power didn't show up in tests, but the Wisp power might. "Why were you out running in one of the worst neighborhoods in the city, far from your fancy hotel room?"

He rubbed the front of his hoodie. "I like it here. The Holt doesn't feel dangerous. There always seemed to be someone lurking around my fancy hotel room, and that lawyer who got me out of jail got me a room here. I would say that I don't need a lawyer since I already had one, but he did what my lawyer couldn't. I'm glad someone shady is helping me right now."

Vinnie choked on a laugh. "You're glad someone shady is helping you?"

One corner of his mouth lifted, and she had the feeling that the attempt at a smile was for her benefit. "If someone shady is trying to pin murders on me, maybe it takes someone shady to help me. I'm pretty sure they were going to keep me in jail for a while. Not sure my money was going to help."

Will had come through. He'd said he would, but hearing it made her feel better. "Why were you following me?"

His eyes traveled over her face, resting on her lips for a moment. "I saw you, and… I just saw you."

He looked as confused as she felt. Vinnie took one step toward him and stopped herself. She wanted to wrap her arms around him, tell him it was going to be okay and have him tell her the same, but she also wanted to run as far away from him as she could.

Conor took a step toward her so they were close enough to touch, but he kept his hands to his sides. "I saw you and you looked like a miracle. And this place…" A frown twitched on his face and was gone. "Run with me?"

His eyes searched hers for acquiescence for a moment, and he must have seen an answer because he turned and jogged back the way they had come, slow enough for her to catch up.

Vinnie followed. She shouldn't. She should stay as far away as possible, but he hadn't given her time to explain that, and she didn't want to hurt him more than she already had. She caught up, and they jogged side by side, their steps and paces syncing as they fell into a rhythm.

They ran like that for five or six blocks before Conor turned down a side street and slowed to a walk.

The street was narrow, buildings crowding in on both sides, the shop fronts had their doors flush against the wall and nothing but small plaques to say what they were. There was no one on the streets here and very few windows.

Near the dead end of the street, Conor stopped and pointed to the wall beside a plaque that said the business inside was haberdashery. A hat maker in the Holt? That was weird, but not worth coming down the alley. Vinnie gave Conor a questioning look.

"Not the shop," he said. "The graffiti."

The wall was covered in graffiti: gang names, fancy lettering, plain swear words, and penises. And in the middle of it all was a bright pink alpaca — chipped and faded — with angel wings. Only a few bits of flowers remained over the faded pink of the body. Cerulean had been here.

The fire surged in her body and Vinnie's fist clenched with the desire to burn the paint off the wall. Or she could just throw a fireball at it and blow a hole in the side of the building to get rid of the painting. How could Cerulean be so stupid? So blind that he would trust someone who had killed so many people. Kara had kept her promise — she had promised to take away his pain. Too bad that meant taking him away from everyone else and the stupid, selfish little prick —

"Vinnie?" Conor touched her shoulder, and she spun, shoving at him as hard as she could.

He stumbled back, more from surprise than any actual strength in her push. "I'm sorry. This one wasn't on his website. I thought you'd want to see."

Her skin felt like it was on fire. Vinnie squeezed her eyes shut, and pulled the power back in, struggling to contain it and get control of the rage. "Thank you. I'm sorry. I did want to see it."

"You didn't push very hard," he said. "I'm not hurt."

She opened her eyes again. "This time. But you almost died because of me. You were arrested because of *me*."

"Hey, we don't know why I was arrested," he said. "And I may not remember all of what happened that day, but I know you wouldn't hurt me on purpose. You're the only one I know who might know a shady lawyer. I'm out of jail because of you. Just... tell me you didn't call your dad or something stupid."

"I didn't call my dad," Vinnie said. But had she done something stupid? Maybe. "It doesn't matter if I want to hurt people or not. They get hurt because of me."

"Would people stop hurting if you let her win? How many did she kill?"

"Eight. That I know of."

"Eight." He turned away, looking off in the distance. Finally, he said, "Some memories are coming back. Most are just fuzzy impressions, but I remember you trying to save me. Fighting her. And I remember flying. There was so much pain and I knew I was dying, but I saw the ground rushing by underneath me and I wasn't afraid. For as long as I live, I will never forget that feeling. That was you, right? You were a dragon. I don't know how I know that. Most people seem to think it came through an anomaly, but it was you."

Vinnie nodded, not sure what else to say. He knew, and he wasn't running away.

"Vinnie." He stepped closer to her, hand going up to tuck in the hair that had escaped her hood. "You might be right that they're after me to get to you. Some of the people who came in to talk to me weren't asking about Maddie. They asked about Kara and they asked about the dragon. I think they're looking for you. You have to disappear. The worst that will happen to me is I'll go to jail. It will be so much worse for you if they find you."

She thought she'd disappeared when she came to the Holt. She'd left home and come here and she thought she was invisible, but Kara found her. It hadn't been a coincidence that Kara had come here, to the city that Vinnie was living in, but how Kara had known was still a mystery. She'd implied that she'd used some kind of Twisted power, but hadn't elaborated. As long as Vinnie didn't know how Kara had found her, there was no way to keep anyone else from using the same means of finding her. Conor was right. She needed to try again to disappear, but first she needed to clean up her mess.

"I can't do that," she said.

"Fine," he growled. "How can I help?"

"I have help. It's not my dad, but I obviously don't have the power to hire lawyers on my own. The best thing you can do is keep your eyes open. Text me if you see anything that might help us prove it was Kara."

He stepped away from her. "Someone else is allowed to help, but not me?"

"I don't care what happens to him." She squeezed her eyes shut and then opened them again. "That sounded bad. He's made it obvious that he's using me to get what he wants, and I'm doing the same. He has connections I don't understand, and can get around things."

"You're making dangerous deals to save me?" His voice was quiet. "I'm not worth it, Vinnie. I know you'd throw yourself in front of a bullet for someone else, but I'm really not worth it. Run. Save yourself."

He meant it. She wasn't the only one who would throw

herself in front of a bullet to save someone. "You already know my answer to that."

He nodded and then stepped forward, wrapped his hands around the back of her head, and kissed her. His mouth was hot, hungry on hers and Vinnie kissed him back, wishing this was how it could be, but it wasn't.

Conor released her and stepped back. He adjusted his hood. "I'll text you if I find anything out."

And then he was gone, jogging back down the street and disappearing around the corner.

CHAPTER FIFTEEN

The apartment complex came into view as Vinnie turned a corner, and she slowed to a walk. She had plenty of time to shower and get breakfast before Will arrived, so she moved more slowly, enjoying the sensation of pleasant fatigue.

As she ascended the steps, something by the door caught her eye, but it wasn't until she was right in front of it that she could see the problem. Someone had broken into her apartment. The frame of her door was splintered at the locking mechanism and stood ajar by just a few inches. She should call the police. Vinnie blinked at the thought. She'd been stalked and attacked and this is what made her want to call the police?

Instead, she waited a moment for her heart rate to come down, opened her senses wide, and searched the apartment. No one was there. Whoever it was had been fast. They had to have seen her leave and then gotten in and out.

Vinnie pushed open the door and stepped into her apartment.

The two boxes that she hadn't unpacked had been pulled

away from the wall, opened, and the contents were strewn all over the floor.

Kitchen drawers were open, but there hadn't been much in them. Her numb legs carried her to the bedroom where the closet doors were thrown open, some of her clothes were thrown on the floor. There was a brand new fist-sized hole in the bedroom wall, as if the thief hadn't found what they wanted and punched the wall in anger. Vinnie had no money, no electronics, nothing worth stealing.

Had it been random? It didn't make sense that someone would come, see an almost empty apartment and search anyway. Or maybe it did. People were desperate. Maybe it was random. Or maybe it was whoever was trying to set Conor up? Someone who wanted information, or proof. Or whoever had been following her, or left a rat on her friend's porch or… there were too many possibilities.

Vinnie pulled her phone out of her running shorts, but there was no one to call. And it wasn't like she was defenseless if they came back. She put the phone back and went into the living room to repack her boxes. That done, she gathered them up and moved them, one at a time, to block the door and keep it closed.

That wouldn't keep out anyone who wanted to get in, but neither had the lock.

She went back to her bedroom. The mattress looked like it had been shifted a little. She went over and pulled it out enough to get to the hidden nook. The baseboard hiding place opened at her touch, the crystal and sketchbook still inside.

Satisfied, Vinnie closed it, grabbed fresh clothes off the floor and went to the bathroom to take a shower.

When she was done and pulling on her clothes, she heard the scraping sound of boxes being moved by the front door.

A Mesmer was in her apartment, she could feel the energy as they came inside.

She dragged her shirt over her head, pulled the Mesmer's power and pressed her ear against the door.

"Vinnie?"

Will. The person in her house was Will. Relief flooded her, and she released his power. She unlocked the door and stuck her head through.

Will stood in her living room, eyes roving the empty space. His eyes landed on her.

She stepped out of the bathroom. "Do you always just walk into people's homes without being invited?"

He pointed at the door. "It was unlocked."

Vinnie stared at him for a moment and then burst out laughing.

His cheeks twitched like he was trying to share in her amusement, but also didn't see what was funny. "Now you laugh?"

"That's true," she said. "It was unlocked, but an unlocked door isn't an invitation inside."

"The door is broken. You could have been hurt, and you didn't answer my texts."

She patted her pockets but, of course, she hadn't put her phone back in her pocket yet. Vinnie went back into the room and retrieved it. There were two texts from Will, one asking if she was awake, sent while she was running, and the second saying he'd be early. She ran her hands through her wet hair. "I was showering."

"In an apartment with a broken door…"

"The bathroom has a door and a lock. Where else am I supposed to shower?"

"With a friend?" he said. "Oh right, you're pretending you don't have any. You can stay with me. I have plenty of space."

Was he serious? He looked serious. "Because a cheap motel is safer."

"You've seen the security I've put in. The hotel has plenty of empty rooms."

She would probably be safer there, assuming she trusted Will, which she did not. He seemed sane most of the time, until he was taking over her body to kill someone. Plus, the hotel was outside of the Holt. "It would take me too long to get to work from there."

"Greg can drive you to the library."

"My other job."

He blinked.

"The library donations aren't enough to cover living expenses unless I'm sharing them. I work at a convenience store at night."

He looked around the place. "That's why you can't come and train with me more often? I thought you were just being difficult."

Being difficult. People had accused Vinnie of being a lot of things — impulsive, naïve, but she didn't think someone had ever accused her of being difficult. "Thanks for the benefit of the doubt."

"You insist on taking the bus when Greg could pick you up. You wait for an emergency before getting training that is useful to you —"

"I get it," she snapped.

"Always angry with me," he muttered under his breath. Louder, he said, "You may or may not have realized, but I have a lot of money. I asked you to work for me and you agreed. Generally, when you work for someone, they give you money. I think I pay more than enough that you could quit your job."

Vinnie let out a breath and stalked to the kitchen, where she pulled a jug of sweet tea out of the fridge. He'd never said anything about paying her. They were exchanging favors. And if he were going to pay her enough that she could move somewhere else, he wouldn't have offered for her to stay at the hotel. He was obviously making stuff up.

She took a swig straight from the jug. "You never mentioned any money."

"I forget things like that," he said. "That's why I have assistants."

He forgot he intended to pay people. "And if this hadn't happened, would you have remembered that you intended to pay me?"

He shrugged. "Eventually."

Right. Sure. She believed that.

"Here." he pulled a wallet out of his front pocket, grabbed a few bills, and handed them to her. "That's for the first two weeks."

Vinnie stared at the money in his hand. They were hundred dollar bills, probably enough for a month of rent. "You just carry that kind of money around?"

"No one will rob me."

He was a Mesmer, so had some protection. "You make them think they don't want to?"

"Something like that." He stretched his hand with the money toward her. "Are you going to be difficult?"

Oh, she was definitely going to be difficult. Vinnie leaned her hip against the counter and crossed her arms. "So, now and then you'll just randomly give me cash like some kind of sugar-daddy?"

He took a few steps forward and put the money on the bar. "I'll have Greg set up a deposit to your bank account."

"I don't have a bank account."

"You receive donations for the library."

"Not in my name." Was he going to ask why?

"We'll pay you through that since you have access. Unless you just prefer cash."

Cash was less traceable, and taking electronic donations for the library was already risky since she wasn't reporting income, didn't have a nonprofit, wasn't paying taxes, and didn't want her dad to find her. "I prefer cash."

"Fine. Greg will pay you every two weeks."

Goodie. "Soo… am I going to have set hours? When do I work?"

He shook his head. "No set hours. You just need to work when I need you."

"Except when I'm working at the convenience store or the library."

Will waved at the pile of cash. "Is that not enough money?"

"For what? I don't know how long this job will last. I need other income, income I can rely on." The annoyance on his face was strangely satisfying. Maybe she was being difficult on purpose.

He closed his eyes and pinched the bridge of his nose. "I'm obviously good for the money, but, let's just do it this way. I will pay you for six months in advance. I know you won't quit the library, but I need you available as much as possible. I'll also hire someone to take over some hours at the library. If, at any time in the six months either of us decides it's not working out, you still get to keep the money. You might want a safe deposit box for that or something. If, after six months, you want to leave, I'll give you another month's salary, which would hopefully be enough time for you to find another low-paying job that is far beneath your abilities and potential. Does that sound fair?"

Vinnie deepened her voice. "'Far beneath your abilities and potential.' You sound like my dad, except he was a controlling asshole and you're…. probably not an asshole."

"Should I also get you a therapist so you can talk about your daddy issues?"

Touché. "Eww, don't say daddy issues. And no, no therapist and no to hiring someone to work at the library. The rest sounds fair." She didn't want to give up the job she'd found on her own, and she didn't want to feel like she owed him anything, but she was exhausted from work and having a Wisp power she couldn't control. That might cloud her judgement in the future, and she needed some control in this negotiation. "It almost sounds fair. If after one month I find working for you intolerable, I will return five months' worth of money to you and you never bother me again."

"Even if we get this solved, you're going to need my help in the future, whether or not you find me tolerable."

No. Vinnie was not going to be beholden to him or anyone to protect her and the ones she loved. She didn't know how she would figure out what she needed to know if this didn't work, but she would find a way. Somehow. If that meant that she had to work for, and learn from Will in the meantime, she would do it.

"I guess we'll see about that," she said.

He shook his head in exasperation. "I'll wait for you in the car."

CHAPTER SIXTEEN

Lingate prison didn't look how Vinnie thought a prison would look. The prison building itself was made of pale brick, at least the part of it she could see over the fence. She'd expected it to be surrounded by chain link and barbed wire. There was barbed wire, but it sat on top of a solid metal fence that was pearly white and seemed to have almost a pink sheen.

"Why is it pretty?" she asked.

"I don't know," Will said.

On the drive over he'd told her that there would be a Mesmer inside who would read her mind, in spite of her clearances, they still had that one last check. Vinnie swallowed her dread.

"Why haven't they moved them yet? I know it's complicated, but they've had a month. Did they want to keep them here to ask about Kara?"

"Only two are still here — the Wisp and the Mesmer. The rest have been moved. They should have been able to move them by now, but someone requested extra precautions at the highest security level, which should have taken a few weeks at most, but somehow the paperwork got lost and was resubmitted. Then was denied, then there was an appeal, and that's where it stands."

"Sounds fishy," she said.

He laughed. "Not really. Welcome to bureaucracy."

"I guess I have to go in." Vinnie willed her body to move, but she sat, frozen.

"Are you sure you don't want me to put a block in your mind?"

"No." That lit her fire. She stepped out of the truck, not wanting to hear more muttering about how difficult she was, refusing to do things the easy way. He really couldn't seem to grasp that she didn't want him anywhere near her mind.

"You can't just block the Mesmer," Will said as he caught up. "And you don't have any practice with the techniques we talked about."

"Hilda wasn't really fooled by your eating dinner routine when she tried to read your mind." When they'd first tried to question Will, he'd imagined his dinner to keep Hilda from hearing his real thoughts. It hadn't worked against Hilda — she'd known something was up, but maybe the Mesmer here wasn't as strong. If they only got impressions like Vinnie rather than clearer thoughts like Hilda, it would work.

"You're Vasum, just take the Mesmer's power. They'll just think they're having an off day, but likely won't say anything."

And she should have thought of that herself. She might be able to set up a loop where she read what they expected to see and fed it back, but she hadn't practiced that either. Better to just keep it simple.

They'd made it to the front of the compound. Will showed the guards some official-looking papers and Vinnie showed her government ID. They passed through the security check and metal detector in the gatehouse. An armed guard walked them down a corridor to the prison.

Inside the building, they were led to a smallish room, with maybe ten worn gray chairs.

"Wait here," the guard said.

Less than a minute passed before the door opened again. Another guard poked her head in. "Ms. White? If you'll follow me. Mr. Jones can wait here in the lobby."

They stepped back out into the corridor and the guard led her three doors down and let her into a room that was empty except for a white box with the front cut out. Vinnie stepped inside the box as instructed.

A wiry woman dressed in what appeared to be a guard uniform led in a young girl, who couldn't be over fifteen. They stood the girl in front of Vinnie. Dancer. Will had said a Mesmer would test her. The Dancer girl stared at her for a moment.

"Clean," she said and was led out.

Vinnie started to step out, but the guard held out a hand. Next, a man who looked to be in his thirties with sallow skin and long scraggly hair came in.

His movements were slow, but when he looked at her, his eyes seemed to pierce her soul. This was the Mesmer. Her mind dropped into thinking about eating a donut for a second until she noticed the collar at his neck. It looked like it was leather and had metal rivets and two blinking lights.

His smile was cruel. "Shock collar. They can kill me in a heartbeat and don't let me forget it. I see you don't like that. Suspicious."

Vinnie pulled in a breath through her nose, and let one out through her mouth, trying to clear her mind of the sudden spike of fear.

"Why…" She clamped her mouth shut on the question.

Any further show of compassion would only make him more suspicious. Stick with the plan.

Vinnie pulled his power, but not all of it. She needed to leave enough that he thought he still had control. He shouldn't notice because he wasn't expecting it the way Hilda did.

He frowned, and Vinnie let his thoughts in. He enjoyed making people afraid. Her discomfort made him feel power-ful. They may have a shock collar on him, but he could make sure this fancy government agent didn't get in if he wanted.

He wanted her to be scared. Vinnie modeled her thoughts on what he was expecting and amplified them so he would hear what she wanted him to. She was afraid because Twisted were evil. He could hurt her in here and no one would know. He could break her mind and no one at all would know it was him.

"Why are you here?" he asked.

"I'm an investigator with the USSF trying to ascertain if there's any threat from the Twisted who attacked the Warrior games."

"You think they didn't work alone?"

Danger. Dangerous question. His excitement had increased when he asked it. He wanted there to be a bigger conspiracy. No one would tell him anything, but her mind was easy to read. He could pluck the lies right out, finally. Maybe he could join them. They would save him.

"This is just a routine check." Vinnie sent the thought that there was definitely something going on, but she couldn't let that slip and that she needed to distract him. "They should have been moved by now. I had to fly in, miss my anniver-sary dinner with my boyfriend."

The Mesmer smirked. "It's very important that we know if there is anything else going on." He wanted to make her squirm.

Fine. She could play the game. "That's not protocol."

"Ah," He crowed. "So there is something."

Vinnie let her mind splutter about protocols and getting fired, then deliberately thought of donuts again.

"That's a good trick," he said. "How long have you been with Hanna's Soldiers?"

Who? Vinnie didn't need to fake her surprise.

His eyes narrowed and his thoughts turned smug. He'd gotten her. If she was with the USSF, she'd know what he was talking about.

She didn't need to fake her panic, either. Donuts, donuts, donuts, soft center, teeth sinking in. Vinnie pulled as much of his power as she could without taking it completely.

"I don't know what you're accusing me of. I've passed rigorous background checks and safety tests. I've never even heard of this Hanna's Soldiers or whatever. I lied, okay? I'm just an executive assistant. My boss is sick, and they didn't think this was important enough since the FID is all over it. I'm just a formality." She sent him all her panicked and fearful thoughts. A moment of punching Will in the nose slipped in accidentally. Punching him for not helping her prepare better would be satisfying.

The Mesmer grinned evilly, "That your boss? Okay. You passed."

And he was out the door. Vinnie slumped in relief. Done. The hard part was over.

Unless there were more surprises later on. More security checks that Will hadn't told her about.

The guard came back and led her to another small room and handed her a jumpsuit and some kind of hood. "Make sure all of your flammable clothing is covered and your hair is completely tucked under. Knock on the door when you're ready."

Vinnie did as instructed, dragging the heavy jumpsuit

over her body, and tucking her hair up under the elastic of the hood. This must be for the Wisp. The Wisp would have a collar too, which meant that if they tried to hurt her, they would be hurt far worse. That didn't guarantee her safety. Some people were desperate, and might try anything.

When she was ready, she knocked and was led down two more hallways to a room with a heavy door and no window. The guard pulled the door open, making sure to position herself behind it as Vinnie walked into the room.

A young man with deep red hair sat at a table with his hands cuffed in front of him. Vinnie stuck her head back out the door. "I thought I was talking to both of them."

"I don't know anything about it. Not my department. I was told to bring you here and here I have brought you."

Great. So helpful. Vinnie walked back into the room. Her chair scraped the floor as she pulled it out and sat.

"Hi, I'm Anne."

Flames flared in the Wisp's eyes and his mouth parted as he sat up straighter for a moment before returning to his nonchalant pose. "Kiernan."

Vinnie wished she'd brought a folder or something she could put in front of her. Open it, close it, pretend to be engrossed, so she didn't have to look at him.

Kiernan smiled. He seemed happy to see her. "What brings you to my humble abode today, Anne?"

This was the guy who'd blown up the crews of the Warrior games? His face seemed kind and open, his voice soft.

She used her Vasum power to search the compound for Amanda, the Warrior Games Mesmer, but the only power she found was weak, most likely the prison Mesmer again. His power was already depleted, but she pulled what she could and eyed Kiernan.

"I'm with the USSF trying to determine if what happened at the games is a threat to national security."

His demeanor showed no panic or surprise, but the thoughts were too fuzzy to back up her impressions.

"And you thought they'd have Amanda, the Mesmer, from my crew, in here too. I heard you tell the guard. Did they tell you you could see her?"

Will hadn't said she'd get to talk to them all, but he had said there were two here and she'd assumed.

"My boss was expecting me to talk to all the Twisted responsible. The Wisp, the Mesmer, and the Ferr." A small spike of chatter in his thoughts about the Ferr. The news reports had said the responsibility for the fire was strictly the Wisp and the Mesmer, though that didn't prevent the others from being sent to a rehabilitation camp. At least they wouldn't be going to dead enders like Kiernan and Amanda.

Kiernan leaned back in his chair. One index finger made a slow scratching motion at the table — a tic maybe, showing his mind working.

"Do you know why they are only letting me talk to you?" she asked, hoping an easy question would get him talking.

"Per USSF rules, they keep strong, dangerous Mesmers sedated to keep them from getting into the heads of people who could have knowledge that would help them escape."

If she was actually USSF she should know that, but his voice was gentle as ever, not accusing her of anything.

Where did she start with the questions? Lou thought people would be after Conor, and a Pro-Twisted group might have the resources to do that.

"The Mesmer that let me in said something about Hanna's Soldiers," she said. "Do you know why he would think that? Did they have something to do with the explosion?"

"I caused the explosion."

"All by yourself?"

He leaned forward, his eyes dropped to his own finger worrying at the table. "It's been really busy in here since they locked me up. I've had the local police come in. The FID asking if Kara murdered children, a USSF agent asking if I knew where Kara was, and now a second person claiming to be from USSF asking about an explosion." His eyes slid up to the corner of the room and then back to Vinnie. "People may think they're getting away with something, but the staff might take note. Maybe they're used to it because maybe the USSF's head really doesn't know what its backside is doing, but the last I checked, it was illegal to work in an enforcement capacity if you're a Wisp, and if somehow those rules had changed, you would have a registration tattoo on your hand. I've turned the camera off."

Vinnie's eyes shot to the corner. Her panic had increased with every sentence, he'd uttered.

"Friction," he said. "They'll think it just malfunctioned."

"Are you threatening me?" she asked, but she didn't feel threatened. It wasn't Kiernan himself who made her feel panicked, but that she could be trapped in here if someone out there realized something was off and made a call.

His confusion was obvious. "Why would I threaten you?"

To blackmail her? To get her to get him out? Because he could? None of those sounded logical to her, but people weren't always logical.

"Why do you think I'm a Wisp?"

He tilted his head at her again. "Kara didn't send you."

She'd come in here thinking they had been unwilling participants in the explosion. He seemed kind, but that sounded a lot like disappointment in his voice. If he was helping Kara willingly, how much could she possibly learn from him? The truth seemed like her best bet.

"No. I'm Lavinia Forbes. I'm here because Conor Hahn

has been arrested for a murder he didn't commit, and I need to find out who is setting him up. I don't think it's Kara."

"Damn." He slumped again. "That sounds just stupid enough to be the truth."

"Why do you think Kara would send someone in to talk to you?"

"Because she protected me. She protected all of us."

Not the answer she was expecting. Kara had tried to kill her and her friends, had killed Maddie and crowed about it, proud of the work she was doing, but she had said she was trying to help Twisted — had vehemently defended them when Lou was attacking and saying they were evil. Vinnie thought those were just words to justify killing people to get power.

"All the crews or just yours?"

"She was just one person. She couldn't save us all. Not yet."

The Mesmer power told her there was some doubt in his mind, an incident, maybe more than one. He remembered arguments but she couldn't get a clear reading on his thoughts.

"You think it's okay that she murdered Twisted, then? Because she protected you?"

"She didn't murder anyone." His eyes were fiery, but in his mind he was thinking of a guy — suicide?

Vinnie remembered an unusual suicide of a guy in Atlanta when she had been researching the murders. Would telling him she knew that Kara had killed people change his mind? Or would he figure out she knew more than she was saying, and that she'd killed his hero and lose trust?

"Who do you think did, then? We both know it wasn't Conor."

He looked away, breath hissing between his teeth.

Thoughts of being murdered and thrown into the bay with concrete on his feet.

The bay? There was no bay here in the middle of the country. Someone had been watching too many gangster movies.

"I don't think La Mafia can get to you in here."

His head jerked back toward her. "Why are you asking me questions if you already know the answer?"

He really thought a small local syndicate was murdering people all over the country.

"I can't figure out the connections. I need to know. They shouldn't be able to reach you in here. You don't mix with the rest of the prison."

"You got in. They could get in. You could be with them." He frowned as if the thought had just occurred to him.

"You don't believe I'm with them, but if I was…" Vinnie leaned forward and dropped her voice. "That means someone high powered is helping them. Who?"

He clamped his lips shut and shook his head. She needed to bring back helpful Kiernan.

"How did you know I was a Wisp?"

He rolled his eyes, disbelieving.

"No. really," she said.

"You're serious?"

Vinnie shrugged one shoulder.

"Any institutionalized Twisted would also know how I know you're a Wisp, which means you have not met any other Wisps in your life. True?"

Not true, she hadn't met any other Wisps when she was a Wisp, though, which meant that how he knew had something to do with Cerulean's power coursing through her.

"Are you going to tell me?"

"When you looked into my eyes, what did you see?"

"Flames." He gave her a tiny head tilt that let her know she was right. "Does it only work with other Wisps?"

"As far as I know. At least, I've never known a Wisp who could see anyone else's powers. Am I really the only Wisp you've ever met? How are you still alive?" His eyes roved over her. "You're a little thin. You need to make more focal points so it doesn't eat you up. If you found the information on the internet, it was probably vague. I don't know, I'm not allowed to use the internet, but you can make the focal points colorless with practice if you don't want to mar your skin. You really have to practice, though." He pointed it at his wrist. "It's worth it. They don't let institutionalized get tattoos, no matter the cause, unless you're lucky and get leased out to a good boss."

What was he saying? A focus so the power didn't eat her up and tattoos. Cerulean had been covered in tattoos. As she looked closer at his wrist, she thought she could see the shimmer of something, but she had searched the internet for ways to control Wisp power and hadn't found anything about focuses.

"A focus is some sort of tattoo? I can see you have at least one on your hand."

"How are you even still alive?" he whispered. "You must be very weak."

"I barely have any power at all."

"A focus works with your subconscious to control the power so you don't have to. The easiest way is to make a mark on your skin. Whatever effects you can use the power for, you put the intention into your focus. That locks that ability so your subconscious can't use it and burn you up. If you have a strong ability, you need more to take care of all the subtle variations. If you're weak, you would only need one for heating your body up when you're cold or something. The more power you have, the more subtly you can use it, so if you were strong you might need one for various temperatures, for example."

"If you're strong, you would be covered in tattoos?" Cerulean's tattoos had covered at least half his body, maybe more.

"Yes. Let's try one for body heat." He put his hands on the table, palms up. "Roll up your sleeve, so it's easier to see."

Remove the barrier that kept him from burning her? Did she trust him? His thoughts seemed placid and there was no doubt in her mind. She pushed her sleeve up and took his hands.

"Imagine it's freezing and focus on your wrist."

Vinnie did as instructed and as she watched a small butterfly bloomed on her wrist. "Did I do that? I didn't think about a butterfly."

"Wow, you know zero." He pulled his hands back. "Wisp power is sympathetic. That's how we can boost other powers. We can send the power out into objects and people. It's easier with other Wisps, like most abilities are easier to use on our own types. Probably some kind of adaptive trait to help us survive. You provided attention, I matched my power to yours and made the focus. You should be able to feel how it works and make more if you need them."

Sympathetic. It sounded similar to what TK had told her about how to use Ferr power to match heartbeats to establish trust with another person.

"Thank you," she said. "You seem like a good person. Why would you cause an explosion that hurt people?"

"They keep us locked up like animals. We need to make our voices heard." The words were rote, like he'd repeated them many, many times, and there was a flicker of something in his mind. Maybe more doubt, but it was just a whisper in his thoughts.

"You're part of Hanna's Soldiers, then?"

"Hacks. I mean. Yes, yes, all hail Hanna's Soldiers."

What was he trying to do here? He wasn't trying to make her believe he was part of that group or that he believed what he was saying. Vinnie tried to pull more from the Mesmer, but pain was starting at the edges of her mind, a consequence of using the power.

"So you weren't under the influence of Kara McKnight when you blew a hole in the stadium floor?"

Angry thoughts, thoughts of betrayal. He wasn't an innocent, not completely, but she didn't think he intended to cause an explosion.

"I had nothing to do with murdering children."

He still didn't think Kara had done it either, but there might be some doubt. "Do you really think La Mafia is going to come after you if you talk to me?"

"You think I'm crazy," he said. "Just like everyone else does."

"I've seen some pretty crazy things," she said.

His eyes met hers. "When we first came to this town, a mob boss disappeared."

Nieves Delgado. She and her friends had gotten evidence that he had been involved in human trafficking, but he had disappeared before the police could arrest him.

"They say he was involved in human trafficking," Kiernan continued. "But what they don't say, what they were trying to cover up, is that he was trafficking for the government. They're the ones who made him disappear. I think Kara was onto them. She said there was some big thing going on with some agencies that would kill or take away what little freedom we had left and that's why she needed our help. We had to stop them."

He was right. She thought he was crazy, but if she told him that, he would clam up. "What does that have to do with human trafficking?"

His eyes cut to the door, then up to the camera and then back to her. "They can't make Twisted children disappear here. Even though they took me when I was little, they still sent reports and photos back to my parents. Sometimes I could even see my parents. They don't have the same constraints with children from other countries."

And he thought Kara was trying to save them.

The door opened, and the guard entered. This time she too was dressed in a flame retardant jumpsuit. "Time's up."

Vinnie had so many more questions.

Kiernan slumped back in his seat. For a moment, flames danced in his eyes and then went out. For a moment, he'd had hope. Kara had given him that. Now he would go to a dead end prison where he would spend the rest of his life for a crime he didn't commit.

Vinnie pulled all the Mesmer ability she could and leaned across the table. She put her hand over his.

I'm sorry this happened to you. I'll do everything I can to make sure that the bad guys lose.

The flame flared in his eyes again, but he showed no other reaction. She knew it had been a mistake. A risk she shouldn't take. A risk with no benefit, TK might say and if she was wrong about Kiernan, she might agree. But if she was right, that he was a person who had thought he was doing the right thing, maybe she could at least give him some peace.

The guard led her to change and then back to the front lobby. Will was not waiting for her, but he'd sent a text that he would be in the car. The voicemail indicator was on too. Vinnie listened to it as she walked down the corridor out of the compound. They'd let her walk out on her own with no accompaniment.

"Hey Lavinia, It's Terrance. We need to talk, it's important. Call me as soon as you get this."

TK, who was in love with the ex-wife of a former mafia boss. The same mafia who Kiernan thought was trafficking children for the US government. Kiernan was probably crazy, but maybe TK knew something.

She dialed the number. TK answered after two rings.

"I have a few hours before I have to go to work," she said. "Let's talk."

"I'm a little busy at the moment."

"You said to call as soon as I got the message. It could be days before I'm free again." She couldn't keep the edge out of her voice.

"I'll give you an address. Meet me there in 45 minutes."

CHAPTER SEVENTEEN

The tattoo on her forearm itched, even though it hadn't been created with a needle. Vinnie rested her hand over it. There was nothing there, no Wisp power, it was just a mark, and yet she felt a tiny bit of relief, like she wasn't working as hard to hold the power down.

Will turned the SUV down a road that had seen better days. The address TK had given her was north of the suburbs, outside the city limits. Buses didn't travel this far, which TK would have known. If she hadn't been with Will, she would have had no way to get out here unless she called a ride share.

The vehicle bumped along the broken asphalt and Will hummed along to the sixties rock he'd been blasting the whole way. Most of the shops they passed were housed in cheap warehouses, the kind that were metal siding with no central heat or air. In the distance, a new construction site had sprung up in a spot that had once been trees. If that was their destination, then most likely Jory would be there. He was a construction foreman, and TK was a news anchor.

Will flipped on the turn signal to turn into the construction site just as an unfamiliar car pulled up to a small office trailer and cut the engine.

The two people in the car were exactly who she'd expected to see here. The way Jory was dressed, however, was unexpected. She had never seen him in anything but jeans or sweats, but he was wearing slacks and a button-down shirt. So was TK, but that's what he wore most of the time.

"Looks like your friends are up to something on a Saturday," Will said.

Vinnie pursed her lips at him. "Thanks for the ride."

Jory had gone to unlock the door to the trailer, but TK hung back and waited for her.

"New car?" she asked as she approached.

"Loaner." TK raised an arm and pulled her close for a side hug.

Vinnie tensed. TK was not a hugger. Her friends were definitely up to something on a Saturday. "Is it Gina's?"

His arm stiffened, then he squeezed and released. "If you have something to say, just get it out of the way now. Everyone else has had their turn."

Buried anger flared in her. He'd lied to them. He'd lied about why he wanted to go after Nieves Delgado and he'd lied to her about the reasons he took her to the house Kara had kept Maddie in. The house was Gina's and so was the ring he'd given Vinnie to practice using Ferr power on. He'd wanted to know if Vinnie had run into Gina at some point, but he hadn't told her that beforehand.

But Vinnie didn't want to fight and she knew he'd felt justified in keeping it from them. Would he also keep it from them if he knew something about La Mafia?

"I was just curious," she said. "It hurt that you didn't tell us the whole story, but everyone seems to have their secrets."

"Gina and I are not in a place where she would loan me her car."

But they were in a place where he would try to get rid of her ex-husband so she would be safe? Vinnie didn't understand, and she opened her mouth to ask just as Jory poked his head out the door.

"Are you guys coming in?"

Vinnie followed Jory into the trailer, with TK right behind her. The trailer seemed smaller on the inside, with a tiny microwave and fridge on one end. A desk with a computer sat in front of the micro kitchen. A couch and a tiny coffee table took up the middle and there was a door on the other end that Vinnie assumed led to a bathroom.

Jory sat at the desk, putting two folders in front of him, one very fat and one very thin.

"I didn't know you owned slacks," Vinnie said as she sat on the side of the couch closest to the desk.

He must have heard the question in her voice because he answered, "We had some stuff to take care of at the bank."

"You know you don't have to dress up to do stuff at the bank anymore." She couldn't imagine a bank refusing to do business with someone in jeans.

"It never hurts to dress nice, Vinnie."

She tugged at the sleeve of her shirt. The nicest one she owned, navy blue, also a button down, but she wore jeans with it. This was the nicest outfit she had. Did she look like she worked for the USSF? The guys who questioned her at the library had also been wearing slacks.

"Why am I here?" She asked TK, who had sat down beside her. She had a feeling he wasn't the one who wanted to see her.

Jory answered, "I contacted an old acquaintance to ask if he knew Conor Hahn was being set up for a murder he didn't commit."

Who would Jory know with that information? "Someone in La Mafia? Is that why TK is here? Because his girlfriend was married to their leader?"

"Vinnie — " TK said.

She held up a hand. "I'm not mad. I'm just trying to understand."

"An older acquaintance than that," Jory said.

From before he went to prison? Vinnie didn't think he'd known anyone who could get that kind of information.

Jory was tapping the folder on his desk.

"Jory did something stupid," TK said.

Which meant someone dangerous. Someone that would make Jory nervous about telling her, which meant it was bad. "Just spit it out."

"People don't just escape from Maximum Security Twisted prisons," Jory said. "That's why they call them dead end camps. They don't make mistakes when they are checking to make sure you're dead. They don't make mistakes taking the bodies to incinerators. There is no way that I should have been able to escape the cart. They didn't take chances even with the dead."

"Someone helped you escape," Vinnie said.

"That's his theory," TK said. "My theory is, he was dead, which means this guy wanted him dead and is going to come after him now that he knows he's not."

"I was not dead. Zees can't come back from the dead."

TK quirked an eyebrow. "And Ferr can't control people. Until they can."

"That's not the same. We are talking about no life in a body."

They were just going to go on like that, not addressing the real issue.

"Stop." Vinnie looked Jory in the eye. "You contacted someone who may or may not want you dead to ask why

Conor is being set up? Why would you do that? I had it under control."

"Did you?" Jory asked. "Because the last I heard, you had no clue and had gone to some snake who is using you so that he could use you more."

"I was going to text you." She probably wasn't. "Will got me into the prison and I talked to the Wisp who caused the explosion. I have leads. You didn't have to put yourself in danger."

His look was incredulous. "You walked into a prison where they might have figured out who you are, to talk to someone known to associate with someone who wants you dead and you are mad at *me?*"

"That was safer than what you did!"

"You don't know that!" Jory thundered. "You don't know the person I contacted like I do."

"With Vinnie on this one," TK murmured.

Vindicated. TK and Jory were best friends. If he agreed with Vinnie, she felt sure she was right. That didn't make her feel any better, because that meant what Jory did was really risky.

"I don't want you to get hurt," Vinnie said. "I was hanging out with Conor when Maddie was found. I am in this whether or not I do anything. I don't have a choice. You do."

"I don't," Jory said. "I can't cower in fear while you risk your life to keep someone from going to a cushy jail for a few years."

That was the second time someone said the consequences for Conor would be small. "I'm pretty sure most serial killers end up on death row."

"Wait," TK said. "Are they charging him with the other murders too?"

She flopped back on the couch, deflated. "The FID agents who talked to me asked about other deaths. Maybe."

"Damn," TK breathed.

Vinnie couldn't agree more, and now Jory had potentially put himself in danger. His fingers still played with the edges of the folders in front of him. He'd found something or they wouldn't have called her here. But there was one thing she wanted to know first.

"Why would someone want to kill you when you were already going to be in prison for the rest of your life?"

"Because they are people who will do anything for power, Vinnie. High-powered people who will crush anyone they can get away with crushing."

"What he's saying," TK said. "Is there were people who were running clandestine experiments on Twisted in the prison. Jory ingratiated himself to one of them — "

"I made friends with him," Jory said.

"You know as well as I do that people who have power over you, and perform experiments on you, are not your friends."

They stared at each other for a moment before Jory looked away.

"They were almost found out," Jory said. "Some prisoners that were part of the experiments disappeared, offices were broken into to make it look like theft, computers smashed, papers shredded. The man I knew said he would get me out. I trusted him and then I was jumped by the guards, beaten until I was close to death, and dumped on the cart to be incinerated. The incinerators went down, and I was left there for I don't know how long — at least a day. After the incinerators were fixed, the guards that drove the truck became violently ill en route, and I crawled out and climbed over the fence that was supposed to be electrified but was not."

That sort of sounded like someone was trying to get him out, but there was one issue. "You think your friend had you beaten to death to save you?"

"I wasn't dead."

"But," TK said. "If that was the plan, he never shared that with Jory. Sounds like a whole lot of coincidences to me."

Jory didn't know if his friend had actually tried to save him or kill him. "And that's who you got information from?" She asked, even though she knew the answer.

"Yes," Jory answered calmly, as if he didn't notice her trying to glare a hole right through his head. He held out the folder.

She took it without snatching it and flipped it open. Vinnie stared at the page, trying to make sense of what she was reading. The first document inside appeared to be a prison dossier. A familiar face stared back at her.

"Charlotte Knight," she said. "She didn't change her name much. Kara McKnight."

"It's easier to stick to something close to what you know," Jory said.

His real name was Jordan, but he'd never told them what his last name had been.

Kara had been in a dead ender, just like Jory. She killed a classmate when she was fifteen. The notes from the psychologist who evaluated her said it appeared to be self-defense. They also noted a history of doctor visits for sprains and broken bones, consistent with abuse that had stopped around the time she was twelve. Her mom committed suicide when she was twelve, and Kara — Charlotte — had been in foster care since then. It had been the opinion of the evaluator that she was a good candidate for special rehabilitation.

"Special rehabilitation?" Vinnie asked.

"There were sanctioned projects and unsanctioned ones," Jory said. "But don't let Kara's evaluation fool you. Whether you got to leave for a sanctioned project or not depended less on your crime and more on how much power you had."

Kara had gotten into some other prisons with some high level authorizations. They'd thought she had a good forger. "You don't think they let a known murderer work in operations high enough to actually have enough security clearance to get into a maximum security prison."

The look on both the men's faces said they did believe that.

"That's ridiculous," she said. "Dangerous. She was unstable. Why would they be so stupid?"

TK snorted.

"When Will asked me to help him go after Kara, he said the police couldn't handle her," Vinnie said. "They would need to have someone strong enough to take her, and people like her on. I couldn't even talk to the Mesmer in the prison because they didn't think they could control her."

Jory said, "They need the power, but they don't want the public to know."

"She had the clearances," TK said. "She had a weapon dangling around her neck."

"The Wisp at the prison thought the government was working with La Mafia to traffic Twisted children," she said.

She expected another scoffing laugh, but TK and Jory looked thoughtful.

"That would be one way to do it," TK said. "Without relying on dangerous criminals."

"He seemed to think she was trying to save Twisted from the government, not helping. And Lou thought it was some subversive group after Conor specifically." Something was still bothering her. The pieces still didn't seem to fit together quite right. "Kiernan was also sure she wasn't a killer and we know she was. We have this evidence she was taken for special projects, and the USSF is involved in addition to the FID. If La Mafia was helping her get children to experiment on she wouldn't have had to take Maddie."

"The Wisp doesn't sound like he was very reliable," Jory said.

Familiar power pinged on Vinnie's senses. Hilda was outside. "Hilda's here. I guess she's late."

TK frowned. "We didn't tell her about any of this. She doesn't know we're here." He stood, moved around the coffee table, and opened the door.

Outside was a figure dressed in a form fitting black outfit with white dragon wings on the back. Hilda had a black ski mask over her head and was looking into the trees behind the construction site.

Jory had gotten up from his desk so he could see out the door. "Hilda's the White Dragon, I knew it."

"My money was on Nell," TK said.

Outside, Hilda threw her arms up in front of her face and then her body was engulfed in flames.

CHAPTER EIGHTEEN

Jory shoved past TK and ran toward Hilda. The flames around her disappeared, probably snuffed out by removing the air around herself. She appeared unharmed.

TK descended the steps of the trailer and Vinnie followed.

Four people had emerged from the trees on the other side of the construction site, wearing street clothes and ski masks.

"All Twisted?" TK asked.

Vinnie hadn't felt them approach, and couldn't sense them now. She pushed as much awareness into her ability as she could muster and got the same low throb she'd gotten from the Mesmer who'd attacked her.

"Yes, but they're blocking me. It's hard to tell what kind they are. Stone. Dancer—"

Run! Get in the Car! Hilda turned to run. A gust of air knocked her off her feet and sent her sprawling.

Jory, who had been next to her, was pushed back a few steps.

TK grabbed Vinnie's elbow and pulled her toward the car. Jory had planted his feet and wasn't moving.

Hilda climbed to her feet. *There are more behind the building. We have to get out of here.*

Two more attackers came from around the side of the trailer.

"Ferr," Vinnie said, feeling the dull throb of power coming from one of them. The other was blank, no power at all.

TK had opened the two doors on the passenger side and scrambled around to the driver's seat.

Jory still hadn't moved. He stood with his shoulder hunched, and he flung a hand toward one of the original attackers.

There are too many. Hilda's thoughts were frantic and she was broadcasting thoughts meant for Jory to all of them.

Whatever Jory's reply was, it wasn't what Hilda wanted. She turned, ice-blue eyes bored into Vinnie, who stood beside the open car door.

Run, save yourselves. Hilda turned back toward the attackers, throwing her hands out. Two attackers were thrown off their feet.

"The hell we will," TK said, slamming the door he'd just opened.

What could she do? How could she help? Her friends were better at using their own power than she was. Pulling the power from the attackers would be too slow to be useful. "Dancer, Stone, Mesmer, Ferr, Zee. That's all."

"We know there's a Wisp."

Six attackers, all the types. A full crew and there was only four of them. Was the Wisp just better at blocking? The Mesmer was knocking Jory and Hilda around. Maybe she could take enough power to weaken them. She started there, but pulling the power was agonizingly slow.

TK grunted. "My power seems to have no effect on them."

"They have some kind of block." The air around her warmed. Her Wisp power responded, flaring up in her without conscious thought, and she pulled the power in the air into her own body.

The Wisp crumpled to the ground.

"Did you do that?" she asked TK, because taking power out of the air shouldn't have caused the Wisp to collapse, but she wasn't sure what she'd done.

Before TK could say anything, he stumbled too and then righted himself. His face was waxen, and he sat backwards through the open car door and landed in the driver's seat.

Hilda, Jory, and the other four attackers were fighting on one of the house foundations.

Hilda's legs went out from under her. *Get the Zee.*

The Ferr had turned his attention to the battle on the foundation.

They're blocking me, but I can try. The attacking Zee stood back from the rest. Vinnie tried to feel around the block, but it wouldn't help much. She couldn't pull fast enough.

TK emerged from the car, swung his arms and steadied them on the roof, gun raised. He pulled the trigger, catching the Ferr in the shoulder. Then he yelped and dropped the gun. The Wisp's eyes were open, boring into TK.

I'm having trouble getting in their heads too, but I can use the air around them just fine.

Whatever the attackers were using to block them, it only seemed to effect things that worked on their bodies directly. That meant there wasn't much TK could do.

One of the attackers, the Zee, gasped and clutched his throat. The Dancer launched himself at Jory. Vinnie switched targets, trying to pull as much from the Dancer as she could. The Dancer punched Jory a few times in rapid succession.

Jory seemed unfazed by this. His fist flew out, sending the Dancer to the ground. He stepped over the Dancer and headed toward the Stone, who was on the other side of the foundation.

Hilda was blasted back by something Vinnie couldn't see and fell on her back in the dirt.

They have too much juice.

Trying to pull power from the attackers wasn't helping much, but she had another ability. If her friends had more power, they could do something. They might stand a chance.

The battle had moved off the house foundation. They couldn't take away Jory's ability to use his own body. That meant they couldn't blast him over with air, and the Dancer couldn't knock him down. Vinnie had a feeling it would only take one hit from the Stone to take him out, though. He just had to not get hit. Jory's attack was pushing the other crew back, but he had to be getting tired.

Vinnie calmed her panic. She had survived the last time she had used the Wisp power. She would survive this one. She opened up to the power, trying to let a small amount free, but the power roared through her, out of control. Almost out of control. Vinnie held as much as she could and pushed it at Hilda. Hilda, who had just been getting to her feet, stumbled.

Vinnie grabbed more and pushed to Jory, who pivoted, throwing another punch that took the attacking Zee down.

There was a blur and the Wisp sprinted onto the foundation and off the other side. She barreled into Hilda, taking them both down.

The Stone had knocked Jory down, but he was back on his feet. Vinnie channeled the Wisp power, preparing another boost just as another figure in black came running onto the construction site.

Nell.

Nell wore an outfit just like Hilda's, black with white wings on the back. Hilda had lifted the Wisp with a cushion of air and Nell ran straight to her and kicked, sending the Wisp sprawling into the fight with Jory.

Get to the car. Nell will hold them.

The Zee was trying to get back to his feet, and Jory kicked him to keep him down and took a few steps back. Another blast of wind hit him but she could only tell by the ruffling of his hair.

Hilda had backed off toward the car. *The Zee is holding TK.*

Vinnie gathered some of the Wisp power raging through her, and a fireball formed in her hands, which she threw at the Zee. He dodged, but it must have been enough to break his concentration because the car engine started behind her.

Jory back off. Get to the car

Jory scrambled back and Nell moved forward so that she was between the attackers and the car.

Can you boost Nell?

The roaring in her body had calmed. The Wisp power was depleted. Vinnie dug deep, pulled all she could muster, and shoved it toward Nell.

Nell crouched, jumped high in the air, and came down on the ground, slamming both fists into the earth. For a moment, there was no sound, then there was a concussive boom. The earth shook, knocking the attackers off their feet. All but the other Stone.

Hilda and Jory scrambled into the back seat of the car.

Nell was backing away from the Stone, prepared in case he did something else.

Vinnie felt the attacking Dancer's power clear in her mind — something had happened to the block. She pulled all his power, pulled some from Hilda, and the memory of how to form an ice spike was in her mind a second before it coalesced in her hands. She threw it at the attacking Stone, who held up a hand and let it hit him.

He stood still and watched as Nell continued to back

toward the car. Vinnie climbed in the back and pulled the door closed, leaving the front passenger side door open for Nell.

The other attackers were dragging themselves up.

Boost me. I'm going to shield her.

Vinnie gave Hilda everything she could muster.

One of the attackers was up and poised as if to come at them again. Nell's fists clenched.

"We can't take them," Hilda said. "Let them go."

Nell unclenched her fists and whirled, dashed the last few steps to the car and threw herself into the front seat. TK hit the gas before her car door even closed and they were roaring down the street.

"What was that?" TK screeched as the car tore down the road.

"I think that's what they call an attack," Jory said. He seemed calm, but the muscle in his jaw was spasming.

Hilda pulled her ski mask off. "About thirty minutes ago, we got a notification that a robbery was in progress at this location."

"This is outside the Holt," Vinnie said. Zandia said the White Dragon only operated in the Holt.

"We don't discriminate," Nell said. "We just can't really get anywhere else in a timely manner, usually." She pulled the ski mask off.

"I knew it was you," TK said.

Nell frowned at him. "Is that really how you want to play it?"

He pressed his lips together.

Vinnie glanced back and forth between them.

"TK already knew," she guessed when it didn't look like he was going to answer.

"Or was in on it," Jory said. "Looks like we've been left out, Vinnie."

"Would you have wanted in?" Hilda asked.

He shrugged, leaned back against the seat, and closed his eyes.

Vinnie would have wanted in, but she was the one who'd left them, not the other way around. TK didn't look like he was going to confirm or deny their speculation, and they had other things to talk about.

"This had to be a set-up," Vinnie said. The Wisp power fluttered inside her, but there wasn't enough left to overwhelm her. Her head felt cloudy, but she pushed the next words out. "You got a notification to be where we were. The only one not here is Shaw."

"We've been very careful with our identities as the White Dragon," Hilda said. "People think it's only one person, so one of us can be out in the open when the other does something. It had to be a coincidence."

"Big damn coincidence," Jory muttered.

A shudder went through Vinnie and she wasn't sure if it was fear or the aftereffects of the Wisp power.

"I don't think it's a coincidence," TK said. "They know who we are, they know where we live."

Vinnie's seat belt clacked in time to her shaking body.

Hilda glanced sideways at her. "If they know where we live," she said. "They didn't attack us there. Should be safe."

"Plus, we rang their bells," Nell agreed. "We might have been a tiny bit outmatched, but they'll think twice before messing with us, and we don't have anywhere else to go. Anymore."

"We could go to my place." Vinnie's words came out a little slurred, and her vision blurred further. "Need ice."

And then the world was gone.

CHAPTER NINETEEN

The smell of chocolate under Vinnie's nose brought her mind back into her body, and she opened her eyes. Hilda hovered over her, holding a soft chocolate cookie. Vinnie was on her back, somewhere soft. Home. Jory's house. On the couch.

Hunger pierced her stomach, and she grabbed the cookie, took a big bite, chewed twice, and swallowed.

The flavor hit her taste buds, and she gagged. "Salt, too much salt." Vinnie rolled to the side and pushed herself up.

Hilda held out a glass of tea and Vinnie took it, swallowing a few gulps.

"You used a lot of Wisp power," Hilda said flatly.

Did Hilda realize Vinnie hadn't pulled the power? The look on her face said she knew something was off.

"Why was that so easy for you when pulling from the others was hard?" Hilda asked. "And you were burning up in the car. Wisp power never did that to you before. What did they do to you?"

Her relief that Hilda didn't know the truth was short-lived. She needed to tell them.

"I didn't roast myself. That's progress. Where are the others? It will be easier if I tell you all at once."

"In back, Nell used a lot of power, too. She's grounding."

Hilda had also used a lot of power, but she looked like she was fine. How long had Vinnie been out?

"Almost two hours," Hilda said, answering her question. "I'm not fine. I'm pissed."

That was obvious from the stiff set of her shoulders. Vinnie didn't think she was going to escape that wrath when she told them about the power. "When did Nell learn to make earthquakes, or whatever that was?"

Hilda turned on her heel and started for the backyard. "Looks like we all have a lot to talk about."

Like how did she and Nell get a notification app up and running so fast, and more importantly, why had they? Vinnie clutched her tea as she followed Hilda down the hall.

"And who were those people and why were they attacking us?" Hilda said. She'd gone through the kitchen and opened the door to the backyard.

"We've ordered pizza," TK said as they approached. He sat on a blanket under the only tree, while Nell lay on the ground. She'd removed her black top and was in a white tank top and black pants.

Jory lay beside her with his eyes closed. Vinnie sank to the ground next to Jory, managing not to spill her drink.

The cookie was still in Vinnie's hand and it smelled good. She took another bite, wincing as she chewed and swallowed.

"Why are you baking all these cookies when you're bad at it, Nell?" she asked, eyeing the ground for somewhere to put it down so she'd stop eating.

Nell rolled her head toward Vinnie. "I'm not bad at baking cookies. I used to bake with my grandma all the time. I know how to bake cookies."

Vinnie made a face at the cookie she was holding and then held it out to Nell. "You want to eat this, then?"

Nell huffed and looked back at the sky. "Yes, THAT cookie is bad."

"Are you going to tell us or not?" TK muttered, not taking his eyes off his phone.

Nell tensed for a moment and then she relaxed into the ground. "Cer loved homemade cookies. His mom would bake them every Sunday, but he never got them living with us because none of us baked. He tried to make some once when it was just the two of us. I was busy and didn't offer to help and they were a mess, burned and flat."

Hilda looked at Nell like she was crazy. "So you're making cookies the way Cer would make them? That's dumb. Make them the way he would have wanted them instead. Then at least someone could eat them."

Nell sat up. "I'm not messing them up on purpose Hilda! I can't…." She balled her hands up and pressed them into her lap. "I can't focus."

Vinnie took another bite of the cookie and gagged.

"Stop that!" Nell snapped. "It's not edible."

"It's still sugar," Vinnie mumbled around a bite of cookie. The salt didn't seem as bad this time.

TK set his phone in his lap. "Maybe since we're examining everyone's psychological problems because of Sam's death, Lavinia can tell us why she thought that Wisp who attacked us was normal."

Vinnie couldn't think of a single time TK had called Cerulean anything other than his given name. It jarred her. Sam. Sam had had a family, once, parents he'd accidentally killed because he couldn't control his power. She'd known he was dealing with the pain of that, but she hadn't known how hard he had to fight every day to keep the Wisp power under control.

If Nell hated her before, she was going to hate her even more now. Having Cer's power felt like proof she was responsible for his death. If she'd known how to give it back, he would still be alive.

Hilda's eyes widened. Of course she'd heard Vinnie's thoughts. Vinnie hadn't been trying to bury them this time.

"I'm not sure, but I couldn't tell she was a Wisp, and I couldn't pull any power from her."

"But you were using Wisp power." Nell shifted her position so she could stare Vinnie down.

"Kara kept going on and on about how she wanted me to teach her how to hold power and keep it. I didn't know why she thought I could do that. I took his power from her, and I thought I put it back in him, but he died anyway." Vinnie took a big gulp of tea. "Then I felt something burning inside me, and it kept getting stronger. I couldn't control it. I almost burned the library down."

"You have Cer's power." There were tears in Nell's eyes and Vinnie's eyes pricked in response.

"I didn't mean to hurt him."

Nell sat up and turned her back on Vinnie.

"You think you can't recognize or pull from a Wisp because you already are one now?" Jory asked.

"I don't know," Vinnie said. "That's the first time I tried. I talked to the Wisp at the prison, but I already knew what he was, so I didn't check, and the people who attacked us had some kind of block. I could barely sense them. The Wisp could have just been better at blocking."

"Does having that power boost your own abilities?" TK asked.

Did it? She didn't have to think as much about sensing other people's power. She could shift and see the power more easily. "I think so." Nell still wasn't looking at her and

Vinnie wanted her to say something, even if it was anger. "Nell? I'm sorry."

Nell buried her face between her knees, back hunched in a protective posture.

Vinnie watched Nell, feeling helpless. What would she do if she didn't think Nell hated her? She put down the cookie and empty glass, crawled forward, and put her hand on Nell's back. Nell lifted her head enough to twist around and bury her face in Vinnie's shoulder. Vinnie's eyes burned as she wrapped her arms around Nell.

"Maybe we should all make cookies," Hilda said. "My neighbor taught me to make snickerdoodles."

"I can make brownies," TK said.

"I don't know how to bake," Jory said.

Nell snuffed. "Now Vinnie can tell us some sob story about how she wasn't allowed in the kitchen and the maid would sneak her cookies."

That was almost true. "The maid hated me. I had to sneak my own cookies."

Nell choked on a laugh. "We have to teach Vinnie and Jory how to bake." She pushed herself to stand and held her hand out to Vinnie to help her up.

"What? Now?" TK said. "Shouldn't we recover and talk about what we're going to do about being set up?"

"We can talk while we move." Hilda stood. "Jory can watch from the chair since he can't recover as fast."

Jory got to his feet. "I want peanut butter cookies."

"NELL. NELL!" TK grasped Nell's hand, which had just been about to dump sugar into the brownies they were making. "I already added the sugar to the chocolate. That sugar goes in the peanut butter swirl."

"Oh," Nell breathed. "Right." She shifted to put the sugar in the second bowl.

Hilda was busy pulling ingredients out of the fridge and cabinets and piling them on the counter. She reached over Nell's head to get peanut butter while Nell stared into the peanut butter bowl.

The pizza had arrived while they were arguing over what to make and talking about what they all knew. Vinnie grabbed another slice and put it on her plate.

Jory picked up his phone. "While you guys cook, let's go over what we know." He'd taken notes while they were talking, and he read them now. "Kara McKnight disappeared from a maximum-security prison where she was being held for murder four years ago. My contact believes she was taken out for an experimental program. She joined the Warrior games just over two years ago and began murdering Twisted to take their power. Conor Hahn, who runs a non-profit that is attempting to find ways of more easily identifying Twisted, has been set up for the murders. Kara may or may not have been working with a group called Hanna's Soldiers who are trying to... do what?" He muttered. "Vinnie's apartment was broken into this morning. Nothing appears to have been stolen."

"Both the people who attacked us today and individuals who attacked Vinnie last week could block Twisted power. However, their blocks don't work one hundred percent and Hilda picked up some thoughts about a weapon which we suspect to be the crystal that Kara was wearing."

"And don't forget the government is buying children from La Mafia." Hilda smirked as she handed TK the peanut butter mix.

"The more I think about that, the more ridiculous it sounds." TK snatched the bowl from her and poured it on top of the chocolate in the pan.

"Why? Because your girlfriend might have been in on it?"

"Hilda," Jory said.

She sighed. "Fine. But if we interrupted some clandestine operation, that's another reason people might attack us. We shouldn't narrow our focus to people who may have been working with Kara or are after Conor. We have plenty of potential enemies."

"I can believe that the government would try to get Twisted children," TK said. "But Nieves hated Twisted so much he tried to kill his own wife, who he loved. I can't see him working with Kara."

"Unless he didn't know what she was," Nell said.

TK held the brownies out to her. "Do you want to do the honors?"

She took the pan from him, and he moved out of her way and sat at the table while she put the pan in the oven. Nell twisted the oven timer.

"That timer doesn't work," TK said.

"I've got the timers set on my phone," Hilda said.

"Pfft. I'll just keep track of the time in my head."

"Not all of us can keep track of our heartbeats to tell the time, TK."

"You can both keep track," Nell said. "It's not a competition."

"If it were, I'd win." Hilda put her phone on the table with a large timer ticking down. "Because everyone can hear the timer on my phone." She walked back over to the fridge, pulled out a bottle of wine and took a swig before leaning back against the counter.

Jory rubbed his hands over his face, but Vinnie could see it was mock exasperation as he wiped away a smile.

"They were attacking me," Vinnie said. "It was my apartment they broke into, and they attacked me separately."

"Do you have a crime fighting app they messaged to get

you to the construction site?" Hilda asked. "Because I do, which means they were after me, Nell, and…" she glanced at TK. "… Nell."

Vinnie's eyes darted to TK to see if he would confess, but he seemed very intent on the pizza slice he'd grabbed.

"Because you're connected to me," Vinnie said.

"Not everything is about you, cupcake."

"Not everything, but this is." She needed to get out of here. She shouldn't have lingered — she was putting them in danger, and she had to go to work.

"Stop being an idiot!" Hilda snapped. "You say you want to move away, but you move two blocks. You think it matters to the people who want to hurt you if you live with the people you care about? If they want to get to us, they are still going to know it will hurt you and that you'd come running if any of us are in danger. It's pointless."

Vinnie had never intended to stay so close, but now didn't seem like a good time to say that. She rolled her eyes dramatically. "Please, it's at least seven blocks."

TK laughed.

"It also weakens us," Jory said. "Not being in contact. We wouldn't have survived this if it weren't for you. Two blocks is at least close enough you could get here if we needed you, but you have to answer the damn phone."

"You should move back in with us," Nell said. "You're not safe over there alone."

"I thought you hated me." The words squeezed out past the lump in Vinnie throat.

"I thought I did, too. I can't hurt the woman who killed Cer, but I wanted to tear the world apart." She gave the plate in front of her an irritated nudge. "It's like I couldn't think straight, but seeing you in danger…I'm thinking straight now. No one messes with my friends. I will open the earth and bury anyone who tries."

Vinnie swallowed hard. She didn't want to be alone, dragging herself into bathtubs full of ice because there was no one to help her. She'd thought she was doing the right thing, but they were all attacked anyway. Maybe they were right, she should move back in, face whatever was coming together.

It was hard to let go of the idea that being here would put them in more danger. "I'll think about it."

"We'll take Jory's van and get your things tomorrow," Hilda said.

"That's settled then," Nell snuffed. "TK should move back, too."

"Not a chance," TK said. "I'm perfectly safe, and I'm not alone."

He wasn't alone? Hadn't he just said he and Gina weren't in a place to be borrowing cars but he was implying they lived together. Unless he was living with someone else. But no, he was in love with Gina. Vinnie was sure of that. She opened her mouth to speak.

Jory cleared his throat. "Right, where were we?"

"People trying to kill us," TK said.

Hilda tapped the side of the wine bottle in her hand. "They weren't trying to kill us."

"It definitely felt like they were trying to kill us when that Ferr stopped my heart," TK said. "What makes you think they weren't?"

"Because we're not dead. We were outmatched in every way. They knew how to coordinate their abilities and they could partially block ours, and they were used to working together."

"Maybe they were after that crystal," Nell said. "But that doesn't explain why they attacked us. They didn't get close enough to look for any crystal or try to take anything."

"Maybe if we could figure out how they knew who we were, that would be a start?" Vinnie asked.

"They attacked at my work site, and they signaled to the White Dragon." Jory tapped one finger on the table. "We can only be sure they were after three of us."

"Except it was probably the same people who attacked me before." Something occurred to Vinnie that might answer the question of who they were after. "Where's Shaw? If they were after all of us, why not her too?"

"She's not responding to texts." Nell's jaw clenched. "But that's not unusual these days."

"So, we don't know anything useful," Jory said. "We don't know why they attacked. We don't know how they knew who we were, we don't know who they are, and we don't know who they were after."

The timer on Hilda's phone went off just as the front door crashed open. Nell and Jory leaped to their feet.

"It's Shaw," Vinnie said.

Nell reached the kitchen doorway just as Shaw made it down the hall.

Shaw barreled into Nell, wrapping her in a hug. "You're okay. When I turned my phone back on there was a text saying it was Vinnie but it wasn't her number, but it said you guys needed my help and I went to the address and it was full of police and you guys were nowhere."

"Why didn't you call or respond to my texts?" Nell said into Shaw's shoulder.

Shaw pulled back, releasing Nell. "Maybe it wasn't you? I mean, the number was right, but..." She strode into the room and wrapped her arms around TK's shoulders, startling him. "You're all safe. What happened?"

Jory sunk back into his chair. While he summarized what had happened at the construction site and everything they knew, Shaw nibbled at a slice of pizza.

"Someone was following me a few days ago," Shaw said. "Minka thought I was being paranoid. No one attacked me or anything."

Vinnie drained the last of her tea, hoping it would give her some energy. "They're after all of us, then, and we don't know why."

"That's one question down," Hilda said. "That leaves what they were after, how they found us and who they were."

"I can dig into some of the higher security systems," Nell said. "I've been working on some things. I can see what I can find on government projects and subversive groups."

"You're a hacker now?" TK was frowning, but it was a thoughtful frown.

"If people are coming after us, I want to be prepared," she said.

Will was also supposed to be digging for Vinnie, but they already knew that. "It doesn't feel like any of this is fast enough. They are attacking now."

Shaw stopped picking at the crust. "We don't need to know who they are or what they want. We need to get them to come after us again and be ready."

Hilda grinned. "Bait."

Jory swore.

Vinnie didn't like that plan either, but at least it would give them some control. "We can get word out that we have the crystal, since Hilda picked up thoughts about a weapon. We can be seen with Conor. Imply we know secrets we shouldn't know. If one of those is the right thing, maybe they'll make themselves known."

"We are all dead." TK looked around the table slowly. No one argued with his assessment. "I can get the word to La Mafia. Vinnie can talk to investigators since they left her a card, and maybe Conor can get us to see some people at the Warrior Games."

"It's probably the best plan we have." Jory looked as worn out as Vinnie felt. "We need to be careful we don't stir things up and have even more people coming after us. Maybe we should save the details for tomorrow morning after we've rested."

"You guys look beat," Shaw said. "What's burning, by the way?"

Nell's head thunked down on the table. "Brownies."

CHAPTER TWENTY

Their first stop today was the library. When Vinnie had called Manny last night to say she couldn't make it in and give her notice, he'd told her she didn't need to cover the next two weeks because someone had come in looking for a job.

That was a lucky coincidence.

She had training scheduled with Will after the normal closing time of the library and they'd all decided Vinnie would go as scheduled. Shaw and Nell would go with her and try to convince Will to teach them all. None of her friends trusted him, but they couldn't deny he seemed to know more about Twisted power than they could find on their own.

TK had come with Vinnie to the library because the Federal agents had been here, and he might be able to distinguish their signatures in other places. Any information was good information. Then they would pick up Nell and go see Conor before going to Will's hotel.

They were only a few steps into the alley when TK's steps slowed and stopped. He stood with a hand over his mouth and nose, breathing shallowly. His Ferr power was either causing some odor to be overwhelming or a lot of power had been used nearby.

"TK?"

"I've never been to your library."

He hadn't, neither had Hilda. "Is it an anomaly?"

"No. Did this building catch on fire at some point?"

TK, like most Ferr, could sense energy. Everyone had a unique energy, which allowed him to tell when people had been somewhere or touched something recently. He could also sense when power had been used in a certain location.

"I almost burned it down, but it was just one book that caught on fire." Vinnie resisted the urge to use one leg to scratch the other. She'd taken the time last night to create a tattoo vine that went from her ankles to just below her knee. Each thorn, leaf, and flower controlled some nuance of the Wisp ability. It had taken her hours, but it was worth the trouble. For the first time since she'd had the power, she felt like she had some control.

His nostrils flared. "Maybe that's it."

That didn't seem likely. He'd never reacted that way to Wisp power, and the fire had been small. Vinnie sent her senses out, but there was no one. Unless someone was blocking her. She couldn't imagine anything bad happening here. The library was her place of comfort. Only Will had ever violated that. Even the FID coming there hadn't felt like a threat. TK would know if what he was sensing was an anomaly and he didn't seem worried. She was over-reacting.

"Let's get this over with," TK said.

Vinnie went down the steps first so she could open the door. Her muscles relaxed as she stepped into her sanctuary.

"Gah," TK doubled over, hands on his knees. "Why are you always dragging me to places like this?"

"Are you saying there's something wrong with my sanctuary?"

"It smells like burning hair," he said, and frowned. "Like the anomaly at Gina's house. I think I recognize the power signature, but I can't place it."

Kara had used Gina's house to hold Maddie before she killed her. She'd opened an anomaly there and the smell of it had made TK sick.

Vinnie shifted her vision so she could see power and looked around. It all looked normal to her sight. Her eyes caught on a slight haze in the corner, but when she tried to focus on it, it was gone.

"I can feel a lot of power here that shouldn't be," TK said. "And people who should never have been here. Feels like they were here yesterday."

"Who — "

A clatter of books from the back of the library interrupted what Vinnie was about to say. She called up the Wisp power and started for the sound.

"Vinnie!" TK protested, but he followed her.

Vinnie rounded the bookshelves and froze. Zandia stood in the back corner, her face a mask of fear and shock.

Vinnie dropped the power and held up her hand to TK so he wouldn't attack. "Zandia, what are you doing here?" And how much had she heard? Did she understand what it meant? Zandia already knew Vinnie was Twisted, but TK's secret was his own.

"You're late," Zandia said. "He said you'd be here to show me how to run the computer."

Which of the twenty questions going through her head to ask? "How did you get in?"

"Your friend gave me the key. I guess I should have waited outside on the first day. I was just so excited to be working again."

The first day. Working. Vinnie's brain engaged. Will had said he would hire someone to run the library for her. And she had said no. The reason she planned to meet him later was that she was coming here. In spite of everything that had happened since then, she wasn't remembering that wrong.

TK cleared his throat. "I'm going to take a walk. I need to get out of here. Text me when you're ready to go."

He didn't seem worried about what Zandia might have heard, but that could just be because the energy signatures in the library were distracting him.

Vinnie needed to figure out how to get Zandia out of here. She didn't want someone else running her library. It was ridiculous, with everything going on, but this was her sanctuary and it felt as if it had just been ripped away from her.

Zandia crouched down grunting as she picked up the books she'd knocked off the shelves. That's what had clattered.

"Let me do that," Vinnie said as she crouched down and picked up some of the books.

"It's my fault, I can get it." Zandia grabbed onto the side of the bookshelf to pull herself back up with the books in her hands. "You don't look happy. You know I won't tell anyone."

"I trust you." Vinnie stood with the rest of the books and handed one to Zandia to re-shelve. "I thought you were enjoying your retirement. That you never wanted to work again?"

Zandia took a second book from Vinnie. "This isn't a real job, though I'm grateful for the money. Alouette has been sick and the vet bills are terrible. It was a godsend to be offered money to spend more time in a place that I loved. I never loved a job in my life. I'm so glad you offered it to me first, but you didn't have to send Superman to convince me. I guess that he wasn't just looking for a book after all?" She winked. "I had a lot of admirers in my day, too."

Vinnie felt the trap boxing her in. There was no way she could tell Zandia she couldn't have the job, especially since Will was paying for it. Will must have known that when he set this up. He'd known Vinnie wouldn't be able to refuse and he would get his way.

"He's not an admirer," Vinnie said. "He's not even my friend."

"You're mad." Zandia put the last book on the shelf slowly. "I don't have to have the job. I'll survive. I always do."

Vinnie tried to keep her irritation at Will out of her voice. "You're not going to just survive. You're going to thrive and do a great job working here." It might be nice to have more help than Meg could provide. Maybe she'd get used to someone else in her space. That didn't mean she was letting Will off the hook for going behind her back, but that wasn't Zandia's fault. "Will and I only talked about hiring someone yesterday morning. We were supposed to talk more about it first, but I'm glad you're here."

The tension went out of Zandia's stance. "He said you'd show me the ropes, and then you were supposed to meet at two?"

They were supposed to meet at six. She was going with TK and Nell to talk to Conor at two.

"I'll show you how to check people out, and I will meet Will at the time we agreed to, which is six."

Zandia cackled. "Don't let him push you around."

Checking people out was all Meg did when she came in, and that would be enough for now. She'd have to show Zandia how to use her database. She'd built it herself from a free online program, and it was quirky. She didn't remember how to set up a new profile on the computer, so Zandia would have to use hers today. Had she deleted her search histories?

Vinnie was surprised how unworried she felt about that.

"You know how to use the card catalogue and that rebooting usually fixes it," she said as they walked to the front of the library. "I'll have to write out other troubleshooting for you, and I can show you the rest another day."

"You have somewhere else to be? The library was supposed to be open today. You weren't going to close it down again, were you? Ed would be devastated."

Ed had started coming to the library a few weeks ago. He mostly came on Sundays and Zandia had bumped into him that first day and suddenly she was coming every Sunday too. Vinnie had been going to shut the library down again today. The realization of how many ways she let people down when she did that made Vinnie uncomfortable. She scratched at the new tattoo on her leg with her foot again.

"You still get the admirers," she said.

"He's just a friend."

"Uh huh," Vinnie opened the database.

"Are you sure it's okay that I'm here?" Zandia continued.

"I'm glad you're here. I wish you had told me about Alouette. You helped with the fundraiser. We could have had a collection for her, too." Alouette was Zandia's cat. She loved that cat. Vinnie turned back to the computer explained a few more commands. There wasn't really much to it. "If someone new comes in, just add them through here. And that's it."

That was it. Her whole life explained in a few short minutes. In her head, the database was quirky and complicated, but it only took a few minutes to explain how to check people out.

"What about the books people return?" Zandia asked.

"Those are heavy. I can do that when I get in."

Zandia gave her a flat look. "You have a cart, I can manage."

"I'll show you the check-in spot, and you probably know where things go on the shelves as well as I do."

A few more minutes and Vinnie had showed Zandia everything that she needed to know to make it through the day and was back out on the street.

She pulled out her phone to text TK. In the message app was a text from Will saying that the library was taken care of and could she meet him at two instead? That was it. He'd done what she told him she didn't want and just assumed that would be fine. Vinnie pressed the message box to reply and tell him exactly where he could go.

But they needed him. Her friends were in trouble and they needed all the help they could get. Asking Will to teach them what he knew was their fastest path to being able to use their powers to the fullest extent. And she probably shouldn't piss him off. She should just tell him she had other plans and would meet him later.

Vinnie stared at the message box for a moment and then closed it without responding. He could wait. That seemed fair enough. She texted TK that she was done and shoved the phone back in her pocket.

The text was unnecessary. TK's car was in the same place and he was sitting in the front seat.

Vinnie slid into the passenger seat. "What happened in there?"

"Old books have a lot of energy signatures." He started the car.

"That's not why you freaked out."

"There were signatures there that shouldn't be. Sam, Gina, others I haven't seen in years, but it's like they were there yesterday. I called Gina, and she says she wasn't there.

Whatever it is, it has nothing to do with the people who attacked us."

"Uh-huh." Maybe that was true. Maybe it wasn't. Vinnie didn't like the thought of weirdness in her sanctuary. Maybe they'd run the information by the others later, see what they thought. Right now, they needed to pick up Nell and go see Conor.

CHAPTER TWENTY-ONE

Although Conor preferred to stay in his hotel near the Holt, they'd asked him to meet them in the one provided by the Warrior Games. They were more likely to be seen there, which would bait the trap.

The hotel was one of those multi-storied ones in the mid-price range, which made it one of the nicest ones in the city, but it was still bland in the way of chain hotels everywhere. Nell, TK, and Vinnie got into the elevator and Nell pushed the button for the fourth floor.

A phantom itch started on Vinnie's ankle again, and she lifted the opposite foot to scratch.

"Stop that," TK said. "You aren't a dog."

Nell gave her a sideways elevator look, the kind where you look at someone without looking at someone. "Is it bothering you? It's not a real tattoo."

"It itches," Vinnie said. "But only when I think about it."

"So stop thinking about it," TK said.

"Thank you. So helpful." She pulled her phone out of her pocket and scrolled to the text messages, glaring at the three from Will.

TK sighed loudly. He'd already told her to message Will or let it go.

"Sorry," Vinnie muttered. "I guess I'll just stop thinking about that, too." She shoved her phone back in her pocket just as the elevator door dinged.

Conor's room was near the end of the hall. The door was cracked open and someone moved around inside. Vinnie knocked on the open door.

Conor appeared in the living room in line of sight of the opening. "Come in."

The room looked almost like a tiny apartment, similar to hers but much nicer, with a couch and chair. It didn't have much of a kitchen though, just a small two burner stovetop, sink and mini fridge. Two doors led to what was probably the bathroom and the bedroom.

Two framed horror movie posters hung on the wall behind the television.

Conor followed her eyes. "No, they aren't part of the original apartment. I take them with me wherever I go. A little piece of my childhood."

TK walked over to one of them. His eyes roved around the outside of the frame and then continued to the second poster briefly before returning to Conor.

"There's a lot of clashing signatures in here."

"Signatures?" Conor asked.

"I didn't explain everything to him," Vinnie said. To Conor, she said, "TK is Ferr. We thought if he came along, he could see if he recognized any of the power signatures or mundane energies."

"Ferr. You're a local celebrity."

Did his voice seem a little tense? Conor's mom had been conned by a Ferr and there'd been a disagreement with one in the games after a player had died of a heart attack. Of the Twisted, Ferr were the ones Conor seemed most uncomfortable with but he didn't seem outwardly upset that Vinnie had brought TK. She would have told him beforehand, but she'd forgotten to ask TK if he minded Conor knowing, but since TK had mentioned the signatures himself, he apparently didn't mind.

TK grinned. "If you're careful, people only know what you want them to know."

Conor shook his head, but his lips were almost smiling. "Unless that person is a Mesmer, or a Dancer, or Stone apparently." At this his eyes went to Nell. Vinnie had told him that Nell was working on her ability to detect lies. "So, a lot of people have been here?"

TK nodded and sat in a chair. "It'll take me some time to sift. You guys can go ahead and do your thing."

"I don't think it will work," Nell said, almost under her breath as she sat on the couch. Vinnie followed, sitting beside her, and Conor took the other chair.

"Vinnie said you want to see if you can tell if someone you don't know is lying. How good are you at telling if people you do know are lying?"

"Not very." Nell looked sheepish. "I'm not even really sure that's what it is. It's just a feeling."

"She got it right around seven out of ten times when she tried it with our friend Jory this morning, but she knows him," Vinnie said. For some reason, Nell was better at detecting the difference in men than women, but they weren't sure why. "We aren't sure how well it will go with voices she's not familiar with, but we need all the help we can get. And we wanted to ask you some questions, anyway."

"And I'm happy to help, of course, since you're helping me." He looked at the floor and rubbed the back of his neck. "But this isn't your problem. You should stay as far away as you can."

TK scoffed. Vinnie glared, and he wiped the amusement off his face and closed his eyes again.

They'd already had this discussion. She wasn't sure what Conor wanted her to say to that.

Conor continued. "Your friend — the one who got me out — can get me papers and false ID. If this goes sideways, I can leave the country and start a life somewhere else."

Vinnie's heart gave one hard thump. "Is that what you want?"

"Of course not," he said. "But I don't want you or your friends to get hurt, either."

"Where's Hilda when you need her?" TK muttered.

"Aren't you supposed to be focusing?" Vinnie snapped.

Nell held up her hands. "I think what TK is saying is that Hilda would say Conor is being stupid. This isn't about him, therefore his leaving would do absolutely nothing to keep you safe, just like your moving away did nothing to keep us safe. We were still attacked."

"You were attacked?" Conor's body coiled, like he was about to launch himself at something.

"We were attacked by a Twisted crew last night, all six types. They may have been looking for an object that Kara had. Maybe you saw it on her? A pendant that was a large green crystal."

"She wore a lot of jewelry, different things at different times."

"The crystal allowed her to take power from Twisted."

His mouth parted and Vinnie realized she may have just dropped a bomb. Most people didn't know that objects could have power. She hadn't known until she met Kara and saw her use the pendant.

"Power can be taken from Twisted?"

Vinnie flinched internally. She should have seen that one coming. He was researching easier ways to identify Twisted because he thought it would make the world safer. What would be safer than no Twisted at all?

"If the power is taken completely, then the person dies. That's how Kara killed Maddie. That's how she killed Cerulean."

"What if only part of the power is taken, making the Twisted unable to use the ability significantly?"

Nell stiffened and pressed her lips together.

"Is that what you want?" Vinnie snapped. His mouth opened as if to reply, but she pressed on. "They would be depleted similar to when they use the ability for themselves. Mesmers would have headaches and brain fog all the time. Dancers would be dehydrated. Wisps would burn themselves up, because their power would keep trying to regenerate. Twisted ability is not something layered on top of people that can be removed. It's part of who they are."

"But it's possible. Please, let me finish." He clasped his hands together in front of him and stared at them. "There were times when I was playing — the other team would be doing really well. Their Twisted crew was doing amazing, just destroying us and then they would just fall apart. The coordination was there, but the power was not. We all just thought they didn't manage their energy well, but sometimes I felt almost like I had an extra boost of something -- more agility, more power, hits didn't hurt as much. I was just wondering. That's all."

"Only Wisps can give their power to others," Nell said. "And only other Twisted... I think. Vinnie?"

Could she give a boost to a non-Twisted? A memory surfaced. When they'd been fighting Kara, she said she taken power and people had died, but she'd used the power to help Conor. Everyone had a tiny spark of Twisted energy, so it seemed possible.

"I don't know," she said. "I've never heard of anything like that, but we've been learning a lot about what's possible the last few months. Kara had other kinds of power stored in the crystal, which had to come from somewhere so she could have taken it from crews. Can you get us in to talk to these other crews?" Vinnie asked. "Maybe we can find out if they noticed a loss of power or if they knew anything about what Kara was up to."

"They let me keep the apartment, but I'm not supposed to go near the teams or crews." He said. "I can talk to Lou. She might be able to get you in."

"Lou is not going to help us."

"She has issues, yes. She hates Twisted, yes, but she is also loyal and practical. She'll do it to help me, even if she doesn't like you."

He must not have spoken to her since he'd gotten out of jail if he thought she would help. "She's already told me she won't help. She thinks it's best to stay out of the way because she doesn't want to get caught up in the bigger scheme and she doesn't think there's any hope for you, so you're not worth the effort."

Conor had started shaking his head again, halfway through. "You're wrong. She's just scared she won't be able to make a difference. Her uncle and her dad went to jail when they were falsely accused of felony theft, so she's a little fatalistic, but it'll only take a nudge to get her to help."

"Let me guess," Nell said. "Her uncle and dad going to jail was the fault of Twisted."

"Not that I know of."

"People don't need reason to hate," TK said. "They do it to feel superior."

"She'll help," Conor repeated. "That's more important than how she feels about Twisted."

Vinnie didn't know how to argue against that. He was probably right, and she hadn't hesitated to go to Lou when she thought she might have answers. Why was she balking now? Because Conor had suggested it, and she didn't want to think that he agreed with Lou about Twisted, not on any level, but she already knew he did.

"Fine. Will you ask her for us?"

"Of course."

Vinnie turned to Nell, "Ready?"

"I don't know," she said. "I've heard him talk, but I'm still not that familiar with him, but let's try it." Nell addressed Conor. "Are *you* ready?"

"Sure." He sat up straight and pulled his shoulders back.

She leaned forward. "Can you state your name for me?"

"Conor Hahn."

"What color is your hair?"

"Blond."

"What month were you born?"

"April."

"Do you love your mother?"

"Yes."

"What's your favorite ice cream?"

"Pistachio."

"Ew," Vinnie said.

Nell grinned. "Okay, now I want you to lie to me."

"What's your name?"

"Alexander Graham Bell."

"What color is my hair?"

"Blond."

"Do you hate Twisted?"

He froze for a second before answering. "Yes."

Nell's forehead twitched into a frown and then smoothed. "For the next questions, tell the truth or lie. Your choice. What's your favorite cake?"

"Chocolate."

"Do you love Vinnie?"

Vinnie sat up straighter. "Nell!"

Conor kept his focus on Nell. "No. I barely know her."

This time, Nell's frown lasted a little longer. "Did you kill Maddie?"

"No."

"Are you sure?" Nell asked.

"No."

"What's your favorite sports team?"

"The Sloths."

That had to be a lie. He played for the Tigers.

"That's the truth?" Nell asked.

Conor grinned. "It is. It's my mom's favorite team and I am my mother's son."

"Are you aware of any reason someone would want to set you up for Maddie's death?"

"No," he said.

Nell watched him.

"Kara could be vindictive," Conor said. "If she were alive, she would try to get back at me for betraying her, but she's not alive so, no."

"I didn't think we were here to grill him," Vinnie said.

Nell shrugged. "I can't tell if he's lying. I thought something sounded different when he said he didn't know why someone set him up, but the second answer sounded true."

"Maybe you need longer answers?" Conor said. "You said you hear something different in people's voices. You get more voice with a longer answer."

"Maybe," Nell said. "Why do you think Kara is dead?"

He paused again, thinking about that. "I don't actually think she's dead."

"Truth?"

"Yeah, I don't know why."

"One of your hunches?" Vinnie asked. He'd told her he had hunches about people that were correct sometimes, which could be imagination, but his hunches also seemed to lead him to anomalies. "Did you feel the anomaly when you walked into the house?"

"I don't remember walking into the house."

"Lie?" Nell said.

"Vinnie lied to me," his voice was soft, and his eyes had gotten a faraway look. "I remember thinking that." His eyes snapped back to Nell. "I remember fragments, but I don't remember enough to know if I felt the anomaly. You're hearing a lie even when I think I'm telling the truth."

Nell's face scrunched. "So not when you're lying, but when you don't know what the truth is. That's not helpful."

"It helped you get more information, because you know to dig deeper," he said.

"I guess so," Nell said. She glanced at Vinnie like she wanted to say something, but she kept her lips sealed. The confidence she'd displayed when she was asking questions seemed to have evaporated.

"So what's next then?" Conor said. "I'll ask Lou to get you in to talk to more of the crews and…?"

She wanted to tell him everything, the whole plan, but she didn't really know him any better than Shaw knew Minka. "We're going to talk to our associate who got you out of prison, and apparently offered to get you out of the country."

"He didn't just offer. He was sure that was going to be my only solution."

Nice. Great. "I love it when people have faith in me."

"It does seem like a long shot," Nell said.

Vinnie opened her mouth to argue.

"You know she's right, Vinnie," TK said.

TK had told her she was too much of an optimist, but Vinnie didn't think that was accurate. She was very aware that all the people she cared about were in danger, very aware more of them could die, that she could die or lose everything. "I have to believe we can solve this or else what is the point of even trying? Back-up plans are fine, but making them the default is like giving up before you even start, which means you don't try as hard as you could."

"I believe in you, Vinnie," Conor said.

"Lie," Nell murmured so low, Vinnie was probably the only one who heard.

"If we have everything we need here, I'm ready." TK stood.

Conor stood, too. "Did you find anything?"

"Two federal agents, some from La Mafia and, I think, at least two of the people who attacked us, though I was distracted at the time."

"It is related, then," Nell said.

"Looks like it."

CHAPTER TWENTY-TWO

Vinnie recognized the silver SUV from across the parking lot, but she waited until they could see that it was Greg at the steering wheel before she pulled her phone out of her pocket and hit the dial button.

"Stalker," Nell said. "We'll wait in the car."

Will answered. "There you are."

"We had an agreement," Vinnie snapped. "I would quit my job, but I didn't want you to hire anyone for the library."

"No, we agreed I would get people to work for you so you would be fully rested for our training."

He couldn't be serious. And now she knew why someone had miraculously shown up to take her job at Walt's, too. Manipulative, meddling jerk. "That was not the agreement. I would not have agreed to that. I love working at the library."

"Hold on," he said.

Hold on. Hold on? He went against her wishes, sent his goon after her and he wanted her to hold on? She would not —

"I am sorry," Will said. "You are right. I am sorry I had other things on my mind and I remembered the conversation differently. I thought you had agreed, but I can see in the memory that I was wrong. I forgot."

What the hell? "I made it very clear. You didn't forget. You thought you could manipulate me."

"I know why you would think that," his voice was measured. "I have told you before that I am ill and sometimes have memory issues. I remember that we discussed several things in your apartment and I clearly remember you saying I wasn't an asshole, and you would take the money."

"I said no one working at the library and no therapist."

"It's none of my business if you get therapy or not. Why would I —? Never mind. I'll tell your employee her services aren't needed. Fair enough?"

He sounded genuinely confused. Vinnie wanted to stay angry, but the feeling dissolved.

"No, it's fine. She likes working there."

A shadow fell over her. Greg had gotten out of the SUV. The fire inside her kicked back in, sending heat into her limbs. Her body was telling her to run. Vinnie tamped down the feeling.

"Tell Greg to back off," she said.

Greg turned and headed back to the SUV.

"I'll come to the training now, but I'm not riding with him."

"He did what I asked him to. It wasn't his fault."

When she'd first met Will, Greg had kidnapped her off the street by stealing air from her lungs. This was Will's pattern, trying to control her and then begging forgiveness. How many times had it happened now? And still she continued to let him into her life. She was an idiot. Another thought occurred to her.

"How did he find me?" she asked.

There was a beat of silence.

"We should discuss this in person."

The last time Vinnie heard those words was when a boyfriend had thought she was going to break up with him. He'd been right. "Tell me."

"I've been in your mind. I can find you."

Vinnie dropped the phone down from her ear and pressed the off button. She was impressed with how steady her hands were as she put it back in her pocket. Her friends sat in TK's car, waiting for her so they could go ask Will to teach them to fight together more effectively. They had been the ones to defeat Kara, not Will, but they couldn't have done it if Vinnie hadn't already been holding the power from the anomaly.

No matter what she thought of him being in her head or of him being able to track her, they needed his help.

She walked to the driver's side of the SUV. Greg lowered the window a crack. "Tell Will I'm on my way."

TK HAD DROPPED them back at the house so they could take Hilda's car to the hotel and he could go talk to Gina, get the word out they had the crystal.

Nell had pulled the car into the parking lot slowly. Her eyes were on the upper floors of the hotel. The day was already getting dim and several lights were on upstairs.

"I thought no one else was staying in the hotel?"

"There are always other Twisted around when we train," Vinnie said. "I never see them, but they're usually on the upper floors."

"Bizarre," Nell whispered, her eyes not straying from the windows as she drove.

The steering wheel had drifted to the side and was headed straight for a dented powder blue car.

"Nell. Stop!"

Nell slammed on the brakes. The blue car was the only

other one in the lot. Greg must have had something else to do after all.

"Do you think that's his other employee's car?" Nell backed up and turned Hilda's car into the next space over. "You'd think he'd pay them enough to get something decent."

Shaw was inside the hotel already and there was a Zee with her. "I think it's Minka's car. Shaw brought Minka."

"Goodie, Which door?" Nell got out of the car and headed for the hotel.

Vinnie pointed at Will's fake room door. "You've seen her bad side, too?"

"I haven't met her," Nell said. "Just… I don't like the way Shaw acts and it seems like she's trying to control her and," she paused at the door to the hotel. "This is sensitive. We could be in real trouble. Why did she bring a stranger along? I'm not comfortable."

Nell must not know how much Shaw had already trusted Minka with. This seemed small in comparison. "We had to let other people in, eventually."

"But she barely knows her." Nell pulled open the door, and they stepped inside.

The interior of the hotel was silent, the air smelled stale.

"Should we have knocked?" Vinnie asked. The door hadn't been locked, but it seemed polite.

"Maybe." Nell glanced back at the hotel door. "Too late now." She headed for the secret door in the bathroom Vinnie had told her about and they stepped into the cavernous main room.

Some crates had appeared since the last time Vinnie had been here. They were stacked against one outer wall, giving the room a warehouse feel. Next to the crates, Will, Shaw, and Minka sat on the gym mats with their eyes closed.

"Are the two of you coming in?" Will, whose back had

been to them, turned his upper body enough that he could see them.

Shaw opened her eyes and bounced to her feet. "Hey you made it. We're learning to visualize."

How long had Shaw and Minka been here? They'd agreed on a time, so they shouldn't have arrived much before Vinnie and Nell.

"Are we all here, or do we need to wait for more?" Will asked.

Vinnie hadn't told him about the others coming along today, but he didn't seem bothered they were there.

"This is it," Vinnie said. "I didn't think you'd mind the extra firepower."

"It will not be useful today if the others want to come back another time," he said.

Minka finally opened her eyes. "No way. I wanna learn to close portals."

Right. She was supposed to be asking him to help them learn to fight together. After the misunderstanding about Zandia, she didn't think he'd argue.

"Vinnie will learn to close the anomalies," Will said.

"When do we get to the dragon?" Minka asked.

"Minka," Shaw muttered, a rosy spot blooming on her cheeks.

Will looked at Vinnie. "Transforming into a dragon is an incredibly inefficient use of the power."

Vinnie couldn't disagree, but she'd been scared and not thinking straight when she'd transformed herself. That didn't mean she appreciated his condescending tone.

Minka rolled her eyes. "You lack imagination. It's super cool and intimidating. If you could be a dragon, you could rule the world."

"Until a rocket took you out. Or an anti-aircraft gun, or

Mesmer controlling the wind and Stone with an enormous sword. Or a Zee weakening the muscles in your wings or — "

"I get it," Minka snapped. "You lack imagination. You don't have to keep telling me you do."

"Like I said. There's nothing for your friends here today, Vinnie." A note of irritation had slipped into his voice.

Vinnie had been a little angry with Shaw for bringing Minka, but watching her needle Will was worth the trouble.

Nell sunk down on the mats. "We were hoping in exchange for our help that you would give us some information and help us learn to fight together since the deal you made with Vinnie to help clear Conor is looking pretty useless."

Minka grinned at Nell. "I like you."

Will's composure slipped at last, but his glare was not for Minka or Nell though, he directed it at Vinnie. "Being well paid isn't enough? And you think it was easy to get you into that prison?"

The absurdity of the statement struck Vinnie, and she snorted in disbelief. "You're asking me to change the fabric of the universe— "

"Repair," he cut in.

"Fine, repair. Seems like a pretty big job. Bigger than helping me clear one person's name or a few thousand dollars. Besides, you know I didn't agree to help you for the money. I agreed because I need help, and this is the help I need now."

"Okay." He didn't look any happier than he did a moment before. "But you agreed to train with me daily, and this is the time we agreed on. We can work with your crew another time."

Shaw cleared her throat. "Sir. There may not be another time. They were attacked yesterday."

The irritation on his face seemed to freeze into something harder. "Who attacked you?"

A chill washed over Vinnie as the temperature in the room dropped several degrees.

"Oh shit," Minka murmured.

"I - I -," Her gut was screaming at her to run. That if she got the answer wrong, bad things would happen. Vinnie didn't want to get what she was about to say wrong. She really didn't want to get it wrong.

"We don't know," Nell said. "They lured us to a construction site, wore masks. They were well organized, a full crew of Twisted. I don't think they were as powerful as us, but they knew what they were doing. I think we only got away because they were holding back."

"I'll find you a bodyguard, if you won't come stay at the hotel, I'm putting security up at the apartment."

Vinnie opened her mouth to protest.

"She's staying with us..." Shaw's voice trailed off at the end. "If you give us information and train us, then she'll be safe."

His intense green eyes focused on Shaw and she shrunk. "I didn't say I wouldn't, I only said that, one, that wasn't the deal." He held up one finger. "And b, today is not the day for it."

Minka grinned. "I think you forgot how to count."

The corner of Will's mouth quirked. "Did I?"

"But isn't this an emergency?" Shaw said.

"If you want to learn to work together, you need your Mesmer. I can't teach you much that will be useful in such a short amount of time, but I can give you some study material."

Minka groaned and flopped on her back on the mat. "I thought I was done with school."

"Aren't you a Mesmer?" Nell said.

"I won't be there when you need to fight. It wouldn't be helpful."

"Vinnie can also be a Mesmer," Shaw said.

"I'm not teaching Vinnie how to control your power while you still hold it!"

Minka tensed on the mat, but didn't move. They all sat in stunned silence for a moment.

Then, in a small voice, Shaw said, "You don't have to yell about it."

Will rubbed his fingers into his eyes. "Now that that's settled, you are all free to go."

Minka sat back up. "No way. I'm not missing this."

Will looked at Vinnie, eyes asking her to do something. She wasn't in any mood to help him out, but the training would go better if he wasn't irritated.

Is there some reason they shouldn't stay? she thought at Will.

A frown line appeared between his brows, but other than that, he didn't seem to hear her. No help from there then.

"Nell?" Vinnie asked, turning to her friend.

"I'd like to stay too," Nell said.

Vinnie shrugged at Will.

"Fine. There are chairs there." He pointed to a side of the room. "You can bring them closer and watch but keep silent."

"What are we working on today, boss?" Vinnie asked, putting more than a hint of sarcasm in the last word. She knew she needed to stop needling him, but the word had slipped out. She took in a big, loud breath and pushed it out. "Sorry. Thank you for agreeing to help. So…more energetic connections?" They'd gotten nowhere trying to use Ferr power to help her remember, and Vinnie didn't relish wasting more time on something that wouldn't work.

"That didn't seem to be working the last time. You don't want to remember the connections. Let's start building from the ground up, and hopefully that will get you to let go of whatever is holding you back."

"Excuse me." Shaw raised her hand.

"What we'll do," Will said, ignoring her. "Is try to use sympathetic power to teach you to manipulate power in objects. You'll pull the power and then try to vibrate the same power in the natural world."

He reached into his pocket and pulled out a stone, putting it between them.

"Excuse me," Shaw said again.

"Pshtt," Minka said. "Let him struggle if he doesn't want help."

He turned to them. "I said you could stay if you were quiet. I know more about Magiera ability than you could learn in a lifetime."

Shaw sunk into herself again. Vinnie forced the fire down. She wanted nothing more than to stand up and tell Will where he could shove his training.

"My grandma used to say that even the king can learn something from a peasant," Nell said.

At Will's glare she shrugged. He turned back to Vinnie. "You'll pull stone, and then try to vibrate this stone."

"Did you just call Shaw a peasant?" Minka murmured.

"She just meant that you don't have to have all the knowledge to know something someone with more doesn't know, Minky." Shaw reached out and squeezed the other girl's hand and they both relaxed into their chairs.

"Are they going to be quiet?" Will said.

"I can focus with them talking." Vinnie closed her eyes and took a few deep breaths, in through the nose and out through the mouth. He wanted her to pull Stone and Nell was sitting right there, but there was also someone with Stone energy on the upper floors. His people were amazing at blocking. That was something she would love to learn. She could just pull from Nell, which would be easier but she wanted to leave Nell her power. Plus, getting better at pulling from someone who was blocking their power was useful.

Her eyes popped open. "They were blocking their power, the people who attacked us, like your crew blocks, but it was fuzzier, like…. Feeling the power through a haze."

"That's not an easy skill," he said. "You've made dangerous enemies."

Nell shifted in her seat.

"I also have dangerous allies." Vinnie closed her eyes again, focusing on her breath, letting the anxiety and fear soak into the background before pulling the power, slow and smooth.

The power sunk into her body and Vinnie opened her eyes. She let her vision soften enough that she could see power threads. There seemed to be no power in the rock, but she knew it was there. After she'd pulled the power from the anomaly she'd seen power in everything. Was this why she'd had a hard time turning off the sight after she'd become a dragon? She was vibrating in all the frequencies?

"Focus," Will murmured.

She drew in another deep breath, trying to relax her vision further. It felt as if nothing had happened, but there, at the edge of the rock, she saw some Stone energy.

"A live plant would have been easier," Nell said.

"Easy roads lead to weak results," Will responded. "Can you see the difference between the power inside you and the power of the rock?"

She couldn't see the power inside herself, she felt it. That must be what he meant. Her hand sought the rock, lifting it off the mat, feeling the cold smoothness as she brushed her thumb over the surface.

"You're supposed to— "

"Shhhhh." The rock in her hand didn't feel any different,

didn't feel powerful. It was just a rock with swirls of weak power. She'd been working on moving the Wisp power in her body, but she hadn't tried boosting her own. TK had asked, and she thought that it was giving her a natural boost. What if she tried to use it on purpose?

Wisp power was a push. It wanted to go out and escape the body. Vasum power was a pull. It wanted to draw in, to shore up. What did either of them feel like in her hand?

She'd partially contained the Wisp energy with her tattoos, but the wild force of it still made her gasp. When it hadn't been part of her, it had been easy to move it where she wanted it to go. Why shouldn't her own power be like that? The hand that held the rock became warm with the Wisp energy. Vinnie connected her own power to the Wisp energy, they clicked together as if they'd been waiting for this moment and orange and purple blended together in her hand. She'd never seen her own power. The orange and purple danced around the green stone energy but slid off.

Of course, sympathetic power. Like connects to like. She could pull power in people because they were close enough to her to be alike, but in something not human, it was too far away. That was what Will was telling her. She needed to use Stone power with a push, like the Wisp power. Vinnie pushed and green twined with the other two colors radiating off her palm. They latched onto the green of the rock and Vinnie pulled.

The rock shattered with a pop, and Vinnie flinched.

"Daaaamn," Minka said.

"I told you to vibrate it, not destroy the rock," Will snapped. "You need to vibrate more gently. You need control."

Vinnie blinked, trying to focus on his words, but she couldn't quite grasp what he was saying. Vibrate, why would she vibrate? Her head swam, and she swayed.

Nell was beside her, with her arm around her. "Why don't you have something grounding in here if you planned on having her work with Stone?"

"I took it," Vinnie said. Her tongue felt thick, numb. "I took the power. Vibrate. Why would power vibrate?"

"You took it?" Will lifted the rock fragments from her hand.

She hadn't realized she was still holding her hand up. Vinnie dropped her palm, wiped rock dust on her pants. She should have brought some tea in with her.

"When Kara was opening the portal, she was pulling power into her. You said you wanted me to open a portal."

The frown line between his eyebrows was a deep valley. "What did you do with the power?"

Her chest constricted and her throat closed. Vinnie gasped, trying to draw in air.

"Push the power back out," Will said.

She was still holding both the Stone from his associate and the Stone power from the rock. Vinnie let go of both, and her throat opened. She wheezed, doubling over to the side, coughing. Her throat felt like it was full of dust.

A bottle of water appeared in front of her face and she grabbed it, twisted the cap off and took a big drink, before looking up to see who had handed it to her. Greg. He must have finished whatever else he had to do.

Will picked up a piece of the rock and held it up to the light. "You can't hold on to power that comes from a non-human source. It will tear you up inside." He closed his hand around the shard. "I think that's enough for today. Next time, do what I ask."

He was already standing. Vinnie bit her lip to keep from arguing. He was right. She'd gotten caught up in the memory of pulling the power from the anomaly and forgotten what he'd asked her to do.

She took another swig of the water and pushed herself to her feet.

"Don't forget the book," Greg said.

"Thank you, Greg." Will went over to a nearby crate and picked up a book, and held it up. "You left this at the hotel."

Shaw sprang to her feet. "Cer's sketchbook!"

She was across the mat and snatching the sketchbook out of his hands before anyone else reacted.

"Did you help with the drawings?" he asked her.

She shrugged and held the book to her chest as she turned on her heel and headed for the warehouse door, Minka close on her heels.

CHAPTER TWENTY-THREE

As soon as they were out of the building, Minka snatched the sketchbook out of Shaw's hands. She strode across the parking lot to her car, slammed the book down on the hood and furiously flipped through the pages.

"What the hell?" Nell said, as they hurried after Minka.

Shaw reached the car first. Her steps slowed in time with Minka's page turning. Vinnie was a few steps behind. After one more slow flip, Minka stopped on the page of the boy on the ground with the dead eyes staring.

"Is it…?" Shaw said.

"It's not him," Minka said, her shoulders hunched.

"It's not who?" Nell asked.

Shaw touched Minka's shoulder. "That's good, right?"

Minka slammed the book shut and rounded on Shaw, pushing the book at her. "Either your friend sucked at drawing faces, or it isn't him."

"Why are you mad?" Shaw sounded forlorn.

"I'm not mad," Minka snapped. "Why does everyone always think I'm mad? Get a ride home with your friends. I have things to do."

With that, she walked to the driver's side of the car, got in, and pulled the door closed gently. She'd already started it and reversed out of the parking space before any of them moved.

"Shaw…" Vinnie started.

"She forgets I can read emotions," Shaw said. "Everyone always forgets that."

Shaw trudged to the back door of Hilda's car, pulled it open and flopped onto her back in the back seat.

Nell's shoulders were hunched as she got in the driver's seat. When they were all in the car, she addressed Vinnie, "When do you want to get your things from the apartment?"

It was Sunday, which meant she had to be at the library tomorrow. Wait, no, she wasn't sure if she needed to be at the library. She didn't know when Zandia was working. Everything was happening too fast.

"I don't have much. We could do it tonight."

From the backseat, Shaw's voice came, dull and monotone. "You should rest. You'll need your strength tomorrow."

"I only have three boxes, not counting my clothes. It would take less than 30 minutes."

"Fine," Shaw said, resigned. "Don't listen. No one ever does."

"Let's just grab your clothes on the way home," Nell said. "And the pendant."

Vinnie grabbed her cup of tea from the console and took a long drink. Nell was trying to soothe Shaw, not argue.

Vinnie had handed the pendant to Shaw after pulling it out of its hiding place. She and Nell carried her clothes and put them in the trunk of the car. Grabbing the boxes and her few dishes and food would have only taken a few minutes more, but she didn't argue.

Shaw had barely spoken and Vinnie felt helpless, not knowing how to help.

Back at the house, Jory and TK's vehicles were in the drive and she could feel Hilda in the basement.

Inside, TK was sitting on the couch, a black planner open on the table as he talked on the phone. He nodded to them as they came in.

Shaw went straight for the stairs.

"Can we move Cer's bed to Shaw's room?" Vinnie asked. "Do you think she'll mind?" No one had moved into Cer's room after she left. Nell and Hilda still shared a room, and Jory had his own. She'd slept in Cer's bed in his room last night.

"You should ask her that," Nell said. "I'll go help Jory in the kitchen."

Vinnie should ask Shaw that, but she hated the helpless feeling of not knowing how to help, and their last conversation at the library was fresh in her mind. She had failed Cerulean when she thought she was helping, and Shaw was not as easy going as she had been. Try to help the Dancer deal with her emotions. That's what Nell was really saying, but she didn't feel capable.

Her feet carried her up the stairs, anyway.

Shaw had left the bedroom door partially open. That seemed like a good sign. A few weeks ago, Vinnie would have just walked in because this was her room too, but now she knocked softly on the door and peered in at Shaw, sitting on her bed with the sketchbook propped in her lap.

"You look like a puppy that's expecting to get kicked," Shaw said. "Am I such a terror now?"

"No." Vinnie stepped into the doorway, just inside the threshold of the room.

"I wish people would stop bleeding their pain all over me." Shaw turned her attention back to the sketchbook.

Vinnie took a few more steps into the room. Screw it. If Shaw was going to get mad, she was going to get mad. She walked in and sat at the foot of the bed. "I thought you had learned to block emotion."

"Some, but it's like if your neighbors were playing loud music and you stuff your ears full of cotton. It only muffles the sound, and you can't hear your baby crying."

Vinnie had done that for years. She blocked off her own ability to sense other people's powers because she couldn't control when she borrowed it. Now that she no longer blocked it out, it was like an extra sense, extra information that was available to her in any situation. All she had to do was pay attention.

"I'm sorry, I don't know what I can do to help."

"Maybe try getting control of the shit inside your head."

The barb stung and was a surprise. Shaw never would have said something like that to her a few weeks ago. "It sounds like the issue is yours, not mine. My emotions are none of your business." Vinnie regretted the words as soon as they were out. "I'm sorry, I'm tired too. I'm tired of feeling responsible for everyone."

Shaw's jaw jutted forward, and she glared at Vinnie through watery eyes. "You don't need to save me."

"Everyone is worried about you. You're never around, you didn't tell anyone about getting fired from your job."

"Everyone worries because they think I can't take care of myself, but I can. I'm really not some stupid child."

"You aren't a child," Vinnie agreed, even though it was difficult not to think of Shaw as a child. "But not telling the people you live with that you lost your job isn't very responsible, and it's normal for people to be worried when you cut them off and hang out with someone who..." She caught herself. Telling Shaw that she thought her girlfriend was controlling and possibly abusive might push her farther away.

"She's not always like that." Shaw set the sketchbook face down on the bed. "She's worried about her brother. He's in a dangerous situation and she's afraid he's going to die."

Vinnie had two questions, but asking Shaw why she thought letting someone treat you badly because they were having a hard time was okay would probably push her away, so she asked the other question. "What does that have to do with the sketchbook?"

"Minka thinks I can see the future." Shaw turned the sketchbook over on the bed and put it in front of Vinnie. It was turned to the page of the dragon bursting out of the house. "I get strong feelings about things. I told her about the sketchbook and how you'd gone through the roof of Nell's house just like the drawing."

"Cer drew those." Even though Vinnie had the same thoughts about the drawings being prescient, she didn't want to believe they were.

"I told him what to draw," Shaw said. "We... don't be mad... it's not like it was heroine or something... we took some mushrooms... and I think he boosted my power, and I got all these weird visions."

She put her finger on the dragon on the page. "I think the dragon actually had a human face, but Cer didn't draw it that way." She turned the page. "She was sure the boy on the ground would be her brother. Something about her made me think of the drawing and I told her that and she got all freaked out."

"But she was angry that it wasn't her brother dead."

"If you know what's going to happen, you have a chance to prevent it." Shaw frowned at the page. "If you only know there is danger, then how can you prepare or stop it? I know you only see this angry girl, but you've only met her twice. Both times she was standing up for me. She believes in me and she doesn't shut me down or doubt me when I say something. She stands up for me but she also expects me to stand up for myself. Even though I'm not brave."

Minka had stood up for Shaw when Will had told her to be quiet and none of the rest of them had, but she'd also lied and said she wasn't angry, knowing Shaw could tell that wasn't true.

"What were you going to say? At the warehouse?"

"Spending hours and hours trying to form connections and relearn something you already know is dumb. It would be way faster to clear out the emotional block that keeps you from remembering."

"I'm not sure I want to remember." Vinnie realized it was true. Will was trying to teach her to do something she wasn't sure she wanted to do. The power was scary as hell and had felt out of control.

Shaw rolled her eyes. "That's why it's a block, Vinnie."

"I'm glad you didn't say it in front of Will."

"I would love to have that kind of power." Shaw picked up the sketchbook again, turning it back around to face her. "If I had that kind of power, then I would matter like Cassius mattered. He said his world was dark and terrible, but at least he could do something about it. I can't do anything at all."

Cassius was the man Shaw had met who could become a dragon. He'd come through an anomaly from a different universe and Shaw had helped him get back to his own world. But at the library a few days ago, Shaw seemed to be saying she didn't want to be a hero. Maybe she only wanted to be a hero because people told her she had to be. "What would you do if you had that power? If you could be a dragon?"

"Maybe I'd fly into the camps where they keep Twisted and tear them all down and we could fly away to some island where they'd never find us. Or go to South America where they hate Twisted less."

"Magiera," Vinnie said. "Maybe less hate starts with better language."

"Maybe, but what if I use that in front of people accidentally and I get locked up?"

The fear was there, always there, that they would say the wrong thing, do the wrong thing and someone would report them as potentially Twisted and they'd test them. The only thing that kept people from being tested more was the expense and difficulty of the test. How would things change if it were easy? Maybe people would fight back if they knew they couldn't hide.

"The Wisp at the prison knew I was a Wisp," Vinnie mused. "He looked in my eyes and he knew."

"Minka can tell if someone has power when she is around them. I'm not sure what you're saying, though? What does that have to do with using the word Magiera?"

What was she saying? It was a thought that had been nibbling at the edge of her mind since she'd learned that power could be not just in people but in objects. There had to be people who knew, powerful people, and there had to be people who knew Wisps could find Wisps. People who knew Vasum existed.

"The things we've learned over the past few weeks... about the history and different abilities. People have known about us for a hundred years. We've gone from the beginnings of cars, and iffy telephone systems to this." Vinnie pulled her phone out of her pocket. "We've made incredible advancements in technology during that time. Governments have had access to both Magiera and knowledge all that time. How could they not know what we are capable of? That they wouldn't know they don't need expensive equipment to test people to see if they have power — they just need a Wisp, a Vasum or a Zee. They have to know this by now, even if it's not public knowledge. Why would they hide how easy it is to find us?"

"Maybe we're really good at hiding things from them?" Shaw said.

"Some Magiera are found when they are very young. They wouldn't know to hide it."

She thought about Kiernan again, the way he hid that he could use markings on his skin to control his power. Maybe Shaw was right, that this wasn't widely known knowledge, but someone had to know.

"Weird," Shaw said.

They each sat, lost in their own thoughts. At least Shaw seemed less upset, but there was something else Vinnie wanted to know. Something that would remind Shaw why she was upset, but she said she didn't want them trying to protect her.

"Can you really see the future?" Vinnie asked.

"Dunno. Maybe. Cassius said that some Dancers could recognize shifting patterns, but it's not really telling the future. It's just feelings and hunches. When I helped Cassius get home he needed an anomaly, and I had built a prediction program and it didn't work, but I could look at the dots and get a feeling about which ones were right. After he was gone, I saw Harry pop up and I felt like I had to come here."

Shaw hadn't mentioned this before. She'd shown up on the doorstep, same as Vinnie had, and they hadn't asked too many questions. They needed a Dancer to keep Harry under control and there she was.

"I never mentioned it because I was embarrassed." Shaw said. "It sounds silly"

But it didn't sound silly. They needed her, and she came. "You thought you were meant to be here?"

"Something like that," Shaw said.

"And now?"

Shaw toyed with the edge of the sketchbook page. "I pushed Cer to be involved, to be a hero, and in the end he was, wasn't he? But if that's what I was meant to do, I don't know if I want it and now it doesn't feel right. That's the thing about reading patterns, I get confused if it's a pattern or if it's just what I want making me feel like it's a pattern."

That sounded similar to what people always accused Vinnie of. She was too sure. Too rosy, too optimistic, thinking what she wanted to happen was going to happen. "Maybe it doesn't matter either way? I want to give up some days. I don't know if we can figure out what's going on but I know we can affect the world. If I don't believe I can make what I want happen, happen, why would I even try?"

Shaw turned the page to where the boy lay on the ground, bleeding. "I don't want this to happen, and that makes it seem even more likely."

"I think it's easier to pay attention to what we fear, but if what you sense are shifting patterns, working toward something positive would change the pattern. Either way, I don't think it hurts to work for the best."

Shaw was shaking her head.

"If you don't believe in your hunches," Vinnie continued. "Why did you insist I come home to rest?"

"That's just logic, Vinnie. We have a lot to do and you gave Conor a task today. He's highly motivated to make it happen. Your phone will ring any minute and he'll tell you Lou got you in to see the crews. Plus you have to go check the library and go by work to get your last pay."

"Lou won't help me get in to see the crews. She hates me."

Vinnie's phone rang in her pocket. She pulled it out and stared at Conor's name on the screen. "That's eerie."

Shaw rolled her eyes and flopped back on the bed, and Vinnie answered the phone.

CHAPTER TWENTY-FOUR

Manny beamed at Vinnie from behind the counter as soon as she walked in. Jory and Hilda had taken off work so they could meet with one of the Warrior Games crews this afternoon. They'd already been by the library where Zandia was settling nicely. Now she just needed to pick up her pay, and they'd go straight to the hotel where the crews were staying.

"There she is! Let me get your things." Manny bent over and rummaged around under the counter.

Things?

He popped back up holding an envelope and something small and metallic.

"What's this?" Vinnie took the envelope of cash and held out her hand.

Manny placed the object in her hand. Everything around her receded as she looked at what he'd given her.

"It's your earring, right?" Manny said. "It's been inside the cash register for a week. I guess you kept forgetting it."

"Yes, it's mine," she said numbly and turned. Matt Jones had given this to her, claiming he'd found it in the parking lot. She'd had so much on her mind she hadn't even bothered to glance at it.

"It was nice having you here, reapply anytime."

"Thanks, Manny," she mumbled as she stepped out into the sun with the tiny crystal pressing into her palm.

What's wrong? Hilda and Jory sat in the van, waiting for her.

It will be easier if I show you. Vinnie climbed into the back of the van, scooted to the middle seat, and held out her hand with the earring.

"Where did that come from?" Jory's voice was harsh.

The earring Matt Jones had given her was the perfect miniature replica of Kara's pendant.

"That's what it looked like?" Hilda said.

"A man came in when I was working and handed it to me saying he found it in the parking lot."

Jory snorted. "Someone dropped a small version of Kara's pendant in the parking lot outside your place of work. Subtle."

Vinnie was already shaking her head. "It's possible he just found it, but I don't think so. I ran into the same guy again at the used bookstore. I went to get some children's books for the library, and he convinced me to help him buy a restricted book. As we were leaving, he asked if I'd found the owner of the earring."

"What book?" Hilda asked.

A clue had been sitting right there this whole time, but what did it mean? Matt Jones had given her the earring the same night she was attacked. Would it have played out differently if she'd taken the earring with her? Or if she'd known what it meant the day he talked to her at the bookstore?

"The book was The Destiny Papers by Cole Hanna."

Jory hissed. "The book was a test to see if you would break the law."

"Why would he do that?" Vinnie's eyes were drawn back to the pendant.

"Hanna's Soldiers want to destroy the government," Hilda said. "Maybe they are trying to recruit you. Or us. Or gauge your reaction to the pendant."

"Sounds like we were on the right track." Jory tapped his fingers on the steering wheel. "But now we have more information."

Vinnie stared at the pendant as if it would give her a better reason for being in her hand. Matt Jones had given himself away, and then showed up again. It just made no sense to her, even though, objectively, Hilda and Jory's logic made sense.

"I can try doing a city-wide search like I did for Maddie," Vinnie said. "Or boost TK since we have this which will have Matt Jones's power signature."

Hilda looked pointedly at Vinnie's bony wrist. Searching the city for Maddie had taken a lot of power and her body might not be ready to take that on. With the Wisp power more controlled she should be able to get back up to a more normal weight but it could take some time.

"Let's come back to that later," Jory said. "Does the earring have power like Kara's crystal did before it was destroyed?"

Vinnie shifted her vision. Small white wisps of something curled off of the earring like steam, but it didn't look like much. "There's something, but not much. We should get rid of it, we don't know what it does."

Hilda lifted the earring from Vinnie's hand. "You don't throw away power just because you don't understand it." She held it up and spun it in the light of the window. The trails of power coming off of it splintered into rainbows before coalescing white again.

"I think it might just be the power in sunlight I'm seeing," Vinnie said. "Whatever it is it's weak."

Jory held out his hand. "We need to get to our appointment. I can keep it safe until we find a more permanent solution."

Hilda huffed, but she gave him the earring. He shoved it in his front pocket and started the Van.

Parking was hard to find in this section of the city, and Jory had to park several blocks away from the building the crews were in. The building itself looked like an old hotel with three steps leading to a small landing and an ornate front door.

Lou leaned against the building beside the steps.

"I didn't realize Ms. Sunshine would be here in person," Hilda muttered.

"Maybe she's just here to introduce us."

Lou pushed herself upright as they approached. "Welcome to the house of horrors. This way, if you please."

She bowed deep, waving with her arms to indicate the door before going up the steps and punching a code on the keypad. The door clicked and Lou pulled it open.

Inside, there was a small open foyer with a few threadbare chairs. A man sat at a desk in his guard uniform looking bored. His eyes became more alert as they approached, though his posture didn't change.

"Hey, Lou, these your friends?"

Behind the man, to the right was an entrance to a hallway. Stretched across the opening was a gate with metal bars and a lock.

"Indeed, they are." Lou said, answering the guard's question. "You ready for us?"

How do we get rid of her? Vinnie thought at Hilda.

Not a clue.

The guard got up to unlock the gate. "The kid's a little keyed up today so Sabra might be on edge."

"Noted," Lou said as they walked through the door. She led them down the hall to the back of the building. The door opened to a dining area with cheap metal tables and plastic chairs. Some tables had been moved aside and six chairs were arranged in a semi-circle in the middle of the room. The people in the chairs looked at them with hard, flat eyes.

A dark skinned woman with short hair that stood around her head in a halo, slouched further in her chair. "The bitch queen cometh and she's brought friends. Hoo-ray."

Lou held up a remote looking thing with a button.

"You know you don't scare me, Louann, do it."

"Allow me." Jory had the remote for the shock collar out of Lou's hand before she could react. He grasped the remote with both hands and pulled, breaking it apart.

Lou just shook her head at him, but the woman in the chair chuckled.

"Did you bring me a wannabe hero? I wondered why we were getting an extra meeting. These aren't new teammates, are they?"

Lou sat at a chair behind a table. "No," she said. "They're investigating the murders that have been happening around the games for years."

"I thought Conor did that," said a wide-eyed girl with a squeaky high voice. Her skin was pale and pasty, looking almost bruised in spots. The young man beside her pinched her arm.

"Sit," Lou said to Vinnie.

The only other chairs in the room were the ones behind the table where Lou was sitting. They would be behind a barricade of the table while the crew was out in the open, exposed.

Vinnie grabbed a chair from behind the table and put it in

front. Hilda and Jory did the same, putting their backs to Lou and leaving her alone behind the table.

What have we got? Hilda asked.

The leader is the Mesmer. Two men to her right, Ferr and Zee. Man on the left is Stone. The squeaky girl must be the Wisp because the woman at the far end is a Dancer.

"I'm Vinnie," she said. "We don't believe that Conor killed anyone, do you?" Here she looked the Wisp girl directly in the eyes and saw the answering flames. The girl's eyes widened, and she sat up in her chair, wriggling.

That one is going to give us away. Sabra is not responding to mental inquiries. Thoughts from the others are muddled and fuzzy. She might be holding a mental shield over them.

"It's always the ones you least expect who stab you in the back," the Stone man rumbled.

"We think it was a set-up," Vinnie said. "Someone who was after something that belonged to the actual killer."

"We don't know anything about murders," Sabra said. "You want to talk to yellow crew for that."

"Yellow crew is in prison, gone," Lou said. "Maybe you want to join them? We all know they were not the only ones involved."

Sabra crossed her arms and leaned back, pressing her lips together. They wouldn't be able to convince them to help as long as Lou was here, and they thought they were her friends.

Hilda turned in her seat. "And how do we know that, Queen Bitch?"

Lou's eyes darkened. "These six were also close to Kara. That's why I brought you to them, Servant Bitch."

Images of Lou choking on the floor popped into Vinnie's head. *Hilda, she's not worth it.*

Hilda turned back around to face the crews.

"Kara." The Ferr man spat the name, his face twisting in disgust.

"Of course, Kara," Sabra said. "I told you she was trouble."

"She was nice to me. She gave me jellybeans," the Wisp girl said.

"That's what the worst ones do," Sabra said. "They give you treats so you'll think they're your friend, then they steal your soul."

"Like she did to Amanda," the girl said.

"No more talking," Sabra said. "They can't punish us."

"Not today," the Dancer said.

Lou stood, chair scraping back. She looked Vinnie in the eye and pointed to a camera in the corner, then tapped the top of the table. "You won't be punished, whether you talk or don't talk. This is not my fight."

She picked up the broken remote for the shock collars as she left.

That was easier than expected, Vinnie thought.

There's a microphone under the table. Hilda said. She scooted her chair forward

Vinnie felt a wall of air go up. It would block whatever they said while they were in it. She and Jory moved their chairs forward so they would be inside the wall.

"Can you get the camera, Vinnie?" she asked out loud.

"I've never tried to manipulate electricity."

"I think they'd notice the camera feed going out," Jory said.

"You're all Twisted," the stone man rumbled. "What are you doing with the likes of Lou? She obviously doesn't know."

"Means to an end," Hilda said.

There was a pop in the corner where the camera was—used to be.

"I got it," the Wisp girl said.

"Rachel," The Ferr said. "Don't do that. It's not worth it."

Rachel lifted one shoulder. "They won't risk hurting me this close to the championship games, and then they'll forget. Or George will protect me. Or we can just say it was her." She pointed at Vinnie.

Sabra's dark eyes bored into Vinnie, and she felt the whisper of something in her mind, then the Wisp power surged, heating her chest, face and body.

Vinnie stood from the chair before she could stop herself. She slammed up her blocks and the fire cooled.

"Well, looks like we have a wild, wild Wisp." Sabra said.

What happened?

She controlled the Wisp power in me.

I would say not possible, but... let down the blocks.

NO.

Vinnie...

"No," Vinnie said.

"If you guys can stop screwing around?" Jory said. "Look, we need to trust each other here and we don't have all day. Yes, we are Twisted. Two days ago we were targeted by a sophisticated wild crew. They might have been looking for a pendant that belonged to Kara McKnight, which we now have in our possession. Our lives and the lives of others are in danger. If you have knowledge that can help us stop these people, we would be grateful."

The Ferr man scoffed. "Grateful. What do we care about your gratefulness? As far as I can see, our lives are the ones in the greatest danger here."

"Why?" Hilda asked. "You're valuable. They wouldn't hurt you. We saw the stink they raised just about the arrest of the others, and they were deemed dangerous. What would put you at risk?"

Sabra held up a hand to the Ferr to stop him speaking and kept her own lips shut.

Jory pulled the earring out of his pocket. "Kara used something like this to take a friend's power and kill him."

"Not possible," Sabra said. "The pendant can only channel power voluntarily given with the help of a Mesmer."

"Like Vinnie just voluntarily let you use hers?" Hilda asked.

Sabra bared her teeth in a caricature of a smile. "She did."

"I did not," Vinnie said.

"It's not my fault you are an untrained babe. I would not have been able to do that with any of my crew," Sabra said. "But unless there was a Mesmer present, Kara didn't use her pendant to kill your friend."

"She had Mesmer power," Vinnie said.

Sabra shook her head.

"How did she do it, then?" Hilda asked.

"What will you give us for that information?" the Ferr asked.

"Mikael, you know what she did," the Dancer said. "We should help them."

"And you know what we are risking," Mikael snapped.

"All the grown-ups are fighting," Rachel sang. "All the children are dying."

The Dancer woman ran her fingers around her wrist, circling it, like a bracelet. Then she grimaced and clutched at her head. "Damn, Sabra, stop."

"Behave, then," Sabra growled at the woman before addressing Hilda, "We are not weak, like yellow crew," Sabra said. "She manipulated Amanda, but not me. People have come, promising us things if we would tell them what we know, but you don't even offer us anything. Just give us sob stories about things we, and you, have no power to change. If you want us to be cruel and give you answers that will kill you, then you have to buy our cruelty."

"You would withhold information that could save lives?" Hilda asked.

"Whose life?" Sabra asked. "I just told you the information will get you killed. Seems like you're dead whether I talk or not."

"I can get you into the Lost City," Jory said.

Heads whipped around, eyes boring into Jory. The Stone man laughed.

The what? Vinnie asked Hilda.

A city in Canada run entirely by Twisted. Supposedly, the government leaves them alone. Impossible to get into.

"If you could get us into the Lost City, " Mikael said. "Why aren't you there where you're safe instead of here being hunted?"

Jory leaned back, throwing one arm over the back of the chair. "We fulfill our obligations and our obligations here are not done."

The Stone man scoffed.

Sabra held up a hand before he could say anything. "I'm listening. How are you going to get us there?"

"We have powerful friends. Money, resources, Twisted. We'll get you out and I'll take you there myself."

He can't make that promise, can he? Vinnie asked Hilda.

Sabra leaned forward. "If you could really do that, I recommend you forget your obligations and get out of here right now. Don't blink, just stand up and take your friends and run."

Jory leaned forward, matching her posture. "And why would I need to do that?"

"Sabra..." Mikael said.

She looked up at the camera as if to make sure it was out. "Kara is not dead. I don't care what the news said, until I see her dead body and her eyes staring into hell. She's still alive."

Boost me, Hilda said.

Vinnie gathered Wisp power and pushed it at Hilda.

She said she would kill us all if we told anyone. Sabra's mental voice was distorted as if coming through water. *If she doesn't get you, whoever she betrayed to get those power filled objects is bigger and nastier than any of you and if she doesn't get you, they will. If you don't get us out of here like you said, we're probably dead too just for talking to you. Whatever power you think you have, it's not enough.*

"I pushed her through the anomaly myself," Vinnie said. "Closed it around her, took her crystal."

"You're the dragon," Rachel said. "I knew it had to be a Wisp." She nudged the Dancer. "I told you it was a Wisp."

"They'll want the bracelet more than they want the crystal," the Dancer said. She shoved Sabra. "If you try to stop me from talking again, I'll drown you."

"What bracelet?" Jory asked.

"She was wearing a silver bracelet." Vinnie could picture it, flashing on Kara's wrist. She tried to remember if she had seen Kara use it, but some of what had happened was a blur. "What did it do?"

"It pulled power from people," the Dancer said. "That's probably what was killing people. I heard her threaten someone once. She said once she got the power transfer going, she couldn't stop it."

Hilda shot up out of her chair. "Is there a back way out?"

From the front of the hotel came the sound of doors and fast moving feet.

Almost as one, the Warrior Games crew slid off their chairs and landed on their knees on the floor with their hands on top of their heads.

"I told you not to blink," Sabra said, just as the door burst open and people in black combat gear flowed through.

I'll stop the bullets — can you melt the bars? Hilda said.

There were two windows on the back side of the cafeteria, both covered with metal bars. There was no way they'd make it out.

Vinnie started to move her shaky hands up to the top of her head.

For fucks sake, Hilda snapped. *At least stop acting guilty.*

As Vinnie's hands came back down one of the people in combat gear shouted, "Jordan Lewis, put your hands on your head and get on your knees."

CHAPTER TWENTY-FIVE

I *can stop the bullets, Vinnie.* Hilda insisted. *Jory can take out the guard. Ready?*

Hilda had lost her mind. There were at least eight people with guns aimed at them. There were probably people outside too.

We'll deal with that when we get out there.

Hilda —

We are not letting them take him. He'll be executed.

"It'll be okay," Jory murmured. "Don't try to fight them." He dropped to his knees and put his hands on top of his head.

Lou pushed through the door. "This is ridiculous. These are my friends. What is it you think he's done?"

Agent Turner from the FID came through the door behind her. He stepped around the men with guns. His eyes went to Vinnie before dropping to Jory on his knees. "Murdered three people, and escaped from a maximum security Twisted prison by faking his own death. He's Zee, ma'am, and a wanted felon."

Lou pulled up short and the look of betrayal she shot

Vinnie might have been comical at any other time. She wiped the look off her face and stood straighter. "You can't arrest him here. He's my guest."

The look of confusion Agent Turner gave her probably looked the same as Vinnie's. "This isn't some medieval castle. This is the United States of America. We can arrest people wherever we find them."

One of the men in combat gear came forward and kneeled to pull Jory's arms behind his back and cuff him. Then he helped him stand up.

Drop the power Vinnie. He doesn't want to fight.

I'm not — But she was. Her body vibrated with power. She'd pulled from all the crew except the Wisp. Vinnie released the power she hadn't realized she'd been holding.

The man who'd cuffed Jory walked him toward the door. When they reached the door, he looked back, eyes meeting Hilda's.

"Wait." Hilda said. "Let me say goodbye." She rushed forward.

"Ma'am— " Agent Turner started and the Dancer woman shrieked an earsplitting shriek.

Hilda reached Jory, wrapping her hands around his waist as he leaned forward, resting his head on her forehead for a moment. Then she pulled back, and they led Jory out.

When the last federal agent went through the door, the guard appeared, his gun drawn and held down at his side.

"You all need to leave," he said. "You too, Lou."

Lou shook her head in disgust and they left the way they'd come in.

When they reached the front steps, Lou turned to Vinnie. "I should have known you'd consort with murderers," she spat. "Are you Twisted too?"

Vinnie knew she should say no. If she admitted what she was, Lou could turn her in.

"You defend a society that protects murderers all the time," she said. "The men Jory killed sought his brother out and murdered him. What would you do if people murdered someone you loved, and everyone knew but wouldn't do anything?"

"She'd cower in the corner just like she did when Conor was arrested." There was no heat in Hilda's voice, just a dull fatigue. "Let's get out of here Vinnie."

Vinnie trudged down the steps after Hilda. When they reached the van, she glanced back at Lou, expecting to see anger at Hilda's comment, but Lou was watching as they loaded Jory in the police truck, arms crossed tightly against her rib cage.

Hilda had gone straight to the passenger side of Jory's van and sat, eyes unfocused. When Vinnie pulled the driver's side door closed, the silence was absolute. It wasn't the natural silence of an interior space. Hilda had blocked the sound from outside. Vinnie waited a few moments to see if Hilda would tell her whatever she'd blocked off sound to say but she didn't even twitch.

Vinnie started the van and drove. Thoughts tumbled in her brain. She'd seen the security of the prison, maybe she could figure out how to break Jory out? This wasn't the same as the situation with Conor, where they had a hope of clearing his name. Jory was Twisted and guilty of what they accused him of doing. He'd escaped from a maximum security prison designed to hold people like him. They wouldn't take the chance again. Jory would be executed.

Maybe she could cut off the electricity. She could practice with Hilda and they could use the Mesmer power to be somewhat invisible. Nell could knock the doors down, or TK could... could he use the Ferr power the way Kara had?

Vinnie shivered as she parked the van behind Hilda's car

in their driveway. TK was here, his car sat beside Hilda's. He was in the living room.

Hilda still sat frozen in her seat.

"I'll become a dragon again," Vinnie said. "I'll rip the roof off the prison and carry him off."

Hilda slid out of her seat and closed the van door behind her before going inside.

Vinnie watched her go, waiting until she was in the house before she got out of the van and followed. By the time she got inside, Hilda was nowhere to be seen, but Vinnie could feel her in the basement. She walked the few steps to the living room entrance. TK stood in front of the coffee table, obviously just having gotten up.

"What happened?" he asked.

Vinnie opened her mouth, but the words didn't come out. She shut it, swallowed, and tried again. "They arrested Jory. For killing the guys who killed his brother and escaping prison."

TK collapsed back onto the couch. "Lou?"

"I don't think so. She made a half-hearted attempt to stop it. Seemed as surprised as we were. And I'm not sure how she would know who he was. She'd never met him."

"I told him not to contact that guy from the prison. He tried to kill Jory once, of course he'd try again," TK said. He shook his head and tapped a button on the laptop in front of him.

"You really think it was his friend?" Jory had seemed certain the guy was trustworthy and TK had never actually met the man.

"Most likely," he said. "Nell has been looking up some things for me." He nodded at the computer. "I can ask her what's in the system about Jory. Have you told Shaw?"

"You think knowing who turned Jory in will help us get him out?" Vinnie pulled up Shaw's number and pressed the call button. The phone rang three times before going to voicemail.

TK waited for her to finish leaving a message before answering her question. "Jory is gone, Vinnie, there's no getting him back. We need to move fast or it will be all of us in there.

The world felt like it was tilting on its axis. Jory was his best friend. How could he just give up without even considering any alternative? He didn't even look upset.

"It's Jory."

"We can't help him," TK said. "You can't just will things to turn out the way you want them to."

"You didn't even give it two seconds of thought! You went straight to writing him off."

"You just keep tilting at windmills." He typed something into the computer. "I'll be busy trying to save your ass, too."

"He'll be executed. It's like it doesn't even bother you."

He cleared his throat and because she was staring at him she saw the tightening of his jaw before he forced his face back to neutral. "Of course it bothers me. That's my best friend, but it hasn't even been two days since we were attacked. Other people I care about are in danger. I have to solve the problems that I can solve, that I have any hope of solving."

Vinnie wanted him to be wrong, but if there was a way to solve this, she didn't know what it was. She wanted to talk about getting Jory out, even if there was no answer. Maybe if they put their heads together, something would come to them. She needed to call Will. He would probably say there was nothing he could do. Maybe talking about what they knew and trying to solve the problems they could solve, like figuring out who was attacking them, would help her solve the problem TK thought was impossible. The answer had to be there, somewhere, hovering just beyond her understanding. She just needed to think.

"The crews think Kara was working with someone powerful or pissed off someone powerful. She had those objects." But they'd already suspected that, since she had a note in her file about being a candidate for special projects. "How did she get away with those murders so easily?"

"There didn't seem to be a lot of attention paid to the murders, but if it was someone internal to the government who could manipulate the data… if it's that big…" He paused. "Let's hope it's not."

"When we were trying to figure out who killed Maddie, Nell said there were people who knew, but it was kept hush hush." She told Vinnie that right before Kara had lured Vinnie out to Nell's house. "There were people looking at the murders but the details were kept away from databases local law enforcement had access to.

"We seem to keep coming back around to it being government."

They did, but it still didn't feel right. "But if it's government, why so clandestine? There was a guy who came by my work and gave me an earring that looked like Kara's pendant. He found me again later."

He closed his eyes briefly, and then opened them, and typed something on the computer in front of him. "The best thing for us to do would be to leave, hide, but I can't run. Gina won't leave. Her family is here. Her mom is sick." He tapped another button. "Nell found something. There was an anonymous tip to the main branch of the local police force about Jory. Not her district. It was passed up the chain to the FID. The tip came in Saturday morning. The day we were attacked."

"Do you really think it's the guy from the prison? Maybe it's not related to all of the other things going on." Vinnie unglued her feet from the floor and stepped into the room, sitting in the nearest chair. "Why would anyone want to turn Jory in? What do they gain? Even the person he knew from prison. Jory wasn't going to talk."

"If someone I tried to kill had information like that about me I wouldn't want them around."

Vinnie eyed TK, trying to imagine him hurting another person to protect himself. She couldn't, but if he was protecting people he cared about, maybe. Another thought struck her.

"Saturday Morning. What would have happened if the police had come to the construction site in the middle of the fight?" Goosebumps popped up on Vinnie's arms and she rubbed them.

"They would have gotten us all," TK had stopped typing to look at her. "That's how it could be related, if that was the plan. I'll see if Nell can get the actual content of that tip."

"Maybe it's a coincidence. Maybe someone at work saw him use his ability." Not likely. Jory was careful. Very careful. "I should call Will."

TK's only response was a grunt.

A deeper chill washed over Vinnie, making her shiver. Understanding dawned. "Something is wrong with Harry." Another wave of energy hit her. "Hilda's down there."

She launched herself off the couch and ran, sliding to a stop in front of the basement door. She wrenched the door open, and the power coming from the basement almost knocked her over. Steeling herself, Vinnie scrambled down the stairs.

Hilda stood near the wall across from the anomaly. She hurled something into Harry, then bent over and picked up a hunk of brick from a pile of debris at her feet. The roar of raw power in the basement was deafening.

Where had the debris come from?

Hilda hurled the brick at Harry and the anomaly flared, sending another wash of power over Vinnie.

"What are you doing?" Vinnie screeched.

Hilda flicked her eyes to Vinnie and then up over her shoulder to TK, who had followed. "Pissing him off."

"It's not alive, Hilda!" It was an inside joke, but it wasn't funny right now.

Why would a brick cause this? Vinnie shifted her vision as Hilda picked up another chunk and hurled it, and Vinnie saw the push of Mesmer power Hilda was using to make the bricks fly faster. The brick went through the anomaly and the Mesmer power pushed into Harry, disrupting the other powers.

"It doesn't need to be alive to be pissed." Hilda's voice carried to Vinnie without the need to shout. She picked up another brick and hurled it without using her power. "It's strange, some chunks work and some don't."

She didn't even know she was using her power. They were all going to die. Or get arrested when someone noticed the power and then die.

"We can't bring it back down," Vinnie shouted. "We don't have a Zee anymore. Stop."

"We don't have a Zee," Hilda said. "But we have you, don't we? You can bring it down by yourself if you would just stop being a coward. You can use the power. Just like you could have used power to save Jory. You just need motivation to stop being a coward. You've taken power from an anomaly before."

She'd lost her mind.

"It almost killed me!"

The Wind in the basement had kicked up and Hilda shouted her next words. "I saw you pull all that power at the hotel. I saw it in your mind. You could have taken them all out and saved him. You know how to do it, you just won't."

Hilda hadn't been there for any of the training sessions with Will. She didn't know the power of the crew and the power of an anomaly weren't exactly the same. "It's not the same power! Vasum were only meant to use the power that's in people."

"Bullshit," Hilda hissed. "That's what Will wants you to believe. He wants to keep you weak, just like the rest of them. They ALL want us to be weak so they can use us."

She sounded like Kara and Vinnie almost shivered again, but not from the power Harry was kicking out.

Hilda picked up another chunk.

Vinnie needed to stop Hilda, calm her down. She stepped between Hilda and the anomaly. "Stop. Where did you even get those?"

Hilda's eyes narrowed, and she lifted her arm as if to chuck the rock right through Vinnie. She swayed, her eyes fluttered, then closed, and she crumpled. TK stepped forward, wrapped his arms around her and lowered her to the ground.

The wind died down, but Harry was still pulsing energy into the room.

"What did you do?" Vinnie said, horrified.

"Just made the blood rush to her head."

He'd knocked her out. He'd used his power to knock her out. "She is going to kill you."

"She can try. Looks like you're getting a crash course in closing an anomaly."

"She is going to kill. You."

He gave her a flat look. "She'll see reason. Do you think you are up to helping us close this thing?"

"We don't have a Zee," Vinnie said.

"Shaw thinks she can convince Minka to help." He held up a phone to show a text message. "They started this way when Shaw got your message."

Minka. Of course. Minka was a Zee. She didn't want Minka anywhere near Harry. Wind pushed at her back and the anomaly screamed its power. They needed to get the power under control and Vinnie couldn't do it alone, no matter what Hilda thought. Minka was the only option they had.

CHAPTER TWENTY-SIX

When Hilda didn't immediately wake, Vinnie had gone upstairs to get a pillow and put it under her head. She was just starting to worry TK had hurt her when Shaw arrived with Minka.

Shaw paused at the top of the stairs. "TK wasn't kidding. You pissed Harry off big time." She continued down the stairs and across the floor to wrap her arms around Vinnie.

"Hilda lost her mind, was throwing stuff into it," Vinnie said. "TK knocked her out."

Shaw pulled back and looked over her shoulder at him. "She's going to kill you."

TK lifted his eyes to the ceiling, as if praying for patience. "I'd like to see her try. Someone had to do something. She was out of control."

"She just lost another friend. Should she be calm?" Her voice was gentle, with an easy confidence Vinnie had never heard from her before.

TK looked away. "We need to fix this."

Hilda groaned from the floor. "I'm going to kill you."

"That's what people keep telling me," TK said. "I thought

you had more imagination than that." He held out a hand to her to help her up.

She glared at him, but took his hand, letting him pull her to her feet. "I guess I'll have to surprise everyone and let you live."

His eyes showed amusement and Hilda's face softened from anger to neutrality. "If we're going to do this, the Zee probably needs to be down here and not up there."

Minka had frozen at the top of the stairs, eyes fixed on Harry. She seemed not to hear them talking.

Shaw went back up the stairs and took Minka's hands in her own. "Hey, it's okay. We've done this before. It's easy."

Minka's eyes focused on Hilda. "Isn't she the one who opened it?"

"Nope, he's been here awhile." Shaw stepped backward, so she was on the next lowest step, then another step drawing Minka down with her.

Minka jerked her hands out of Shaw's. "This thing has been down here the whole time. Are you crazy? It's not safe."

"It's perfectly safe." Shaw took another step back.

Minka took a step down, following Shaw. "Anyone could just come into your house. The people who are after you, who want to hurt you could just walk right in and you left the door open. Do any of you ever guard it?"

"The people who are after us are in this world," Nell said from behind her.

Minka started and turned. Vinnie hadn't noticed Nell arrive either. She'd been too focused on Minka.

"What difference does that make?" Minka said.

Shaw held out her hand, inviting Minka to take it again. "The anomalies open to other worlds, people who are after us here can't get in through the anomaly."

"They can be opened to the same world."

Alarm pinged inside Vinnie. "They are tears in time,

which sometimes lead to alternate universes. Not transportation devices."

Minka's mouth fell open, and she looked around at all their faces. "You seriously don't know?"

"There have been a few that opened to different locations in our world, instead of others," Hilda said. "But they are rare and this one opens to an alternate world. No one is going to come through. We aren't as stupid as you seem to think we are."

Of all the things Vinnie thought she understood, what the anomalies were was one of them. They learned about them in school science class. What they were, what they did, things that could and could not happen. Possibilities began rearranging themselves in her mind. Kara had fallen through an anomaly, but it couldn't have been to another place in this world, could it? Why had no one mentioned this? Vinnie felt like she never knew enough, was always two steps behind.

"How do you know that?" Minka screeched.

Hilda picked up a brick. "Because this —" She turned and hurled it into Harry. "Came from there."

"Stop!" TK said. "You can be reckless with yourself all you want but stop trying to kill the rest of us."

Hilda had been through the anomaly. What would have happened to Hilda if it had closed while she was over there and she had been trapped on the other side?. Vinnie shook away the thought. They needed to get Harry under control. Then she could worry about the possibilities.

"You've been through it?" Minka asked.

"Nothing but rubble over there," Hilda said. "No people, no animals that I've seen."

"How often have you been through it?" TK said.

Hilda lifted one shoulder.

"See?" Shaw said to Minka. "It's safe. We need your help.

Heroes together." She held up a fist with the palm toward Minka.

"Warriors forever." Minka shaped her hand into a fist, held it up and bumped Shaw's hand in a closed-fist high-five.

Well, isn't that adorable? Hilda's sarcasm was clear even in her mental voice.

You're just jealous.

Maybe, Hilda said, surprising Vinnie.

You and Nell seem to have a cutesy thing of your own, White Dragon.

Hilda's eyes narrowed.

Shaw had gotten Minka to the bottom of the stairs, but Minka's panicked look had barely softened. Her breathing was shallow, and she refused to look at Harry.

"Awww," Hilda said. "You're going to hurt Harry's feelings."

"Harry?" Minka squeaked. Her eyes darted to TK.

"The Portal — anomaly," Shaw said. "We call him Harry because he's a big, hairy problem."

"What do we have to do?" Minka asked.

"Hilda will connect us. She'll guide you in using the power. You just have to relax and do what she asks."

"Creepy," Minka whispered.

"Yep, that's me, Kiddo. Totally creepy." Hilda faced Harry. "Shall we?"

They spread out, forming a loose circle around the anomaly.

Minka stood next to Vinnie. She reached out and took her hand. Minka's hand was surprisingly rough with callouses. She looked so soft otherwise.

They couldn't really surround Harry if they were holding hands. As the others to spread out, Minka seemed to realize her error. She shook off Vinnie's hand and glared at her as if it were her fault as she moved into position between Vinnie and Shaw.

"Ready," Hilda asked.

Everyone acknowledged they were ready.

Vinnie felt Hilda in her mind, not like when she talked to her and not like how she felt all of her friends, but as if Hilda was sitting on the right side of her head next to her ear. It was a strange sensation. Her presence wasn't subtle. Vinnie could tell she was there, unlike whatever Sabra had done.

Vinnie, you're not going to freak out on me, right? Hilda said.

Vinnie's eyes flicked to the others, hoping no one else had heard that. She had attempted to help with Harry before, just as an experiment. She'd pulled Shaw's power and stood in her place, but she'd flipped out when Hilda seemed to take control of her mind. Since then, she'd had them all in her head, controlling her body. This should be a walk in the park.

I'll be fine, she thought at Hilda.

TK's power flowed into her. It felt like warmth and the last time she'd felt like this flashed in Vinnie's mind. Kara. Kara had used Ferr power to control her. Rasping sounds of panicked breathing filled her ears, and it took her a moment to realize it wasn't her.

Minka was gasping, trying to catch her breath. Shaw's power flowed through Vinnie, cooling the warmth of TK's power. Minka's breath slowed, but Vinnie could hear her heartbeat through the connection. Then Nell's power grounded her and made her feel solid, like she could handle whatever was coming.

I've got you. Ferr power won't hurt you. Hilda's voice was soothing, and it echoed through the connection.

Vinnie didn't know if Hilda was talking to her or Minka, maybe both. After a few more breaths, Zee power flowed through the circle, creating a tingling sensation that crackled through Vinnie's bones. Jory's power had never felt like that to her, but she had never been in a circle with him.

Okay, Vinnie, call your power into your abdomen but don't release.

The power responded to Hilda's voice, seemingly without Vinnie actually doing anything. She had a feeling Hilda only used words so she wouldn't feel out of control.

You still don't trust. You have complete control, but it will happen too fast for your conscious mind to understand. The power will flow out now.

The Wisp power surged through the connection and the other powers flared. All the hair on Vinnie's body stood on end as the energy flowed through the room. She hadn't shifted her vision to see the power threads being pushed back, but she could feel it. She could feel all of it. All the others were in her mind and their power felt like part of her, but separate. When she used her own power to pull, it felt like trying to control a foreign object, but this was almost as natural as breathing.

The Wisp power in her pushed and caught the raw energy coming from Harry and tucked it back into place. Vinnie focused on her thoughts and could almost catch the thought telling her where to go and what to do. Hilda's mind was there, nudging her own mind to do the work. She was in control — and she wasn't.

The flow of the power was exhilarating. They pushed and tucked in small bits. The anomaly would flare and they caught it and pushed it back until Harry shrunk to his normal low ebb. The flow of power bouncing between them slowed as they each started pulling their power back.

An urge rose in her to push harder, to close Harry completely. She had to keep her friends safe, and this wasn't safe, having this pulsing monstrosity down here. She tried to push at the Wisp parts, but she wasn't sure how to do it, to work with the others without Hilda guiding her.

Wait. She didn't want to close Harry. Vinnie recognized the warmth of Ferr power.

The connection to the others abruptly severed. The backlash hit Vinnie, and she stumbled back, chest on fire. The room spun for a moment then cleared. She felt the loss of power keenly, like she was missing some essential part of herself.

TK had fallen to his knees, clutching his head. "Damn, Hilda."

Hilda's face was hard. "I didn't make you pass out, did I? You had no right to try to close Harry."

"I didn't," TK said through clenched teeth. "I didn't mean to. It's just, it's not safe. Without a reliable Zee—"

"Don't ever do that to me again," Minka shrieked, and launched herself at TK.

"I didn't — " TK said as Shaw grabbed Minka by the waist.

"Minka Minka. Shhh, shhh. He didn't mean to."

Minka twisted away. "Bullshit. Your friends are messed up." Tears had pooled in her eyes and she swiped them away and ran for the stairs. Shaw looked helplessly at TK before bolting after her.

"Good job, dipshit," Hilda snarled.

TK closed his eyes and let out a breath. He looked exhausted and defeated. "We don't have a reliable Zee to keep it from getting out of hand."

"I really don't think he meant to," Nell said from the floor, where she'd also fallen. She didn't get up, just lay there on her back.

Hilda sat down heavily next to Nell. "He meant to. He's been trying to convince Jory to close it for years."

TK closed his eyes as they all waited for him to respond.

"It was just a momentary thought. We could close it and have one less thing that threatened our safety, but with all the power flowing through all of us, it got away from me."

"We can't remove everything remotely dangerous from our lives," Hilda said. "You see how much power it has. If we can use it, then we make our own safety."

"That is madness. What if someday we can't find some teenager with a hair-trigger temper to help us? What if one day another of us dies, and Vinnie isn't carrying the power inside? I told Jory we needed to close it, but he wouldn't listen and now we are on shakier ground than ever." He turned to Nell, looking almost desperate. "Nell?"

Nell looked apologetic. "We have people more advanced than us chasing us. We need all the help we can get."

"How is this helping us? We don't know anything about it. It's been here years and all we do is keep it contained. What if others can use it against us?" He spun, looking Vinnie in the eye. "I can't believe I'm going to say this, but Vinnie, can you be the voice of reason here?"

What did she think? In spite of all the pain of today and fear and the worry that they were all going through, since she'd come down here her tension had lessened. And just a moment ago she'd seen all the potential — what they could learn from using the power. She didn't think TK was wrong, and she wouldn't want to put her future in Minka's hands, but if Harry got out of control again, there were other ways to get help.

TK was doing what he could to keep them safe, in his own way. "Aside from today, it hasn't really been a danger to us. Why are you so determined?"

He hung his head, and for a moment, she didn't think he was going to answer. Then he said, "I was here when it opened. It came from violence. How can something that came from violence be good for us?"

"Bullshit," Hilda said. "I'm out. I need coffee and a painkiller."

"If you won't do as I ask, at least have the courtesy to listen."

Hilda turned back toward him, looking like she was ready to fight. "Fine. Upstairs. I still need coffee and a painkiller."

CHAPTER TWENTY-SEVEN

"I'll help her get what we need," Vinnie said.

When she got to the kitchen, she went straight to the fridge to get some sweet tea for herself and carrots for Nell. TK would need a drink for his iron pill. She should just take the whole pitcher.

A rattle and thump sounded as a pill bottle slammed on the counter behind her.

Hilda had both hands on the counter and was staring at the unopened bottle of painkillers as if she could glare it open. Then she grabbed the bottle and tried to pry off the cap. The bottle jittered in her shaking hands.

Vinnie set the tea and carrots on the counter, picked up the pill bottle, opened it with one thumb, and put it on the counter.

"Damn childproof caps." Hilda poured out three pills and clamped her fingers around them so they wouldn't shake out. She popped them in her mouth, grabbed the tea pitcher from Vinnie, sloshed some into a glass, and took a big swig.

"I'll make you coffee," Vinnie said, opening the cabinet to get the instant coffee out.

Vinnie had never seen Hilda like that. They'd had to get Harry under control plenty of times and while she had passed out from exhaustion once or twice, she'd never shaken like that. Maybe it wasn't fatigue making her shake.

"So..." Vinnie said. "You and Jory?" She turned away from Hilda, filled a cup and stuck it in the microwave.

Hilda snorted. "Poor Vinnie, so worried that I might have emotions. Here." She shoved her hands in the side pocket of her leggings and held what she'd retrieved out.

The earring. Vinnie replayed the scene in her mind. Jory must have gotten the earring into his hand somehow, and when Hilda wrapped her arms around his waist, she'd taken the earring.

"I'm going to sit." Hilda took the coffee and headed for the living room.

The front door of the house opened and Vinnie felt Shaw pause near the living room before coming all the way back to the kitchen. Without a word, she helped Vinnie load everything on a tray.

"TK is going to make a case for closing Harry," Vinnie said as she lifted the tray. "Is Minka okay?"

"She didn't want to come here at all," Shaw said. "I can't fix other people's emotions."

Vinnie carried the tray to the living room. Nell was on her back on the floor again, but she sat up and took the carrots, tea and multivitamin. Shaw helped Vinnie pass everything out.

When that was done, Hilda said, "All right, you can tell us why you think violence opened Harry and why you think it matters."

"Why it matters," TK muttered, shaking his head. "Four years ago, La Mafia was run by a man they called Papa."

"Of course Papa ran Oh la la mafia."

TK's jaw clenched. "Papa had murdered a friend of Sam's.

A girl who was well known and loved here in the Holt. Sam had started hanging out with this kid name Sergei—"

"The same Sergei who might be running La Mafia now?" Hilda asked.

"Yes," TK said.

"Are you telling me a kid might be running a crime syndicate in our city?" Nell said.

"Yes," TK said. "Can I finish?"

Nell mimed locking her lips.

"Sam was even more unstable than he was when he lived here with us. After the girl died, Sam started painting walls and either Sergei or Sam noticed that when he did, people felt happier near the painting, but only for a short time. Sergei could use his power to manipulate bones and since Wisps can push their power, he came up with this idea of using their combined powers to put Wisp power into paintings around the Holt. It sounds insane, but almost worked."

"The paintings," Vinnie said. "That's why it feels good to be here. I just thought it was… intuition or something."

"It worked," TK repeated. "But not very well with just Sam and Sergei. It took a full crew. I was the Ferr and Gina was their Mesmer. Papa got wind of what was happening, and that one of his own lieutenant's wife was involved and he ordered them to stop. And I was hotheaded and said we should refuse, but to minimize danger, instead of us all being at the painting site, we got the idea to infuse the paint instead."

"Wait…" Hilda held up a hand. "You have known how to create magic objects this whole time?"

He almost growled, "It's dangerous to mess with things you don't understand, if you'll let me finish?"

Hilda was thinking about the objects, but Vinnie was just stunned that TK had never mentioned that he helped with the paintings.

"By that time Sam had introduced me to Jory, and I had gotten a job at the news station. We were buying this house," TK continued. "Jory didn't want to be involved with what we were doing, but we used the basement to infuse the paint. We didn't succeed, but we kept trying. It was here that Papa attacked. He had Gina and her son, who was four, tied up in the basement in order to lure the rest of us in and kill us. He didn't expect Sam and Sergei. I don't know everything that happened. I was knocked out early. When I woke the basement and all Papa's men were charred to a crisp. Gina says that Sam lost control, he almost killed her and Charlie. And the paint, even I could feel the power' coming off it. Jory got rid of it. Three days later, Harry appeared. A lot of power was used in the basement. People died, and that thing appeared. We were trying to figure out how to close it and then Jory changed his mind said we should keep it open and I couldn't convince him." His eyes looked a little wet, but this was TK. Surely he wasn't crying. "And every time I go down there I'm reminded of what I almost lost."

Vinnie wanted to say something, but her mouth felt like it was glued shut. The others seemed to feel the same — they were all silent.

Nell slid a carrot in her mouth and crunched, the sound loud in the quiet room. Breath whooshed out of Shaw.

Hilda cleared her throat. "So, what you're saying is you know how to create power objects."

"People died!" TK said.

"And we'll join them if we don't find an advantage. Besides, creating the objects didn't kill the people."

"You don't know that. We need to close it. It's dangerous."

"Maybe we could vote on it?" Shaw asked.

"This is not a democracy. It's my house. We are not closing it," Hilda said. Her voice had a slight quaver. Vinnie might not have heard it if she hadn't seen how shaky Hilda had been in the kitchen.

TK stared at her for just a moment before standing. "Right. You guys can kill yourself. Have fun. Don't call me."

"TK," Nell stood, but she didn't go after him. "Why do you have to be such a jerk?" She said to Hilda. She looked like she was about to storm out, too.

"Because she's scared," Shaw said.

"I'm not." But Hilda's voice was barely audible.

She was, but Vinnie wasn't sure why. "Why did you say the house was yours?"

"Jory signed it over to me a few weeks…" She frowned. "No, it was just a few days ago. The day we were attacked at the construction site."

"And TK agreed," Vinnie said. "Because he knew Jory was contacting his friend at the prison, and he was worried something would happen."

"He gave it to you?" Nell said, her face radiating hurt.

"Oh, Harry," Shaw said. "He wanted you to protect Harry. Why would Jory want you to protect Harry?"

"I think he would have just wanted to make sure we had a place to live," Nell said. "But I would have protected Harry if he asked me. He could have given it to all of us."

"He was in a hurry," Hilda said. "I had enough money that it looked like a purchase."

Vinnie got a flash of an image in her mind. Men chasing her down a street that was not much more than rubble. But they weren't chasing her. They were chasing Hilda. The memory wasn't her own, Hilda was projecting again. Jory had told her he found Hilda in the basement with a sword not long after Harry appeared. Why would strong, independent Hilda hide in some stranger's basement? How would she even have gotten there? And she'd been to the other side, seemed comfortable with it.

"You know we've got your back no matter what," Vinnie said. *If you'd told TK why you need Harry to stay open, he wouldn't have left. He would be here protecting you with the rest of us.*

"No matter what?" Hilda asked.

"Hilda," Nell sighed. "Of course."

You tell them, Vinnie, Hilda said. *I can't tell them they are at greater risk because of me.*

"Jory knew Hilda would protect Harry as if her life depended on it," Vinnie said. "Because it does. Jory changed his mind about closing the anomaly because someone from the other side came through and if she stayed here, she'd die, but it wasn't safe for her over there either."

Understanding dawned on Nell's face. "Those nights where you stay out all night, and you come back looking ragged and beat up. You're not out partying."

Hilda just gave her a flat look.

"Are you guys saying Hilda is from another universe?" Shaw asked.

"That's what we're saying," Nell agreed.

"But how did you know you'd survive over here?"

"I didn't," Hilda said, "But I knew I wouldn't survive over there."

"You just go back and that's enough?"

Hilda sat up straighter and pushed her shoulders down, trying to look relaxed. "I can stay on this side for about five days now, and then I need 8-10 hours on the other side."

"Five days now?" Vinnie asked. "It used to be shorter?"

"The first time I only stayed around thirty-six hours."

Nell was shaking her head. "That can't be right. You were here for almost three years before we had to get Harry under control."

Hilda looked pained for just a moment. "It was more stable first. Small. I had to crawl through and it would close on its own when I went to the other side. I didn't even know…"

"You're safe," Shaw said.

Hilda glared at her. "I'm sorry I put you all in danger."

She had been putting them in danger the whole time she was here. Every time she went through had the potential to cause a flare up. Vinnie didn't begrudge her that, as she was trying to survive. Tonight, though, Vinnie had thought she didn't know what she was doing when she threw those bricks through, but she saw it. She saw that throwing the bricks was causing Harry to flare out of control. Hilda knew they no longer had a Zee, and she'd done it, anyway.

"If Minka hadn't agreed to help, what would have happened, Hilda?"

"You would have suddenly remembered that actually you know how to close one or you would have pulled power from a different Zee and we would have handled it, Vinnie."

"You bet our safety on something I have never been able to do." Vinnie's hands burned with the need to do something. She clenched them and focused on sending the energy to her leg tattoos.

"Did I bet my life on you?" Hilda said. "Yes, clearly a mistake. I guess I made the same mistake Jory made today."

Now she was going to make this about Jory? "There was nothing I could have done! Should I have risked us all? What would you have done if we had to run and you couldn't be close to your anomaly?"

"Guys!" Nell said. "This isn't helping."

Hilda stood. "Whatever. I need sleep."

Before she was out the door, Shaw stood. "Me too."

They were giving up. They didn't have a plan or any idea how to get Jory out. They were all just going to give up.

"We have to make a plan," Vinnie said.

"We need rest," Nell said. "One day won't make a difference. We'll regroup in the morning."

Vinnie watched Nell walk out of the room. She didn't believe they would regroup in the morning. With every minute that went by, it would just become easier to let Jory go. Every minute without a plan or hope was one minute he was closer to death.

She sat, staring into the darkness, waiting for an idea to come.

CHAPTER TWENTY-EIGHT

Shaw's nose whistled in her sleep. Vinnie had been listening to the sound for hours as she lay on her mattress.

She'd given in and gone to bed, but her mind wouldn't shut down and let her sleep. Visions of a dragon ripping the roof off of the prison, snatching Jory up and carrying him to safety, tumbled through her thoughts over and over.

Nell had tried to pretend she hadn't given up, but she had. Vinnie needed a plan that would motivate them to try, but her mind just kept playing the same image in a loop. That wasn't a plan, that was a ridiculous fantasy.

Wasn't it? She sat up in bed, rubbing her hands over her eyes. The idea was a fantasy, but so was being able to sleep tonight.

She threw the covers off. As her feet touched the floor something caught her eye. A faint glow came from the top of the dresser.

Vinnie slid off the bed. The only thing she'd left on the dresser was the earring, so she knew what it was before she was close enough to see it. She shifted her vision, but it still only gave off the faint white tendrils of weak power. Her hand hovered over it for a second before snatching it up and holding it up to the faint light coming in from the window.

There was something in the center that looked like a small piece of metal, but she couldn't tell for sure.

The room suddenly seemed suffocating — a place of lost hope. Vinnie put the earring back on the dresser, quickly dressed, shoved the earring in her front pocket, and headed down the stairs and out onto the front porch.

The night brushed against her skin, calling to her. She'd only intended to sit outside and see if it helped her mind stop racing, but that wasn't what she wanted at all. She needed to get away from here.

Vinnie started walking. Her feet carried her a few blocks away from home to a street with a strip of businesses. Nestled into the strip was a small bar called The Rope. The owner of the bar had been fortunate enough to get a location next to a parking lot. Only two cars were in the lot — one Vinnie recognized as the weeknight bartender's, the other was unfamiliar.

The inside of the Rope never smelled good. The floor was concrete, the lights dimmed, and somehow the place always smelled wet. Vinnie liked the unpretentious air—she could be invisible or not, depending on where she sat.

The one other person inside was a woman who sat alone in a dark corner scribbling something in a notebook. She'd brought her own tiny light to illuminate the page she was working on, but her face remained in shadow.

Vinnie sat at the bar, right under the spotlight.

Candy, the bartender, sidled over and took her ID. "Credit card?"

Vinnie laid enough cash for several drinks on the bar. "Whiskey sour."

"Haven't seen you in here in a while, Lavinia."

If Candy had really remembered her, she should have remembered that she always paid cash. She'd just read her name off the ID before putting it in a basket behind the bar, and she hadn't even checked the ID to make sure it was authentic.

"Life's been busy."

"Ain't it always." Candy made Vinnie's drink and went back to her stool in the corner, where she pulled out a ragged paperback and flipped it open.

Vinnie stared into her drink, trying not to imagine turning into a dragon and ripping the prison open again. Stupid. The cells were in an interior part of the prison. Even if she could get enough power to transform herself into a dragon again, she'd end up killing people just to get to Jory. And then what? He could get away, go into hiding somewhere else. Maybe they'd shoot her down or the power would kill her.

A cool breeze from the front door opening hit her back. Even on a Monday night, people couldn't resist their drinks.

From the corner came the sound of papers being gathered in a hurry, crunching as they were shoved into a bag, and then the click of a light snapping off.

Vinnie took another sip of her drink, pretending not to notice the sound of a chair being pulled out from a table.

"If he thinks I'm walking over there to take his order, he's going to be waiting," Candy muttered.

Vinnie glanced behind her to the table where the newcomer sat and a feeling of inevitability washed over her. Mark Jones looked back at her, his exaggerated features looking almost garish in the dim light. She downed her drink and pushed the glass forward on the counter.

Candy got up to get Vinnie another drink. As she set it down she murmured, sounding like she was talking to herself, "Don't lose your senses when there's a wolf at the table."

"I'm not sure it matters," Vinnie replied. "He's already outwitted me. I can't even figure out the game."

"Don't play the game, then." Candy went back to her chair.

Don't play. Even TK didn't go that far. He rolled the dice, but only the games he thought he could win. The odds had always been stacked against Vinnie, hadn't they? People thought power made you safe, but it was the opposite. Power made you a target. The more power, the bigger the target and the more people you had taking aim.

If you had no power, you could hide, you could play it safe, you could be invisible and live out your life with no one trying to take you down. But Vinnie hadn't chosen to sit in the shadows tonight. She was done trying to hide.

"Can I get a beer, too?" She said to Candy. "Whatever's cheap."

Candy reached into a mini fridge, pulled something out and popped the top, placing it down in front of Vinnie.

Vinnie grabbed the beer and her whiskey and slid off the stool. Mark, or whatever his real name was, watched her approach with a knowing look in his eyes.

She slid the beer across the table. "It's self-service here. If you want something different, you'll have to get it yourself."

She sat in the chair opposite him.

He tilted the bottle to look at the label. "This is fine. I don't really drink, but this barely qualifies."

"You're in a bar on a Monday night. You don't drink?"

"I'm not here by coincidence, or here to socialize."

Vinnie lifted her drink but thought better of it and lowered it again. "You got here really fast if it's me you wanted. I had no plans to come here."

"We've been waiting for a chance to talk to you alone. As

soon as you left your house, I was alerted. That's quite a walk for a woman alone in the ghetto in the dark." He looked around the bar. "I hadn't really pegged you as someone to come to a place like this."

She'd been coming here with Jory, Hilda, TK, and Nell since she turned twenty-one. Vinnie could almost picture them all around this very table, laughing and talking.

"I guess you're a bad judge of character. Someone seems hell bent on destroying everyone I hold dear. I needed a little help to think more clearly."

He leaned forward, and a pendant swung forward off his chest. The symbol on it looked familiar to her but she couldn't place it. "I'm an excellent judge of character. You think alcohol helps you think more clearly?"

The meaning of the symbol came to her. They used it for some of the hand tattoos they put on registered Twisted.

"Stone," she said and there, just at the edges of her awareness, she could feel the power in him. He wore a pendant that mimicked the pattern they put on people with Stone ability, and he was Stone.

He leaned back, and the pendant thunked against his chest and the feeling was gone. He seemed as ordinary to her senses as he had the first time she'd met him. The pendant was blocking her ability. Vinnie was willing to bet it would block any of the other powers that had a direct effect. He was one of the ones who had attacked them.

"This?" He said, pointing at the pendant. "I'm surprised you knew which one it was. Most people can't tell the difference. Do you know where they came from? What they represent?"

Of course, she knew they were the same as the Twisted tattoos so that couldn't be what he meant. "Maybe you could tell me your real name first, and then you can lord your superior knowledge of oppressive tattoos over me."

"And I heard Hilda was the snarky one," he said. "I'm Andre, and believe it or not, I'm here to help you."

The sound of Hilda's name coming from his mouth ignited the fire in her. He attacked them, he manipulated her, he had the nerve to say he was here to help? But if she wanted answers, telling him to go to hell wouldn't get them.

"Please, tell me how you can help." She didn't bother hiding the sarcasm in her voice.

He pointed at the pendant. "Yes? No?"

Did she want to know what it meant? She could probably find the information on the internet, but he clearly wanted to tell her. Vinnie rolled her hands in a circle, indicating he should continue.

"It's a demon seal," he said. "When power first started manifesting in people, some thought they were possessed by demons and that if they put the seals on them, they could control the demons inside. That was after they tried exorcism, of course."

"Of course," she agreed. "Why are you wearing it?"

"Some people have a terrible sense of humor. When they were deciding on objects to imbue with power, they also wanted to know the class of person who was going to be wearing it at a glance."

Which didn't answer the question she'd intended. "What does it do?" She had a pretty good idea what the seal did, but he didn't have to know that.

"Prevents other Twisted from using their power on me... to a certain extent. You couldn't boil my blood, but you could still throw a fireball at me."

Which confirmed what they'd thought, and maybe that he knew she had Wisp power since he used fire examples. If they were also the ones who'd attacked her on the street after work, she'd also used other power on them. Maybe he wasn't aware of that.

"If these can be made, why not make them for the general populace, make them less afraid?"

"Our skill isn't there yet. It takes considerable power to make something like this. The Twisted involved tend to die way too often for some people's comfort."

She couldn't tell from his tone or demeanor if he was one of the people uncomfortable with Twisted dying. Kara certainly hadn't minded. Was he talking about the same people who had most likely freed her from prison?

"And," he continued. "Most Twisted would resist making this design in particular, since if they are reversed and pressed against our skin, it also makes it difficult to use our own power."

Vinnie sat up straighter. If they could get the pendants off, it would bring them closer to a level playing field and if they could reverse them, they would have an advantage. This was dangerous information, and he'd just thrown it out there as if it was nothing. Which meant this conversation was risky. He didn't seem like the trusting type. Maybe he didn't intend for her to walk out of here.

"You're very free with your knowledge," she said.

He shrugged one shoulder. "You won't remember this tomorrow."

Vinnie gathered her power and put up as much of a block as she could between her and anyone trying to tamper with her head. Her chair scraped as she stood. "I guess we're done here."

"It's too late for that," Andre said in a low voice. "You should sit."

She didn't want to sit. She wanted to burn him alive. "Are you the one who got Jory arrested?"

"No, but whoever did, did me a favor. If you want to save your friends, I can help." He waved at the chair.

Friends. Plural. Not just Jory. He was threatening them

all. Her bravado from earlier evaporated. Why had she left the house alone? Had she not learned anything about taking risks? If the others were with her, maybe she would stand a chance against Andre and his crew. No. He wouldn't have talked to her if she hadn't. She needed to stay calm. The only thing he was threatening her with right now was erasing her memory.

"Did I come here of my own free will?"

"Absolutely," he said. "Magnus put the thought in your head that it would be nice to get away for a bit, but you always had a choice."

No one had touched her, so either Magnus was a Ferr who could persuade at a distance or a Mesmer as strong as Will or Greg. If he could do that, he could erase her memory, just like Andre said, but it would have been easier not to tell her names and information about how the pendants worked. As long as he was confident she would only remember what he wanted her to remember, he might be freer with information.

"Are you with Hanna's Soldiers?" she asked.

"We can talk about that later, if you like," he said. "But first, let's get you the information you need to get your friends out of prison. May I see your phone, unlocked, please."

Again, he said friends and not friend. She only had one friend in prison. Was he threatening all of them with prison? She didn't even have the energy to glare at him across the table. He had the upper hand, and he knew it, but she sat, frozen.

"I just want to record what we say next so that you'll have a record," he prompted. "It won't do me any good to tell you if you don't know what I said."

Because his Mesmer friend was going to erase her memory. "It would have been much easier if you hadn't shared information about the pendants with me. Then you wouldn't need to erase my memory."

"My face is information, too. I needed you to recognize me so you would talk to me, but I don't need you connecting what I'm about to tell you back to me."

And she absolutely wanted to connect this back to him. They needed all the knowledge they could get.

If she went along with this, he would let her go and she would have a chance to stop him and whatever his end game was. Memories were never completely erased. At least, that's what everyone kept telling her. Maybe if she could create connections back to this memory she could retrieve the information later. Kiernan had told her how to use tattoos to lock her power down, could she use one to infuse a memory? This might be her only shot at getting this information, so she had to try. Vinnie started the tattoo on her inner forearm where her hoodie would hide what she was doing and where she would be sure to see it tomorrow. Then she unlocked her phone and slid it across the table.

True to his word, Andre opened the voice recording app and placed the phone on the table between them.

"If you want to save your friends, do exactly as I'm about to instruct."

CHAPTER TWENTY-NINE

Pain lanced through Vinnie's head, waking her up. The last thing she remembered was stepping out on the front porch intending to go to The Rope. In the middle of the night? Had she really done something that stupid? She was lying on her back, jeans digging into her waist. Opening her eyes was going to be agony, but if she didn't do something, she might die. Maybe if she moaned loud enough, someone would take pity on her and bring her a painkiller. Vinnie groaned, rolling to her side.

Cer's bed felt a little too firm and Vinnie cracked her eyes open and then squeezed them shut again. She was not at home, she was in her apartment.

She'd never drank so much she blacked out. Hilda would laugh and call her a lightweight. No, in normal times, before everything went to hell, Hilda would have laughed. Now she'd be too pissed at Vinnie's recklessness. Vinnie wasn't happy with herself right now, either.

She needed to text and let them know she was okay. Vinnie rolled to her back and patted the pockets of her jeans. No phone. At least she'd had enough sense to take it out of her pocket before collapsing. What would drunk Vinnie have done with it?

Her eyes scanned the bare floor, but the phone wasn't there. She was going to have to get up.

Vinnie pushed herself into a sitting position. Pain lanced through her head, followed by a wave of nausea. She pushed off the bed and scrambled toward the bathroom, making it to the toilet to hunch over and heave. Nothing came out and after a few painful moments, she sat back, exhausted.

The corner of her phone peeked at her from where it hung halfway over the edge of the bathroom counter. Her body relaxed at the sight of it. Maybe she could convince someone to drive over and get her a painkiller.

"Ridiculous, don't be a baby," she muttered.

Vinnie scooted forward until she could reach the phone and pull it off the counter. There were three panicked texts from Nell asking where she was.

Ugh. She was going to have to confess to Nell that she'd left the house and gotten drunk last night. Her thumb was poised to open her messages when a reminder popped up.

"Urgent. Check your voice memos," Vinnie read. She never used the voice memo app. Why would drunk Vinnie want her to check her voice memos? She tapped the message app and told Nell she was alive.

A second reminder popped up to check voice memos. Vinnie did as she was told and found there was one from last night.

She pressed play and a male voice started talking. Before he even finished talking, Vinnie paused and hit the call button on Nell's message.

"I think my memory has been erased," she said when Nell answered. "Can you come get me?"

. . .

THE WOOD GRAIN of their old, scarred table might make permanent dents in Vinnie's cheek, but that was a small price to pay for never having to move again. The painkiller had done nothing for her headache. Hilda had her hands in Vinnie's hair, trying to figure out how to fix what happened, but memories weren't her strength.

"We have to call Will," Nell said. "We know he or Greg is good with memories."

None of them wanted to ask Will for anything, but Hilda had been muttering about permanent damage.

"Do it." Vinnie's voice echoed in her ear through the wood of the table.

Nell grabbed Vinnie's phone, since she had Will's number programmed in, and stepped out of the kitchen to make the call.

"Andre." Shaw's fingertips brushed the tattoo on Vinnie's forearm.

They'd found it when Vinnie had arrived at the house and taken off her hoodie. Why would she put a name on her forearm? It didn't have any Wisp power associated with it. At least, not that she could tell.

"You were scared," Shaw said. "But you believed him. This was his name, Andre."

Hilda's fingers tightened. *There.*

"Andre Tolemic." The name popped into Vinnie's mind. She could almost see his face. A sharp stab of pain lanced through her head and she moaned in agony.

Hilda let go and stepped back. "It was right there, but I can't figure it out."

"We need to figure it out," Vinnie said. On the recording, She'd agreed to give Andre the location of Kara and return the power objects — plural — that were in their possession. They couldn't do either of those things. They're best hope was figuring out what she'd forgotten. There must be a reason he'd erased her memory, some clue, if she could just remember.

Nell came back in and put the phone back on the table. "He's coming."

Vinnie almost moaned again in anticipated relief.

"The guy on the recording gave us all the plans and security information for the prison bus that's moving Jory in five days," Nell said. "And you can't remember anything at all?"

"Andre Tolemic." Vinnie said. "His name."

"It's a trap," Shaw said.

"Maybe. But why?" Nell breathed. "If they want Kara and the objects, how would setting a trap help them get it?"

"They wouldn't have wrecked Vinnie's head if they weren't hiding something," Hilda said. "If we know what else she knows, maybe we'll know if it's actually a trap."

Vinnie felt a familiar presence in the driveway. The pain in her head was so intense it took her a moment. "TK is here."

Hilda had apologized to him and explained why she needed Harry, but she had still been uncertain he would come.

Vinnie lifted her head as TK came into the room. He took one look at her and shook his head.

"I guess you got your wish, a plan to save Jory," he said. "And now the enemy knows everything about us."

"They don't know everything," Nell said. "Or they would have known that she lived here now and not at that apartment."

"It's easier to drop her off there without being seen and they were tracking her closely enough that they knew where she would be," TK said.

The table had been comfy, nice and cool against her cheek. Vinnie put her head back down. "They tracked me through the crystal earring." She'd picked up the crystal on her nightstand, but there was more to her knowing than that. Maybe this Andre character had something about it.

"What power does that?"

"Kara…" Vinnie said. She wanted to say that Kara had said that people always thought there was a power reason, but that was the opposite of what she said. She'd said Vinnie didn't think of ways that used Twisted abilities. "Normal chip. Surveillance. Not power."

There was a knock on the front door. Shaw got up to go get it. She returned moments later, and Vinnie could hear other footsteps but she didn't want to lift her head again.

"A Mesmer erased her memory?" Will said.

"Yep," Hilda said. "I can't quite tell what's going on in there, but I can tell they did something. She's in a lot of pain. Nothing seems to help."

"Greg?" Will said.

Ah, of course Greg had come. There was a pause, and she felt the lightest flutter in her mind. She wouldn't have noticed if it hadn't felt like someone rubbing sandpaper across her brain.

"They've made a mess," Greg said.

"Can you fix it?" Hilda asked.

"The pain, most likely. I can at least ease it. The memory pathways are damaged. They would take days to repair."

"They're moving Jory in five days," Hilda said. "We need as much information as we can get as soon as we can get it."

"You are not thinking of attacking a prison bus," Will said. "They'll hunt you down, and you're not that hard to find."

"It's Jory." Shaw's voice sounded small and lost.

"I can try to make different connections," Greg said. "Go around the damage. It might be enough that the memories will come back on their own."

He meant he needed to poke around in her head to help her retrieve the memories. She hated that. She hated it so much and she had hoped she could retrieve the other memories without having to do this. But this was Jory they were talking about.

"Do it," Vinnie said.

Greg walked around the table until he was behind her. She lifted her head again, not wanting him to lean over her.

"I can do it without touching, but this will be faster."

"We should let them work." Will nodded to the door and left. Nell, TK, and Shaw followed close behind.

Hilda stayed. "You don't mind if I watch?"

"No," Greg said, which either meant he didn't mind, or she couldn't watch.

Hilda took it as permission and sat.

"I'm going to start with blocking off the pain and we'll see where that gets us." Greg put his fingertips on her temples and drew in a deep breath, letting it out in some strange kind of groan. "I thought you were going to watch Ms. Forbes's thoughts, not mine."

"How is that useful?" Hilda said.

Minutes stretched by with no response from Greg. The pain subsided, first the sharp spike at the base of her skull, then some of the more diffuse pain. Her nausea wasn't fading with the head pain.

"Your body will catch up," Greg said.

A few more minutes went by and the pain was almost gone.

"Whoever did this was a hack. It hurts because they tried to smash the pathways to the memory rather than excising the threads to it. Are you remembering?"

A dim image of Mark Jones sitting across from her at The Rope flashed across her mind.

"I see the guy who gave me the crystal earring, Mark — no, Andre. His name is Andre."

Pain lanced through her mind, but it was erased almost as

fast as it appeared. Another flash of memory, an amulet swinging out of his shirt.

"An amulet, I don't know what it means."

"Try not to think about him for a minute. I think I see where the memory is coming from."

Of course, because he'd told her not to think about it, that's exactly what she thought about.

"Do you remember when Jory decided he was going to grow cauliflower, and it all came out this weird brown color?" Hilda asked.

Jory had insisted the cauliflower was fine, just a funny color, but when they'd tried to eat it, it was bitter. "TK refused to eat anything from the garden that year. Jory was so mad."

"Try thinking about Andre now," Greg said.

Vinnie's thoughts went back to the bar. She could see him sitting across from her, looking pleased with himself. "Andre Tolemic. He was so sure I'd never remember, so I goaded him to give me his full name."

The thought didn't hurt, but the rest of the memories weren't there.

"I've done what I can," Greg said. "The rest of the memories should come back."

Greg had already disappeared out the front door by the time Vinnie convinced herself to get up. Hilda walked with her down the hall to the living room where the others had convened.

Will sat on one of their worn out chairs, somehow not looking out of place. "Better?"

"Yes, thank you for coming and bringing Greg." Vinnie settled onto the loveseat with Nell.

"Remember anything?"

"A name. Andre Tolemic." She'd already had the first name on her arm, so really, she'd only remembered the last name. "He wore some sort of amulet and I think that's important."

"Not that helpful," he said. "But it's an unusual name. I might be able to find something."

"That wasn't part of the deal." Vinnie pointed out.

"But we appreciate the help," Nell added, shooting a glare at Vinnie.

"Vinnie is of no use to me dead or in jail," Will said. He turned to Vinnie. "Your friends were just telling me about the offer. If you deliver the objects and Charlotte Knight, Kara, they will make sure the trail for the bus hijacking doesn't point back to you. Hanna's Soldiers will claim responsibility for that, and they have evidence to exonerate Conor. Except you don't have the objects and Kara is gone."

"And they'll probably turn us in anyway," TK said. "They've already lied, attacked us, and stolen memories. If they could have gotten what they wanted, they wouldn't be negotiating. After they get what they want, they have no reason to follow through on their promises."

"Why do they think you have the objects that were in Kara's possession?" Will asked.

"I used more than one power when they attacked me in the street. That's something someone with the crystal could do." That had been on the recording too, how Andre knew she had the crystal.

"I'll get you all out of here," Will said. "I know how to hide better than your friend did, apparently. We'll get your friend out and get you new identities."

"Hilda and I are not leaving," TK said. "The rest of you can go."

"Minka's here," Shaw protested. "She won't leave her brother."

"You barely know her," Hilda scoffed.

Shaw opened her mouth, but Vinnie interrupted, "We'll find another way."

"It's not safe," Will said. "It doesn't take a genius to figure out that Jory is your friend. You all lived together. This is the first place they'll look, and it's a big enough crime they will not mind the cost of testing all of you. At that point, they don't have to prove you did anything. If you do this, your life is over. Unless you leave."

Hilda couldn't run. They wouldn't care that she needed Harry to survive. Maybe they'd just toss her through and close the anomaly. She said there was nothing over there.

"That's a chance I'll have to take," TK said.

"Don't be ridiculous," Hilda said. "There's no reason for you to stay. I'm sure your girlfriend will see reason. You all run. I'll stay and hold down the fort."

Lines of tension had appeared around TK's mouth. "This isn't about Gina. I'm the best chance you have to convince them to look away. I'm not running."

Vinnie didn't think his chances were good at all, but that probably wouldn't be a good thing to say. "Maybe we can just see how it goes first. See if Andre keeps his word."

"His word was that you would be blamed unless you give him something you can't give him," Will growled. "If you won't do what it takes to save yourself, I will not help you."

Hilda rolled her eyes. "What help can you even offer?"

"I can help you learn to work together, and we have a name. I can find him. And if I can find him, I can point the evidence in his direction."

"If you can do that, what are we even worried about?" Hilda asked.

"Everything else we just talked about? I doubt this will be the end of it."

They were just going to keep going around and around with no resolution. Vinnie wouldn't run if Hilda couldn't go.

"I wish I'd known about the bracelet. Maybe if I could have gotten that too, it would be enough."

Shaw sat up straighter. "Bracelet?"

"The Warrior games crew said she had a silver bracelet that she used to store power," Vinnie said. "The crystal could store power, but the bracelet could hold more and she could just take the power. That's what was killing people because she couldn't stop the power transfer."

"And she was opening anomalies." Shaw got a faraway look and then sprung up. "Hold on."

She dashed up the stairs.

After some bumps and drawers being slammed, Shaw came back down the stairs. Her face was flushed, and she was holding something against her abdomen. She stood in front of Vinnie and held her hand out.

"Did Kara's bracelet look like this?" she asked. In her palm was a silver cuff bracelet. Vinnie had only seen Kara's bracelet in the middle of a fight, so she couldn't be sure, but it looked the same.

"Where did you get that?" Vinnie asked.

Shaw clamped her hands back over the bracelet and sat back down. "Cassius. He gave it to me. I thought it was just some ugly thing that had sentimental value. I don't know if this is what he was using to open anomalies. He needed one anomaly for power, he said, and he had to have all sorts of coordinates."

"May I see the bracelet?" Will held his hand out.

Shaw clutched it closer to her abdomen.

"We need to know," Nell said gently.

"Don't touch." Shaw held her hand out, palm up.

Vinnie leaned forward and shifted her vision so she could see power. Faint purple threads swirled around the bracelet.

"Vasum power," Will said.

"If it stores power, and Kara could use that power even

though she is not Vasum," Vinnie said. "I wonder if it stores enough power to become a dragon?"

"Cassius wouldn't go around killing people," Shaw said.

Shaw had said before that Cassius's people moved between worlds regularly. It didn't make sense that they would kill people all the time to do that.

"But he didn't have to if he could pull power from anomalies to store in the bracelet," Vinnie said. "Kara pulled power from the anomalies, too. If she could do that, why pull from people?"

"We don't know the bracelets are the same," Nell said. "It's an easy design to wear and carry around."

"And you're forgetting a person can't hold on to power from an anomaly," Will said.

"It made her bleed." Vinnie remembered the blood coming out of her ears. (Check) "And if most of the power is stored in the bracelet…"

TK cleared his throat. "Maybe we can get back to the real problem?"

Shaw closed her fingers back over the bracelet. "We have everything they want. If we give them the bracelet and the crystal, they'll leave us alone."

And Shaw would lose her best chance of getting her wish to become a dragon. Vinnie rubbed the palm of her hand against her chest, but it didn't help with the ache.

"For Jory." Shaw held the bracelet out to Vinnie.

"Now that that's settled." Nell reached beside the chair she was sitting in and picked up an accordion folder she'd stashed there. She opened it and pulled out what looked like a sheaf of paper, which she then unfolded and laid on the table, revealing a map. The map looked like it had been printed on their home printer, which was running out of ink. There were several roads marked with a red marker.

"I couldn't sleep last night, either, so I dug into some

databases. I didn't find much. We know that the prisoners are taken north from here, so there are only a few routes they could take that are direct, unless they backtrack. From there I scoured the internet and the dark web…" She paused, frowning. "It was a lot of work and I had it narrowed down to two paths the bus could take, but I didn't need all that since this Andre guy told you where it would be. I couldn't find the likely times, but I figured we could camp out the two routes or the prison."

Some of the tension in Vinnie's body eased. She'd thought everyone had given up, but Nell had been working on a plan.

"And if Tolemic lied about the time or place?" Will said.

"If we don't attack the bus," Hilda said. "He doesn't have leverage to get us to do what he wants. The bus will be there, and if Jory isn't on it, we'd know and wouldn't attack. He doesn't have a reason to lie about the time or place."

"Right." Nell marked a spot on the map. "Andre told us the best place for an ambush would be here. But this one is almost as good and would give us an advantage in case they sell us out."

"I guess we're doing this," TK said. He didn't look happy, but he wasn't threatening to leave.

"We're doing this," Hilda agreed.

CHAPTER THIRTY

It was the perfect night for an ambush. The moon was bright enough to give them some visibility on the dark stretch of road. The spot Nell had chosen was behind a blind curve. Trees were sparse, but the curve should be enough to hide them until the bus was almost on them. Will would make sure the bus driver and guards didn't see them at all.

If he ever showed up. When they'd committed to trying to rescue Jory, he'd agreed to help, surprising them all. In the few days they'd had to prepare, he'd helped with the strategy and helped them learn to coordinate their power somewhat.

Now they were waiting for him to arrive and do his part. Greg was back at the entrance to the prison, watching for the bus to leave. He'd texted a few minutes ago to let them know it was on the way. But Will had not arrived yet. He should have been here by now.

A Mesmer entered Vinnie's awareness. Will. Finally. He was farther up the road so she couldn't see him yet, and she shouldn't have been able to tell it was him so easily. The only other people she could do that with were her friends, and Will was not one of her friends. That she could tell it was him meant her subconscious had decided to trust him and let him in. Great. Just great.

Will appeared around the curve of the road. He wore a baseball cap that had the head of a dog on the front and two long floppy ears on the side.

Minka snorted with laughter.

"What is that on your head?" Vinnie snapped as he approached. Her irritation was unreasonable — he didn't have to help at all, but she didn't like it that part of her trusted him.

"It's my disguise. I'm poodle man!"

Minka laughed again and Shaw giggled.

"You are one weird dude," TK said.

"You're late," Vinnie said. "The bus will be here."

"Plenty of time." Will turned toward the road. "A second for me to hide us, a minute or two for Nell to get in place, a few minutes for you to pull all the powers you need."

Shaw let out a shaky breath.

"We've got this," Minka murmured, but she sounded uncertain.

They spread out to give each other room to work, but stayed close enough that Will could hide them by reflecting light off the air. Nell was the only one to move farther away. She crossed the road and crouched in the shadows on the other side.

The last few days they'd met at the hotel to work on their timing and coordination. If they didn't get it just right, they'd end up killing Jory instead of saving him.

On the bus was a Mesmer that worked for the prison, the bus driver, and two guards. Jory would be wearing a collar around his neck that would kill him if the bus stopped or if anything happened to the guards, unless one of them pushed a button disabling the system first.

Andre had told them to use Wisp ability to short circuit

the collars, but Will didn't think she should be trying to juggle that many abilities and didn't like that they'd have to trust that Kiernan would be on the bus too. Vinnie didn't mention she didn't have to pull Wisp energy, it wasn't a conversation she wanted to have with him just yet. And besides, Vinnie didn't trust her ability enough to try to short circuit a collar that could kill Jory. When practicing on her own, she'd only managed to fry things.

And none of them trusted Andre. Some of her memory had come back in fuzzy images, but not enough to trust what he said to her. If it was so easy to disable the collars, then they would be of no use to control Wisps.

Andre had given them a reasonable sounding plan but hadn't known the full extent of Vinnie's capabilities. The plan they'd come up with didn't seem much safer. It relied on Vinnie getting one of the guards to push the safety button and she would have only seconds to convince them. It was better than a sure death if she messed up short circuiting a collar.

Jory came into Vinnie's range of awareness.

"They're almost here" she said out loud to Hilda, who would pass it on. "There are two Mesmers on the bus."

So far, everything was exactly as expected. The two Mesmers would be the guard and Amanda, the Mesmer of Yellow crew. She couldn't feel Kiernan.

"Can you tell which Mesmer is the guard?" Hilda asked.

One of the Mesmers was much stronger than the other. Vinnie pulled power from the stronger of the two. Hilda would be focused on coordinating so it was up to Vinnie to scope out the bus. The stronger Mesmer's mind was sluggish and hungry. "They've sedated the prisoners. So, yes." That was unexpected.

Hilda's breath hissed through her teeth. "Jory might be

able to scrub the drug from his body once we get the collar off."

"It's time," Vinnie said. No more time to worry about what could still go wrong.

She pulled Ferr power from TK, combined it with the Mesmer power she held and buried her mind into the Mesmer guard's, trying to get a sense of their thoughts and feelings. She called to their blood and asked that it match her own. They were kin, they were one tribe, their hearts beat together. A flash of sick feeling washed over Vinnie, and she pushed it away. No time for sympathy.

Nell hobbled onto the street as if she was hurt and stepped in front of the bus.

Vinnie sent a wave of compassion at the Mesmer and the thought the bus was going stop and it wouldn't be the prisoner's fault. She should press the safety button.

But the bus didn't slow, there was no squeal of tires or slowing of momentum. The driver shouldn't have hesitated to hit the brakes. The prisoners were of no importance, and it wouldn't matter if they died to save an innocent.

Luckily, they weren't counting on the bust stopping. What mattered was that the Mesmer press the button, and they had not. Their thoughts were that the prisoners deserved whatever happened to them.

Vinnie sent feelings of panic that the guard was going to die if they didn't press the button. A concussion of air sounded in front of the bus caused by Hilda throwing up an air shield in front of Nell.

The bus slammed into the air shield and slowed briefly before breaking through and plowing into Nell's outstretched arms. Her legs stretched behind her, feet grinding furrows in the road as the bus screeched to a stop. The front end of the bus was crumpled when Nell stepped back from it, unharmed.

The Mesmer power was yanked from Vinnie and she could no longer hear the minds of the prisoners. Her heart dropped to her feet. He couldn't be dead. She still sensed Jory, but would she still feel him even if he wasn't alive?

And then they were running onto the road. A pop of gunfire came from the bus's window and then abruptly stopped.

Vinnie found the bus's cameras, and they exploded with a pop as she sent Wisp power into the wiring.

Nell had grabbed the bus door and stepped out of the way as a guard toppled out. TK had knocked one out, while Will got the other.

"You can't make me, you can't make me," the Mesmer prison guard screeched.

She came flying through the door a moment later, thrown by Nell.

"Get the code out of her!" Nell shrieked.

Will, who had come out of the woods at a slower pace, bent over, putting his hand on her forehead. "912028."

Vinnie stepped over the guard and climbed onto the bus.

Nell punched in the code for the door that stood between them and the prisoners and pulled it open.

Jory swore.

"You don't look happy to be rescued." Vinnie eyed the collar around his neck.

"This is a trap, and you walked right into it."

"That's what Shaw said." Vinnie slid around Nell and after a quick glance at Kiernan and a woman who must be Amanda, she leaned over and poked at the metal around Jory's neck.

The collar around Kiernan's neck released and thunked down on the bench next to him. "Allow me." His voice sounded muzzy, and he swayed as he stood. He touched Jory's collar for a moment and it popped off.

"Let me get the drug." Jory grabbed his wrist for a moment. When Kiernan straightened, he didn't sway.

"Do they know you can do that?" Vinnie asked Kiernan.

Kiernan shrugged and slid around her, headed for the door. "I wouldn't try it when the collar was active. It's rigged against tampering. That would be suicide."

Had Andre known that when he instructed Vinnie to use Wisp power on it?

"Hey, Kiernan, don't leave me here." Amanda stood and stumbled after him, not waiting for Jory to scrub the drug out of her.

"The information we were given told us to attack a few miles back. If it's a trap, maybe we switched things up enough." Vinnie exited the bus. The others were standing outside, waiting.

"Someone gave you information?" Jory said as he stepped down onto the ground.

That would take too long to explain.

"Yes," Vinnie said. "Not anyone trustworthy."

"What are you going to do when they figure out where you are?"

"Use our superior firepower?" He really thought this was a trap. Vinnie spread her senses out, but other than them and the Mesmer guard, she couldn't sense anyone else with power.

Nell pointed her arm to the curve of the road. "There's a black car over there, keys are in the ignition."

Kiernan, who had been hovering nearby with Amanda leaning on him, turned and pulled her in the direction that Nell pointed.

"Just show me," Jory said.

"They're almost here," Hilda said. "Don't be stubborn. Run."

He looked at her for a long moment.

"We have a plan. You'll screw it up if you stay," she snapped. "Go!"

Jory's jaw clenched, but after one angry shake of his head he went, loping down the road in an easy run, quickly overtaking Kiernan and Amanda.

And then Vinnie felt it, the fuzzy signature of blocked power. Hilda was right, they were here. She pulled power from the passed out Mesmer guard and put up a reflective shield around Jory. They would still be visible, but Vinnie hoped it would be enough to hide their retreat.

Hilda turned to face the trees opposite the direction Jory had gone, and the rest of them followed.

Vinnie could feel Will step away from the others and move to a position perpendicular to both groups. She took a few steps so she would be in front of the others as dark shapes came into view, wrapped in black, faces hidden. One of the taller shapes moved just in front of the others. Andre, something about the way he moved, was familiar, so that must be him. A memory flashed through her head. Andre sitting at the table in the Rope, an amulet swung out from his shirt and she felt his power.

They're not blocking us with their abilities. She thought at Hilda. *It's the amulets.*

"What are you doing here?" Vinnie called out. "We had an agreement."

A change in air pressure made her eardrums pop. There was a roar of air, but it hit something — a shield of air around them and dissipated.

"We don't want to fight," Hilda yelled. "We'll give you what you want." *Can you get the amulets off?*

Could she? If she used Nell's power to find them, maybe she could melt the chains with Wisp power.

One attacker stepped forward — The Wisp. Vinnie could only tell because she couldn't feel her power. She held up her hands, formed a fireball, and tossed it at Hilda. Vinnie felt into the fire, grabbed it and tossed it back, hitting the other Wisp, who stumbled a second before the fire winked out.

"They're playing with us," Nell said. "What's the game?"

As if her words had triggered something, Andre's crew launched into action. The man she thought was Andre strode forward and slammed his fists into the ground the way Nell had done at the construction site, sending a quake rumbling toward them. Nell put her hand on the ground and the quake stopped before reaching them.

The others were already in motion. The Dancer headed straight for Hilda, but Shaw slid in front of him, sending a swift kick at the other's head. They went at each other, kicking and punching.

The air around Vinnie thinned. The Mesmer was trying to take her air. She pulled power from Hilda to counteract the attack, then she pulled a little from Shaw, combined them into an ice ball and sent it flying at the Wisp, who melted it midair.

The amulets, Vinnie, Hilda thought at her.

A huge wind shear slammed into the other crew, sending them stumbling. Vinnie dropped back behind Hilda and Nell, until she was beside Minka, who stood, paralyzed by fear. Vinnie pulled power from Nell and tried to feel the metal links around the other Dancer's neck. When she found the links, she made the metal hot, then used Dancer and Mesmer to freeze them.

The chain popped, and she felt the full force of the Dancer's power. The attacker crumbled to the ground.

Too slow. She thought. While she'd been doing that, the other crew had knocked Nell out.

Vinnie started for the next one, when the air around her disappeared again.

Can't breathe. She targeted the one she thought was the Mesmer, found the chain and poured fire power into it.

The Mesmer screamed and clawed at his clothes. Vinnie's vision was turning black, but she felt the moment he pulled his amulet away from his body.

"Clear," she murmured.

The enemy Mesmer dropped.

TK doesn't have much left. Hilda said.

What had seemed like a coordinated attack from Andre's crew erupted into chaos. The one Vinnie thought was the Zee threw a hand out and Hilda doubled over, retching. Andre came barreling toward Vinnie. Will stepped forward and Andre slammed into a solid wall of air. Wind lifted him off the ground and hurled him toward the trees.

The Wisp launched a fireball which slammed into the air shield that Will had held on to even as he threw Andre. The fireball hit the ground and the ground seemed to explode with it. It rushed out and around until they were surrounded by a wall of flames.

"Holy shit," Minka squeaked.

Vinnie tried to ignore them and focused her attention on the Wisp, finding her amulet and beginning to heat it up. She heard laughter from that direction, and her own Wisp ability seemed to bounce back on her, setting her mind on fire. She screamed as her vision disappeared and pain lanced through her body.

TK collapsed. He was already on the ground when gunfire ripped through the air. The guards, at least one of them, was awake.

One of Andre's crew threw his arm in that direction and the gunfire stopped. Vinnie couldn't see that far in the dark, but if they had just knocked the guard out, they weren't working with them.

Forget the amulet. Pull the Wisp's power away from her, through a straw, like we practiced. The voice was Will's.

But Vinnie couldn't pull from the Wisp. She couldn't even feel the Wisp's power.

The fire parted behind them, Will had pushed it aside and fresh air came in through the corridor.

"Out," He shouted.

Vinnie couldn't move, she couldn't breathe. The attacking Zee stepped close to the wall of fire on the other side. He held up both his hands and pain ripped through her body.

She tried to crawl for the escape route, but her body wasn't responding. Will's voice sounded again but she couldn't make out the words. Something fell on the ground in front of her. Vinnie couldn't see what it was through her smoke-blurred vision.

Andre's crew were nothing more than fuzzy shapes beyond the fire. The shapes turned and ran back toward the trees they had come out of, but she couldn't tell if they were all gone.

The fire disappeared — snuffed out as quickly as it had started. Vinnie blinked through the stinging in her eyes and the object in front of her came into focus. Will's hat lay on the ground in front of her, its stitched eyes facing the direction of the trees.

CHAPTER THIRTY-ONE

They were all alive. The Mesmer guard on the bus was not moving, and another Mesmer was moving into range.

Another attack? Vinnie needed to get up, to move. They had to get out of here before the guards woke or the attackers came back. Minka murmured nearby and Shaw responded, her voice sluggish.

"Don't touch him." The voice was firm, but not angry or panicked. Greg. That was the Mesmer she'd felt.

"I'm trying to help, asshole," Minka said.

"He doesn't need your help."

"Fine!"

A cool hand touched the back of Vinnie's neck. "Vinnie," Minka murmured. "Your body can heal. It wants to heal. Your body is smart, it knows what to do."

The burning in her lungs and eyes eased as Minka moved off. It wasn't as much as Jory would have done but whatever she had done helped.

Vinnie pushed herself up on her hands. Shaw was helping Nell up. TK had gotten to his feet and was swaying.

Greg crouched, lifted Will's shoulders to get his hands behind him.

"You shouldn't be here," Will said.

"Neither should you." Greg gave Vinnie a pointed look. "You all need to get out of here before the guards wake."

He and Will stumbled off as Minka moved to Hilda to murmur in her ear just as she had the others.

"Can you stand?" Nell asked Vinnie.

Vinnie pushed onto her knees first and then her feet. Nell went to help Hilda up. When they were all on their feet, they moved as fast as they could toward the bend in the road and the waiting van. Will's SUV was parked beside the van and as they approached Greg rolled down the Window.

"He has something that will help you recover, if you'll stop by the hotel," he said.

They knew how to recover, and Vinnie just wanted to go home. "We're fine."

"Come by the hotel, Vinnie." Greg rolled the window up and pulled out.

Hilda let out a pain-filled breath. "If he has something extra, I'm in."

"I'll drive," Minka said.

Nell made a small grunt of protest, but her shoulders drooped and she headed for the back of the van.

MINKA PULLED the van into the hotel parking lot. They'd gotten stuck in traffic and Greg and Will were already here.

He wants to talk to you alone. Greg's mental voice was light, a whisper in her mind.

"You guys rest," Vinnie said. "I'll go get what whatever it is."

No one argued.

She knocked on the door to the decoy room and waited.

Greg answered, looking extra grim. He didn't seem happy to see her, but when did he ever?

"Is he okay?" Vinnie asked.

Greg's mouth tensed. "He shouldn't have been out there."

Which didn't answer her question. These two were good at not answering questions. "He chose to be there. No one forced him."

"No, no one forced him. They just gave him false hope." Greg stepped back to let her in. "By some miracle, he's unharmed this time."

This time. Apparently, he'd been seriously injured the first time they went after Kara. He said he had an illness but never said what it was. How could she plan around something if she didn't know what it was? She felt like Greg was judging her, blaming her, but maybe she was just blaming herself again.

She walked past him to the secret door.

"He's in the kitchen," Greg said before leaving through the front door.

Vinnie walked past the banks of computers that were humming away with their screens off and toward the light in the kitchen. Will was sitting at a table with his forehead resting on one hand. The other hand was wrapped around a cup of brown sludge. He lifted his head as she entered. His eyes seemed to be sunk into his head, cheekbones hollowed out, lips cracked. Her stomach lurched at the sight of him — he looked half dead.

He got up and turned to open the fridge behind him, pulled out a pitcher of the same sludge that was in his cup, and set it in the middle of the table.

Vinnie picked it up and sniffed, wincing at the smell. "What is it?"

"Something I've concocted for Vasum. It has all the nutrients you should need. It'll be useful for the others, too. I'll give you the recipe," he said. There was something in the tone of his words that Vinnie didn't understand. It sounded almost sad.

"Goodie," she said. "I mean, thanks."

"You're welcome, Lavinia."

She wasn't imagining the sadness in his voice now. Vinnie pulled a chair out from the table and sat. "Tell me."

He tapped the chair in front of him. "It's time for me to move on."

"Move on?" What did that mean? He couldn't mean he was leaving. He'd tried for weeks to get her to work with him, had some big, noble plan he was trying to accomplish, had taken the time and money to completely modify this hotel. He had just risked his life to help them free Jory. He couldn't mean what it sounded like he meant.

"Yes, you know, pack my bags and leave. Don't worry. I'll still pay you for a year. You can save it if you survive the next year or spend it all right away. Whatever."

He was saying exactly what it had sounded like he was saying. The room seemed to close in on her. "You're just going to leave? What about the training? The closing of the anomalies?"

"Right." He put his water bottle down, the movement stiff. "Well. Lavinia. You have attracted a lot of attention. They know where you live. Trouble seems to have found you and you revel in it. Putting myself in dangerous situations will not get the job done, will it? And you can no longer close the anomalies. So not only are you dangerous, you're also useless."

Too much was happening, and her mind couldn't make sense of it. Where did she start with that? Useless. She'd started to trust him, started to rely on him, and he was just going to leave because he thought she couldn't do what he wanted. She should be angry, but she just felt lost.

"We freed Jory, we succeeded," she said.

"And you think that's the end?"

No, she didn't think that was the end. She'd made a deal with Andre and he'd double-crossed them and attacked, and then let them go. Vinnie had no illusions that they'd won that encounter. Andre and his crew had let them go. Again.

Will continued. "You used power that you should not have been able to use, combining various abilities. It was impressive. They were sure to notice. Do you really think they're just going to let you roam free? And even if they did, you will not stop, will you? You and your friends? The White Dragon, hacking, taking over criminal organizations? And Andre Tolemic doesn't exist. Even Kara had a trail. He either lied about his name, or this is much bigger than an anti-government group."

Somehow, she wasn't surprised he couldn't find Andre, but he was wrong about one thing — she didn't want to be doing all of this. She was tired of being afraid, of always looking over her shoulder, wondering who was following her. She wanted to let the burden go, but that wasn't an option. At least she knew what she stood for. He couldn't seem to make up his mind. He chased her, made promises, and the minute it got a little difficult, he was ready to run.

"You think they will want to use me? I guess you would know all about that. You say you want to close the anomalies to make the world safe, but the minute it's a little risky, you want to back out. Just the thought of helping people makes you turn tail and run, and you want me to believe you're trying to save the world? Maybe you should try telling me the truth."

He leaned back. "It doesn't matter. You're useless to me now."

"Because it's dangerous."

"No," he snarled, the calm finally breaking. "Because you

lied to me. You didn't tell me you could no longer pull Wisp power. Without that, you can't do what I need you to do."

She couldn't sense Wisp power anymore, but that didn't mean she couldn't manipulate it. She could move the power in the anomalies. That's how it worked. Sympathetic magic, push the power back using the power that she had. That's how anomalies were closed and she could do that, which was what he said he wanted.

"I can't sense the Wisp power in people anymore, but I can see it in anomalies. If I can push it, I'm sure I could pull it."

He looked to the ceiling as if praying for patience. "That's not how it works."

"Why not? And why can't I sense the power in Wisps anymore?"

"Kara took the power from your friend, all of it? And you took the power from her. You must have been holding it when he died."

She could feel that day almost like it was happening again. So much power inside her, desperately trying to give it back. "I tried to put it back so he wouldn't die."

"You cannot pull Wisp power anymore, because that is how Vasum power works. How it was originally used. Vasum would rip the power away from another Magiera, all the way down to the roots. The Magiera died, and the Vasum had permanent access to the ability. There are old records that say some families would gather all the other six types and sacrifice them as a coming-of-age rite for their children. There is a reason Vasum were hunted to near extinction — they murdered others to gain permanent power. But once you have that power, you no longer have that pathway to use the power of others. That's what Elliot Mustaine was doing. I told you about him and the Vasum girl. He wanted to make a super being that he controlled.

"Why would I need to pull it when I already have it? Closing anomalies is pushing."

"Do you realize how much power you've lost? You could have pulled power from 100 Wisps at once and now you only have the power of one."

And if she were going to close all anomalies, it would take a lot of power. "You thought I could close them all at once? Theoretically, I could have pulled from more Wisps but, how would I have handled that much power going through me? That's insane."

"It can be done. But not by you. Not anymore."

Not by her? She and her friends had already figured out things he didn't know. "I was right. You don't care about saving the world."

"Because you think I should stay here and help with your lost causes rather than finding another Vasum who can do what you can't?"

She was getting tired of people telling her she was too optimistic. "I don't have any lost causes. I fight to win, and I haven't failed yet." If you didn't count failing to save Cerulean, but she had done more than anyone thought she was capable of, and yet he still dismissed her. "And no, you don't want to save the world because if you did, you might trust someone other than yourself. You horde your knowledge like a dragon with his treasure, but the greatest things ever accomplished were not done by one person alone. They were done by teams working together. Many minds are greater than one. You won't accomplish whatever it really is you want to accomplish because you don't really trust anyone else."

He shook his head. "You need to go. I'm tired."

She smacked her empty cup down on the counter and stood. "Thanks for the smoothie. Don't bother giving me the recipe. I can do it better."

Vinnie stalked out of the room, past his stupid computers and his stupid fake decoy room. She slammed open the hotel door, not bothering to close it after herself.

Minka, who had been standing outside the driver's side of the van, surged forward a few steps, before pausing, body tense. "You took so long. I thought something happened. That nutcase seems like he could snap at any time. Did he hurt you?"

Vinnie wilted, her anger evaporating as fast as it had come. "I'm fine. Is everyone okay?"

"Fine," Minka said. "Tired."

"Let's go home. We have a lying snake to meet tomorrow."

CHAPTER THIRTY-TWO

Vinnie stepped out of the shower and grabbed a towel to wrap around herself. She'd slept better than she should have and felt more refreshed than she had any right to feel this morning. Maybe she should have let Will give her the recipe for the smoothie. That was the problem with letting emotions get the better of her. She didn't always do the practical thing.

Her face was a haze of blurred features in the steamy bathroom mirror. As she lifted the towel to clear it off, a memory flashed through her mind — Andre again.

His lips quirked in a way that looked self-deprecating. "I know you have them, because I've seen you use their power. If I don't get them back, people I care about could lose their lives. We know too much for them to let us live."

She jolted back to the present, an echo of a headache faded along with the memory. *Remind me not to let anyone erase my memory again.*

You almost done primping? Came Hilda's reply. *If we're going to get this bastard, we need to get moving.*

Vinnie finished, wiped off the steam, and grabbed a comb to pull through her wet hair. Even the dark circles were gone from under her eyes, making the green irises look more subdued in her pale face. That done, she dressed in her jeans and t-shirt and headed downstairs.

Everyone else was there already. Last night they'd been too tired to discuss what happened, and they still needed to figure out what to do now. They'd made a deal with Andre and then he'd attacked them. It didn't make sense.

TK had stayed at the house last night. She could feel him in the kitchen with Hilda. Shaw and Nell were in the living room. Soft noises that were crying or laughter came from the living room, so Vinnie went that way. Nell had her arms wrapped around Shaw on the loveseat, while Shaw shook. Tears, then. Of course it was.

Nell met her eyes. "Minka broke up with her."

That hadn't been what Vinnie expected. Minka had been helpful last night, taking care of all of them.

"She said she couldn't handle the danger," Shaw said. "We were supposed to go to the finale of the Warrior games today. We were supposed to be heroes together."

Vinnie softened. It wasn't fair of her to expect Minka, who barely knew them, to stay around when they had just risked their lives, and were still in trouble. Not like Will, who had a better idea of what he was getting into when he said he'd help.

"The finale is today," Vinnie said. With everything that was happening, she'd forgotten. That meant Conor might leave soon, too, if Andre was true to his word and the murder charges were dropped. Without a murder investigation, there would be no reason for Conor to stay. She supposed they could keep texting and talking to each other, but there was no future for them. There never had been.

"Don't you start crying too," Nell said.

Shaw lifted her head and swiped at the moisture on her face. Before Vinnie had time to process what was happening, Shaw was hugging her.

Vinnie hugged back. The top of her head only came to Shaw's shoulder, and Vinnie leaned into her, relaxing for a moment. She didn't dare let the pain in or it would become a tidal wave and she had too much to do.

"You up for kicking some ass?" she asked Shaw.

Shaw squeezed and let go. "Always."

"We may not get to kick any ass." Hilda had come out of the kitchen and was halfway down the hall to the living room, with TK behind her. "The crystal and the bracelet are gone."

Nell launched to her feet. "How can they be gone?"

Vinnie started down the hall. She could feel Shaw and Nell behind her as they strode into the kitchen. The cabinet doors under the sink were open. They'd hidden the items in the hole in the cabinet's floor around the drain pipes. Vinnie slid her phone out of her pocket and turned the flashlight on as she crouched in front of the cabinet. Not that she doubted Hilda, she just needed to see for herself.

The hole under the floor was empty. She scooted out of the way so Nell and Shaw could look.

"Gone," Vinnie said. "After all that, they just break into our house and take them? What was the point of any of it?"

Hilda had paused in the doorway. "Power play? They wanted to see if we'd do it, and now they have something on us."

"It's not in the news," Nell said. "That the bus was stopped and prisoners escaped."

"What difference does that make?" Hilda snapped. "The authorities still know it happened. They've just kept it quiet."

"But why?" Vinnie wanted to scream, but her voice was calm. "They told us how to get Jory out, but then attacked. They didn't go after Jory, Kiernan and Amanda. They had us again. And didn't follow through again. Then, at some point, broke into our house, and somehow found the objects and took them."

"I'm not sensing their power signatures in the house," TK said. "There's nothing here but us."

Hilda crossed her arms and glared at the cabinets. "If they can block us from using power on them, maybe they can hide their signatures."

The answer was logical, but it didn't feel right. "The house doesn't look like it was broken into, but when they broke into my apartment, the door was kicked in."

"The house has an older lock," Nell said. "Maybe it's easier to pick? Camera!" She pulled out her phone and opened the app that connected to the camera on the front door. She scrolled through, shaking her head. "Nothing but Minka leaving at five in the morning."

Shaw sniffed. "But what do we *do*? Vinnie is supposed to meet them in an hour. They said we had to give them this stuff or bad things will happen."

"We're alive," TK said. "They've got what they wanted. We held up our end of the bargain. We should leave it alone."

"No." Hilda shook her head. "They think they can mess with us. I don't want to be constantly looking over my shoulder. We have to end this on our terms."

"They got what they wanted," TK repeated. "They won't show up at any planned meeting. We have no way to find them, just a fake name."

"We have the earring he gave me." Vinnie stood and brushed herself off. "If he doesn't show up, maybe we can use it to find him. We need answers. If we don't know why, we can't be sure they're done with us. And they broke into our house when we already had an agreement."

Nell scrubbed her face with her hands. "This is insane. We can't suddenly beat them in a fight just because we want it more."

The memory of the man who called himself Andre saying people he cared about would die came to her again. He'd seemed sincere and had no reason to lie about that since he thought she wouldn't remember. She could only hope he'd show up and could be convinced to leave them alone now that he had what he wanted.

"Maybe we won't have to," Vinnie said.

TEN MINUTES past the meeting time and Andre hadn't shown up. He'd said she'd chosen the location on the voice recording he'd left. Considering the location, she had no reason to doubt that was true.

She'd chosen the park where she'd first met Cerulean — where he'd painted her a picture to keep her warm. The morning was chilly, but Vinnie felt warmth at her back. Back when Cer had painted for her, she'd thought she was imagining the warmth that emanated from the wall, but after TK's story about what they'd done, she wasn't sure.

Her life was falling apart, chunks and pieces just kept falling away, and maybe when all was said and done, she'd end up right back where she started — on a bench alone in the rain, cold. This time, Cerulean wouldn't come to warm her up because he was dead. Cer was gone, and now Jory was gone and Will — why had she let herself trust Will, to start to depend on him?

She took a sip of her sweet tea, expecting Hilda to be in her head at any moment, saying they were wasting their time. Her friends were nearby, but not so close that it would be obvious to Andre and his crew. Probably. Maybe Andre letting her choose the location had been a clue that he had no intention of keeping his end of the bargain.

Vinnie ran her thumb along the green crystal of the earring Andre had used to track her. He wouldn't need to keep tracking her, since he already had what he wanted. She should smash the thing, grind it under a rock.

She closed her fist around the crystal just as the soft whisper of feet approached. The person approaching had an echo of Stone power so light it could be coming from someone normal.

A shadow fell over her. "Vinnie?"

And there he was, wearing his black hoodie, looking like a normal human being instead of a backstabbing liar.

"Think of the devil," she said.

"I'm flattered that someone I only met twice would think of me at all." His eyes searched hers.

That's right. As far as he knew, she thought they'd only met twice. She might have recognized his voice on the recording, but as he said, they'd only met twice.

"It's not every day someone asks me to break the law for them."

He sat beside her on the bench. "You remember."

"I never forget a book."

Something flashed across his face that looked like disappointment. "Right. A book."

She couldn't really tell him off as long as she wasn't supposed to know he betrayed her. Playing games would only slow this down. "And your voice was on a memo on my phone."

His lips quirked. "I'm flattered that you recognize my voice after only meeting me twice."

Bastard. Is he flirting?

"You're easily flattered," Vinnie said. *I don't think so. You can hear that?*

His words are an echo in your thoughts.

"And you're lying about something," he said.

Vinnie sat up straighter and looked around. "Is your Mesmer here?"

"I don't need a Mesmer to know you're lying."

He was Stone. Nell said she needed to know the person to know if they were telling the truth, but the abilities varied even within types. "You don't know me well enough to know when I'm lying."

"I know you better than you think." His voice was soft, almost intimate. Vinnie scooted a little farther away and amusement danced in his eyes. "I'm sorry. I didn't mean to make you uncomfortable."

Maybe he didn't mean to, but it didn't seem to bother him much. Was she forgetting something about that night that would make him act overly familiar? The thought made her feel a little queasy. "No, you just meant to lie to me and attack me and my friends."

"I haven't lied to you. Your friends have escaped and the charges against Conor will be dropped as soon as I have the objects and Kara."

"You're forgetting the part where you said no further harm would come to us."

He looked her up and down. "You don't look hurt."

Vinnie's jaw clenched. "Maybe you should stop playing games and be straight with me if you want something. Why are you even here? You told us to attack the bus and then you attack us. You attacked us at a construction site. You attack me on my way home from work. You erased my memory and yet you show up here where I can see your face. What do you want?"

"I was very clear about what I wanted on the recording."

He already had the objects, so there was only one thing left. "Kara. What, you didn't have some alternate plan to get her, too?"

"I always have a back-up plan. Unfortunately, when you are in the picture, they seem to fail. We put trackers on your prison friends. They removed them. And, just to keep the record straight, you attacked my team after you left work that night. Not the other way around."

"That's..." Vinnie frowned. They'd been following her. She'd been scared, but had they actually attacked her? "Two Twisted following me on a dark street in the middle of the night while I was alone felt like an attack."

"At least we had confirmation that you had the power objects, or so we thought. But we didn't, did we? How did you know they were Twisted?"

You have another power object.

It was as good a lie as any. "I have another power object."

Andre gave her a flat look. "Even if I didn't know you were lying to me, we checked last night. You were combining powers, but you didn't have a power object on you."

She stared at him for a moment, trying to sort through the tangled webs of his schemes. After the fire, one of his team had done something that caused her pain. It hadn't been as intense as when Kara was trying to steal her power, but the feeling was similar. They'd been trying to find another power object, or maybe figure out how she was doing what she did. Vinnie wasn't going to tell him how she knew they were Twisted, or how she used different powers. Time to deflect, again.

"That's how you found the objects in our house? You can detect them."

"We wouldn't need to go into your house to know that you didn't have our objects there."

"You took them." The words were out of her mouth

before her mind caught up. There hadn't been anyone on their home surveillance, and TK didn't detect anyone who shouldn't have been there, but who else would have taken them?

"They weren't there. Our Ferr is familiar with them. He can detect the ones we lost from a distance. We didn't need to break into your house."

He had to be lying.

You don't think he's lying.

"Did you break into my apartment?" she asked.

"No. You're saying you don't have them anymore?"

"Someone took them."

Andre clenched his fist and tapped it on the bench. It was the only outward sign of his frustration. "But you know where Kara is."

Sort of, but if she answered that, then he'd know that they didn't have anything. Nothing that they'd agreed to exchange. Jory was out. He was safe, but the rest of them?

"We're on the same side, Vinnie."

"I've heard that one before."

"Fine," he said. "You've heard this one before, too. Give us the objects and Kara, and no further harm will come to you or the people you care about."

Something in her said he was bluffing. Vinnie probed the thought, and more of the puzzle clicked into place. "As you so kindly pointed out earlier. No harm has come to me or any of my friends at your hands. I think you'll also keep up your end of the bargain where it comes to Conor, since we've done our best, and you know he's innocent. You're not with Hanna's Soldiers, are you? You're USSF." Kara had been released for special projects and she had objects that Andre had just said he'd lost. There were actual Twisted working for the USSF. Vinnie almost couldn't process that. It was like someone had told her the sky was green. "That's why the bus hijacking didn't make the news. How you so easily set up Conor." Wait.. had he set up Conor? A feeling she couldn't name said he hadn't. Was he the USSF agent visiting Kiernan in prison? "And I'm guessing you're also the reason a dangerous Ferr got out of prison to go off and murder people. Kara was working with you, wasn't she? That's how she got the power objects. Imagine the uproar if it got out that they are letting a Twisted convicted of murder onto national security teams. Or on national security teams at all. That's why people are in danger if you can't get them back. I don't think you actually want to hurt anyone."

His gaze had grown stony during her speech and the man looking at her now looked a lot more dangerous than she had ever seen him.

Should have thought that one through. Hilda sounded amused.

Thanks, helpful.

"I think you underestimate what I'm willing to do to protect my people," Andre said.

"Maybe I did, but that doesn't bring back the objects or get you closer to Kara."

"You really weren't working for her. How did you lie to me about knowing where she was? I didn't sense you were being dishonest."

She hadn't really lied if she'd told him she knew where Kara was, she just couldn't lead him to her. Her earlier certainty that he would still hold up his end of the bargain was slipping away.

"I know where she went. Kara is dead," she said. "I killed her. Pushed her through an anomaly and closed it."

To her surprise, some of the tension seemed to leave his body. "An anomaly she opened?"

"Yes."

"If we can find the body, that would be even better.

Maybe we can figure out what her patterns were. She must have been frequenting someplace remote if the body didn't turn up yet. Where was the one you pushed her through? The house. It had to be the house. Which means the dragon was from this world." The last part came out low, musing. "Wait. You closed it? You can use more than one power and you closed an anomaly, but you don't have an object."

His questions should concern her, but her mind had caught on his belief that Kara's body would be in this universe. Her thoughts shifted to Minka, standing at the top of the basement steps afraid someone bad would come through Harry. Someone she was afraid of. Minka had known where the objects were, and she was afraid for her brother's life. Why would she be afraid for his life? Maybe he was being threatened by someone who could open anomalies with a silver bracelet.

Then an older memory of Conor saying Maddie, the girl Kara had killed, had come to the games with another girl. He'd sent her the photo. Vinnie pulled her phone out of her pocket, almost dropping it because her fingers had gone numb. She opened her email and scrolled until she found the email. On one side of Conor was Maddie, smiling at the camera. On the other was a sullen blond girl. Minka.

Holy shit. Hilda's mental voice was soft.

"Vinnie?" Andre said. "I won't try to force you to tell me your secrets. I just need to find Kara. Please."

"You could have just asked me instead of going through all of this."

"I thought you were working with her."

"Like you did?"

He sat back down on the bench, moving carefully as if he was trying to hide fatigue. "They told me she was stable. I thought we would be able to help her get past whatever had made her so angry, and she would be an asset to the team. I was wrong. The world is better off without her. No harm will come to you over this. Do you know where the body is?"

TK says 'roll the dice.' He's after her just like we are.

They were after Kara. Which meant that Hilda had come to the same conclusion that Vinnie had just come to.

"I'll tell you if you can answer something for me," Vinnie said. "Why would someone steal a power object that had been sliced in half?"

"To repair it, maybe. If it still had some power, it would be easier to repair than create a new one. It would still take a lot of juice."

"By a lot of juice, you mean Twisted. People died trying to create your amulets." She was stalling. The answer she was looking for was there, she just needed to grasp it. "A lot of juice. Like six Twisted crews all in one place?"

"Definitely, but getting that many who were cohesive enough to concentrate their power—"

"Like the Warrior Games crews?" Vinnie asked. The Warrior Games finale might be the only place that many Twisted could be guaranteed to be there, outside of a reha-bilitation camp or prison. During the games, there were usually only two crews on the field at a time, but they brought them all out for the finale.

His mouth opened. That was a yes.

Roll the dice. "I don't think I killed her. I thought the anomaly would send her to another world and she would die there. But someone who might have been working with her was in our house last night. The crystal is missing. If she has the crystal, she knows the crews, she might try to repair it there."

"That's crazy, even for Kara. She'd never be able to pull that off."

"How determined would she be to fix the crystal if she had it?"

"We'll check it out. What else have we got to lose? I'll be in touch."

Andre hadn't made it to the end of the park before Shaw appeared around the corner. Vinnie rose to meet her. When Shaw reached Vinnie, she grabbed her hand.

"Minka broke up with me to save me. That woman has her. We have to save her."

CHAPTER THIRTY-THREE

"Tell me again why you think a government trained Twisted crew, who beat our asses twice, can't handle this?" TK drummed his fingers on the steering wheel of his car.

"She has MINKA." Shaw pushed herself out of the back of the car, slammed the door behind her, and started for the stadium.

The question had been meant for Vinnie. "They haven't caught Kara yet," she said. "Conor says they have the staging area locked down. It's the only place the crews would have been in one place other than the open arena. I'm sure they can handle it, but..." Something was still bothering her. Something they'd missed.

TK turned in his seat to look at Hilda.

Hilda shrugged one shoulder. "If Kara is alive, she has Minka, who is one of us. You think those assholes are going to care if she gets hurt?" She got out.

By the time Nell and Vinnie and TK got out, Hilda and Shaw were halfway to the stadium.

"Minka, who stole from us and who probably helped

Kara target the other girl, and is probably helping her now," TK said to Nell and Vinnie.

Nell answered, "She broke up with Shaw rather than bringing her here. You saw how terrified Minka was that someone would come through Harry. If Vinnie's right, she's been manipulated and is a victim here, too. Kara could have been manipulating her two ways, through Ferr power and threatening her brother."

Vinnie hoped she was wrong, and Minka wasn't here. She hoped she was wrong that Kara was going to attack the crews to repair her stupid crystal. Would Kara kill the crews to get her power back? She didn't doubt that. What she struggled with was the belief that Kara was alive. She'd been so relieved Kara was dead.

The evidence fits. If you're wrong, then the worst that happens is we get to watch the Warrior Games Finale.

Do you really think she'd risk the crowds?

They'd come to a small door near the side of the stadium. Vinnie sent a quick text and they waited.

"She's power crazy," Hilda answered. "She might risk it."

Do you really think Minka is worth saving if she helped Kara kill Maddie?

You've felt Kara's compulsions. You tell me.

It wasn't that simple. Minka was afraid, yes, but Vinnie had seen the loyalty Kara could inspire, even without using her Ferr power. The promise of freedom could make people do horrible things. But Shaw was not stupid either. She could read emotions and surely would have known if Minka had been faking.

"Kara may be crazy, but she's not stupid," TK said. "We're talking about publicly killing Twisted crews. She got away with causing an explosion. If she's here, she'll have an out. With the USSF waiting for her, maybe she'll back down."

The door opened and Conor looked them over. They

were in ordinary, nondescript clothes with ski masks rolled on the top of their heads to look like hats. "I'm not going to get arrested again, am I?"

"Are you planning on doing something illegal?" Hilda asked as she pushed past him into the stadium.

"No ma'am," he replied. "Not planning on it, but if it's necessary, then I will. Just tell me what you need."

"How did you even get us in?" Nell said. "I thought you weren't allowed anywhere near the games."

He held up a card with Lou's picture on it. He'd told Vinnie Lou would help, and she'd doubted him again and was wrong. Maybe she just needed to admit that she didn't understand people.

He led them down a narrow corridor toward the field. " You'll go in through the service doors. That should be unobtrusive enough. Do you need to stick together?"

"Within a quarter of the stadium," Hilda said.

"We can stagger it, then. Less noticeable if one person is coming out at a time. Go out the doors and then to the steps that lead into the stands. Left, then right," Conor said.

TK went through the doors first. After two minutes, Nell went, and they continued until Vinnie was alone with Conor in the corridor.

"Do you really think she's out there?" he asked. "That she would risk capture just to get a trinket back? You'd think it would be easier to steal another one."

"She's smart," Vinnie said. "She's gotten away with a lot already and I get the impression these objects are pretty powerful and rare, not so easy to get another one."

Unless you meet someone from another world who just hands it to you the way Shaw's dragon had.

"She caused an explosion. That was also pretty public, and she got away with it by making it look like it was the crews," he said.

The more others talked about it, the more plausible it seemed to Vinnie that Kara could pull this off. She could take power from the Twisted crews in front of everyone and get away with it, and Andre and his crew in the staging area wouldn't be able to stop her.

"How can we stop her when we don't know what she'll do?" she said.

"If anyone can, it's you," he squeezed her arm. "Be careful."

Vinnie tore her eyes away and tried to swallow her fear. She'd been lying to herself as much as anyone when she'd said she could succeed because she hadn't failed yet. She'd failed to stop a fully trained crew who knocked her and her friends out. Her defeat of Kara before felt like pure, dumb luck. Dumb being the keyword, because she hadn't even questioned how Kara's portals worked. She'd assumed they were just like the regular anomalies and that they were safe.

Conor pulled the door open for her, and she stepped into the stadium.

The roar of the crowd washed over her. Inside the corridor it had sounded like a heavy buzz, but out here it was dynamic, alive, and she was pinned like a bug against a flat, blank wall. Exposed. Her instincts screamed at her to dive back through the door. Standing here, she was a perfect target.

Vinnie ignored the panicky feeling. No one would be paying attention to the service entrances. No one would notice her. She walked the few brief steps to the right and up the steps into the bleachers.

Andre was betting on Kara attacking just as the crews arrived at the stadium, and he knew her better than Vinnie did since he had worked with her. That feeling of missing something hit her again. She couldn't force the thought to surface. All she could do was pay attention and hope that whatever she needed to know, she'd know it.

Hope is not a strategy.

You've got something better? Maybe you can read my mind and figure out what I know that I don't know.

I can only know what you or I know, and what I know is when this is over and they come after us, you guys need to run, hide.

They'd been over this before. They weren't going to leave Hilda behind. *People need to stop telling me to run. It's getting old. Stick with the plan.*

If Kara wasn't attacking at the entry point, she would be in the crowds, unless someone else got her in and she was lurking in one of the other entry ways.

Her best point of attack might be just as all the crews arrived at the stadium, but that would be tricky. How was she going to do this? TK said that for the strongest positive feelings in the paintings, it took a full crew coordinating, but Cerulean had done small amounts by himself. The Wisp provided the push. The trick was, how was Kara, a Ferr, going to coordinate the Twisted crews in order to repair a crystal?

Vinnie leaned against the railing and carefully opened up her ability, which she'd closed off to keep from being overwhelmed. She'd been practicing selective filtering, but it wasn't an easy skill. Shielding herself from any energy from one direction was easier, but clunky. It would work well enough in this situation. She kept her shield in place for any power coming from the stadium, which would cover most of the crew's power.

Since she couldn't distinguish Kara's ability from any others, she was just looking for a strong Ferr. If she found one, TK could tell them if it was Kara.

A blast of fanfare came on over the loudspeakers to kick off the pregame show. This was where all the Twisted crews would be in the stadium. Even though only two teams made it to the finale, all the teams and their crews would come out for a pregame play, where they had a mock tournament.

This would be the best time for Kara to strike.

Isn't it a little early for them to start? She thought at Hilda.

At least fifteen minutes. What are they doing? she paused, then said, *Maybe the USSF is trying to throw her off, get the crews out before she's ready. TK hasn't found anything. You?*

Not yet. Vinnie shifted her senses farther out. The other side of the stadium would be tricky to search without opening herself up to the power on the field.

The announcer came on and talked about the event. The fence across the main stadium opening was pulled back and people dressed as superheroes ran onto the field.

Not superheroes, Villains.

The crowds booed as the Twisted crews waved and made their way around the field. Their costumes were in various colors to signify their type, just like the last games Vinnie had come to, but that time the crowds had cheered.

Vinnie tuned out the noise and spectacle and continued her search. She was halfway done with the other side as the Warrior games teams came onto the field.

How long does the show last? she asked Hilda.

Varies, but the shortest was 30 minutes.

Thirty minutes was a lot of time for Kara to work with, and not much time for them to find her and try to stop her. Maybe she really was wrong, inventing demons in her head, and nothing would happen.

The feeling of Ferr power touched her senses and Vinnie leaned into it. There, perpendicular to her location.

Ferr. She sent an image of the direction of the energy signature to Hilda, who would pass it to TK.

After what seemed like only a moment, Hilda replied. *Not her.*

Vinnie continued searching. She was getting to the edge

of what she could reach without taking down her shield. When she reached the limits, she pulled back and braced herself to try a filter. Soothing feelings washed over her from Shaw and her anxiety vanished. She could do this.

Vinnie dropped her shield.

The rush of power hit her just as a boom sounded from the stadium roof. Her body reflexively ducked along with the rest of the crowd, but the combination of power and sound sent her all the way to the ground.

"Are you all right?" The man who had been standing next to her at the railing asked. He reached out his hand to her just as another boom sounded. He flinched, turning away from her.

A dark shadow moved across the semi-transparent panels of the dome. The shadow expanded as it drew closer to the dome again. The shape became more distinct, and a shiver of awe went through Vinnie's body.

Dragon.

Her mind denied the thought. There couldn't be another dragon, but the shape of the shadow was unmistakable.

"Dragon," the man beside her whispered. He pulled his phone out and pointed it at the roof.

The shadow on the roof grew smaller again as the dragon lifted and came back down. The thud boomed through the stadium, and then everything went still, as if the crowd was holding its breath, while the dragon wasn't moving. The scratching sound that came next seemed almost silent compared to the booms.

Get ready, Hilda said.

Ready? Ready how? They'd expected to fight a human Ferr, not a dragon.

The dragon's forelimbs moved against the roof and then the roof screeched as a panel was ripped away. As the panel came free, a large, scaly, white hand reached through the opening, grasped another panel, and pulled it off.

The white dragon poked its head through the hole. So much for Kara trying to hide what she was doing. There was stunned silence for a moment, and then people started screaming and pointing. Cell phones pointed at the dragon as it continued to pull panels off the roof.

Bitch. She had to make herself white. The white dragon was our thing.

Hilda's thought shook Vinnie out of her shock. "You think it's her?"

"Who?" the man standing beside her asked.

She'd spoken out loud. Before she could answer, the dragon dropped through the hole. Its wings snapped out and after an awkward moment, it flew, soaring around the stadium.

"Ooos" and "Ohhhs" came from the crowd. Some chunks of people began pushing their way toward the aisles, but others just stared in awe.

"Get out of here. Run." Vinnie's voice was weak.

"You first," the man beside her said.

The dragon swooped low over a section of the crowd, who screamed and ducked.

The announcer came on, telling everyone to remain calm and stay in their seats. The bottom five rows were to begin evacuating, and everyone else should wait. He said there was no danger, and then the dragon opened its jaw and spewed fire into the crowd.

The crowd screamed, and the man beside Vinnie scooted around her, heading for the nearest exit. People began pushing into her, rushing to get to out. She was going to get trampled if she stayed here. She moved with the flow of people, fighting to stay close to the railing. When she got to the stairs that led to the arena floor, she slipped out of the crowd, almost stumbling as someone bumped her.

Vinnie's feet hit the stadium floor, and she pulled the ski mask over her face.

"How do we stop it?" Vinnie said out loud. She needed to focus. *How do we stop it?*

Can you pull the power from it?

That would be one way to stop it. If she stole the power making Kara a dragon, she would no longer be a dragon. The dragon swooped again, spewing fire. None of the fire seemed to actually touch the crowd. Vinnie focused her power on the dragon. The powers were all woven together so tightly she couldn't distinguish them.

I'm not sure I can pull it all when it's woven together like that. Let me see if I can pick it apart.

Maybe before she kills someone?

Vinnie's eyes flicked over the crowd. Hadn't it burned some people already?

"Don't hurt her," Shaw said beside her.

Vinnie barely heard her. She focused on the dragon, trying to feel the threads of individual power.

"Vinnie, it's not Kara. It's Minka." Shaw's soft words startled Vinnie and broke her concentration.

Shit. Hilda thought. *She's right, it's Minka.*

"Don't let them hurt her," Shaw said. "It's tearing her apart."

Vinnie remembered the feeling of being ripped apart when she was a dragon. Andre probably wouldn't care if he killed Minka. Did Vinnie? Seeing that picture of Minka and Maddie had knocked the wind out of her. She may have been coerced, and Vinnie knew how hard it was to break Kara's compulsion. Had she even tried? Vinnie pushed the thoughts away. She was making excuses. It would be easier to stop Minka if she didn't care, but that didn't make it right.

Hilda came up beside her and Vinnie could feel TK and Nell moving toward them. The dragon let out another gout of fire over the crowd.

"It's going over their heads," Vinnie said. "She's trying not to hit them."

"Trying or not, she's going to kill people," Hilda said.

"I can't pull the power from her unless it's disrupted. Even if I did, the fall might kill her. Maybe we can find another way."

A figure in black combat gear ran toward the Twisted crews. The professionals. One of the Warrior games crews collapsed.

Vinnie felt Nell's arrival but kept her eyes on what was happening on the field.

"Is that the USSF?" Nell asked. "What are they doing?"

More people dressed in the same combat gear were running onto the field, along with stadium security. Stadium security headed for the Twisted crews just as another crew collapsed.

Vinnie shifted her vision so she could see the power again. Her vision lit up with white and she winced and squeezed her eyes shut. The image was burned into her brain. Blinding white power flowing across the field from the crews up into the stands.

She tried to push the image at Hilda. *The power from the crews is flowing into the crowd. The dragon is a distraction.*

"We still have to stop the dragon," Hilda said aloud.

"What's happening?" TK asked from the other side of Vinnie.

Vinnie pointed in the direction the power was flowing. "Kara must be over there pulling power from the crews while Minka distracts everyone with her dragon act."

A thud sounded from the stadium roof. Perched on the edge of the hole was a black dragon. As they watched, the black dragon shifted forward and dropped into the stadium.

"Well, shit," Hilda said.

They didn't even know how to stop the first one, and now there were two. "Who is this?" Vinnie asked.

"I can't tell."

TK shook his head. "The energy is familiar, and I feel like I should know, but it's like an echo."

How would people who were not Vasum build up the power to transform into a dragon? A bracelet was the only way Vinnie knew, and there were two bracelets. If the first was Minka, then the second was Kara, or Minka's brother? But didn't Kara need the bracelet to pull the power from the crews to repair her crystals? Vinnie needed to know more about how the objects worked, but she was out of time to figure it out.

The black dragon's wings snapped out as its feet touched the stadium floor. It used the momentum to launch itself back up, and with a few hard snaps of its wings, it barreled into the white dragon. They both crashed into the field and skidded, leaving a gouge in the turf.

Shaw gasped and then she was charging across the field toward the dragons.

"Shaw, stop!" Nell shifted forward, preparing to chase Shaw, but she paused, head swinging back toward the others, indecision on her face for a moment before she turned and ran toward the dragons.

"The energy is flowing toward Jory," TK said. "Vinnie and I will go try to stop it at the source."

He was already moving by the time Vinnie registered what he said and sent her awareness in the direction of the flow. "Jory is here."

Hilda's whole body seemed to clench. "I'll try to connect with the crews and to stop the flow from this side."

Vinnie nodded and took off after TK, catching up with him halfway around the field.

"They're completely frozen. It's creepy," he said, gesturing at the Twisted crew nearest them.

The crews that hadn't collapsed were all standing frozen. One of the agents in black was standing in front of one of them. At least they weren't writhing in agony the way Cer had when Kara had stolen the power from him. Or the way Vinnie had. *Dragon!*

Vinnie and TK threw themselves to the ground as a wall of flame erupted from Minka's jaw right above their heads. The black dragon crashed into her again. Splatters of blood rained on them.

The black dragon had landed on top of Minka, but Minka was bigger and she flipped the black over and began tearing at it with her claws.

Minka paused in her slashing and her head swiveled to Shaw, who had come up behind her. She lifted her tail and used it to shove Shaw to the ground. As she turned back toward the black dragon, Nell wrapped her arms around the tail and began pulling, dragging her off the other dragon.

"They've got this. We need to stop the source." TK was moving again, and Vinnie followed.

They found another stairway leading into the stands and made their way up. Vinnie no longer had to stretch her senses to feel Jory.

As they crested the top of the stairs, she saw him standing midway up the stadium. Jory stood with no one around him, staring off onto the field.

Vinnie broke into a run, sprinting up the stairs to reach him.

"Vinnie wait! We don't—" TK said.

Jory was almost ten rows up from the bottom. He didn't turn as she approached.

"Jory!"

He didn't respond, just continued staring out across the field. Kara must have control of his mind. If she wanted more evidence that she was right, that Kara was out there, it was in Jory's blank-eyed stare.

His head didn't turn even when she stood right next to him.

"Jory?"

"I'm just another distraction so she can get away," he said in a monotone voice.

"Kara isn't here," TK said. "I've searched the entire stadium."

"Not Kara." Jory gasped, and his face scrunched up. Sweat broke out on his forehead and he opened his mouth to say something else, but the words wouldn't come out of his mouth.

"The Mesmer from the prison bus," TK said. "She's here."

Amanda. What did that mean? Was Kara behind this, or had Amanda taken over?

Jory dropped to his knees.

TK dropped down beside him and grabbed his arm. "I can break him out of this. Go get her."

A Mesmer. She was looking for a Mesmer, not a Ferr. Vinnie spun, taking in what was left of the crowds. Out on the field, the two dragons crashed to the ground again, spatters of blood landing next to them as they rolled. The black came up on top, but instead of continuing to attack, it launched itself back up in the air. Minka tried to follow, but her body wouldn't lift.

The black dragon disappeared through the hole in the ceiling.

I don't think the black dragon is coming back. It was in bad shape, Hilda said. *I'm holding Minka, but I haven't got much left. Nell is out. Shaw is almost out.*

Vinnie needed to find Amanda. If she could stop her, then maybe Minka would stop. She moved away from Jory and TK, back to the center walkway, braced herself and shifted her vision again. If she could see where the power was flowing, she'd have an idea where to start.

Most of the power was gone from the field. The Twisted crews were collapsed, but there seemed to still be sparks of power in them. Not dead. Hopefully not dead. The power was lessened enough that she could open her senses wide without worrying that she'd be overwhelmed. She spread her awareness across the stadium, but the only strong Mesmers were on the stadium floor. Vinnie pushed out farther, as far as she could, trying to find Amanda, and there, beyond the bounds of the parking lot, was a Mesmer with enough power to be Amanda.

Too far. She was too far away. Even if Vinnie ran out to the parking lot and got in a car, she couldn't catch her, but maybe Andre's people could. Black- clad bodies were littered on the field along with the Twisted crews, but some were still on their feet.

Amanda is heading west from the stadium. Can Andre's crew catch her? She asked Hilda, who had the best chance of getting through to Andre.

Minka was back in the air continuing her rampage, seemingly oblivious that she was abandoned, but maybe that's exactly what she'd been programmed to do.

The USSF is on it. They'll try to catch Amanda. Vinnie, you're going to have to pull the power out of Minka. Her mind is a mess of rage and pain. She is going to kill people.

There was no one else to help the people trapped in the stadium with an enraged dragon.

Power flowed around Minka, encasing her dragon form in the white light of the combined abilities. The power seemed to be concentrated around her right foreleg. A bracelet, just as she had suspected. As she watched, the white power rippled with orange.

Wisp power. If she could see the Wisp power, she could push it out of Minka, the way she did an anomaly. Vinnie gave it an experimental nudge.

Minka roared and her wings snapped wide slowing her momentum. She banked right, wheeling her body around midair. Time seemed to slow as Minka regained her speed, flying straight at Vinnie.

Cold, hard fear pooled in Vinnie's abdomen. She felt for power, pulled a little of each one from her friends, and felt the resonance with the bracelet on Minka's wrist. She could push the Wisp power out, which would destabilize the rest enough for her to pull, but the fall would probably kill Minka.

Use the Mesmer power to catch her. Hilda said.

I don't have the skill, I don't know how.

Then give me the power.

It's not natural power, it will kill you.

Minka was almost on top of her. Vinnie was out of time. Orange flashed through the power again and Vinnie pushed.

I'll be fine. Vinnie, you have to trust me.

Was saving Minka worth Hilda's life? Vinnie pulled all the other powers into her. There was a pop, and the dragon became Minka again, in midair. She fell.

Dammit, Vinnie trust me!

The unnatural power tore through Vinnie like tiny shards, she pushed it out of her, all except the Mesmer power. She twined the Mesmer and Wisp power and pushed at Hilda.

Pale yellow power surrounded Minka and descended. When the Mesmer power hit the ground, Minka slowed. She floated down, landing softly in the grass of the field.

A wave of dizziness washed over Vinnie. Jory and TK had

come up beside her and Jory steadied her with a hand to her elbow.

"Get out of here before they catch you again," she said to Jory, and started down the steps. Hilda had collapsed on the field not too far from Minka. She was alive. That was all Vinnie knew.

CHAPTER THIRTY-FOUR

Vinnie still had a spark of Wisp energy. She pushed it to her legs to help carry her down the steps to the stadium floor faster.

Before her feet hit the turf, Shaw was up, stumbling across the field to where Minka lay. Some of the Twisted crew on the ground stirred. Not dead. They weren't all dead. Vinnie's legs went weak with relief and she almost stumbled as she continued to the place where Hilda had fallen.

Nell got there first.

I'm fine. Hilda said. *Help Minka.*

Vinnie paused just as Shaw reached Minka. Shaw tugged desperately at the jacket she was wearing, trying to get it off. When the sleeves finally slid off her arms, she crouched, draping the jacket over Minka.

"What did you do, what did you do?" Shaw sobbed.

Vinnie covered the last few feet.

Minka jerked and shuddered on the ground. Her mouth parted as if in a gasp, tears poured from her eyes, containing every color of the rainbow as if the residual traces of power were pouring out with the tears. Her head rolled toward Vinnie.

"Don't—" Minka gasped, and coughed, blood splattering out of her mouth. "Don't hate me."

"I could never hate you," Shaw said.

Vinnie crouched next to Shaw, stomach clenching with pain. This was too familiar. This field was more manicured than the one Cerulean died on but it was another field, and another person Kara had manipulated.

Does Andre have a Zee with him? We need a healer.

Nell and Hilda were coming toward them slowly with Hilda leaning heavily on Nell. They paused and Hilda's face scrunched.

He does. The thought was weak, as if Hilda was miles away instead of a quarter of the way across a football field.

"Why?" Shaw wailed.

"Me," Minka said. "Me or everyone. Kill them, she'd kill them all."

TK arrived at the same time as two people in combat gear. Vinnie recognized Andre's stance, even though his face was covered. With him was a woman who approached Minka and kneeled beside her.

She put her hands on Minka. "It's like her body tried to destroy itself. I'm not a healer, I don't even know what to do with this."

"Vinnie," Shaw said, eyes begging.

Vinnie could use the power. She could do some basic things to heal, but so could the Zee in front of her. None of that would be enough to save Minka.

"Can someone see if any of the Zee in the crews know how to heal?" Vinnie said.

"I'll do it," the Zee from Andre's crew said.

"Vinnie," Shaw wailed.

"I'll try," Vinnie said. Minka was Zee herself, but she had almost nothing left, so Vinnie pulled from the Zee who had gone to look for help. "Can you help me, Minka?"

As if in response, Minka's body convulsed.

"Hold on," Vinnie said. She could try to push the power directly, like she had with Hilda, but she wasn't sure what that would do. Minka wasn't coherent enough to control it. She needed to use the ability like a Zee would. Vinnie imagined the power in her body becoming light and sent it into Minka. "Can you feel the power? We're going to make light. Feel the power turn into light. Your body knows how to heal. You can heal."

"She's not going to survive," Andre said. "Bodies are not supposed to do that."

"If you can't help, shut up." Vinnie wasn't going to let Minka die.

Minka stopped convulsing. "It was him or Sergei. I'm sorry. I'm sorry."

The name dinged in Vinnie's brain. Sergei, the kid who was running La Mafia?

Minka gasped, arching her back. She screamed.

This wasn't working. Maybe if she could tap into Minka's own power and boost it. Zee could at least heal themselves, right? Vinnie felt around for the power in Minka. It was there, but it was like broken shards of the cohesive whole. As if the other powers had become part of Minka and when Vinnie ripped them away, she'd broken Minka's own power.

Minka screamed and writhed and cried.

"I can make it fast, so she doesn't suffer." The Zee had returned. Alone. "None of the crews have enough power left."

"Get her away from here," Vinnie growled. She wasn't going to put Minka out of her misery by killing her. There had to be a way. The words sunk in, and Vinnie saw a different meaning. If she could do it fast enough, it might work. She dug in, grabbed all the shards she could, and pulled.

Minka coughed one last time, back arched, then her body went limp. Her eyes stared blankly. The power clanged inside Vinnie, causing her to gasp. The unnatural Zee power from an anomaly was clinging to the natural Zee power. She scrubbed them and pushed the Zee power back into Minka. Minka's body remained still.

"No." This was not going to happen again.

Vinnie pulled the power from the Zee woman, making her eyes roll up in her head as she passed out. Vinnie took the power and pushed it into Minka. Her body arched and thumped back down, but Minka didn't revive.

"It's not a jumper cable."

Vinnie started at Jory's voice, and fear and relief warred with each other. "You were supposed to run."

Jory kneeled and ran his hand over Minka's forehead, and she took a breath. "I don't think I know how to do that anymore. Give me a boost?"

Vinnie gathered all the Wisp power she had left. It felt pitifully small, but she pushed it at Jory. Then she took the rest of the Zee power she had and gave that to Jory too.

"Neat trick," he said. "I'm keeping the flow of blood to her brain and contracting her heart to make it pump. Lungs…"

Minka took another breath.

"Then we work on repairing the damage. Got her lungs moving, like life support. I just need her body to heal enough to take over." Jory continued his commentary. Explaining to Vinnie what he was doing at each step. "It's easier because she's Zee." He said at last, pulling back his hands. Minka's eyes stayed closed, but she was breathing easily.

Shaw sobbed in relief and leaned over Minka, putting her

head on the jacket that covered her. Her hand had slipped under the jacket to hold Minka's.

Jory sat back on his heels, rubbing his hands over his face, and looked up at Andre.

At some point, the curtains between the field and stands had been lowered and Andre had lifted his mask.

"Are you the boss?" Jory asked.

"At the moment," Andre said. "I'll have to take you back in."

Hilda strode forward and put both hands on Andre's chest and shoved. He didn't budge.

"He only came back to save her life. You let him go once."

"Now maybe he can save the life of my team by letting us take him in. We didn't catch Kara, we don't have the power objects. We are hanging by a thread."

Hilda whirled on Jory. "Why didn't you run?"

"I had a promise to keep." He got to his feet.

Hilda turned, eyes scanning the field, and Vinnie followed her gaze. There were only five crews on the field, when there should have been six. Jory had told Sabra that he would get her to some secret city or something. Was that really what he'd come back for?

"And Amanda refused to run with Kiernan," Jory said. "She said she had something left to do in the city. She seemed… crazed. I knew whatever she had to do couldn't be good, so I offered to help. Kara is alive, but she's sick. Something happened to her when Vinnie pushed her through that portal, but she is recovering."

"And now she has her crystal repaired," Vinnie said. She wanted to kick herself for letting Amanda get away.

"We have insider information now," Andre said, looking down at Minka. "If we can get her to talk. I'd also be very interested to know how she became a dragon."

Shaw stood, hands clenched in fists. "It's not her fault. You can't take her. She's not a bad person."

"Then she won't mind helping us."

Shaw's body tilted forward as if she was about to launch herself at him. Nell wrapped her arms around her and made a soothing sound.

"We can help her," Andre said. "We have psychologists who are used to dealing with Twisted. She's traumatized, and we can help. I promise you she won't be harmed."

TK made a sound like a cough and then another. Vinnie realized he was trying to hold back laughter. "You just said you can't even protect your own team."

"She'll be protected."

"Because you want to use her," Shaw said.

Andre glared. "Your friend—"

"Girlfriend."

"Your girlfriend," Andre continued. "Just attacked a stadium full of people. The people I work for, and frankly few people at all, are going to care if there were extenuating circumstances. She's lucky that she will live."

Shaw's fists clenched, and she tried to step forward again, but Nell still had a hold on her. More black-clad figures had come and lifted Minka onto a stretcher.

As they lifted the stretcher, Minka's eyes opened. She turned to Shaw, who stepped forward and took her hand.

"Save Sergei," Minka said. "Don't let her have him."

Shaw's face crumpled. "I don't know how."

Rage passed over Minka's face and was quickly erased. "Save him."

"I'll save him," Shaw said. "I'll find a way."

Minka let go of her hand and closed her eyes. Metal clacked as the black-clad figures carried her off.

One of Andre's crew was holding handcuffs. They were

going to take Jory again. There was no power left for Vinnie to pull and no way out. After everything, they'd still lost him.

Jory held out his hands. "Everything is going to be fine."

"Was it worth it?" Hilda snarled.

Jory looked at Shaw. "She was."

The agent handcuffed Jory. Hilda made a growling sound low in her throat. She took three long strides, grabbed Jory's face and kissed him, her mouth lingering on his.

Someone whistled.

Shaw snorted, amused for a moment, then glared at Andre. "We'll get him out again. And Minka too."

"I hope not, she's better off with us,"Andre said. "And I could use a Zee who can heal like your friend." He pointed at one of the side entrances. "I would change clothes if you can before you leave, unless you want to be mobbed. People saw you dressed like that. That side is the clearest of people."

And then he was leaving too, following the stretcher down the field. His crew followed, leading Jory with them.

We should get out of here before they figure out they're missing something.

What did I miss?

Shaw flashed a piece of metal at her before shoving her hands in her pocket. The bracelet. She'd taken the bracelet off of Minka's wrist.

"We should get out of here before they change their minds about letting us go," TK said.

Vinnie felt strange, like that feeling you get when you know you've overstayed your welcome, but there was still so much to say. She wanted to chase Jory down and thank him for everything he'd ever done.

"You'll see him again." Hilda's tone warned her not to argue.

"Who needs me to carry them?" Nell said. She swayed and collapsed to the ground.

A surprised giggle burst out of Vinnie. Hilda glared at her and stalked off in the direction Andre had pointed.

"It's not funny," Nell said, but her lips quirked.

TK held his hand out to help her up. "We survived. We shouldn't have. That's almost funny."

CHAPTER THIRTY-FIVE

"Who was expecting company?" Hilda asked.

Vinnie craned her neck to see past TK in the driver's seat. There was a lump of a person on their porch swing. Her senses told her he had no power, but she knew that wasn't true. If she'd had a moment to think at the stadium, she might have recognized him — might have understood what he was. "It looks like the black dragon has come to pay us a visit."

"Is that Will?" Shaw climbed out of the backseat.

"Yeah," Vinnie said. Who else could it have been? If anyone was surprised by her statement, they kept it to themselves.

Hilda made it to the porch first. She crossed her arms and glared down at Will, who appeared to be asleep with his arm thrown over his eyes.

Shaw was less polite. She pushed at Will's shoulder. "Where did you get a power object?"

He moved the arm that had been draped over his eyes and looked at them.

"I don't think he needs one," Vinnie said.

Will winced, squeezing his eyes closed. "I don't."

"Can't wait to hear this," TK muttered. He unlocked the front door and went inside.

"Can you stand?" Nell asked.

Will pushed himself up and then sank back down.

"Figures," Nell muttered, offering him her arm. He took it and she pulled him up and slung his arm over her shoulder. They tilted to the side, almost stumbling.

"You're too short," he said, voice slurred.

"I'm not growing just for you."

Hilda held the door open.

"Is he drunk?" Shaw said in a stage whisper as they filed into the house.

Will choked, trying to hold in laughter. Nell deposited him on the couch, and he slumped against the back in a sitting position.

"I'll get you something." Vinnie didn't wait for his response. She needed to get out of the room.

The kitchen was dark and for a moment Vinnie considered leaving it that way, but the light was out in the fridge, and she wouldn't be able to see. She flipped the kitchen switch and stood there. All the strange little things about Will over the past few months made sense now. There had never been any other team with him. All those times she was pulling power, she was pulling from him... Ferr, Wisp, Mesmer... all of them. His Dr. Pepper addiction was to fuel the Wisp power. How did he make himself seem normal? Or just Mesmer?

Vinnie sent her senses in Will's direction. Or tried to. A wave of nausea washed over her, and she pulled back. She was too tired. It could wait.

She shuffled to the fridge, pulled sweet tea out, and wished again she'd gotten his smoothie recipe. Why was he here, instead of back at his hotel? Vinnie gathered up some food and vitamins. They'd packed some restorative supplies in TK's car before leaving and so the others had already gotten some vitamins and caffeine, but more couldn't hurt. She grabbed some glasses and headed back to the living room.

Everyone was staring at Will, but no one spoke. Will, for his part, had his head thrown back, eyes closed. Vinnie poured him a glass of tea and kicked his foot to get his attention.

He lifted his head, took the glass and a vitamin from her.

"You have better supplies at home. Why are you here?" She asked. And why had he transformed himself into a dragon to help them?

"You're not happy to see me? I helped."

"How did you get the power?" Shaw added. "And why aren't you dying like Minka?"

"He's a Vasum," Vinnie said, still hoping she wasn't right. If he was Vasum, he hadn't been pulling any power in the stadium, and there was only one explanation for having that much power that she knew.

Nell's back snapped straight.

Will's chest rose and fell as he drew in a deep, almost silent breath.

"You would have told me if he was pulling power from the crews," Hilda said. "And there was no anomaly to pull power from. Was there?"

"No, there was no anomaly," Vinnie said. "He doesn't need one. A Vasum can keep power if they take it all and the person dies. "

"You mean when that person dies," Hilda said. "They keep it when the person dies."

"Right. Apparently, that's why I have Cer's power, and why I can no longer sense or pull power from Wisps."

"He already had all the power he needed to become a dragon inside of him." Nell's voice was full of awe.

Vinnie stole a glance at Shaw, expecting to see the same awe, but Shaw looked sad, her eyes distant as if she wasn't completely with them. She had just lost her girlfriend. Even if she had survived, she was in the hands of a government agency, and her brother was still in danger from Kara.

"Vinnie needed the power of an anomaly to become a dragon," Hilda said. "How much more power does an anomaly have than a Twisted, TK?"

"Depends," TK said, and something in his demeanor shifted.

Vinnie's mouth filled with the coppery taste of blood, and her ears started ringing.

"Terrance, please." Will said. "If I wanted to kill you, you'd be dead. I can't take anyone's power anymore. It had to happen all at once. To answer your unspoken question, I don't know how many people died to give me the power I have. More than six. I don't think I set out to take anyone's power. I would like to believe I don't have that in me, but I don't know. I woke in the hospital and my memory of the prior months was gone. The rest of my memories, my entire life, are patchy. Mostly I remember her. I remember Evie. Evie was a child when we first met, Evie becoming a woman. Our wedding day. I remember her and that's all I know about my life before I was this."

Evie. The woman who she'd seen give him the knowledge of how to use Vasum power.

"Convenient," Hilda said. "You have power that can only be gained by killing people, but you don't remember."

Vinnie backed up, not taking her eyes off Will, until her legs were against the loveseat and then sat. The others had settled in various places around the room.

Will's eyes closed. "Maybe we can discuss this when we're all rested."

"You have all that power, but it's limited," Hilda said. "Trading certainty for possibility. Vinnie couldn't have stopped Minka or given the Mesmer power to me, so I could catch Minka if she was locked into only what she was carrying herself."

"Thank you for saving her," Shaw said.

Hilda shrugged.

Will's eyes popped open and bored into Vinnie. "You gave someone Mesmer power?"

The intensity of his gaze made her squirm. "Not someone. Hilda. Let me guess, not supposed to be able to do that."

Will sat forward and put his empty tea glass on the table and reached for the pitcher. He poured more into his glass and then some into a second glass, which he pushed toward Vinnie. "It's not something I've found in any Vasum literature, but if power is put into objects, then it should be possible."

"It wasn't Vasum power, it was Wisp power. Wisp can give their power away. Vasum can hold the power. How is it, with all your resources, you haven't figured that out?"

"Knowledge is power," TK said. "Unless you let it blind you. Some people think they know something and stop looking for possibilities."

"A lot of knowledge was lost when the Magiera were wiped out," Will said. "They didn't write down much of what they knew, and the world has stifled the flow of knowledge. Not wanting to kill people limits what I've been able to learn for myself. If you want to take that risk with your own friends, then that's your choice. I'm not sure that's one that I would have made."

Vinnie bristled. "I trusted Hilda to handle the power."

"And I did," Hilda said. "I think what Mr. Sassy Pants is

really saying is that he's too much of a prick to make friends that are close enough to trust."

"He came to help even though he wasn't getting anything out of it," Shaw said, but even though the words sounded like praise, her tone was clipped.

Will's eyes were bleak. "What do you know about what I am getting out of it?"

"You said Vinnie couldn't do what you wanted her to do anymore."

"Maybe I'm not here for Vinnie." His eyes stayed focused on Shaw.

Shaw squirmed.

"Well then, *maybe*," Nell emphasized the last word. "You want to tell us why you're here and not back at your own place? Don't think we haven't noticed that you could have been helping us much more all along."

"And why a dragon?" Vinnie added. "I hear that's really stupid and showy."

"Here we go with all the questions again," he said, but something seemed to light up in his eyes. "I wanted to see if I could do it. If Evie could have seen me..." His eyes got a faraway look.

"If you could become a dragon," Shaw said. "You could have rescued Jory from the prison bus all by yourself."

"It is stupid and showy," Will said. "I didn't survive this long using my abilities around people who have the power to control me. But when I realized what was happening at the stadium, I had to do something, but I needed cover. I had William make what looked like a mistake in his hacking. Federal agents are probably swarming the hotel as we speak. They'll find what looks like a plan for transforming oneself into a dragon. The evidence will point to someone they won't be able to find. All trace of Greg and me will be gone, but there should be enough there that it looks believable."

Hilda made a face. "You're here because you have no home? Dude, get a hotel."

"I'm here because we need each other."

"And to make sure we don't give away your secret," TK said. "Otherwise, it could have waited."

Now he needed them, did he? He'd looked straight at Shaw when he'd said he wasn't here for Vinnie, and Vinnie didn't like that at all.

"What is it you think we can do to help you?" she asked.

"I don't know, but you left a sketchbook with me that had a drawing of Evie in it. I think Shaw has the gift of sensing patterns in time. I need to understand how it manifests in her to know if there's any significance to it. If you all are instrumental in helping me find Evie, then this is where I need to be."

Vinnie thought back to the sketchbook. The only drawing he could mean was the one of Vinnie in front of a burning building — Will thought that was Evie. Was it?

"Don't take this the wrong way," Nell said. "But I think you're lying."

His face hardened. "I'm not."

Hilda sighed. "I'm with Nell. You don't give a shit about saving the world, and you certainly don't give a shit about us."

"If we find Evie, we might save the world, too."

TK scoffed. "A few more anomalies out there doesn't mean the world is ending. I think you're manufacturing drama so we can help you find your wife."

"Your dead wife," Vinnie said. He had told Vinnie that Evie was dead, right? He definitely had.

"She's dead?" Shaw squeaked.

"She died in this universe, yes."

He was insane. Absolutely batshit insane.

"Whoa, whoa," TK said. "You want us to open a portal to another universe?"

Hilda's eyes narrowed. "And why would we help you? You've been completely useless so far. You didn't help Conor like you promised Vinnie. You haven't taught us much we wouldn't have figured out for ourselves. We could have handled that dragon without you. You just bought us a little time to figure it out. As far as I can see, we get nothing out of this."

"I know more about how your bracelet works than you do."

Shaw's eyes widened. "You could teach me to be a dragon."

"Probably."

Which might be important to Shaw but didn't solve their biggest problem. A government agent knew who they were, and more were likely to come looking. They needed to get out of here. They needed to rescue Jory. "Kara's bracelet killed people to work."

"It didn't have to be that way," Will said. "I'm almost certain. If you can push power into your friends, you could push it into the bracelet. And in case you didn't notice, none of the Twisted crews died today, and someone was definitely using one of those bracelets."

"Shaw becoming a dragon isn't really going to help us much, though, is it?" TK said. "We've got much bigger problems."

Will's eyes turned to Hilda. "The bracelet can also open anomalies. Which I believe would solve your problem as well. If you weren't tied to one place, you could run, hide."

A slight tightening of Hilda's eyes was the only outward sign of her anger. *How does he know about Harry?*

"You said he didn't read minds," she said out loud.

"I don't need to read minds. You don't *look* right, and I felt the anomaly the minute I came into this house the first time."

Hilda didn't look right? Vinnie shifted her vision so she could see Hilda's power. She looked the same as ever. What must it be like in Will's head to have all the abilities all the time? To have enough power coursing through your body that you could turn into a dragon at will? The world must be overwhelming with the constant sensory input on so many levels, feelings, emotions, power signatures. It would be enough to drive a person insane.

"If Hilda could use the bracelet, she could go home from anywhere," Shaw said sadly. "That's way more important than being a dragon."

"It wouldn't be her." Vinnie said, pulling the conversation back to Will's insane goal. "It wouldn't be your Evie. If we found a world where she was alive, it wouldn't be the same person."

"You really think you're so different than you would have been anywhere else?" he asked. "It doesn't matter. If I can just see her, talk to her..."

He's crazy. Hilda's eyes met hers, and her expression shook Vinnie. Hilda was afraid. *He may be able to block me from his thoughts most of the time, but when he talks about her, he can't quite. You know what does that? Emotion. I can't directly sense it, but it's there, and it's wild, dangerous, obsessive.*

"And if we can open anomalies," Will continued. "Maybe we can repair the damage the Rending caused. Just closing the anomalies won't do it if there is still an imbalance. My goal may be selfish, but it could be a stepping stone."

"And you can help us get Jory and Minka out of prison," Shaw said. "And save Sergei."

"I don't know who Sergei is, but I can't get anyone out of a Twisted prison. That's just a distraction."

Shaw's demeanor didn't change, but it was hard to miss

the anger she was putting out. First, TK had lost control for a moment and now Shaw was on the verge. They really needed to stop and get some rest.

"You just said you trusted my drawing meant something," Shaw said. "But you're just like everyone else. It's not a distraction. We need to do this."

"Your emotions can get in the way of seeing a true pattern."

Shaw's anger was unmistakable now. "You lied to us. You want to use us. We aren't doing anything unless you help free Jory and Minka."

"Hilda's life isn't worth it to you?" Fatigue was etched in every line of Will's body, but his voice remained strong.

Shaw stood, fists clenched at her sides.

"I will help in any way I can," Will continued. "But that's not a way I can help. I suggest talking to your new government friends and cutting a deal, like you're trying with me here. You have, or might be able to find, something they want, yes? Besides, they know too much about you. You can try to erase their memories or you can get them on your side. Getting on your side may be the easier task."

"We have more information about where Kara might be than they do," Vinnie said.

"Whatever," Shaw said. "I'm getting some sleep."

Vinnie had the same sensation that she'd had at the stadium of things being unfinished, incomplete. The same feeling she'd had after Jory was arrested. But her friends hadn't given up, and she knew they wouldn't give up now. Her brain was mush, and no one else looked any perkier.

"We can discuss this more when we're not all dead tired," TK said. "Vinnie, can you help me put new sheets on Jory's bed for Mr. Darrow?"

"I'm not—" Will started.

"You're dead on your feet," Vinnie said. She didn't want him here, but he had risked himself to help.

"I imagine they'll be looking at other hotels in the area after your stunt," Hilda added.

"Fine," Will said. "Thank you."

Nell had pushed the chair into recline mode. Her eyes were already closed, breathing even. Vinnie grabbed the blanket off the couch and draped it over her before following TK up the stairs.

CHAPTER THIRTY-SIX

Vinnie hitched her bag up on her shoulder, opened the front door, and stepped out on to the porch. She was the last one out of the house today. Shaw should have been home since she hadn't found another job yet, but she wasn't.

As she closed the door behind her, her eyes went automatically to the camera above the door. The morning after the incident at the stadium, they'd found another dead rat on the porch. The camera had caught the biggest tomcat Vinnie had ever seen delivering the rat. Hilda had been right about that.

The walk to the bus stop and the ride downtown were short, but today the trip felt like it was taking ages. Vinnie sat perched on the seat closest to the door as the bus rattled along. It had been four days since the incident at the stadium, and Vinnie was eager to get back to the library and some small piece of normalcy. Will hadn't left their house, and they all just seemed to have accepted that he was staying with no discussion. Vinnie still had her reservations, but once she'd gotten past her anger, she felt some comfort having someone so powerful staying with them.

She had tried to contact Andre to no avail, and with every day that passed, the possibility of getting Jory free seemed further away. Will had been so sure that Andre would come looking for her since he knew something was different about her, but that hadn't happened. Will's ploy to set someone up as the black dragon had taken some of the heat off, with the news reporting that the parties responsible for the terror at the stadium had been caught.

Nell said that behind the scenes, things weren't so calm. More teams had been sent to the Holt, and they were digging into events of the last few weeks. It seemed only a matter of time before they found something that would lead to Vinnie and her friends.

As the bus rumbled to a stop near the library, Vinnie knew something was off. Hilda and Shaw were nearby. Their energies seemed to come from the direction of the library. Alarm pinged through her and she gathered the Wisp power and coiled it tightly, ready to blast someone if necessary.

Hilda?

Shhh, you don't know I'm here. Hilda didn't sound alarmed.

Vinnie exited the bus and strode toward the library. The sooner she saw they were fine, the sooner she could get out of high alert status. The alleyway was empty, which meant they were actually in the library. Was something wrong with the library? She scurried down the steps and pushed the door open. Inside was dark, the only light coming from the small basement windows.

Fear pinged through Vinnie. She always kept the small lamp on the desk on, because the windows barely allowed any light in at all. She fumbled for the light switch and flipped it on.

"Surprise!"

Hilda, Shaw, Conor, and Lou jumped out from behind the bookshelves and the counter. Everything in the library was covered in tarps, her counter, the bookcases. There were even tarps on the floor.

"It's not my birthday."

Conor narrowed his eyes. "Are you sure?"

Vinnie laughed, and some of the tension left her body. "Yes, I'm sure."

"Good thing this is a wallpaper removal party, then," he said.

That would explain the spray bottles and scrapers on the counter that she hadn't noticed until now.

"We have cake," Shaw said, pointing to a store-bought layer cake covered with a dome of plastic. "Because we know how you love cake."

"Though your taste is questionable," Lou said. "Bad cake, bad location. How long have you been here with that wallpaper up?"

"Two years, and the rent was cheap." She certainly didn't want to be talking to Lou about how the basement had felt like home when she first stepped into it. "I just knew someday a knight in shining armor would come to rescue me from this hideousness."

Conor put his hands on his hips and puffed out his chest.

"I meant Lou," Vinnie said.

Lou rolled her eyes and Conor deflated.

"Harsh," he said, but his eyes danced with laughter.

"How do we do this?" Vinnie asked.

"Allow me." He grabbed a scraper and a spray bottle and went to the back wall.

The others grabbed their tools and moved to opposite sides of the basement.

Vinnie followed Conor and watched as he sprayed the wall paper, used the scraper to pry up a corner and sprayed some more.

"Now we let the water soak in," he said. After a few

minutes, Conor pulled off the first strip of wallpaper. "Is that...?"

"More wall paper," Lou called from across the library.

"It's a good thing I called in sick today," Hilda said from her position a few feet away.

"What's Lou doing here?" Vinnie asked, not caring that Lou could hear her.

"She wanted to help since you helped get the charges dropped," Hilda said. "Or so she says."

"She helps evil people now?"

Hilda shrugged.

Vinnie wasn't sure how she felt about Lou helping for whatever reason. It felt different from when she'd asked Lou for help at the gym because then she hadn't known Vinnie and her friends were Twisted.

"Relax," Lou called. "I still hate you. I just don't want to owe you anything."

"You don't," Vinnie said. "Nothing I did was for you."

"Of course it wasn't," Lou said.

What was that supposed to mean? She was implying that Vinnie wouldn't do something for someone else. Vinnie picked up her spray bottle, prepared to go confront her.

"It's not worth it," Hilda said.

"It really isn't," Conor said. "I think you've gone a long way to changing her mind, though."

"I don't care about changing her mind." Vinnie savagely ripped a strip of wallpaper down. She wasn't really angry at Lou. There was nothing she could do about people like that. She was angry because Conor was retiring from the Warrior Games. He had decided not to continue playing, but he wasn't staying here with her. They texted and called so much over the last few days, she'd started to think maybe there was a future, but he wasn't staying even though he could.

There was never a future. He's not that much better than her,

Hilda said. *And stop mentally shouting. My head still hurts from the stupid dragon bullshit.*

Vinnie took a deep breath. Hilda was wrong about Conor, and Vinnie didn't want to be mad at him.

"Have you decided what you're going to do next?" she asked Conor.

"I'm going to pull my money out of the foundation and start my own. I think."

His own foundation to identify Twisted? He was starting another?

"You were right," Conor continued. "It's not okay to identify people whose control over their own lives will be taken away. I do still think if we want things to change, then people need to feel safe."

"People could just stop being dicks," Hilda said, but there was no heat in it.

"It's not the same as being smart or knowing martial arts." Conor pulled off another long strip of wallpaper. "I just don't think we can agree on that. If someone smart is trying to manipulate you, they can't actually know what your thoughts are when they try to do it."

Neither could any normal Twisted, either. Will probably could. Not a conversation she wanted to have with Conor, though.

"That's true, an intelligent person can't smear their blood on you and take away your will so thoroughly that you would hurt your friends," Vinnie said. It had been scary when Kara had told her to stop breathing, and she did. She never wanted to feel like that again. She wasn't sure it was that different from someone holding a gun to your head to do the same, but a gun was visible and could be taken away.

"Exactly." He waved a strip of wallpaper before dropping it on the floor.

"How are you going to make people safe?" She wasn't sure

she wanted to know the answer to that question, in case it was something horrible, but the words were out.

"What if we could make something like the amulets those government guys have?"

And she really wished she hadn't asked. "The ones people had to die to create?"

The hurt in his eyes brought her up short. "You don't trust me not to kill people?"

"I trust you," Shaw yelled from the other side of the library.

"If it gets out that this is something that's possible, there are other people who wouldn't mind killing a few Magiera to keep themselves safe."

He nodded and turned back to the wall. "Probably true. But if we want things to change, sometimes we have to take a chance. I don't think a research foundation to create protective items is going to excite too many people. Mine probably won't even be the first."

Vinnie turned back to the wall and pulled a strip off. The paper underneath the first layer wasn't quite as ugly. Looking at it almost made her feel happy, in spite of everything. Almost. Clean, bare walls would be better. She could put whatever she wanted up. Right now, she just wanted to see the wall underneath. Instead of pulling off another top layer, she prepped the second layer and pulled it off. There was more wallpaper underneath.

"How many layers are there?"

Hilda snorted.

A throat cleared near the door, and Vinnie turned. Andre stood there in casual jeans and a snug gray t-shirt with a faded logo that showed off a lean, well-toned chest. "I'm sorry, I didn't realize it was home improvement day. I just need to talk to Vinnie."

It's go time, Hilda said.

Vinnie wasn't ready. She'd been preparing what to say to him in her head for days, but now that he was standing there, she wasn't ready, but ready or not, it was time to make a deal.

Vinnie nodded toward the outside. She didn't want Conor, and definitely not Lou, to hear the conversation.

Andre stepped outside and waited for her a short distance from the steps, frowning at the sky as if it had offended him. "Is it always this warm here in November?"

Vinnie shrugged, though he wasn't looking at her. "Maybe tomorrow it will be freezing cold. Who knows?"

He looked down, eyes flicking over her tank top and then back up. "Right. Who knows? Life is full of mysteries. Sometimes you encounter mythological creatures where you least expect them."

Somehow, she didn't think he was talking about the dragon, but she could pretend. "A dragon pulling a roof off a sports stadium was surprising."

"Almost as surprising as a Vasum in a public library."

"Took you long enough." He must have heard of Vasum. He worked for the government. Shouldn't he have access to all kinds of knowledge?

"It took some research. As far as anyone knows, Vasum died out in the 1800s."

"As far as most people know, Twisted didn't exist until 1918." She looked sideways at him. "What are you going to do with that information? If you try to take me in, I will burn this city down. I'm sure your higher ups wouldn't like that much."

He shook his head, a slight smile on his face. "No, you wouldn't. But I don't want to take you in. If I arrest you for cause, which I certainly have, you go into the bowels and you won't do me any good there. However, if you voluntarily join my team, you can work for me and I will protect you."

Vinnie snorted. "A few days ago, you told me you couldn't

even protect the team you already have. You expect me to believe..." But if he had her, he would have some leverage. "Oh, you're hoping that bringing them a Vasum will be enough to get you out of hot water."

"If I had a Vasum on my team who would only cooperate with me and no one else, they would think twice before they hurt any of us. That's true."

"Until I messed up or didn't do what they want me to do?"

His face hardened. "Look, Vinnie. The little trick you and your friends pulled with the fake hotel set up is only going to hold people off for a few weeks at best. What you and your friends did at the stadium was spectacular. People saw us talking. They saw you and your friends interacting with my team. I've been..." Here his jaw clenched, and nostrils flared. "It's been a difficult few days. Neither I, nor any of my team, have given you away, but you better believe they aren't buying the 'we know nothing' story. You're right, I can't guarantee your safety either way, but you have a much better chance if you join us."

So much had happened. She'd been so busy focusing on how to get Jory and Minka that she hadn't had time to consider alternative options. If she joined them, she might have a better chance of figuring out how to get Jory out, and it might take the heat off of the rest of her friends, keep them off the radar a little longer.

Stick with the plan, Vinnie, Hilda said.

The plan. Right.

But Andre wasn't done talking. "If you join us, they won't look for the rest of your friends."

She could save them all. That's what he was saying. All she had to do was give up her own freedom.

And become a danger to the freedom of every other Twisted in this country. They could just take you out on any street and have you point them out. You —

Hilda! It's okay. I've got this.

"I appreciate the offer," Vinnie said. "But we are perfectly capable of taking care of ourselves. You and your team seem to be the ones incapable of staying safe. Or accomplishing much at all. You've had years to find Kara, and it seems like it should have been easy. She used government documents to gain employment with the Warrior games. Given the risk, you know they verified they were real. How did they do that, Andre? How is it you didn't even know?"

All trace of friendliness seemed to have left this expression, but he didn't respond.

"Here's the deal I am offering you," she continued. "We will bring you Kara, and the two power objects in her possession and you will free Jory and Minka."

He continued to look at her, still as stone. Vinnie fought the urge to fidget, to take the words back, to say she'd work for him if he'd just let Jory go.

"Minka is better off in our care," he said.

Did that mean he'd agree to get Jory out? "Why do you get to decide that?"

"Because that's the way life is, Ms. Forbes. Some of us don't get to decide who we do or do not work for. You think I haven't heard all the names and the slurs? Traitor to my kind because I try to keep the world safe. Is that what you think?"

Vinnie had had those thoughts, but she wasn't blind to the reality of some Twisted. He probably thought he made the best decision available to him, but his decision also meant that he had more freedom than the people he took in. "And so, because you have no choice, you want to take it away from everyone else?"

His nostrils flared again. "You know what? Fine. You believe you can be some sort of vigilante hero and get away with it? Go ahead. I'll even make that deal with you, but let's make it a bet. If you get me Kara and the objects, I will get Jory and Minka free. If I find her first, you will work for me."

"I'm not working for you."

"Then, no deal," he turned to walk away.

This was her only shot. They had no other way into the prison compounds or rehab camps. Letting him walk away meant letting Jory go.

"Wait," she said. "Deal. If you catch her, I'll work for you."

He glanced over his shoulder and nodded, and then he was gone, down the alley and out of view.

When Vinnie stepped back into the library, Hilda's eyes immediately sought hers.

We'll get her first, Vinnie told her. They had to.

Of course we will. Hilda turned back to the wall she'd been stripping.

"Ouch," came Lou's voice from across the room. "I think the wall just burned me."

"Maybe there's some heating vents behind that section?" Conor said.

"If it was that hot, this place would have burned down." Hilda moved in the direction Lou's voice had come from and Vinnie followed.

Lou had stripped the wallpaper completely in one section. Underneath all the layers, the wall was painted bright blue.

Cerulean Blue. Vinnie had been feeling something when she was outside talking to Andre. A sense of loss, compounded by a sense of peace. Cerulean. She stepped around Lou and put her hand on the paint. The wall felt a little warm under her palm but not burning hot. It was him. He'd done this. She grabbed the edge of several layers of wallpaper and pulled. A big section of wallpaper came up and behind it there was more blue, but some of it was a slightly different shade and formed a curve.

"It's Cerulean," she said. "He did this."

Shaw stepped forward and started clawing at the paper, pulling off chunks. Some of the paint came away with it.

"Hey," Hilda said. "Slow down. We don't want to mess up the painting. We have time. Let's do this right."

They gathered their tools and began working together on the blue wall.

Shaw was the first to uncover something that wasn't blue. A tiny coral colored fish swam above some stylized ocean flora. A few minutes later, Hilda uncovered something that looked like a dolphin tail.

The work seemed to fly by as they uncovered more of the painting. There were some ordinary ocean creatures, but there were also some colorful fish with long fins, like wings.

When they had uncovered most of it, Lou took a few steps back and whistled.

"It's beautiful," she said.

They all moved back from the wall so they could see the entire painting.

Vinnie's vision blurred. "TK didn't mention they'd painted one down here."

Maybe he didn't know. Remember what he said about the paint? Even I can feel the heat pouring off of this. Hilda said.

You think it's that paint?

"Let's see if there's more." Lou picked up her bucket and headed for the next wall.

Vinnie wanted to yell at her to stop. There might never be more, because Cer was gone. If they uncovered paintings here, this could be the last that would ever be discovered, and it would be like he'd left them all over again.

She put her hand against the painting. Some things, once uncovered, couldn't be covered again. She could put up more wallpaper, but she'd never forget the paintings were there. Shaw put a hand on Vinnie's shoulder.

Vinnie swallowed a lump in her throat. "He didn't do all this work for it to be hidden. Let's go see what else we find."

ALSO BY ELLE WOLFSON

Harbinger of the Storm

ACKNOWLEDGMENTS

As always, I couldn't do this without the love and support of my husband, James. Thank you for believing in me and for your mad typo hunting abilities.

And a big thank you to Julia J. Simpson, my critique partner and friend, for pushing me to be a better writer and a better person, and for being there whether things are dark or light.

The magic is out there